T0365057

# Eminence of

# Evil

*Rise of the Witch-Master*

*Andrew Vincent Metalhorn*

**Written By**

**EMINENCE OF EVIL**
**RISE OF THE WITCH-MASTER**

*iUniverse books may be ordered through booksellers or by contacting:*

*iUniverse*
*1663 Liberty Drive*
*Bloomington, IN 47403*
*www.iuniverse.com*
*844-349-9409*

*ISBN: 978-1-5320-4748-0 (sc)*
*ISBN: 978-1-5320-4749-7 (e)*

*Library of Congress Control Number: 2018904524*

*Print information available on the last page.*

*iUniverse rev. date: 12/12/2024*

"The people are enraged, my Majesty! They talk about your son, and how he studies under that Witch you call a sorcerer."

King Bosren laughed aloud, then plunked his robust rump upon his thrown. "Let them talk. It's only gossip; I shall increase their taxes and order a curfew that should shut them up."

"But, my Majesty, they already pay the highest premium of all the Kingdoms from here to Spain." The King waved his hand in disgust and sneered. "My Lord, there's been talk of rebellion, and as your adviser, I suggest a different approach."

The King lashed back, "And what would that be, old man, that I burn my own son at the stake to appease these idiot rubes?"

"My Majesty, I would never suggest such treachery or treason to your family. I am but a servile servant and adviser to your greatness. But you're not far off to what I have in mind, and it just might save your good name and Kingdom."

By this time, a highly religious mob had been camping outside the castle walls. They had been there for almost two weeks in protest to the King's black magic servant and star pupil, the King's son. They would rant and rave as to how the Devil has a heavy hand on the King's influence. They simply couldn't live under such an impious ruler. Poverty was second nature to them, as it had always been.

God Almighty was all they had, and if the King fell short of the good word, where would that leave them? Nay, they truly lived in the valley of death midst of Devils and Demons from which the King was surely directed.

The castle was a great fortress of formidable design. It stood like a monolith of enduring fortification. The valley below lay like a peninsula enclaved by mountains which protected the castle from invasion with only one way in and or out. Its elongated basin allowed fertile farming and was owned by a handful of wealthy farmers who were mostly dedicated to the King. The Earth was plowed and manicured as none starved due to the great boundaries that were produced. "God's great valley," the peasants sang as they tended the flocks and harvested the crops.

High in the west tower, a flickering light loomed over their campfires like a far-off star in the night sky. Inside was the black-hearted Devil-man of Black Magic that the God-fearing people so much feared. A monstrous man in his late sixties with the skin of a rhino and a mind that encased the foulest malevolence one could imagine.

"Come here, my young Master," he said as he held out his hand in a welcoming manner. "Look down and gaze upon your people and see into their darkest fears."

A boy walked to the window and looked downward. "But Master, all I see is a crowd of people and their campfires."

The old Master walked behind the boy. He grabbed the boy's head with both of his hands and pointed it towards the people below. The old man's rotted breath filled the room. A third eye on his forehead opened as he said aloud, "Gaze from my glorious orb as your inner vision sees into the heart and Soul of man and your true self."

The boy stood with a hand on each side of the block window. His normal sight began to blur into visions of the Devils and Demons. His eyes widened as beads of sweat began to cover his face.

The old Master held a firm grip on the boy's head and said,

"Don't fear your Demons; embrace them! Embrace them with your very Soul, and they will take you to your highest ambitions. Control them; they are your slaves if you so will it. You are destined for Mastery. You are what no one will ever deny. You are an Eminence of evil. The Witch-Master to come!"

The boy's vision blurred into red, blue, and green shapes of a Demonic army, horned and non-horned, fanged and clawed, all in unison. Then, in the midst of minions, one stood out alone on the foundation of its own morality and arrogance. All around him was a frenzy of chaotic Demons, yet it seemed calm as if in the eye of a calamitous hurricane. The boy looked deep into the creature's large black eyes as it stood tall with vermilion burrs and bumps. The corner of its mouth cracked with a slight grin. Its eyes drew the boy deeper and deeper until all he could see was the pitch blackness of a vast eternity.

A silhouette appeared in the distance, coming closer and closer until the boy realized he was staring at himself. The image then faded backward as his gaze returned to the black eyes, then to the creature and Demons, until his sight shifted to the crowd below.

The old Master still held the boy's head. "These are the unearthly sights that only the dead and Celestials see," he said in a low, calm voice that eased the young Master's anxieties. "I offer you the powers that a thousand lifetimes wouldn't bring. Do you wish to continue your studies, or do you walk as a mortal and die like a common man?"

The old Master turned the boy's head up toward the stars and whispered ancient words in Hebrew. He then released him, but the boy's eyes remained fixated and hypnotized by the night sky. He stood silent behind him while the boy's young mind seemed to soak in the secrets of the stars, whereupon he spied a slow-moving comet upon the canopy of the universe.

He slowly turned around, peered into the old Master's eyes, and gave a cynical grin. "Oh yes, Master, I wish to learn. I wish to learn all there is to know and all the knowledge you contain."

The old Master cradled the boy with one hand and hugged him with his other in a unified embrace. The first crucial step had been taken. The young prince passed his test with the assortment of Devils and Demons.

Devin is a prince sixteen years of age, a handsome young man with brown eyes and brown hair. His stride is of the grace of an athlete and was even admired by adult women. The old Master Barabis was raised in the Black Forest by six Witches. His family was killed by the Witches wolves that scoured the land for any horror they could find. The wolves were bewitched and trained to kill families on journeys and strangers who strayed and found themselves lost. But if they came upon a child, they were to bring the Witches their prize. Children were extremely precious to them; their Gods had Soul appetites for the blood and flesh of the innocent and sacrificed them in their rituals.

But Barabis was different. He crawled into the middle of their pentagram and raised his arms, holding up a dismembered limb that was there. This was truly a sign for them to pass their secrets on to this prodigy from hell as they raised him in the deleterious depravity of malignant vileness.

By the time he could walk, Barabis had been taught the language of the Underworld. And when he reached his teens, he would entice young children to the Witches' encampment with promises of games and candy. For his reward, he would penetrate young girls before they met their demise. Debauchery and sex were a part of their rituals as he indulged himself on numerous occasions. If a young girl wasn't available, the Witches would throw themselves at the sex-craved boy. By his seventeenth year, Barabis had cultivated

4

speaking in tongues and learned the mysteries of the Underworld, which was more knowledge than aged gray men took to their graves.

The four Demons from the darkest depths of the highest dominions of hell---Aquiel, Surgat, Agares, Ronove, whispered their dark, sacred secrets in his ear, which strengthened him with black, mystic powers. He was fed human flesh and would drink wine mixed with blood and, for dessert, the loin of the sacrificial lamb.

By his seventeenth birthday, Barabis left his Evil encampment for the Earthly riches of the World. He said goodbye to his surrogate mothers by ripping their hearts out and sacrificing their hollow cavities to his God, Mephistopheles. He'd grown beyond their small-time spells and castrations of young boys for excitement. His Master promised him the highest rank of his counsel in exchange for being the stepping-stone for the Dark Prince Messiah to come. A foresight of vision was bestowed on him, which he embraced full-heartedly.

Barabis knew his future would be guided by his Dark Savior and that his role in life would be of John the Baptist to Jesus Christ, albeit to Evil. He would be forever perceived as a superstar in the Underworld. Barabis traveled throughout old Europe and worked for many Kings. He searched for his apprentice that was foretold to him. He also enjoyed Earthly fruits by leaving a wake of disaster in his path.

By his late sixties, Barabis found himself at his current castle residence, a sorcerous servant to the King. But still, the King feared and dreaded him with the remorse of ever hiring him. Devin took an immediate liking to Barabis. He had never seen a man so mystical and mysterious, a man to whom armies and Kings trembled at the sound of his name. Barabis once held off an entire army of Norse barbarians simply by casting a sickened, soft-spoken spell. When their leader questioned Barabis's powers, he found himself covered in cankerous boils the instant he spoke his name. The boils protruded all over his skin and ruptured with greenish-yellow, milky pus. They exploded in intervals, spraying the sickly secretions on those who surrounded him. In turn, those who were sprayed suffered the same ill-stricken fate as it spread throughout most of their army. The remaining survivors dropped their weapons and ran back the way they came. Considering Barabis never left the castle, this just added to his formidable reputation, for which Devin admired him.

Barabis's servant Kilgore had no tongue, which was cut off by a slave trader when he fell behind on a death march. It was Barabis who thwarted a boulder that was launched at Kilgore's head when their paths met. The slave trader became fainthearted in the presence of Barabis, folding to his knees and pleading for his pathetic existence. Throwing two gold coins at the trader, Barabis pointed to Kilgore's shackles, and they unlocked and fell to the ground. Kilgore immediately dropped to his own knees and grabbed his new Master's robe in submission. From that day on, Kilgore was a servant, fetcher, and executioner if need be. Originally from Tunisia, Kilgore was a slender 6'11" with 170 pounds of pure muscle and a glistening bald head. His acceptance of death in a foreign land attracted Barabis's attention, a sign from his Dark Deity, so he named him Kilgore.

Barabis introduced Devin to pentagrams, rituals, and the secrets of his Master as he also had his first drink of wine mixed with human blood. After his bloody wine-induced ritual, Barabis sent Kilgore to fetch some harlots. For the first time ever, Devin experienced the prowess of his new persona. He laid in bed with the two strumpets, gazing at their full-bloomed womanhood after they truly exhausted him.

Then, with lazy eyes, the boy gazed upwards, and the

women began to float, looking down in disbelief. Devin's eyes widened as he witnessed them crush and fold into one another above his head. He could hear their bones breaking and their anguished howls while they pressed together into slabs of ripping flesh. Their bodies folded into themselves, first from the hips down, then their limbs into each other, until they were compressed into one abhorrent cube. By this time, Devin was now showered with blood as he gripped the silk sheets with wrought intensity.

The human cube started spinning as Devin caught a glimpse of a face that managed to shriek out a gurgling cry of grief. The cube spun faster and faster until it abruptly seized and fell into Devin's lap. He looked down upon the human mass and saw eyes upon him in a fixed, dead stare. He pushed the cube off his lap and scrambled to his feet in a perplexed manner. Devin looked over at Barabis and observed the old Master's eyes return to their normal color from a bright glow of red. A cynical grin came over Devin's face as he depicted a crazed lunatic dressed in blood.

Barabis then spoke in a low, calm voice of authority, "These are the powers I offer you, my young Master. Powers of the Underworld are at your command as humanity will fall at your feet."

Standing in the shadows was Kilgore as Barabis barked at him to bring him the stiffened carcass cube. Barabis then drifted to the tower window, fingers crooked, and eyes rolled to the back of his head. Without hesitation, Kilgore picked it up and took it to his Master. Barabis stuck his hands deep into the cube of carnage and spoke onto its mass as he commanded it to come alive. Then he ripped his hands out from its gore and nodded to Kilgore to throw it out the window. Kilgore obeyed, tossing it like a discarded piece of trash. Barabis then walked away nonchalantly.

Devin wiped the blood from his eyes and ran to the window. Hanging out his head, he caught the tail end of the cube's fall. Then, with straining eyes, he could see two appendages protruding from its mass. Two more limbs began to sprout out as Evilness began to take form. The crowd of peasants scurried to their feet and scattered, shrieking in horror as the cube continued its change. It became a breathing creature again, but instead of two beautiful women, it was now a 16-footed atrocious Monster of odious anger. Its eyes were distorted out of configuration, with one sitting low on its cheek and the other high on its forehead. It's stubbed.

Snout was far to the left, as the mouth seemed to be the only orifice in order. Long strands of ratty black hair rested on its giant, deformed head. Its arms ostentatiously touched the ground as it stood erect, facing the crowd. Screams echoed through the valley as the Ogre Beast began feasting on the flesh of anyone within reach. Mothers collected their babies. Men took up their swords and spears with quick resolutions to kill the Beast.

One after the other, men lie broken from the giant's furious rage and feast. After what seemed an eternity, the crowd disbanded into a disarray of desolation. The field was now empty, except for the remains of cadavers and crying babies whose parents were either eaten or lost in the confusion. The contemptible creature gathered the crying babies and any dismembered limbs and sat upon a mound of human flesh and feasted.

As the cannibalistic Beast gorged, the sound of chains filled the air. The portcullis rose, the drawbridge lowered, and soldiers rushed out in great numbers. They surround the nefarious creature and push their spears and swords into it to no avail. This only enraged the creature, who tore a score of men to shreds.

Barabis then calmly walked out into the open like a savior in the night. He commanded the soldiers to step back, reaching up to the sky. Barabis roared out upon a black mass of clouds as they began to thunder with bolts of lightning. They crashed around him in a fluster of destruction, ripping the Earth. Random charges of electricity poured from his hands, emitting a green spectrum of death. He then muttered, "I'll see you in hell!" A green isotopic cloud then consumed the creature in a luminous glow as it fell, crying out in convulsions. The Beast shrieked dissonant sounds of death as it lashed out the last motions of its short existence. The green cloud dissipated, leaving a dark, charred figure. The smell of sulfur mixed with fetid flesh from the smoldering black mass sent a few soldiers spewing their last meal.

Transforming from Satan to Saint, Barabis appeared as a white fleece angel. The men raised their swords in glorification, except for Kronus, the head knight. His gaze was suspicious, wondering how this creature came to be. Kronus abruptly yelled in an angry tone while his soldiers scurried to attention. He then ordered his men to gather their fallen comrades and have them buried. Barabis turned back into the castle as Kronus glanced upward; he saw the outline of Devin's head peering down as the bloodied prince quickly drew away.

Due to the rumored talk of Devin's participation in black magic, Kronus began to contemplate if the boy was somehow responsible for the carnage that came to the castle. The troops piled the remains of the dead into flatbed horse buggies, and they marched away into the night for a ceremonial burial.

The next morning came with a glorious display of colors, painting the sky with shades of purple, orange, vermilion, and fuchsia. King Bosren perched at the head of a long table opposite Devin, where they feasted on their morning breakfast. The chamber remained silent while their teeth ripped into an array of the finest foods fit for a King and prince. After the servants wiped their faces and hands, Devin tried to make a quick exit, but his father stopped him in his tracks with the question, "Why are you spending so much time with Barabis?"

Devin slowly turned to him as if he'd been caught in some heinous crime. "But father, he is wise beyond his years and teaches me about far-off places I wish to see someday and people I would like to meet."

King Bosren slammed his fist on the table and shouted, "You are my son; your place is here on the throne!"

Devin stood defiant as the words bounced off him like a pebble off a stone, his seething surge of fury fired in his veins. "I don't want you talking to Barabis anymore! I won't have my only son influenced by that Devil-man!"

A pause instilled the air as Devin slowly turned to his father in a stance of defiance and leered. "Devil-man, maybe," Devin retorted, "but he contains more knowledge in his little pinkie than you contain in your whole Kingdom. He is a man of Worldly prowess and power, and I doubt that even you would want to get on the bad side of him."

"Blasphemy!" the King shouted, blasphemy by my own son. I won't stand for such treason!"

Devin lowered his chin and glared at his father with seething hatred and shaking in searing anger. The King stared in disbelief, yet a slight surge of fear ran through his veins. Devin simply turned and walked away.

King Bosren jostled with horrifying thoughts of losing his son to this sorcerous madman he hired. He now realized the heavy hand Barabis had on his son. He pondered in glooming fear, what kind of Witchery. He then jumped to his feet and yelled, "Alisatar!" He cried out laboriously, trudging through

10

the dark, dismal corridors. He finally reached the throne room as Alisatar and two servants rushed to his side.

"What is it, my majesty?" stammered Alistar with a concerned look of fear.

The King caught his breath, "My son has befallen under the spells of Barabis and turned against me with impertinent words of abandonment."

Alisatar was King Bosren's adviser and had served his father before him. A small, hunched man in his late seventies with thin white hair and feeble features, Alisatar stood but 4 foot 7 inches and weighed less than four sacks of potatoes. Alisatar sheepishly piped up, "I didn't want to wake you last night or disturb your breakfast, but we have a pressing problem that needs to be addressed. A hideous creature attacked your people outside the castle walls last night. It killed many of the good citizens and thirty-three of your best soldiers."

The King drew silent as he settled deep into his thrown. Alisatar then told him how Barabis slew the foul Beast. King Bosern pondered the notion for a moment before he asked, "And where did the Beast come from?" Alisatar sheepishly shrugged his shoulders.

Just as the new information took hold, Kronus marched into the throne room, storming mad. He approached the throne and lowered himself on one knee to his King. "Your majesty, may I have a word with you?"

"Yes, yes," the King said as he gestured to him to get up. "I lost thirty-three of my best men because of a creature that the peasants say fell from the sky. I have fought Beasts, serpents, and hellish creatures of all kinds, but I have yet to see them just drop out of the sky. They usually circle before they land, with shrieking war cries. We don't have any enemies of which I know that perform magic like that. Barabis is the only one who has such powers, which raises my suspicions."

"Somebody mentioned my name?" Barabis stood in the archway. He walked toward the throne with all eyes fixed on him in fear, except for Kronus, whose stare was of contempt.

"Alisatar just informed me how you rid us of that foul Beast," the King stammered.

Barabis gazed at Kronus as if he knew all of his thoughts and ambitions. "I am only here to serve you, my Majesty," he said, taking a bow.

Kronus immediately began his tricky questions, hoping to trip Barabis and stumble him with confessions. But Barabis only answered the queries with more questions with his convincing cajoling calumniations.

Barabis proposed that the creature must have come from a nearby castle. After an hour of deliberation and theoretical speculations to Kronus, none of them seemed to fit. The King, however, was too intimidated to accuse Barabis or otherwise. Barabis may have been able to fool the King and even Alisatar, but Kronus remained stern and silent as he watched the slithering snake sing. Barabis bowed and dismissed himself, then glanced to Kronus with a slit smile as he walked away. Silence came over the throne room until Barabis's absence was made. Kronus abruptly drew his sword in anger as he promised revenge for his Majesty's men. King Bosren then sent for his Bishop, hoping that his Holiness might solve their problems through prayer and liturgy. Kronus advised his Majesty to do away with Barabis and reclaim his son. The Bishop and Alisatar quickly agreed.

After hours of persuasion and religious counsel, along with the testimony of Kronus, who saw the young prince hanging his bloodied head out the west tower window, King Bosren finally gave in and agreed to listen to the terms of how they would rid themselves of the black magic tyrant who had resided in his castle. Devin hunched, hiding behind the drapes of his family crest that hung from the ceiling to the floor. After taking in their plans, he crawled through a cubby hole that led out of the throne room and into the servants' quarters. Once there, he ran through the long corridors to the stairwell leading to Barabis' chambers. He rushed up the stairs and briskly burst through the door.

Barabis seemed to be in a ritualistic ceremony as the young prince shouted his name. Initially Barabis ignored the intrusion, sitting in a pentagram chanting ancient tongues of Hebrew. Devin looked to the left, where he saw Kilgore standing like an obedient chattel awaiting orders. His eyes returned to Barabis, and he blurted out that Kronus and his father were conspiring against him. Barabis still held his back to him as he spoke in a supple, baritone voice, "It is not me who is chosen for great grandeur and glory."

Barabis then turned to the boy with his hand extended, holding his eyeball. Devin gazed upon him and saw that he plucked out his own eye with a spoon that lay on his knees. Blood and nerve endings elapsed from his deep black socket, which stained his face with gore. Devin stood speechless as Barabis stared back at him with two remaining eyes, one on his forehead and the other in its rightful place.

"Don't be frightened, young Master! I did it for you so that you may see into the hearts of humanity and into the future of your true calling."

Devin remained repulsed, but his high admiration for Barabis led him to believe he had a reason for his torturous self-mutilation.

Barabis turned away and rinsed his eye socket with water from a bowl. Afterward, he dropped the eyeball into the bowl.

He then reached down to the corner of his robe and tore a square of cloth.

He pushed the nerve ending back into its socket and stuffed the small square cloth into his hollowed aperture. He then tied a strip of cloth around his head.

Devin's beguilement stood him still as he started to wonder if his father's warnings had validity. Barabis slowly walked over to Devin in a shamble of grueling grace, bending over to greet him with his foul green breath and makeshift grin.

"Devin, my Master, I need you to understand. I am the only person in this whole Kingdom that would die for you. I truly want you to rise to your destiny. Come back to my chambers tonight, and I will show you your true self and how this will be the beginning of your post-natural World.

Devin nodded and turned as Barabis continued his dark rituals of invocation.

Word spread like fire threw dry brush as people began to gather once more around the basin of the castle. Only this time, their numbers were far greater tenfold. Even though Barabis destroyed the vile beast, they all believed he caused its life. Great numbers and their pious beliefs forged them dauntless to rid themselves of the Devil Witch that lived in luxury behind the castle walls.

Yuan was the head protestor; he was a large landowner and farmer who ran his farm with an iron fist in a velvet glove. In his early forties and with little education he and his four sons ran the farm along with their peasant help. He rewarded his workers with squatter's rights and livable wages. His wife died one winter night after she gave birth to the youngest, Brier. He entered the World with a cry, and she left with a sigh, which left Yuan a bitter man.

Yuan's father bequeathed him a wealthy man, but with all his wealth, he still felt short, incomplete, and broken-hearted. Yuan had a loud voice, which came in handy as he drove his flatbed buggy throughout the basin, yelling in protest.

He became bitter towards the King after he watched his sons die one after another. This Devil's hand of deathly disease was surely the King's fault, as he imagined him ruling with a two-pronged crown. Yuan would stop anywhere people would listen, standing in his carriage preaching in protest. He fed off their fears and they his adamancy against the Evil that was, gathering more and more followers as he led them present at the basin of the castle walls.

Night fell upon the castle in the usual way, with the sun dipping behind the mountainous walls. Devin lies in the solace of his drape-shrouded bed, asking himself if he would return to Barabis chambers tonight. Somehow, he knew he would never be the same if he did, seeing in his mind the faces of those who met their demise the previous eve. He wondered if he could ever be so ruthless and what the point of it all would be. Did he really have a future to be, as Barabis proclaimed, a great sorcerer of witchery? And is this really what he wanted? He thought about what he would do with such powers as that old cynical smile came back to his face, and he suddenly found himself enjoying the memory of their souls taking their last breath. Right then and there, his mind began its dark descent onto the path of black magic.

Later that evening, Devin's feet found their way back to Barabis' chambers. A strange sense of foreboding came over him as he walked into the candlelit room. Shadows danced off the flickering light. Kilgore stepped out of the darkness and handed Devin a hooded robe, gesturing for him to strip himself bare. Liberated into his birth-given suit, Devin recast himself into the soiled stygian robe. Kilgore took Devin's clothing and his shoes, then returned to the darkness.

Barabis appeared and greeted Devin into his World, holding out his arm and pointing to the pentagram on the floor. Encircled with candles, there were cryptic writings scribbled in blood within the pentagram. Using a low tone of authority, Barabis then directed Devin to sit in the middle of the circle.

With bare feet, Devin lifted his robe from the path of the flames and stepped over the candles. He then squatted in the middle of the blood-painted star and gazed at the opaque orthographic writings. Devin then abided into position as his heart began racing, fearing what was to come. He looked over his shoulder while Barabis had his back to him, preparing some sort of a brew.

Kilgore then approached Barabis with a machete-type knife. The two of them stood in the shadows, with Kilgore seeming reluctant to carry out an order. Barabis finally laid his right arm on the table as he barked at Kilgore to follow through on his demand. Loathing his task, Kilgore raised the machete and came down with one quick stroke. Barabis cried out in agony for a short moment, then became silent as he directed the blood flowing into the orbed bowl.

After he accumulated enough, Kilgore reached an iron rod with a metal cup on its end from the fireplace. He held the glowing orange cup to the stubbed appendage, then pushed upon it as it sizzled, and Barabis gritted his teeth to stem the grueling pain. Kilgore wrapped the stub then grabbed the bowl where the eyeball was now buoyant in blood and held it out towards Barabis. The old Master lifted his lifeless limb with his remaining hand and dipped the still fervent fingers into the redness of gore before raking them across his face and chest. He used his fingers like a paintbrush as he painted himself in the same cryptic writings that were in the pentagram.

After he finished, Barabis turned toward Devin. The boy's

16

eyes widened in disbelief as he started to shake in terror.

"Don't worry, my Master, my life is insignificant. It is you whom I serve." Those words appeared to bring some comfort to Devin as he sat awaiting the unknown.

Kilgore then reached over and disrobed Devin to his waist, exposing his young chest and shoulders.

Barabis held his dismembered arm and dipped the fingers into the bowl. Next, he flung the limb, like a Priest sprinkling holy water, showering Devin's face and torso with blood. Barabis began to chant in Hebrew as he circled the young Warlock to be. After six hundred and sixty-six rounds, he stepped into the circle. Kilgore set the blood-filled bowl next to the pentagram and withdrew into the shadows. Barabis submerged the dead fingers into the red-clotted bowl. He scripted Hebrew on Devin's face, arms, back, and chest as if on naked canvas, mumbling in ancient tongues.

Barabis suddenly became silent, then raised the bowl to Devin's lips. Devin drank down the dark-red liquid without hesitation or remorse, becoming entranced and swayed to the silent song of Satan. His eyes rolled back in his head while he tightly gripped the bowl with both hands and drank down the gore, leaving only the orb.

Barabis reached for the orb that lay at the bottom of the bowl with his dead limb that came to life as if it were still attached and alive. He shouted obscenities of Demonic blasphemy as he walked behind the young boy. He held out the dead limb, which still held the discolored orb, and he continued shouting upward as if yelling at God Himself. He then reached around the boy, cupping the eye against Devin's forehead, while he shouted louder and louder.

Barabis abruptly ceased, and in sudden silence, he dropped the arm in Devin's lap. Stepping outside the circle, he slowly

17

shuffled in front of Devin. Devin gazed upward toward Barabis with his two brown eyes and the third eye green upon his forehead.

"Excellent, excellent!" Barabis shouted. "Come, come. Come hither, my young Master!"

Devin slipped the robe over his shoulders, lifting the lifeless limb as he walked toward the old Master. The boy gazed upon Barabis in his mutilated state of rapture.

"How do you feel, my young Master?" said Barabis as he set his remaining hand on Devin's shoulder.

Devin's new orb fixated upon Barabis as they exchanged sadistic smirks. Barabis then spoke: "Now you have the vision to see all the Worlds as all the Worlds are yours to see."

They conspired until dawn as Barabis elaborated on how to see into his Father's World, hell's abode. He instructed the boy on how to use his third eye. He took him into the hearts and Souls of men. Their dreams and aspirations depicted a picturesque vision of love, lust, greed, power, and the hunger for fertility. Devin also saw the diligent faith of a diminutive handful of pietistic believers who carried a cross in their endless craving for the closeness of God. He saw the mindless drones of people who drowned in their atheistic quandaries as they existed unacquainted with God.

Devin's new omniscience enabled him to glimpse beyond the gates of the celestial city and all of its omnipotence. He raised his arms and shouted, "Oh, Barabis, I can see so much! I can see the Creator himself, sitting upon his throne as his Angels sing praises of his name.

I can see my mortal father's enemies and how they plot against him as he remains unenlightened to the fact. I can see my true Father, our Dark Messiah, who waits ever so patiently as he gathers the rivers of casted Souls to clash against God and his arched Angelic Armies and rise to seize his throne in the Zion city of heaven. I can see beyond these walls and a great deal past the mountains and vast high seas to far-off lands and Kings.

I can see a baby and its mother in a desolate desert, starving for but a handful of water. I can see a young man drowning in a vast ocean, crying out to God his last words. I can see a young virgin being taken for the first time, screaming out in ecstasy.

Oh, Barabis, I can see all the Worlds and all that is in them. I can see, I can see!" The boy drifted left to right as if on a low-hanging swing.

The newly empowered boy burst out in hysteric laughter as his newfound vision flashed Worlds within Worlds.

Barabis then spoke with conviction as the boy ceased, "I gave you the knowledge and many forms of magic from the Underworld that would otherwise take many lifetimes to learn. But know this: we can only see into the near future while the far future is but a vague dream of the present time, for it could change from moment to moment. But we can call upon our predecessors and trade secrets from the Underworld. This is your World now. There are many treasures that will be laid at your feet. The flesh of humanity is for your consumption as you deem fit, while your appetite for destruction will be an endless hunger." And Barabis advised, "When you mix with humanity, simply close your third orb. It will seal to your normal appearance."

Barabis then barked, "Kilgore, bring me my parchments!" Kilgore emerged from his dark corner as he fetched a case of scrolls. "Give them to the young Master."

Kilgore handed Devin a black maple box that was almost large enough to hold a small child. "Take heed, young Master, this case contains a profusion of virulent Demonical secrets. I am just a messenger, but you are the ever-turning wheel that will set the world ablaze."

Devin opened the case, put the amputated arm inside, and closed it as he shut his omnipotent seeing orb. He then left for his chambers, taking Kilgore for his servant. Back in his own quarters, Devin had Kilgore fetch some hot water so he could soak his young, tired bones. He fell into a torpid state of slumber in the hot, soapy suds, his subconscious revering to nihilistic visions of shadowy phantoms. Devin's mind raced through multifarious figures, Devils and Demons in their demented, retched demeanor.

High in the heavens, Devin could see angels singing psalms of glorification to their Savior, along with their trumpets sounding in triumph. He could also see himself before God in defiance as he was forced upon his knees by the Archangel Michael and his soldiers.

In his vision, Devin shouted foul obscenities at God as he spat at His feet in the high courts of heaven. His name was stricken from the Book of Life, and he descended into the deep darkness of Hell. Devin was greeted with sulfur flames and Barabis, who sat on the council convocation of malevolent delegates. A scream then bellowed into his ears, and he awoke. A chambermaid had dropped a tray and ran out of the room.

Devin jumped out of his bath and looked down the hall to see the maidservant crying out, "Devil! Devil!" Devin approached the mirror as his third orb was sealing back to its usual appearance. After returning to his handsome, boyish looks, he burst out in laughter that echoed throughout the castle. He then went to the dining quarters and took his place at the table.

Shortly after, King Bosren entered and stared at Devin,

who had taken his place at the head of the elongated table. The King sat in silence but continued staring, searching for something that he knew not.

"What's the matter, Bosren? You look at me as if you were looking at the Devil?"

"You call me by my birth name? What insolence! I am your father, the King!"

Devin chuckled with amusement, then ceased abruptly as he glared at his father with contempt. "You may be my blood father, but I exalt myself over you and your kingdom."

The King beseeched his son with dire disfavor as he asked why Barabis had shamed him and turned his only son against him.

Devin shook his head and replied, "You could never understand, old man. I simply grew wise beyond your years." Devin then heaved a cloth napkin at the King. Bosren reacted by cringing cowardly as if it had been a dagger.

Devin then shot out of his chair, and it toppled to the floor. He then turned his back in a symbolic gesture of sin and stormed out of the room.

The King yelled as Devin dissolved through the corridors, "You are the heir to the throne! You can't walk away from your position in this kingdom!"

Alisatar hastily shuffled past Devin in a nauseating quake as he heard his King lashing out in anger. Devin simply smiled, willing ill fortune to Alisatar in a moment of thought. Seconds later, he heard Alisatar cry out in pain as he tripped over the chair that lay in his path. It sent him face-first onto the black oak table, and the injury killed the feeble, aged man. A cynical smirk came to Devin's face once more as he heard the shrill of the last syllable the old man ever uttered. Alisatar lay staring at the ceiling, quickly fading, gurgling in his own secretions of blood.

The bridge of his nose splintered straight into his brain, and his body contorted into a coiled posture of death. Running to his side, the King fell to his knees. He then lifted Alisatar's lifeless head and shook him, wailing out his name. King Bosren looked up to the heavens and cried out in tears, "Why, oh Lord, why?!"

Returning to his quarters, Devin sauntered over to a large mirror on the wall. Instantly, at will, he opened the omnipotent orb upon his forehead. He searched for something he knew not until he came upon a fair-skinned minx picking daisies on a countryside hill. He then ordered Kilgore to accompany him as he made his way to the stables.

Once there, Devin snuck up behind Gavin, a seventeen-year-old boy who was the stables' caretaker. Ever since he could walk, Gavin had been a stable hand under his father's guidance. He became the head caretaker after his father met his demise---he carelessly castrated a horse and was met with a hoof to the head, which killed him instantly. Devin was fond of Gavin, who was stout and strong from a life of labor. Gavin was Devin's only link to the peasant World that he was so curious about.

"Blah!" Devin yelled while poking Gavin in the ribs. Gavin hardly flinched, as he was used to unpredictable situations.

"Hello, Master Devin," he said as he stuck his pitchfork into the ground and bowed his head in respect. Devin smiled at him as he handed him a piece of candy from the castle kitchen. Offering this little treat was a ritual for Devin every time he would meet with Gavin.

"I'm going for a ride in the countryside. Would you like to

join me, young Gavin?"

Gavin was shocked by his question because peasants didn't consort with sovereignty as a rule of thumb. "But Master, what would your father say? And what of the people if they saw me with you?"

"Stop calling me Master! You are my friend, and I require your presence for an afternoon of romping through the countryside." Gavin nodded as he fetched Devin's colt. Then, for himself, he returned with a rickety, old workhorse that should have been led out to pasture a long time ago.

Devin shook his head and told him to ride his father's stallion. But Gavin was apprehensive, so Devin took the King's stallion, and Gavin took Devin's colt. Devin gave Kilgore orders to stay and watch the old workhorse as sort of a cruel, harmless joke. The two youths rode off, taking the roundabout way out so they would draw no attention to themselves. They played touch and go throughout the countryside on the grand, gallant steeds.

They stopped at a hearty apple tree and helped themselves to a belly full of the delicious red fruit. They walked their horses, joked around, and talked of things that the young boys found of interest.

They then came upon a young girl around Devin and Gavin's age. She would turn out to be the same minx picking the same weed flowers on the same hillside that Devin had seen earlier in his vision.

"Let us have a talk with the fair lass. What do you say there, young Gavin?"

A love at first sight, Gavin gave himself away. His passion rang out with rapturous joy as his heart harmonized in singing its sublime song. "Oh yes, Master Devin, I mean Devin, I would like that very much. Her beauty is that of a heavenly angel."

Devin half smiled as they came before the young girl. As they approached, she turned to them with a curious eye and caution. "Don't be frightened, pretty girl, we just want to talk," said Devin.

She studied their demeanor as she held a handful of freshly picked daisies and dandelions. Devin quickly introduced them by name before Gavin could blurt out that he was a prince. She then proceeded to pick the lanky weed flowers as her carefree eyes smiled at the two young striplings. They tied their horses to a tree stump at the basin of a hillock. Devin and Gavin both walked to the girl's side, then joined her in picking the varied colored weed flowers.

"What's your name?" Gavin asked in a nervous tone, as his face blushed to a healthy red- rose.

"Celia," she said, giggling in a gaily girlish manner.

Devin remained silent as he studied her slender shape in her sundress, which stirred his loins. Gavin then inquired, as if for future reference, where the girl lived. She pointed over their shoulders in a westward direction, past a hill, in a depiction of delight, as if pleased someone would ask. Gavin stretched his neck in that direction, contemplating the path she indicated as Devin simply nodded. The day pressed on as they rollicked along the rolling hillsides, chasing each other in a youthful game of foreplay. Devin seemed amused as he studied the power of the opposing sex drives. The three then came upon a brook that ran adjacent to the rolling hills in the serene setting.

Devin sat down on a grassy slope while Gavin and Celia walked to the edge of the water. Gavin slipped his arm around Celia's waist as they gazed upon their reflection in the slow-running stream. Devin noticed Gavin and Celia had taken an immediate liking to each other, and the seed of jealousy began to take root as their laughter echoed through his brain. But his newfound powers outbalanced those petty feelings; he knew he could easily ravish the sweet, young plum with no avail. Devin called out to Gavin and Celia, gesturing to them by waving his hand. "Come hither, you pretty, little lovebirds. I have a game we can play."

They both hurried to Devin, and they plopped their young rumps into a circle. They waited in anticipation of Devin's game plan, watching him intently. "The game is called hide and seek," Devin announced. Gavin and Celia looked bewildered, having never heard of such a game.

"It's simple," Devin explained, "I will go stand by that tree and count to fifty as you two go and hide. Whoever I find first, they are, then the next one must find the others."

The brook was the only sound heard until the excitement of the game got underway.

Gavin and Celia jumped to their feet and waited for Devin to reach the tree before they ran in different directions.

Devin braced himself against the tree with his forearm, resting his head on his arm and tilting it to the ground. He then opened his third seeing orb, gazing at Gavin hiding in the willows that grew by the stream. He could see Celia hiding behind a knoll in the tall grasses behind a tree.

"Forty-nine, fifty!" Devin quickly went for Celia, running along the slope until he was twenty paces behind her. He crouched down like a panther as he calculated her next move. He took two giant steps, jumping from the knoll and pouncing with ease, slamming Celia on her back. He cupped her mouth as he ripped her dress with his free hand. She desperately endeavored to scream, but Devin held a firm grip which rendered her helpless. Devin spoke, "Just relax," his magnetic words transfixed her. He thrust himself onto her. *Oh, such great wondrous pleasures God bestowed on us,* he thought as her body jerked with each thrust.

"Enjoy the moment, young Fraulein," Devin cried out as he prodded his tongue into her ear. She wrapped her arms around Devin while she infused her tongue into his throat. Devin groaned out loudly as he released the pressure from his loins. He lay there paralyzed and exhausted as if the weight of the World fell off his shoulders. He rolled off her, lying on his back, staring into the heavens. Celia's body was in spasms as she thrashed about helplessly, and she cried out like a crazed animal.

Gavin stood on the slope in disbelief, staring down upon their young, naked bodies. His heart fell to the ground while his dreams for any kind of future with the young minx were shattered. Devin jumped to his feet, as he pulled up his trousers and straightened himself up. Gavin began to walk away when Devin shouted for him to stop. Gavin turned momentarily, piercing him with a contemptuous glare, then continued storming off.

"God damn it, Gavin, I said stop!"

Gavin turned to face Devin as tears flowed from his eyes. Rushing to his side, Devin whispered, "Don't cry, young Gavin. She awaits your company."

Gavin stared at Devin in shock; the words crushed his ears in disbelief. Devin grabbed Gavin by his golden locks of hair and steered him to Celia who was reeling left to right on her back as if agonized over Devin's absence.

Devin pushed Gavin's primal buttons. His cajoling enchantment transfixed Gavin's mind into transgression as Celia's flesh summoned him into delirium. Gavin's hormonal rage raced through his body like a wild wolf. Devin released Gavin's hair and then let him lose him to the fiery Fraulein.

Devin sat on the edge of the knoll for a ringside seat as Gavin made a slow, torpid march to her lost in mind. Celia then sat up, startled and looked at Gavin and screamed out. Gavin was shaken by her scream and became aware of his true self. He reached out in jester of empathy, but she quickly jumped up and ran away as her screams echoed nausea into Gavin's ears while blubbering his apologies as she ran away. Devin cackled excessively, tears trickling from the corners of his obstinate eyes.

"What kind of witchery have you befallen me?" wailed Gavin in a trepid tremble of fear.

Devin suddenly became silent and stared at him with pity for his mortal morals of benevolence. "I just wanted to introduce you to your dark half that's been dying to get out and have a little fun. I don't know how you snapped from the spell; I guess I must work on that."

Gavin put both hands over his face as he cried out to God for forgiveness.

"God is dead," replied Devin. "He cannot hear you. I am your lord, God, and Master. You bow to me!" These words horrified Gavin as he struggled to find his old friend, Devin. But all he could see was an impish Devil-child in his place, and he wondered how Devin had controlled him.

Devin started back for the horses, with Gavin following silently behind. When they came upon the steeds, Gavin could see Celia on top of the hill with a man, possibly her father, pointing at them. As the youths mounted their horses, Devin looked up the hill and saw the man running toward them. Devin began to laugh; the scene only seemed to amuse him.

"Watch out for that nasty fall," he cautioned. Just as the word "fall" left his lips, the man tumbled and toppled down the hill, shrieks of pain echoing through the air.

Gavin witnessed the event in deplorable horror as his disbelief of reality burrowed under his skin like an unwanted parasite that was making him ill. Celia ran down after the fallen man in desperation while Devin simply trotted off, humming in song. Gavin followed behind in silence, feeling hopeless about helping Celia and her father. He lingered four horse lengths beyond the Evil-spirited hellion, becoming revolted by the harrowing sound of Devin's happy songs filling the air along the way.

When they reached the stables, Devin could see hordes of people gathered in groups, building pyres. Devin seemed amused as he uttered, 'Back for more, aye,' while Gavin took the horses and quickly disappeared.

Kilgore, standing in the shadows of the stable, continued his watch over the workhorse as if his life depended upon it. Devin smiled at him and relieved him from his duty, then disappeared into the castle. Walking through the courtyard, Devin noticed Kronus and his father, the King, holding a weighty conversation, which aroused his curiosity to intervene. He then turned to them, their conference urging him to interrupt. "What's all the hush-hush about? You gloom as if someone died said Devin."

Kronus straightened up like he wanted to belt the boy but remained restrained, awaiting the King's reply.

"Your words ring a distasteful truth, my son. Our beloved Alistar died this morning."

Kronus then blurted out, "He's dead because of you and your careless anger!"

King Bosren touched Kron's shoulder with a gesture so as not to provoke the currently calm boy. Bosren then informed Devin that Alisatar's funeral would be held after dinner that evening and asked if he would attend.

To the King's surprise, Devin did a role reversal, abetting his sorrow and sincerity. "I'm sorry, my dear father. He has been part of our family for almost three generations. May I give the eulogy?"

The King's face lit up with an unexpected, elated expression as if caught off guard by a shot of good luck. "Why yes, yes, my son. I am honored to have you host tonight's sad gathering."

Kronus stared with contempt and suspicion as he studied the boy's face, trying to find a secret that he knew Devin was concealing. Devin smiled back at Kronus, knowing he had already gotten under his skin. He nodded at his father and started to walk out but halted intermittently.

"I will be writing the eulogy in my quarters," Devin informed his father. "Can you send a chambermaid with my dinner? I want to make sure that I give a perfect speech."

The King was almost lost for words as he gleefully agreed.

Kronus continued to stare with suspicion as the boy walked away. "Your majesty, do you think it would be wise to have your son deliver the eulogy?"

Bosren eyed Kronus with a touch of anger and said, "My son will deliver a beautiful eulogy."

Kronus quickly bowed his head in submission before making a quit exit.

When Devin arrived at his quarters, he reached under his

bed for the black case and clutched it from where it was laggardly hidden. He placed it on his bed and opened it as the stench of death escaped and filled the chamber. Rigor mortis and decomposition rapidly consumed the dismembered arm. Without thought, he picked it up and placed it next to him as he lounged in bed, reading the parchment scrolls. His young mind bathed in the knowledge of many degrees of black magic.

The afternoon slipped into the early evening. Devin studied each one of the scrolls in consolidated concentration, losing himself in other Worlds as the words became etched in his mind. Just as he was reading about how important it was to deny your maker, he heard a rattling sound. He looked up, and there in his doorway was the same servant as earlier. She was entering his room with the fear of death in her eyes. Stepping into the chamber, she beheld the arm dancing upon his bed whereupon she once again dropped the tray while running out of the room screaming. Devin roared out in laughter as he pondered how it was possible that one could die of starvation in the castle.

He walked over to the fallen tray, picked up a scrap of chicken, and nonchalantly returned to his research. After three more scrolls had been thoroughly scrutinized, he rolled them back up and returned them to their case, along with the arm.

The funeral for Alisatar was being held in the courtyard. Aristocrats and commoners sat in rows of chairs before the casket. Devin strolled to the front of the courtyard where his father was sitting on his secondary thrown.

"Where is your eulogy?" Bosren anxiously asked, looking at the young prince with concern. "Don't worry, good father," he replied. "It's all right here," he said as he pointed to his head.

King Bosren smiled and nodded as some women passed half-curtsied to his sovereign crown. Devin looked to the rear of the courtyard. He caught sight of Kronus glaring at him, along with two of his patrons. The Bishop stood behind the pillar as the Alter boys swung censers of frankincense of aroma filling the courtyard. Behind the Bishop was a choir of boys awaiting their cue to sing their Heavenly hymns. Musicians played ever so softly seated overhead on a balcony.

The Bishop rang a small handbell, indicating the service was about to begin. Everyone drew silent and scurried to their seats. But Devin remained standing when the Bishop began to recite the Act of Contrition prayer. It seemed like an eternity as the Bishop continued with "Our Fathers" and "Hail Marys," which drove Devin crazy. The choir began to sing, and Devin's secular boredom became very apparent as he yawned at every syllable that was sung. Finally, after the recitation of even more "Our Fathers" and "Hail Marys," the Bishop left the pillar and nodded to Devin.

The King was overjoyed that his son was about to deliver the eulogy for his dearly departed friend. Devin walked to the pillar, his ears ringing from the singing and the gossip about. He stood silent as he peered from behind the pillar, looking over the people. He then began speaking a slow, sarcastic rhyme.

*"Old King Cole was a merry ole Soul and a merry ole Soul was he. But it really didn't matter because his belly's getting fatter, and I killed his advisory."*

By this time, the King was furious. His face turned red with anger and embarrassment while Devin continued with his speech. *"All the King's horses and all the King's men couldn't put Alistair back together again. He lies there broken; this much is true. Now my spell has been spoken, so I bid you adieu."*

One man stood out from the crowd yelling "Witch!" then a woman, then another man until the whole courtyard was in an uproar. Devin just stood behind the pillar as he laughed aloud at the crowd with contempt. He then pushed the pillar to the ground, strolled to the casket, and kicked the leg out from the long table it sat on, which sent the casket crashing to the floor. Alisatar's cadaverous body rolled out of its casket, with Devin pointing in laughter. Women began screaming, panic ensured, and the corpse lay on the floor.

Kronus and his men started for Devin as the hellish Imp vociferated in an ancient dialect and crooked his finger at the cadaver. The lifeless corpse then jumped to its feet! Devin held out his arms as if he were working a puppet on strings while the corpse mimicked his every motion. People began trampling each other in a frenzy of chaos as they frantically tried to reach the archway exit. Devin chortled hysterically, dancing in place as the cadaver mirrored his movements.

Kronus tried desperately to reach Devin, making no headway as the panic-stricken crowd pushed him back. The sound of crushing bones permeated the air, with screams filling the gaps in between. Devin made a running gesture, and the corpse ran toward the horrified people. When Devin jumped, the corpse threw itself upon the crowd. Devin turned around, smiling from ear to ear as the King shook in tremulous trepidation, his face recast to a ruddy red rose.

Kronus finally reached Devin and, with one knockout - punch, rendered him unconscious. The boy lay limp on the floor, as did the corpse. The King rushed to his son's side but was timorous to touch him. He just stood over Devin, desperately pleading with Kronus as to what should be done. Kronus called his men, lifted the boy, and carried him down to the dungeon. There, the prince was shackled, his eyes blindfolded, and he was lowered into a four-by-four pit cell with no bars or windows.

Kronus gaped down at the still comatose boy as he slammed down an iron cast cover on the cell. Three iron rods were slid and locked in place. A boulder was then lowered by chain and sat askew on top of the cover. By that time, the Devil-boy awoke, and he began banging and screaming about in a bemoaning, anxiety-filled voice. King Bosren rushed to the pit and pleaded with Kronus about how they should consider this matter. The King appeared weak and feeble.

Devin heard his father's voice and cried out, "Father, is that you? Please help me, father! I can't see, and it's oh so cold! Please, father, please!"

The King fell to his knees as he sobbed, "My son, my son, my only son!"

Kronus lifted the sobbing sack, and he and a guard escorted the weakened King back to his quarters. The King cried himself to sleep, Kronus watching over him with stoical disgust.

Kronus ordered his top trooper to keep watch over the King as he rounded up the rest of his men in the courtyard. His first order was to emancipate the prisoners so that the entire dungeon was emptied, leaving one sole occupant, the Prince. The prisoners ran in elated exhilaration as they were pardoned by the stigmatizing circumstance. Kronus and his men slowly crept up the west tower with swords and clubs in hand, hoping to catch Barabis by surprise. They broke down the giant oak door, rushing into his chambers. All was dark as they proceeded furtively in their encroachment.

A voice rang out, and Kronus looked in the direction from which it came. There was Barabis, sitting in the pentagram, basking in darkness and awaiting his capture. Kronus's men clubbed, shackled, and dragged him to the dungeon, where he met the same fate in a twin cell next to Devin. The guards sneered, laughing haughtily as they walked away to their standpoint. Barabis could hear the young Prince crying and thrashing about.

"Young Master, why do you cry?"

Devin straightened upright, straining to listen as if he couldn't believe his ears. "Oh, dear friend, Barabis, is that you?" he said, wiping his eyes.

"Yes, Master, it is me. Why do you cry when you are all so powerful? Kingdoms will tremble in fear to the sound of your very name?"

Sobs turned into silence as Barabis strengthened Devin with benign reverence and stories of his surmounting prominence. He then proclaimed, "Our Master Mephistopheles lives in darkness, but he knows he will rise with a vengeance and obliterate his oppressor who perches high in the Zion courts. You, too, will rise and rule this World as Kings and men of government will cringe at the sound of your name. I've seen far into your future. You will prevail over your vicissitude while you sit high up on a pedestal as your enemies bend to your feet."

Devin's tears turned to vindictive anger while Barabis continued to praise him and preached "hate."

"Tell me, young Master, where are the Sacred Scroll Parchments and Kilgore?"

"Oh, Barabis, I forgot all about Kilgore! He must be hiding in the stables, and the black box is under my bed." Barabis then declared, "Your all-seeing orb, we together will guide Kilgore to get the Sacred Parchments."

Devin relaxed into himself as his third eye opened. He could feel the heat form from Barabis as they merged into one vision. Their sight took them past the guards and up the stairwell through the corridors. Devin could see servants picking up the mess he caused in the courtyard along with two women and one man who had been crushed by the fear-stricken fury he induced.

Their vision took them through dark, dismal halls and stairwells into Devin's chambers. They could see the black box that was still in its place. They shot back through the corridors and then outside the castle to the stables, where Kilgore lay in a deep sleep.

"Kilgore," Barabis whispered. Kilgore immediately jumped to his feet and looked around as if Barabis were in the room. Barabis then murmured a chaotic satire of ungodly words that brought Kilgore's body alive in metamorphose. He fell to the ground, and his vocal cords strained to vociferate from the change that was taking place.

Black fur began to cover his body while cartilage and thin-skinned flaps protruded from his sides. His legs shriveled into clawed talons as his torso filled out and elongated into devilish proportions. Thick, black ears grew on his head, and his face narrowed to a point.

The horses in the stable went into a frantic commotion, bucking and stirring about in rigorous repulsion. The now nine-foot bat flopped on his belly, straining to reach the outlet of the stable. Its wings cut into the air in chaotic celerity. The horses bucked in panic while the batted creature made its way past each stall. Once outside the stable, it stood erect, flapping its elongated wings and letting out hellish, Demonic screeches. Its pearly-white fangs glowed in the moonlit sky, and it hoisted its head from side to side in its continuous graded screams. Whirls of dirt and dust clouded around the creature as it took flight towards the castle.

Scathing screeches throughout the valley brought attention to the Beast, which momentarily blocked out the moon as it circled for Devin's window. The rebellious protestors pointed at the nocturnal creature as it gracefully landed upon the ledge of Devin's window. Once inside, the Devil-winged Beast flopped on its belly and made its way towards the black box. By this time, the guards were alerted and making their way into the room. Just as they entered, the batted creature wedged its body under the bed in a beeline for the black box.

One of the guards plunged his spear into the creature's eye. It let out a sheering wail of agony. The Beast sprang upright, throwing the bed onto the guards. Standing erect, it flailed its head from side to side, trying to dislodge the spear.

Its shrieking screeches of horror shocked the guards, who froze like statues from fear. The creature half flew over the bed and bit into the spearless soldier's face.

By this time, Kronus made his way to the action of which his men no longer wanted any part. He jumped past his trembling soldiers and seized the spear that was still lodged in the Beast's head, trying to force it deeper. The Beast jumped backward in flight. The spear dislodged, along with Kilgore's plucked eye. The creature flew in screeching misery, bouncing and bobbing off the walls and ceiling as Kronus tried to stick it again. It finally swooped down and clinched the black box, then plopped itself onto the window ledge and jumped out into flight.

Kronus rushed to the window, hurling his spear into the night. The Batted Beast easily evaded it with ranging radar and swiftness. It shrieked out to the sky as it disappeared into the clouds, leaving Kronus disgusted with anger. Kronus's eyes then widened with inclination, and he commanded his men to follow him. They hurried to the dungeon, only to find his guards sitting at a table as if nothing was wrong.

Upon seeing Kronus, the guards snapped to attention. Kronus quickly ran to the twin cells and peered downward into the pits. After seeing the black magic villains were still in their places, he asked the guards if there had been any activity. The guards replied that all had been quiet. He then ordered them to stand by the cells and make sure the prisoners did not speak to one another, and to watch for any suspicious movements.

Dawn finally broke onto the valley with its usual variegated colors. If not for the night before, it might have been cheerfully spirited. But the angry crowds were a fast reminder of the previous night's mishap and the black magic culprits the castle contained.

That morning, the King ate alone in his depression, the weight of the World seeming to press against his shoulders. He had lost his good friend and adviser, along with his son, to that Devil-man, Barabis. He had an angry crowd outside that wanted his son's head. And he still had to worry about his enemies. Kronus stepped in just as the King finished his hardly-touched breakfast.

"My Majesty, Alisatar has been buried, along with the three who died last night. My Majesty, may I speak candidly?" Silence bestowed the air as the King nodded and gestured for him to continue.

"We had more witchery last night, even though your son and Barabis had been locked down in the pit. Your people want justice, and there's been talk of them trying to overthrow your position as King."

The King flustered in fear as he jumped from his seat. "What! My family has ruled for over three hundred years! What would I do?"

Kronus studied the King's demeanor as he basked in the words he was about to say. "My Majesty, I'm afraid if we don't

37

do away with Barabis and your son, they might storm the gates and rampage the kingdom."

"My son! My son is all I have. Who would be my heir? Who would take my place?"

Kronus restrained himself to not laugh aloud as he corralled the crowned clown into a corner. "My Majesty, I have an idea. Are you still friends with the King of Spain?"

The King flustered once more, but this time, he was confused and faint-hearted. The King shuddered at the thought of what Kronus was about to propose. "Yes, yes! But why do you ask? How could he possibly help?"

Kronus paused, then looked into the tired old eyes under a miss-fitted crown. "Tomorrow, we burn Barabis and your son at the stake."

"Not my son!" stammered the King.

Kronus barked aloud with an upper hand of disrespect for the fading King. "Listen, listen, my Majesty, but what the King's people won't know is that it will be Barabis and a different boy who looks like your son. The Prince will be exiled forever to the New World of America. You sign the proper papers and give me heir to the throne, as if I were your son. Then, and only then, I will have Devin delivered first to Spain and then to the new lands of America. You would have to pay the King of Spain a handsome amount of gold for his ships and crew members."

King Bosren put his head in his hands and cried, "My forefathers turn in their graves. Of all the generations, I would be last." Kronus cast a firm look on his face as if his option was the King's only solution.

"Very well," divulged the King in defeat. "I am very tired,

and my son doesn't wish to rule in my place. I'll have the papers drawn by nightfall that you will be my heir."

Kronus gave one last status bow before making a quick exit with a crooked smile. Soon after, Kronus left the valley with two of his most corrupt men. They went to conspire with Slone, a slave trader. Slone's slave camp was only ten miles outside the valley, en route to other kingdoms spread throughout the land. Kronus's greed for power was only superseded by his hunger for wars and hostile takeovers as he envisioned himself as the King of these lands. When Kronus reached the slave camp, he had a choice of many boys, but none fit Devin's description.

Kronus laid down more gold on the table than one man could carry with two hands as he made clear his requirements. By nightfall, Kronus was back in the valley with a boy who would be close enough to pass for Devin's brother. Papers were signed, placing Kronus just a King's death away from sovereignty. That same night, Kronus ordered his men to take Devin's metal cell box as they placed it on a carriage awaiting in the courtyard.

The same two men who escorted the slave boy from Slone's camp oversaw Devin's delivery to Spain. Devin's mobile prison had a secret compartment in the undercarriage of the wagon, which held four cases of gold. The guards had no knowledge of the gold-coined cargo, or Devin's trip would have surely been short-lived as the senior guard held the sealed document only to be opened by the King of Spain.

As dusk settled on the valley, a thousand peasants, led by Yaun, roared at the castle for justice and retribution. Finally, the portcullis rose, the drawbridge lowered, and a flatbed buggy exited. Two people tied back-to-back wore burlap sacks on their heads, with a hooded executioner standing by their side. The crowd went into a frenzy, as the smell of death would soon fill the air. The carriage halted at the neatly piled pyres, and the riotous mob surrounded the buggy, shaking and cursing its contents. The executioner ordered the guards to lift Barabis and Devin's sacrificial lamb to the pyres. They tied Barabis to a wooden stake, then the kicking, faultless boy, who bellowed through the burlap sack for God to help him. The executioner pulled the burlap sack off Barabis's head, giving him a last chance to repent and ask for forgiveness. But Barabis laughed hauntingly, gazing in contempt at the crowd and the executioner, the look of a diminished madman. He then opened his repugnant orb, and the mob repelled backward in horror. Barabis began shouting Demonic parables of blasphemy to the sky.

By this time, people were in a frantic commotion by his ungodly sight and Demonic ridicule. The executioner quickly lit the fires, which saved him from taking the hood off the boy. The innocent lamb began to shriek as Barabis bellowed out in laughter that echoed throughout the valley. Twenty-foot flames blazed while he shouted out in praise for the Princely Eminence of Evil, Devin Demas.

The haunting laughter continued, and a burst of flames stretched high in the form of a fiery hand that roared with Giant inferno fingers. The hades hand of hell extended outward, ripping through the crowd with tormenting, anguished death. The fiery hand began incinerating anyone within reach and everyone it touched. Wails were heard from the very mouths of those who just moments ago boasted of the deaths of the Prince and Barabis.

Hundreds lay charred and disfigured while the rest of the mob made a desperate run for the countryside. Black clouds of smoke hung in the air, with the stench of hair and flesh consuming the valley. The executioner removed the hood from his fiery, engulfed frame. Kronus lies dead and would never touch the crown. Finally, the hellish hand died out as if it seemed satisfied with the toll if left in its path. The valley lay still in the quiet sound of death, the remainder of the population disbanding into obscurity. The people deserted the kingdom in fear it would be haunted by the two ghosts-Devils, Barabis and the Prince. The only remaining people were King Bosren and one servant who was so old that death would almost be welcome. Corridors echoed with loneliness as the King sat on his thrown with no one to rule. The castle was truly haunted by the horror of its past, and would never hear children singing or symphonies in composition ever again.

Nearly forty miles away, the carriage that was en route for Spain would soon stop for the night. The sun peered down behind the horizon as the guards stretched their road-weary bones. The two guards lifted the iron confines from the carriage to give the boy rest and a hot meal. They opened the metal box and chained Devin to the carriage without word or struggle. The senior guard sat on the other side of the campfire as he stared in silence at the little Monster Imp. He then bragged how he would slit Devin's thoughts if he spoke or tried any of his bewitching antics.

The other guard went into the forest to fetch some firewood, all the while whistling winsomely without a care. After heaving an armful, he started back, still whistling until he became wrapped in black Devil wings. The Batted Beast squeezed tight as it squished the guts from the squirming man. The Giant Beast then bent its head down to the top of the squirming man's cranium and sank deep its fangs into his skull. It ripped open the top of the skull as the man's squirming ceased. Kilgore sucked his brain slowly, savoring every slosh of slop he could muster.

The Deviled-winged Beast then stretched out its black appendages as the extracted carcass fell onto the bloodied Earth. Loud screeches consumed the night as it belched out its Devil cry unto the black sky. The remaining guard jumped to his feet, his eyes darting about the forest as Devin sang out, *"You're going to be a dead man."* The driver's hair stood on ends in daunted terror as he rubbernecked about the forest and sky. Devin kept singing, *"You're going to be a dead man; you're going to be a dead man."*

By this time, the guard was perturbed by the mouthing boy. He reached down and slapped the singing boy's face. Devin simply turned back to him and sang even louder, *"You're going to be a dead man, you're going to be a dead man! Dead man! Dead man!"*

The guard started to backhand him once again until the batted creature descended from the black sky and toppled him to the ground. It flapped its wings in a frantic frenzy, pinning him down and biting into his face.

Devin gaily changed the chorus: *"Told you so, told you so, I see your departing "Soul", told you so, told you so, I see your departing "Soul"."* The Devil Beast ripped the man's larynx, which dangled from its mouth while it jerked its head left to right as if it were a bird with a worm.

The nocturnal creature feasted brain caviar while Devin changed the chorus to *"Kilgore ate your brains, Kilgore ate your brain, ha, ha, ha. Kilgore ate your Brains."*

After the bat creature was satisfied with its fill, it stretched out its wings and flew off into the pitch-blackness of night. One song later, it returned with the black box in its claws, dropping it ever so gently at Devin's feet. It then circled overhead and flopped itself upon the ground, subsiding in submission to the presence of its Master.

By sunrise, Kilgore lay naked, curled in the fetal position, and worn out from the night's activities with a gaping hole where his eye once was. Devin woke to the sight of a half-eaten cadaver and a naked Kilgore at his feet. Devin nudged him with his foot as he half sang, *"Wake Up, my unfeathered friend, wake up."*

Kilgore jumped to his feet, unashamed by his nakedness. Devin then snapped, "Get these blasted chains off me."

Kilgore rushed to the dead guard's corpse, reached into his jacket, and grabbed the keys. After Devin was freed, Kilgore put the guard's bloodstained clothes on himself. Kilgore's face then appeared puzzled as he patted his pocket from a protruding package that positioned itself to his attention. He immediately handed it to his Master.

Devin smirked when he recognized his father's handwriting and the family seal. He jumped up and down with joy after reading of his impending freedom from his father and the newly found gold. The Devil Imp opened his orb to the vision that bestowed him with overwhelming joy. He could see the carnage Barabis left behind, along with his father sitting alone upon his thrown. Devin thought of turning back and ruling the kingdoms that lie throughout the vast lands. But Bosren intrigued Devin with the letter regarding the New World of America meant only for the King of Spain's eyes. As clever as Devin was, he had a different objective in mind.

Rather than give his gold to another fat King, he would hire his own ship and crew. So, he and Kilgore would continue their journey to the west until they reached Spain.

Three weeks later, Devin found himself at a pub near the shipping docks of the coastal ports of Barcelona. He left Kilgore with the gold-secured buggy as he walked into an unsavory type of tavern. He laid a gold coin in front of a cut-throat type of sailor.

The sailor's eyes lit up like fireworks as he contemplated a swift sword into the boy's belly if it would net him any more gold. The sailor led Devin on a wild goose chase, walking him through the docks of legitimate vessels sailing to legitimate locations. They walked past a cargo crate out of public view when he turned with a sword, pointing it to Devin's throat.

"Oh, ye simpleton," Devin lay claim as he clinched the tip of his sword. The boy then held the tail end of a cobra as it spat in the scoundrel's eyes.

"Please don't hurt me," the sailor begged. The serpent remained stretched out and suspended as Devin held firmly to its tail. The mendicant fell to his knees, and the snake bit the air around him.

"Please don't hurt me," he winced with newfound respect.

Devin smirked and rhymed, *"Listen here and open your ears, my craven little mouse. If you abide by my commands, you'll surely be endowed. Your frayed, worn pockets will rapidly overflow with the bulk of bullion, your precious gold. But don't dare "cross" me, my craven little mouse, or ye befallen, a deadly forceful trounce."*

Devin askance with competence of his capabilities as he slapped the sailor's face for his audacity of pernicious attempt. Devin then cast the snake upon the dock as it metamorphosed back into a sword.

"Take heed, Ole simpleton Sailor. Do not bequeath me with any more treachery, understand?" "Yes, yes!" said the vacillating rat. Devin then commanded, "Now go find me a ship!"

The sailor nodded as he started to grab his sword but changed his mind and hurriedly began to scurry off. Devin raised his voice as the sailor drew twenty paces away. "Oh, Ye Simpleton, I think it best we don't mention anything about this," he said as he pointed to the sword. The sailor waved his hands, gesturing and bewailing he would not, and then he fearfully hastened away.

44

The next day, Devin waited in the pub along with Kilgore until the sailor showed up with a man who was soiled and seasoned by the sea. Devin brought two satchels of gold with him. They sat at the table as Kilgore stood silently by his side. The soiled seaman introduced himself as Captain Sam Gutter. He gawked at the gold and quickly agreed to take Devin anywhere he wished. The first sailor took his finder's fee and hurried off without a word. Captain Gutter's eyes widened to the size of the satchels of gold. He would say what he needed to get the boy and his gold out to the open sea before cutting them into chum.

Carefully choosing his words, Devin negotiated his voyage. He told Captain Gutter he would require the captain's quarters. Since the scalawag had a swift murder in mind, Captain Gutter quickly agreed.

The next morning, they were out on the open sea. Devin had never been on the ocean before, so he stood at the stern watching the waves. Just two miles out, the captain made his move. He and five of his men emanated across the deck with swords in hand. Kilgore commenced to place himself between the swords and Devin. But Devin anticipated the possibility as he was more confident with the powers he possessed.

Devin raised his arms and commanded the ocean for his bidding as the Sailors halted and farcically laughed at the crazed boy. They then continued for Devin's throat as they slowly shuffled across the deck in a scourged showdown of death. Blue servile servants made of ocean water suddenly crawled upon the deck. The pirates drew nearer until the Aquatic Soldiers washed the attackers off their feet.

Devin needed the captain and his deckhands for the journey to the New World, so he placed the fear of his powers into their black hearts. The blue Titan servants washed away the captain's attack and left the Pirates lying bewildered on their backs. They crawled to the far side of the deck, staring at the puddles with their newfound veneration.

Devin charged the cowardly captain, who still lay on all fours, and grabbed him by his beard. "I think best that you listen, and you listen well," the boy announced. The captain nodded as Devin held firmly. "Now you are going to take me to the new lands of America with no fuss, right?"

The captain nodded again.

"If you try anything like this again, I will maroon your bloody carcass on a rock in the middle of nowhere, got me?" The captain detested looking weak in front of his men but nodded in submissive prostration.

"If you do as I say, one of those cases of gold will be yours. If not …"

Devin looked out at the ocean. Captain Gutter jumped to his feet and then barked orders to his men as the ship steered toward the west, making an about-turn.

For the next few weeks, the Sailors stayed clear of the Devil-boy and Kilgore as they performed their duties with precision. The captain wasn't happy about giving his cabin to a runt of a boy and his servant, but considering the alternative, what choice did he have?

By the next day, a storm was brewing, and the Sailors were doing their best to get ready. Strong winds from the north started to push the ship off course.

The captain approached Devin and told him to prepare for a rough ride, but to Devin, it was of trivial importance, and he rendered no concern. That evening, giant waves thrashed the ship about like a small toy. The captain rushed to Devin once more and said he didn't think the ship could weather the storm.

Devin smirked and replied, "Fret not, old foolish fool as he walked past him and started for the deck."

On deck, all hands were scrambling to take down the sails and batten down the hatches. The wind whipped Devin's long, dark hair as he struggled to the bow of the ship. He commenced singing in strange tongues as he waved his arms about. He continued for a time as the captain began to lose his fear of the boy. The vessel suddenly ceased its vicious rocking. The captain was dumbfounded as the storm continued its fury. Captain Gutter ran to the ship's side and looked down, the sight astounding him. The Aquatic blue Titans had returned to the ship and had lifted it upon their shoulders.

They methodically hoisted the vessel with ease while the storm continued to rage around them. The ship seemed to make even better time than with wind-filled sails on a clear, windy day. The storm endured for two days as the tireless Aquatic Soldiers made headway to the new lands of America. The weather finally broke one evening, and the Sailors began to chant, *"Red sky at night, sailor's delight. Red sky in mourn', sailors be warned."* The Titan Soldiers dissipated into the ocean as the Sailors' chants became upbeat in mirthful song. The captain emerged from under the deck as he checked his sexton and compass to the geometric trajectory of the stars. His jaw dropped when he realized they had traveled almost four thousand miles! He ran down to the captain's quarters to tell Devin the incredible news, knocking twice before rushing in. To his horror, Kilgore was in batted feature hanging upside down from a rafter as Devin had his third orb open, reading his Parchments. Captain Gutter slammed the door in repugnance while Devin burst out laughing. The captain then ran back up to the deck, and he spewed his last meal overboard. He had intended to tell Devin they would stand to make millions from his Aquatic servants but decided against it when he thought of the Witchery that was involved.

With calm, clear skies, the sun sparkled on the ocean with its morning light. The deckhands unfurled the sails and then continued with their daily chores in a cheerless capitulating conduct. Two days later, they reached the shores of the New World. The captain ordered the crew to set anchor, and the deckhands rolled up the sails. Devin and Kilgore walked up on deck as the captain was studying the shoreline with his pocket telescope. Sam Gutter's lips cracked from the salt air and sun, but it didn't stop him from licking them as he anticipated his payment in gold.

Devin nodded his head. "Foolish, foolish man. I said to take me to the New World, not before it."

Devin reneged his word as the captain stuttered, trying to tell him that his dinghies would take them, but the young Warlock refused to listen. He flailed his arms about as his Aquatic servants raised the ship and rushed it toward the shoreline.

The captain pleaded, crying out, "You promised! You promised!"

But Devin held firm his decision as the vessel continued towards the coast. The ship hit the sand, yet it still pushed ahead, the Titan blue Soldiers carrying on. The blue servants sustained the ship as far as they could, soaking in the sand upon each step. The Titans vanished into the pearl-white beach as the ship lay marooned, tilted slightly on its side. By this time, the captain didn't care if he lived or died as he drew his sword and ran for Devin's throat. Devin belched out bewitching words, halting the captain in place and making him cry out in agony. His frame contorted, folding backward into itself. The sound of breaking bones filled the deck while his crew watched in harrowing horror. The mass of human flesh folded three folds until it lay still, silent, and cubed as its life's blood secreted around it.

48

"Anybody else has anything to say?" Devin announced. "No? Very well, then. Let us see this New World of America, shall we?"

He ordered everything off the ship---lanterns, food, clothing, even the ship's sails, and rope---until all was stripped. Everyone stood puzzled, staring at the ship and at Devin. One sailor finally had the guts to ask, "What's to come of us?"

Devin laughed and answered, "Well, if you're not good little Sailors and don't do as I say, you might not find yourself folded like your good Captain!"

Devin suddenly jumped up on a small crag, shouting words of ancient dialect as a dainty dragon made of fire danced out from his lips and set the ship ablaze as the Sailors' hopes of returning home went up in flames with the ship.

Devin then gave a satirical speech, let me reintroduce myself. *My name is Devin Demas of malevolent grievance; let me tell you about my Demons. They are black and blue and misconstrued and love to dine inside you! So if you do, or if you don't, what would be thy end result, a life of gold or crease in the fold, matters not to me at all!*

Devin smiled and gazed upon the worried-faced frowns as they fluttered amongst themselves with fret filled mutter. Devin burst out, "1637, This is not the year of our lord! Nay, no, not, this is the year of me, your lord! You will flourish from me, live for me. Faithfully follow me, me, me. Get it? Got it! Good! Now, let us look at our new homeland, shall we?"

They stared at the burning vessel in disbelief, grabbed the cargo, and began heading inland. They traveled through rough terrain, foothills, forests, and swamps until dusk came.

"Very well, this spot will do," Devin commanded.

They stopped at the bottom of a ravine and on a solid slate

of granite, where they set up camp. Kilgore disappeared into the dark forest before nightfall, as he would soon turn into a batted Beast. He would feed on rabbits, snakes, rats, and rodents of any kind, and maybe even human brains, if the opportunity presented itself.

"Where did your servant go?" a Sailor asked.

Devin smirked, then said, "Ole Kilgore, he just went to get himself a little snack. He'll be back by morning."

The Sailors looked at each other bewildered, remembering their late captain telling them of a nine-foot bat in his cabin. They sat around the fire, keeping a careful watch on the sky and on Devin. They cooked some slop they brought from the ship and sat close around the flames. Devin could see fear in their eyes, and that's exactly how he liked it.

Devin, however, did want to break the ice, so he asked the crew their names, all twenty-nine of them, minus one captain. One by one, just like taking roll calls, they answered, their faces glowing in the campfire light. There was Matthew, Mark, Luke, and John almost every Bible character of one time or another. If it wasn't for their ruffian pirate appearance and their murderous lust for gold, one might mistake them for saints.

Devin then opened one of the cases, and all faces lit up with the luster that lay at their new Master's feet. Even though there was no place to spend it, their lust beat strongly in their hearts, and they would take that lust to their graves. Devin reached in, grabbed a handful, and tossed a coin to each of the Sailors.

After three handfuls, the scavengers received one gold coin each, compliments of King Bosren. Afterward, Devin recited a three-song speech about how they all could be wealthy beyond mere trinkets of gold.

50

Most didn't understand a word Devin spoke as their barbaric, simple minds kept their eyes on the four encasements of riches. The crew lay fast asleep, except for one whose eyes couldn't tear themselves away from the cases of gold. Matthew reached into his boot and grasped his eight-inch knife. He bit down on the blade and made a slow, quiet crawl to Devin's throat. Although he had visions of being the hero, saving his Clan from this tyrant boy who plagued them, he just wanted the gold.

Just as Matthew was approaching the slicing distance, a screech rang out in the night sky. The sailor turned his head upwards in time to see black claws sinking into his shoulders. He screamed as the Batted Beast lifted him off into obscurity. His cronies woke in horror, witnessing Matthew's departure into the sky. That night, Kilgore's mutation would feast on the delicacy of Matthew's brain. Devin simply lifted his head, smirked, then lay back asleep. The fear-stricken Sailors slept not a wink, staring at the Devil-boy and keeping watch on the night sky.

The next day, all was quiet, without even a syllable uttered, the humbled crew continuing their death march into the New World. Kilgore led the pack while Devin sang gleeful songs and trailed behind the herded group. He then began to feel sorry for his cargo-toting slaves, so he had them halt when they reached a clearing by a brook. Devin sauntered to the water to have a look, with the Sailors following suit. They filled water jugs and tried unsuccessfully to catch some fish.

Devin stepped into the cool, clear water, blithely beaming before him as he uttered, "Bequeath us your bounty, oh Crooked Creek."

A hundred hands made of water commenced throwing more fish on the bank than the Cronies could carry. The men jumped up and down in elation until a loud roar erupted behind them. A giant black bear stood erect, coursing toward the scent of the brook's bounty. Devin grabbed a fish from one of the trembling men. He then charmed the giant Beast with words and the flesh of fish. The giant bear ever so gently accepted his gift, clenching the still-wiggling fish from its new Master's hand, then turned and walked away.

From there on, the men would almost depend upon the boy's protection unless the perpetrator was the boy himself. Day after day, they pressed westward through rain, mud, and rough terrain. Their feet began to blister and swell. Some would talk of escape, and if it were to happen, it would be well after nightfall. Devin decided it was time for a two-day rest as his feet also began to ache. So, they camped by a lake where there would be game and water to sustain them on their journey. Devin kept them well fed in fish, but they began to tire of fish that was plentiful. Red meat is what they craved; to sink their teeth into a well-cooked carcass would be heaven.

Just as they were about to ask Devin if they could go out and hunt, three Indians approached the encampment. One of them carried a wild boar slumped upon his shoulders, a gift they were to offer if greeted in a civil manner. The Indians had been watching the group ever since they landed ashore and regarded Devin as a Master of Mother Earth's creatures. None of the Crew had ever heard of these Indian type people, but still, they welcomed them into their camp. The wild boar would be enough to kindle a new friendship as they feasted through the night. Devin remained mute during their sumptuous meal while the Indians and Sailors communicated with hand signals and a few muttered words.

By nightfall, the Indians departed, and Kilgore vanished as usual into the night. The Sailors joked into the wee hours, and even Devin laughed at some of their tall tales. The next morning, Devin woke up early and bathed himself in the lake. The child in him still loved to play, so he made his own

52

playmates out of the water. After an hour of toying in the lake, he finally grew tired and made his way back to camp.

It was then that Devin learned four of the Sailors had deserted and set out to find their new Mohawk friends, laboring to carry two cases of gold that they stole. Devin became infuriated when he discovered their disappearance, along with his gold. Kilgore rushed to his side as he heard his Master roaring at the remaining sleeping Sailors. They woke to the sound of Devin's fury, squinting their eyes in the morning light and the young Warlock's rage. "What do I have to do, kill you all just to make a point?" he roared.

One of the trembling Sailors then confessed, "We're sorry, Master. We didn't know that they would go ahead and do it."

Devin yelled, "Do it? Do it? You mean to tell me you idiots knew they were plotting, and no one came forward to tell me?"

One vacillating jellyfish then blurted out, "I'm sorry, Master. I tried to talk them out of it, but they just wouldn't listen."

Devin's fury flared along with the flames of the fire that suddenly consumed the confessor's head. The confessor cried out in tumultuous agony as he ran about the encampment tousled in terror. He then rushed to the lake to submerge his burning head.

Devin sat in the middle of his loathing sheep. He crooked his arms like a tree and opened his all-seeing orb. The trepidation of the Sailors made them jump back when they took in the horror of his third eye. Devin scoured the countryside until the running rats came into focus. He proceeded to ring out a composition of a deadly spell of rhyming of hateful verse: *"Trees, trees, oh lovely trees, bring my enemies to their knees. And if they yield your branch and leaves, break their bones and kill them, please."*

Devin closed his orb and opened his eyes. He leaped to his feet and gazed about the encampment, only to find his men hiding from him. "Come out, come out, my frightened little rabbits. We have rats to catch."

The Sailors slowly rose from behind rocks and trees as Kilgore clapped his hands in a violent gesture for them to comply. The crew grabbed the cargo and started off with their heads hung low. Devin opened his orb once more as a grin came down his face. He sealed the orb and changed direction. The group came upon a thicket of willow trees. There they were---all four men dangling from a weeping willow and its whip-like branches, horror-stricken expressions on their faces.

Devin then cracked his own joke as he smiled devilishly, "What kind of rats don't run no more? The dead kind! Ah-ha-ha!"

After Devin retrieved his gold, they continued their journey. Four more bad apples dangle from the tree, left for the consumption of the forest. Devin began to sing as the terror-filled Sailors toiled and trudged in loathing torment.

*"Thirty Sailors set sailing across the open sea. The captain tried to trick me dead. I folded him in three. One got eaten, one set* scorching, *and four rats that hang broken ... and now twenty-three, and now there's twenty-three!"*

Devin repeated his twisted song many times as he sang in glee. The remaining twenty-three were aghast at his song as they pondered who might be next. Even though Devin's body ached, if he knew the men ached as much as he, that would be good enough for him to keep his merciless march alive with pleasure. Dusk came upon them once again, and Devin approved a spot at which to camp for the night. The Sailors were pained by hunger but dared not utter a word of complaint. Gazing at his downcast crew, Devin could sense their hunger. Kilgore came to his side and was given instructions to carry it out. The despondent men dared not to look or listen, hanging their heads toward the ground. Kilgore walked off into the woods while Devin said nothing and sat himself down by the fire. All eyes remained looking downward as Devin smiled in the dead silence that imbued the campfire.

He then spoke softly, "You're all probably wondering where we're going. All I can tell you is I'll know when we get there." The men just looked at each other, wondering who would speak on their behalf. Luke finally spoke up with carefully chosen words, "Master, are we to see our homes and wives ever again, and if so, how would we return, getting farther and farther from the sea with no ship?"

Devin remained silent as all eyes fixed upon him, awaiting his reply. He burst out cackling, "Why, Luke, I didn't know one-eyed, toothless vagabonds would have wives waiting at home for them! Who would marry the likes of you?"

The whole camp broke out in laughter, forgetting their worries for a moment. Shrieks then filled the sky, and the laughter died into panic. Yet Devin began to chuckle once more, seeing their fear-stricken faces. His humor horrified them as the men were preparing for their deaths, or at least a struggle for their lives.

Devin roared hysterically, trying to push out the words: "Dinner's here."

His guffaws finally subsided as his Devil-winged pet made a star appearance, dropping a one-hundred-pound doe from the sky. Gaping holes covered its back from Kilgore's giant claws. The sight sent shivers up the men's spines as blood-curdling cries filled the night sky. Some of the men spewed at the thought of this gift from hell, while others just accepted it as if they had no choice. Once the aroma of roast venison permeated the air, they all joined in for the feast. The Sailors swapped stories from the sea as they picked clean the bones from the once vibrant doe. Devin remained mute while their laughter surrounded the campfire, and their swashbuckling tales soaked up the night.

Weeks went by as they continued their journey into the unknown. Only Devin vaguely knew what lay ahead. Finally, they came to a valley that resembled the home he had left behind. He decided that this would be his new realm of residence for his reign of reprisal.

Devin ordered the sailors to build a mansion of smaller fashion but with the same specifications as his father's castle. But Sailors, being only Sailors, looked at one another dumbfounded. Finally, Luke spoke, explaining how his father was a builder and hated that his son chose the life of a Sailor. But the knowledge did not escape him, Luke said.

He had worked for his father until he turned twenty. Soon after, the crew began to tear into the Earth with picks and shovels upon the spot of Devin's choosing. They built the foundation with slabs of slate, the walls of stone from the riverbeds, and lime mixed with clay and sand for mortar.

By the time they finished, Devin was twenty and well-studied in his parchments. Amazingly, the remaining twenty-three Crew members were still alive due to the fear that kept them loyal. The local tribes didn't mind Devin's Motley Crew of pirates as long as they didn't travel on sacred grounds and stayed clear of their women. But it was only a matter of time before the unruly hellions would pillage, plunder, and rape. One day a young Squaw was getting water from a river that lay adjacent to Devin's valley. Two of Devin's crew pummeled and chastised her, leaving her for dead. Her father, a head chieftain, tried to consult with Devin in a civil manner, but Devin basked in tyranny as each year Evil grew deeper in him.

One morning, Kilgore had not returned home from his nightly prowess of nocturnal activities. Devin loved his friend, if not for him, his journey to the New World might not have been possible.

Devin sank into a deep meditation as he searched for Kilgore with the aid of his omnipotent orb. He searched throughout the lands until he saw Kilgore, riddled with arrows, at a tribal camp. Since his visions never failed him, he took precautions in handling the situation. He went to his hand-painted pentagram, which was drawn in the blood phlebotomized by his pawns. He then began a pugnacious ritual, placing the gifts given to him by the neighboring tribes into the pentagram. He went into a trance as he convoked the depths of Hell to assist him in his quest for virulent deaths.

He took articles from each Tribe, and he beat them together while shouting foul obscenities of Demonic dialect. The boy appeared a lunatic in the pale candlelight light, crying and shouting while ripping out his hair in clumps, infusing his hatred into the spell. After three hours of rampaging nefarious hexes, he came forth from the ritual room exhausted with tear wrought face but strong with a sense of retribution. He walked outside and sat by a raging campfire as one of his men shaved the rest of his hair to a glistening bald in honor of Kilgore.

By evening, smoke signals pervaded the countryside, while the air seemed disturbed with violent hatred. The next day, the valley echoed with war cries as warriors from each tribe slaughtered one another in a meaningless quest that they knew not. The only survivors remaining were the women, children, and feeble, old men who couldn't pull the string of a bow to save their lives. Devin then offered rewards of the flesh to his men, and they took their choice of women for sex slaves and children for sacrifice. By this time, Devin's remaining twenty-three never questioned his motives as they partook in their Master's endeavors, becoming devout followers in Devilish debauchery. Devin had a traditional funeral pyre built to honor Kilgore, and they celebrated with fruit wine made from raspberries and apples.

Seventeen more years elapsed into Devin's manhood while more and more settlers colonized a village just east of the valley. Devin paid no mind if they knew the valley's interior was off-limits. Along with the settlers came trade, whiskey, women, and the much-dreaded Catholics and Christians. They poured in from all over Europe, but mostly it was those Damn British---they were like ants on an apple, crawling everywhere.

Devin knew he had to get documents drawn up in writing stating his ownership of the valley. He became part of the rising community and paid one gold coin for every fifty acres he owned. After all was paid, he owned over fifty square miles. Along with his acclaimed acknowledgment came responsibilities.

He projected his conspicuous prominence as a pragmatic pioneer in the progressing province, yet he decided to be low-key in his witchery. If word spread of his ungodly endeavor, he would surely become a hated man. Even though the Indians knew of his Demonic ways, he conceptualized that they would be no threat.

Their genealogy would have to flourish two more generations before they could cause any retaliation. Devin's priority was to cause commotion within the ranks of the community and slow the progress of Church and State. His second priority was to place his newly educated pawns into power to do his bidding for pernicious intent. He often banged heads with the Clergy, and if they caused too many problems, they would meet with an accidental death. But too many accidents would lead to too much talk in the community and would force him to take different actions. There would be payoffs and blackmail, using Indian squaws for bait. And, of course, if all else failed ... persuasion through his Black Arts.

Devin could overthrow the Christian preachers and replace them with his own version of Spiritual vision. However, the Catholic Priests were handpicked by the ecclesiastic officials of the Vatican, as his hands half-tied.

One day, Devin was returning home from a town council meeting when a young woman caught his eye - a strawberry blonde so beautiful she caused Devin to feel weak in the knees from the sight of her. Devin had never known love before, except from his beautiful mother, who died away when he was six. She was the most amiable person he had ever known, and she glowed with the elegance of a true Queen.

Devin jumped in the young woman's path as he stated that her beauty was like that of a solitaire Goddess. He then tipped his hat in a courteous gesture, slightly bowing his bald head. She was a bit taken aback that this wealthy man would take an interest in her as she half curtsied. Her face turned scantily red with insecurity and reverence.

Devin inquired her name as he peered into her Soul. She nervously replied, "Dianna," while she half curtsied once more.

"My name is Devin, Devin Demas," he returned as he kissed her hand like a wolf in sheep's clothing.

"My father is the Pastor at the new Catholic church," she answered. "Are you Catholic?"

He quickly pulled his hand away as if caught off guard. "Yes, I am, but not much of a practicing one these days. I'm just so busy."

"God is never too busy for you," she said with judging eyes.

Devin nodded as he noticed she wore an amulet gently resting above her cleavage.

"Well, I really must be going," she said as she half curtsied once more.

"Will I be seeing you in Church?" asked Dianna with soft, curious eyes.

"I don't know," replied Devin in an unconvincing voice. "As I said, I'm a very busy man." Dianna glared with prudent eyes as she walked away.

Devin now controlled half the businesses in the yet-to-be-named town. He owned the fur trading union, a saloon, and a general store, which all operated in the names of his subsidiary pawns. The next day, Devin was in his study, mulling over his Parchments with a glass of twenty-year-old French brandy. He gazed out the window, daydreaming.

Pacing about, he contemplated universal knowledge, with a selected Parchment lying flat on a black oak table. He savored a mouthful of the exquisite elixir, and suddenly, he noticed that when he looked at the Parchment upside down, it read as an entirely different inscription parallel to the other. Devin was excited beyond all his expectations. He began to read the Parchments as if he was finally able to read a new book after reading the same one for years.

New incantations and secrets were expounded upon as he fumbled through each Parchment with anticipation. He then came upon the last Parchment, written by the very hand Devin kept in his black case. It divulged the secrets of immortality along with the revelations of the unearthly battles to come. It forbade his future and his hand in the acts he had yet to perform. It revealed a chaotic upheaval, where Evil triumphed over Good as mankind faltered to pestilence and war. It told of a man who would live through death unto the End times to

Come and the Worldly undoing of God's will. It mentioned the Prince Prophet and how he would have the answers to all the World's troubles. It also gave the recipe of the steps for immortality through the destruction of his very Mortality.

An epiphany extended through Devin's imagination as he realized the prophecy that Barabis had preached to him oh so many times during his younger days. He now realized the real struggle between good and evil and its plight to compete for the hearts of Mortal Man. Devin then opened his all-seeing orb, gazing at the key ingredient to his prophecy, waiting unexpectedly, kneeling in a church. A pure-at-heart virgin, yet to be tainted, Dianna prayed diligently with faith. Devin would have to pursue Dianna to be his unwedded wife for unholy matrimony to fulfill his ungodly endeavors. The parchments explained how Devin would have to win the love of a virgin, impregnate her, and then use his own Child for the forsaken price of his own Immortality.

On the next day, Devin stepped through the new Catholic Church doors as he searched the pews and the interior of the building. He then found what he was looking for a true creature of God; she stood in utter beauty as she led Bible studies with the little children. Devin caught her eye, and a big smile came to her face in an expression of surprise. She told the children to read a page from their Good Book as she excused herself to have a chat with her caller.

"To what do I owe this unexpected treat?" she said as she approached him like a mouse to a python. "Well, I thought we might have a picnic if you weren't busy," said the python to the beautiful little mouse. "I'll be finished here shortly. If you want to come back in an hour, I could put together a basket."

Devin nodded, acknowledging his return for what would be a date. He walked to the saloon for a nip of whiskey and an update on his Profits. Daniel was one of the smartest in

Devin's Cult, so he ran the saloon in selfless loyalty.

After an hour of going through the books, he walked back to the Church, where Dianna waited on the steps. They loaded the carriage and took off for the midpoint of a mountain that overlooked Devin's great valley. There, he told stories of his homeland as they dined under the blue skies. By the end of the afternoon, her heart would be his for the taking. Afterward, they returned to her Church home. Devin gently kissed her and said goodbye. He turned his carriage around back to the saloon for a personal victory celebration.

At the saloon, he brushed shoulders with the local Aristocrats and commoners, debating a name for their growing town. The closest name to anything anywhere on the map was Demas Valley. Anderson, Lark, and Horry were just a few of the names mentioned, the very names of the drunkards who suggested them.

Devin seemed amused that men felt a need to immortalize their names to cover their shortcomings. He headed home, thinking it had been a successful day.

That night, a vibrant young woman lies in bed, her mind seeing Devin's face in her grand fantasies of marriage. Dianna had been pursued by male callers before, but none of them were so becoming or worldly-witted. She fell asleep hugging her pillow, and dreams of Devin and their barefooted children playing danced through her head. Devin simply fell asleep dreaming of Damnation, World domination, and killing God's Creation.

Devin tirelessly studied his scroll Parchments, sometimes not coming out of his study for days at a time. When he did surface, he would be breathing Dianna's air as her love for him grew day by day. Astrological trajectories and configurations, along with the passing of a Comet, played a key role in Devin becoming Immortal. Sacrificial rituals would have to be practiced by his followers to ensure his passing into immortality.

They would need sacrificial lambs to perform the Ceremony, with live Participants for Sacrifice. But of course, volunteers were not to be found for such a process, nor could one advertise, so they would have to capture one.

Indians and Poachers who wandered carelessly onto Devin's Valley provided practice pigeons until the ritual was perfected. All that was left was articulating the timing and conception along with the configuration of Constellation. Hence, if Devin could have the fidelity of conviction to let go of his Mortality. For two more months, Devin would have to wait for the effusion of conception to take place for fate to fulfill his Prophecy. He would continue to court Dianna through misguided assumptions of their everlasting love, even though some feelings did begin to elapse into his still human heart. To appease Dianna's guardian, he donated large sums of gold to the Church, which granted him blessings.

Being the Prince of lies, Devin led her on, and her expectations grew with every passing day. Devin tried desperately to see the future beyond the deadline of his foresight, but all was black with no image. Two months finally went by at a snail's pace. Devin invited Dianna to his mansion to woo her with the inducement of savory wine, fine foods, and the misleading promise of a prosperous future together. It was indeed a hot August evening, with hormones jumping like Mexican jumping beans in a frying pan. The two sat at opposite ends of a long, black oak table, drunk on wine and full-on lamb.

After they had wined and dined together, they lay upon a Black bear rug sprawled out before the fireplace. Devin then began to seduce Dianna in a low voice. His mouth found hers quickly as his tongue went deep. She surrendered in the same manner. He crawled atop her and thrust his pelvis, creating a frenzy of friction. He cupped her breasts as their hips became one in a motion of facilitating movement. Then she abruptly ceased, remembering her virtue and her dreams of marriage to the man with whom she was accompanied; her shame would surely rear its ugly head if she gave in to her lust. But Devin had a destiny to fulfill, and the heat of the moment demanded relief of his loins into her fervent, virgin crevice. He stuck his tongue into her ear as he lifted her dress and spread her legs. At first, she resisted, but her animal urges coerced her into giving in to his needs, and she spread her legs wider and wider. The fire of their bodies fueled each other's flame, Devin pumping her in penetrating passion. He submerged himself deeper and deeper as she cried out his name. He stirred her veins with a pleasure she had never known, inhaling him into her very Soul as he released his very essence into her. They jerked upon every jolt from his loins as he locked into her until he was truly drained.

Darkness turned into daybreak while they lay by the dwindling fire, exhausted from their Procreation. Dianna awoke feeling guilty from the night's activities. She swiftly got dressed and hurried home in Devin's carriage in tears.

Devin awoke to the sound of the horse and buggy tearing down the road. He smiled as she disappeared around a bend, basking in his success of the conception. A week went by, and Devin hadn't called on Dianna, which left her angry and confused, with the sick feeling of betrayal. He never even bothered to retrieve his carriage. So, Dianna worked up her courage to return the buggy, and that would give her an excuse to unleash her anger. One midday afternoon, she drove to the mansion impassioned in rage, her thoughts racing a rocket's red glare. Upon her arrival, she stormed through the front door. Instead of knocking, she decided to surprise him with her intrusive anger.

As she stood at the entrance, she gazed around the seemingly empty home. She pursued in silence but held tightly to her anger in the event of Devin's appearance. She came to a corridor that split off from the dining room that had three doors on each side and one at the end. She peeked in each one as she made her way to the end. She came upon a study, four bedrooms, and a storeroom. All that was left to inspect was the last room at the end. She slowly opened the door, hoping to find Devin off guard with her unannounced arrival. Instead, she found Devin kneeling naked on the floor in the middle of a pentagram, with one more eye than she knew him for. She gasped for air, then turned to make a mad dash to the front door.

Devin quickly turned to see the tail end of her dress vanish around the corner. He closed his orb, jumped to his feet, and chased the frightened kitten. Devin then shouted out a command and the solid oak door held itself closed, preventing her escape. Dianna grasped the handle to no avail, with Devin close behind her. She continued to turn the handle in a frantic frenzy until Devin grabbed her from behind. He picked her up from around the waist as she kicked and screamed in a fit of fear. He then pulled her away from the door and threw her onto the sofa.

Devin stood naked before and began to laugh in a mocking manner. She looked at his face and saw him in his normal natural state. Her expression changed to one of quandary. She struggled to evaluate what, if anything, she saw. She announced her confusion as she rubbed her head. "I thought I saw …" She halted as she realized what she was saying.

Devin bantered with playful facial gestures and asked her to stay. Dianna considered another mad dash to the door but decided against it as she began to think, *am I seeing things?* After the Prince of lies convinced her that he was a saint and she was not, he realized her state of fear stirred his loins. He sat down beside her, caressing her thigh and whispering in a low voice of bewitching arousal. Her trepidation dissolved into hormonal cohesion as they began to draw into each other. Devin ripped at her clothes as she obeyed his will and let him ravage her as he climbed atop of her, then in. He pumped into her like an animal as she jerked upon his every thrust. On and on, like a nymphatic Demon, he tore at her as she stared at the ceiling, detached in mind. An hour later, Devin rolled off her exhausted and drained. He sat up as she stated, "Devin, I think I'm pregnant," in a nervous tone. Soon after, she went into a tizzy, wailing about how being pregnant and unmarried would bring shame to her and her family. Devin quickly said he would marry her just to shut her up. They tousled once more for two hours on and off until Dianna announced she had to go. Devin then told her that she could keep the carriage as a gift.

Another month went by, with a mild southern winter approaching. Devin was at a council meeting where the members were voting on a name for their town.

The ballots were all in, and Devin and two others democratically counted the choices for the town title. Only a handful remained when Dianna's father burst in, his anger obvious as he made his way to the consulate.

"You, Mr. Demas, are a disgrace to our community and my family."

Devin just sat there while jaws dropped, and whispers filled the room. The Pastor then addressed the room, shouting with resentful rage in a self-righteous voice. "These vermin of a man seduced my God-loving daughter into sexual acts as he promised her marriage, but he donates gold to the church and gives my daughter two horses and a buggy. And we're supposed to accept that in the place of husbandry? Nay, I say, Mr. Demas. I won't let you make a fool of my daughter. You will marry her, or God's curse will riddle your very Soul."

Devin sat silent as this man of the church reprimanded him with fire and brimstone and all the trimmings of Damnation. This would be the first time since his own father's rage that anyone raised their voice to him. Still, as a prince of sovereignty, he wasn't about to stand for it much longer.

Devin blurted out as he jumped to his feet, "Listen here, old man. Your daughter begged me for it. She stalked me like the whore she is!"

"Lies, lies!" the Pastor shouted. "You speak with the tongue of Satan. My daughter is a Puritan in the eyes of God. You tainted her! You tainted her with your stagnant lies and promises."

Devin burst into laughter as he threw a stack of ballots into the air. "Father Lang, I have about as much intention of marrying your daughter as I have to run a knife across my throat."

Just as he delivered that statement, Dianna stood in the doorway, tears flowing from her hazel eyes. Everyone turned and looked at the tortured Soul whose heart lay out before them, feeling compassion and pity for the love-stricken girl. She ran out the door, wailing while Devin sat in silence, awaiting the next outbreak from the outspoken man of God.

Pastor Lang shook his fist, shouting a slanderous speech at the serpent that tempted his once pure daughter. His veins popped out on the sides of his neck, and his face turned red. His knees buckled, and he grabbed his heart. He cried out, "Lord Jesus!" and fell to the floor. The Pastor of the yet-to-be-named town lay dead at their feet, with Devin seeing the situation in a whole new light.

The next day, the people declared their town Lang Township, and they mourned at the burial of their beloved Pastor. Dianna felt the World torn out from under her again as she now stood pregnant and fatherless, with no husband. She dropped a handful of dirt on the grave in grief while her tears ran like rain pouring.

Except for his clan, Devin was no longer viewed with envy or respect. He was now looked at with fear and contempt. The townspeople went so far as to try and blackball him from council activities. Dianna became known as a martyred saint, taken advantage of by the tyrant snake who had stolen her innocence. Devin fumed from the unexpected turn of events and called for a meeting of his Cult subjects. They met at Devin's mansion, clothed in hooded robes and surrounding a blazing pyre.

Devin walked from the mansion stern and stout, with an expression of rage, as his voice rang out in command: *"Listen here, my vicarious, clawed lames. I have come to the summit of arbitration as I gazed high into the Zion heavens of our Maker. As so, I also felt the furious flames of hell. The time is soon upon us as my destiny for Immortality draws near. I will be exalted, the Zenith of mortal man, as the Zephyr winds send the vassalage of my transgression to the four corners of the world. My influence will take command while I send world leaders flailing to destroy the other. For I am the Witch-Master, I am the taker of life, I am a Curse Caster, I am a Demon in Flight. And so I say onto to you. Redeem yourself, from yourself, and be as I. For I am a Granet Mountain "unmovable" in will. I am the spellbinder in my constant quest for the Divine prize. And so I say to you. Dares partake in the ritual of self-sacrifice and walk tall with Devil's pride, indulge in the flesh of delight, and be as I."*

Like a preacher receiving hallelujahs, Devin was cheered into the night, exclaiming his message of Unholy Sacrament. The moonlit sky cast an eerie light on the carnage of Devin's speech. The faces of his followers flickered in the shadows of the high flames, appearing twisted and grotesque. Their Demons came alive from the hatred they consumed and culminated. Low tones bellowed from their Soul as they poured forth the Psalms of Hell. Devin gazed upon his herd with joy, swaying to the unhallowed songs that filled the night sky.

Two of his Zealots brought forth a young Indian boy to the middle of the herd as they continued to sing around the flames. One stepped behind the boy and tilted his head to the sky while the other slit his throat. They filled a challis half full of wine with the sanguine fluid and handed it to Devin. He was the first and the last to drink after it rounded the circle to every hooded deviant. They repeatedly chanted unto dusk as their sacrificial lamb lay charred in bright red coals. Far off in the distance, a disfigured man was watching the hooded herd disperse as the morning sun rose off the horizon. A man who married himself to a diet of revenge took in the sight of his ungodly nemeses, Devin Demas. He, too, broke away with the sun as he scurried back to his clan.

That morning, Dianna moved from the church to a countryside cabin with her mother and her unborn child. The cabin was donated by Lang Township, with generous support from the fur trading union and its silent partner, the town's Devil, Devin Demas himself. Devin waited patiently through the long winter months, making sure she ate well from his deceitful donations.

Spring finally came, and Dianna's belly looked as if it were ready to burst. Devin's disciples checked in on her and often would arrive bearing a plethora of gifts, along with poultry and livestock. Every now and then, she would cry herself to sleep, wondering where she went wrong and why she gave in to her temptations. But the thought of her newborn child kept her sane through it all, and she thought of names for the child and the games they would play together.

One early spring night, she and her mother lie fast asleep in the confines of their home while nearby, four horsemen crept to the cabin on steed and carriage on a mission to carry out their orders. Two of the miscreants each carried a dead Indian woman slumped over their shoulders as they followed their fellow encroachers into Dianna's room. Two men grabbed Dianna, and the third laid the Indian woman in her place. The fourth threw the Indian corps on the ground, then grabbed Dianna's mother by her hair and slit her throat. They then torched the cabin ablaze, and they rode off towards the mansion. Dianna kicked up a fuss of forlornly foil, truly thinking she would die on this dismal night.

Devin awaited their arrival while standing beside a flaming pyre. As they pulled in, he gazed at her flailing body in the rear of the carriage. The men took her into the mansion, down the long corridor, and into the ritual room with the blood-painted pentagram. There, they tied her to a bed that lay adjacent to the blood-painted Pentagram in the middle of the floor.

*She struggled and screamed with all her might as she whaled out in pain, such a most sorrowful sight, as night turned to day and day back to night. Her tears flowed like rain, a deluge of plight. Her only human contact was two times a day, with the delivery of gruel upon a cold steel tray. But as time fills her with fear, her baby bucks near. Where were her Angels? And why cannot God hear" her most dire petitions?*

The constellation was in the proper trajectory for the comet's appearance in the next three days. All that was left was the delivery of the sacrifice. The time had finally come as Dianna brought forth her new baby boy at eleven o'clock at night. She bent her shame as her baby was delivered into the hands of the very man who killed her mother. She pleaded with him not to hurt her child as Devin walked into the room. Clad in a hooded robe, Devin knelt in the bloodied circle as his head disciple held the baby while the others walked in. The ritual had begun.

The baby cried for his mother and his mother for her child

while the men in hooded robes circled their Master. They completed the circle and passed the child around one to another, shouting out obscenities in denial of their Maker. After the baby made the full circle, he was in the hands of the first handler.

"My baby!" Dianna cried out. "Please don't hurt my baby!" But her words were empty, holding no substance in their plan. Devin disrobed and was handed his ill-fated child. He stood up shouting in broken tongue, raising his boy up over his head.

Dianna suddenly felt more kicking in her stomach, and she realized she was having twins. She screamed in wretched distress as her firstborn was being dismembered. Her eyes recoiled in repulsion while Devin bathed in his own son's blood, his disciples dancing around him, each holding a portion of the once whole child. Dianna held in the second the best she could as the others continued their sacred, iniquitous sacrilege. They completed 666 rounds, and she couldn't hold onto her baby any longer while its head began to plunge out of her body. But in their toil, the oversight of her labor went unnoticed. They halted in silence in a circle around their Master. The hooded head deviant raised his knife and then buried it in Devin's chest. Devin let out his last Mortal cry, and his disciples proceeded to carve out his heart.

Dianna shrieked at the harrowing horror that was presented to her eyes as her birthing baby spilled out untangled. The foremost perpetrator caught sight of the other baby, turning his attention to the new, living Soul. The floor shook with a rumble, crumbling where Devin's hollowed carcass lay. Hell opened its gates, and his dead body fell into a dark descent. The head hooded deviant made his way to the new baby as two of his colleagues fell into Hell's aperture. He smiled as he tilted his dagger to her. Dianna let out a wretched scream in repulsing terror as he cut the umbilical cord to the second child.

He then raised the infant until an arrow pierced his neck. His face changed to a contortion of pain, and his body slumped onto Dianna. Dianna lifted her head as an Indian approached her.

All went black while she fainted from the murderous frenzy. It was the confessor, with his multitudes of Mohawks. They had killed every hooded robe in sight and were whooping out in victory. The earth continued to shake while the confessor spoke in Indian. He commanded his warriors to grab Dianna and her child. They barely made it out of the mansion as it crumbled into itself, leaving a fragment of what it once was. An Indian gently laid Dianna on the ground, and she came to consciousness. She immediately cried for her baby and started toward the ruins. The confessor stepped in front of her with her healthy boy, handing him to his sobbing mother. The child looked up without a care in the world, his mother cradling him and crying out in joy. They stood at the foot of the ruins, the confessor shaking his head in disgust.

Devin's Soul Ascended into Heaven, where Archangels met him with disgrace, apprehending him and taking him before God. The Archangel Michael held his position with authority as he forced Devin to his knees before his Maker. Devin gazed unto the throne of God, and the brilliance of light shone through his Soul.

The blackness of his sin distilled itself into the open as there was no place it could hide. He shouted obscenities at his Maker, but Michael battered him to silence. God's son raised his fist in anger, rebuking him in His Father's name.

He then pointed to the Book of Life and struck Devin's name from a page. He condemned him to Hell; the Angels lifted him and carried him away. Devin just smiled, knowing he fooled God himself because once his Soul descended to Hell, his Prophecy for Immortality upon the earth would be fulfilled.

The Angels took him to the dark edge of heaven that dropped off into a vast blackness. Michael stood like a flawless statue, looking down on Devin with contempt and disgust. Devin yelled out a pledge at the almighty Angel: we will" meet again, and I promise" I will run my sword through you in a grand glee of delight.

Michael pointed his finger toward the vast darkness to which the soldiers cast him. Devin then descended into a negative state that consumed his Soul while it stretched to the depths of despair. He drifted directionless into a vast ocean of voided blackness, his Soul floating buoyantly with no variability. A cold hopelessness began to stir within him. His spirit weighed heavily with a lifetime of wrongdoings. He began to feel forsaken and betrayed as the emptiness consumed him in the black curtain of infinite enormity.

Shrieking screeches sounded off in the darkness as a winged creature seized Devin's drifting Soul. He could hear its giant wings cutting through the black dimension. Its cry sounded somewhat familiar, and he wondered, could it be? They glided down into a canyon filled with glowing red lava, the coals bringing sight back to Devin's eyes.

He looked up at the clawed Beast which held him. It was Kilgore who glanced down at his old Master. Devin felt relieved to see the familiar furry face as they raced through canyons and caverns. They then came to a giant palace carved from brimstone, and they flew through a large, gaping entrance eroded with time.

The batted Beast set Devin down before Satan's throne. He looked to his right, where he saw his hollow corpse stretched out upright within a towering oblong circle of liquid platinum that bowed and raged swiftly of great centrifugal force. Devin stared at his dead body as Barabis shouted, "On your knees before our Master, our King!"

Devin looked up as Barabis stood at the foot of the exalted one whose throne sat high upon a mound of crusted earth. The throne's wide basin narrowed to a pedestal as it stretched high, then widened to the hellish curvature of tortured Souls where Mephistopheles ensconced in all his glory. The fallen angel was both magnificent and grotesque at the same glance. A shining beacon endowed his Divine Celestial structure from which he was blessed in his creation by the very hand of God.

Satan cast his great head high, barring his twisted two-prong crown. His long snake tail reflected dark-shaded colors from its scales as it coiled around the pedestal of his throne. Devin dropped to his knees and kissed the Devil's clawed feet as he praised his Dark Messiah's name, "Mephistopheles." Barabis spoke, "On your feet. Our Master is very pleased with you, Devin Demas. You have defied your Maker since childhood and never looked back. You have brought pain and suffering to humanity and angered the highest Courts of Zion. Your disposition of insolence impressed our Master, and his most wicked subjects threw out time and me. I'm very proud of what I created in you." Satan pointed to Devin's suspended corpse as the tortured souls screamed out from his throne. Barabis then commanded, pass your Soul through your once-living skin as the shadow of your very essence takes hold in your unhallowed vessel.

Your new living vessel will reign upon the surface of Yahweh's creation, unknown to our Zion oppressors. The gift you are about to receive shall keep you restored in the long journey you are about to begin. Your Soul shall remain protected by my side at the foot of our Master until your other opens the gates that bind us here. Only then can you return as you shall to the vessel of your once-living skin. Now," do our Master bidding amongst the living and plant his seed into the

74

hearts of mankind and take what is rightfully ours. Let the gift of Satan take hold of the Devourer of souls. Take hold of the serpent that will replenish you in the eleven generations of your journey.

Devin's Soul turned and walked upon a small ramp that bridged into the silver oblong circle. He then passed through the cold corpse while leaving his very semblance into the hide of the hollowed human shell. Devin's Spirit then drew back to Barabis's side weekend and drained.

Satan then slithered off his throne of tortured souls and glided slightly from the ground, slowly in Demonic form. It dragged its grotesque clawed toes into the dirt while whipping its tail behind him. The Old Serpent encroached into the silver circle and the outstretched corpse. He gripped the cadaver's head and pinched open its mouth as he vomited vile secretions that drizzled down his long Devil chin. A pure white snake with expanded hoods upon each side of its head and glowing emerald eyes as it peered its head from the mouth of Satan. It then stretched long and into the mouth of the corpse as the Devil yoked with death and spewed the vile snake into the bowels of the hollowed hole. Mephistopheles Sat back to his thrown and perched himself as he awaited the emanation of his creation.

A corpse no more. Devin opened his eyes, gazing at Hell's palace as Barabis was beside himself with joy. Devin's awakened corpse and Soul turned to each other and took in the spectacle sight before them. Satan then pointed upward as if releasing the hounds of Hell as the batted Beast followed command and clenched Devin's awakened corpse. They then ascended towards the surface, reaching venal velocities faster and faster, ripping through time in their approach. The earth's crust gave way as they drew near, while Devin saw the sun blocked out from a solar eclipse.

Kilgore gently set Devin upon the earth, then soared high and plunged back into the gaping cavity of darkness. Devin gazed around his dwelling; his mansion was now wasted in a pile of rubble. Over in a clearing, he could see a makeshift shed. Out walked the last hooded-robed man who had somehow survived. The disciple dropped two buckets of water as he once again knelt before his Master. Devin was perplexed as he gazed at his servant, for he had aged over for what seemed like ten years since that fated night of sacrifice!

"Master, you returned; you returned just like you promised! Oh, Master!"

Devin asked what year it was as he continued to look around. "Why, Master, you've been gone for twelve years! This is the year 1666."

Devin's mind contemplated the time-lapse as it only seemed like hours to him. "Rise to your feet!" he commanded his follower. His subject rose, sensing his life would now be over. Devin smiled as his face contorted into snakish features while his arms became scaled, and his left fist turned into the head of a snake. Three-inch fangs dripping with craving, the snake's head hissing while swaying in the air. His right arm turned into a hellish, ill-natured husk sword. The robed man nodded his head and stretched out his arms in a welcoming manner. The snake expanded its hood, then ripped into the man's left shoulder and held him up as Devin raised his ill-natured sword and sliced downward his other shoulder, tearing deep down the man's torso and slicing him half. The man, somehow still alive, sits as his body splits. The snake's fist ripped out the heart that lay open and beating. Devin opened his mouth to a gapping aperture as the white snake with bright emerald eyes swallowed the man's Soul before it could escape to be judged, devoid of its very existence.

The white serpent ripped left and right as if it finally feasted after a millennium of starvation. It then returned to the cavern of Devin's Demon frame as the Soul would never be traced and judged in the high courts of Zion. Devin then drew a pentagram with the dead man's blood on the earth. He held the bloodied heart in his hand and sacrificed it to the eclipse until its passing.

Devin now walked the earth with no beating heart or Soul, only the white serpent that infused the man with the appearance of a thirty–three–year–old. He would age no more; he strolled to an old donkey that was used for laboring a water well pump.

He mounted the old plug upon its quivering back and disappeared from the Valley. He melded into the world like a creature of comfort in the bounds of an Ungodly convener. Devin became a Diplomat, advising top World officials of corruption and deceit. His first recommendation favored the slavery of African tribesmen for profit. He then stirred the Boston Massacre, intervening by enraging the crowd before he stepped out quietly. He was in the counsel that talked General Robert E. Lee and others into the Southern Confederacy and its plight for ill-fated reasons of war. He was in suspicious conversations with John Wilkes Booth at a pub before the Abraham Lincoln assassination at Ford's theatre. He was incumbent to the Kaisers of Germany in the times of World War I. He was Adolf Hitler's cellmate for a year before Hitler rose to power with fresh ideals and the book Mein Kampf.

He was Joseph Stalin's adviser during the mass starvation and massacres in Russia while he lived comfortably in St. Petersburg. Ethiopia suffered the iniquities of epidemic starvations and pestilence during the devastation of his visit in the eighty's.

For over three hundred years, Devin brought misery and treachery to humanity and grew more powerful with every passing day. He bestowed himself into the millennium, his societal corruption cultivating his covenant into the jugular of the world. The ranks of his followers numbered into multifarious digits as his flock proliferated his work unto the four points of the compass. He emerged to be the most powerful force on earth, with technology aiding him in industrial science, stock markets, government contracting, and the prescription field of medicine. A silent subsidiary in the prosperous business of life and death, his corporation, True Alliance, became a key player in the world's economy.

Devin's corporate signature was that of a silhouette of a man standing atop the World, a flame of fire emitting from his cupped hands.

While Devin's corporate headquarters was in Manhattan, its chain had links to Tokyo, Frankfurt, London, Barbados, the Caymans, Los Angeles, and Vancouver. Devin would travel country to country, following each solar eclipse with a sacrifice to sustain him during its passing.

After three hundred years of rampage upon the World, he decided to return to Demas Valley, along with an assemblage of disciples. There was Nina from the Italian Alps, Hector from Mexico, Ora from Norway, and Syck from the northern coast of California. They were all Prophets from their own reign in the crafts of witchery, whom Devin came to know from his travels and inner sight. He had a two hundred-million-dollar mansion built in the Valley, which brought envy to the simple minds of Lang Township. Construction was completed in the warmth of summer, the huge structure laid out like a beautiful canvas, hand painted by Vincent van Gogh. About a hundred yards behind the mansion lay the grounds of his old residence, buried in a thicket of brush and overgrowth. They christened the modern mansion with orgies, drugs, and holy blessings of sacrificial sacrilege.

Thomas Syck was a stallion of a man whom women found hard to resist. He stood six foot four inches tall with long blonde hair and blue eyes. Each one of the four Disciples was given a brand-new vehicle. For Syck, it was a classic Viper. Ora received a Lexus, Nina an MKZ Lincoln, and Hector a Suburban. They also were bestowed a six-thousand-dollar tax-free allowance per week, along with all the cocaine they could stuff up their noses.

Syck went to check out the town in his black Viper while cranking Metallica's classic Master of Puppets. He raced up to seventy in a forty-five zone. A cop abruptly pulled out from a dirt road adjacent to the highway as Syck sped passed in a fierce mode of metal mirth.

Jamming to Metallica, he hadn't noticed the sirens that sounded off behind. The officer was getting increasingly infuriated as he floored the pedal and pulled along the side of Syck.

"Fuck!" Syck yelled as if he were more angered at the gate crashing his song than over the possibility of a ticket. He drew over to the side of the road, closed his ashtray that was full of half-smoked joints and roaches, and watched the officer approach him with caution and a hand on his holster.

"You didn't see me following you with my flashers on?" the officer asked sternly.

"Hell, no," Syck said sarcastically. The officer spoke firmly, "Well if you didn't play your stereo so damn loud, you might have heard me."

"Yeah, well, if you were cool, you wouldn't give me a ticket. But I know you cops have a quota, so ... Ah, spare me the talk and give me the damn ticket, huh."

"License and registration," barked the officer. Syck glared

with daggers as he reached for the glove box. "You must be one of those folks who moved into that million-dollar mansion, huh?" Syck grinned, then added, "Oh, I guess country folk can add after all."

The officer looked askance at the sarcastic Hellion as Syck handed him some papers and smirked. A cop for four years, Johnny was usually good-hearted and fair about things. But in Syck's case, he became perturbed at the city-slicked, smart-ass. He walked back to his squad car, ran the plate and name through the computer, and red flags flashed with warnings. Syck had assaulted an officer in nineteen-ninety-seven in Los Angeles, where he served six months in the county glasshouse for that little number. In ninety-eight, he was busted for solicitation as part of an illegal escort service in Hollywood, where he received a slap on the hand.

In ninety-two, he served a two-year bit at a Juvenile correctional facility for the statutory rape of a fifteen-year-old girl who just happened to be the daughter of the Dean at UC Berkley. On and on, the computer spit out the dates and places of a lifetime of criminal history. But it showed no warrants for his arrest, so Johnny just wrote Syck a speeding ticket.

Johnny walked back to the convertible. Syck glared through the rearview mirror at the "approaching ass wipe behind a badge."

"Well, Mr. Syck, you have an interesting background there in sunny California," Johnny said as he handed him the ticket. Syck ripped the ticket from Johnny's hand, lashing out sarcastically, "Yeah. What the fuck does that have to do with now?

Johnny studied the bad apple and then warned, "Well, you better mind yourself "here" in Horry County, understand?" Syck chortled, then blasted the volume on the stereo as he revved his engine. Syck had so many horses under the hood that you could almost hear the theme song to Bonanza as he rode off onto the horizon. Johnny just shook his head while Syck drove away. He wondered what he was doing here in Horry County and why.

Devin admired Syck for his fearless pugnacity in the face of consequence. He could be looking at a death row sentence, and he'd still tell the judge to fuck off. He was raised the son of a Witch in a fashion of Ungodliness, learning at an early age how to Master his powers and bring ill fate to his enemies.

Nina was raised by Catholic monks in the northern Alps of Italy. She learned from an early age to hate religion and clergy from being repeatedly raped until the age of seventeen. One night, one of the three monks who took turns with her decided to creep into her room and have his way in his usual manner. But she was fed up with the stench breathed old men, so she waited with a butcher knife as she lured one to a death of dismemberment.

After her story went viral, Devin took her in. He called upon his council of lawyers, who quickly got the charges dismissed on the grounds of self-defense from repeated rapes of the Monastery Monk. She had been a loyal little Witch ever since.

Devin saved Hector from the garbage dumps of Mexico City when he was eight years of age. Devin respected his will to survive and his ability to read people. When Hector was just eight years old, he tricked tourists into traps for muggings laid out by his older brothers. So, Devin decided to buy him from his parents for a couple of thousand dollars and a pickup truck, which they demanded as part of the deal.

Ora was raised in southwest Normandy by her father, a shepherd farmer, who loved her dearly. But the region was

81

riddled with witchery, and she became influenced. By the time she was eighteen, she had a website to which Devin became accustomed. He was amused by her zeal for the Black Arts of Divination, so he emailed her an offer she couldn't refuse … an account with a weekly salary, a new car, and a ten thousand dollar signing bonus.

Devin taught his disciples diligently every day, spewing his secrets into their Souls. They, in return, would help bring Devin's grand design cast upon the world.

Syck pulled into town with a chip on his shoulder the size of a boulder. He laughed at the hicks who lined the streets in their daily existence.

He was looking to get laid and play some pool when he came to a tavern called Buckeye Buck. All eyes were fixed upon him as soon as he walked in. He promenaded through a thick haze of defiance, ordered a brew, and surveyed the bar. Two farmer-type hicks were sitting at the corner of the bar, eyeballing' a table of portly women laughing in the drunkest manner. In the back of the bar were three rugged bikers accompanied by two hot pants that fancied his attention.

Syck walked to the pool table and busted out a wad of cash, which brought turning wheels of ill-fated contemplation his way. Syck broke the ice by inquiring about any "action" and smiled at the women.

A giant long hair slammed five hundred on the table as he provoked Syck with sardonic sarcasm. "Put your money where your mouth is, surf boy!"

Syck pulled five Bennies from his wad, then put them halfway in his mouth as he perched in the saucy kitten's face. She reached out smiling, gently plucked them from his mouth, then tossed them in the pile. One of the crony bikers snatched the pile of cash and began counting with an assertive demeanor.

Syck smirked at the counting fool, then turned and seized the first cue stick that came to hand. The two kittens eyed Syck's confidence with enticing wonderment as they giggled among themselves.

The prodigious biker silenced their gayety with a snide harsh stare, grabbing his cue and barking out the rules: "Best four out of seven wins! You break, surf boy."

Syck smiled at the two nymphets as if the bikers were of no concern or matter while he barely took the target to the cue ball. He then broke the rectangle of assorted colors as the panting purring kittens whispered their approval of his ass. The greasy giant biker smirked as all the balls remained. Then he commented about how glad he'd be to take Syck's money.

Syck burst out laughing at all his cockiness and cool certainty. He then stopped suddenly and said, "If you can take it, take it; if not, I take the dough and the ho-ho-hos. But you know, I'll still buy you bums a round so you can sulk in your suds." The giant goon glared at Syck as the two buttercups looked at each other with hopeful eyes, comparing the potbelly bikers to the blue-eyed blonde. Syck lost the first three games in a row, hardly minding count as he grazed on the confidence of the oversized buffoon. The biker gave a smug grin, then said, "Well, surf boy, looks like one more game, and I'm five hundred dollars richer."

Syck smiled as he held out five more bills, signifying he was upping the ante. The biker patted his pockets and told him that was all the dough he had.

"Well, you're not all cleaned out," said Syck as he wolf-eyed the women. One of the bikers stuck out his chest like a cobra expanding its hood and blurted, "Listen here, you fuck! They're not for betting."

Syck fanned himself with a spread of greenbacks as he tempted the biker in a taunting fashion. One of the bimbos blurted out in excitement, brazenly volunteering herself for the bet. The other then added in a dare, as if wanting the goons to lose, "Yeah, come on, Ronnie, you could beat him."

Ron stood watching Syck and his green fan wave with a spellbinding swoon as greed consumed his big dumb animal frame and the willful lambs fell wayward. The big oaf finally nodded silently in agreement. Syck smiled briefly and threw the money on the table.

As the next game played out, Ron had sunken all but two as he then stepped back silently as he awaited the blonde bomber to fall.

Syck sarcastically acted in tomfoolery, gesturing like a tight-roping clown to the table while the strumpets juiced to his parody. He then cracked the cue ball onto the others, and three sank upon the command of his stick.

Syck pranced around the table, looking for his next shot, as he commented, "I'm finally getting a little lucky there, huh Ronnie boy?"

Ron just glared in suspicion as he racked a new game. Syck cleared the table with newfound ease. He would intermittently seesaw each game just to keep Ron's hopes alive. The biker grew angry after every shot. He missed each pocket from Syck's hindering fated will. Upon the blonde Devil's next shot, Syck put his cue behind his back, and he kissed into the air at the strumpets while the last eight ball fell into his chosen pocket.

The giant biker's veins flared as his slow mind contemplated his loss. He stared at the cue ball and the remaining striped spheres, then blurted out his sore losing conclusion, "You played me for a fool, pretty boy."

Syck nodded his head, smirking from ear to ear, then said, "No, I just beat you like a red-headed stepchild, and now, it's pay-up time."

The biker stepped forward as he poked his finger into Syck's chest. "I ain't paying you shit head," he said. "In fact, if you were smart, you'd walk out that door and keep that pretty face in one piece." The three bikers all laughed in unison as Syck did the same, with an overtone of lunacy. The biker began to push his finger into Syck's chest once more until Syck reached down and seized the prodding appendage and snapped it like a dry twig. Ronnie wallowed away as the other goons made their attack with cue sticks. Syck busted his cue stick over one's head, and he smashed the other in the face with a cue ball.

Then he went over to Ron as the bumbling biker readjusted himself to strike upon his assailant with his good hand. Syck simply grabbed Ron with one hand around his throat and the other his injured finger and twisted it counterclockwise.

Syck bent forward to the blubbering giant and said, "Potbelly boy says what? Here, here's the money, take it, take it," wailed the pain-filled ape.

Syck bent Ron's broken finger backward until his knuckle splintered out of the skin, then punched him, breaking his nose. Ron cried out and sprawled away. Syck turned to the two floozies while picking up the cash and said, "Well, come cum, my ladies, my sugar babies."

They looked at each other and burst out laughing. The willing strumpets stepped over the broken bikers as Syck turned about face, and he extended his elbows. "Shall we, sugar babies?" They each wrapped an arm around him as they started for the door. Syck stopped at the bar and tossed the thousand dollars on the counter before the bartender. The man behind the counter smiled ear to ear as he reached for the money. He nodded his head as he told him how he hated those punks. Syck grinned and returned a nod from his blonde head. He held his finger to his lips and whispered shh, then disappeared with his new frumps. By that time, evening and fallen upon the town, and the threesome walked out to Syck's Viper. The two females debated who would sit on whose lap as they crowded into the sports car.

Syck reached over their laps to the glove compartment and fished out a big bag of coke. Their eyes lit up like the fourth of July as Syck handed them a straw. The biker bimbos giggled while whispering to each other about how they made the right choice in leaving those imbeciles behind. Syck reached a speed of one hundred and twenty as the trio laughed hysterically, sniffing and snorting around each curve. When they arrived at the mansion, their eyes widened more than just from coke at the great spectacle they beheld.

After Syck parked, he and the two doxies quickly piled out of the Viper. The floozies giggled like schoolgirls as they followed their attraction to the door.

"Is this house your house?" one asked in glee, looking about. Syck just smiled as he turned the key.

Upon entering the mansion, they saw Ora sprawled out by the fireplace while Nina and Hector sat adjacent to her on a sofa. The cupcakes were greeted like two long-lost friends as they walked into the room. Soon, they all sat around a mirrored table of coke, the newcomers divulging their names with enthusiastic eroticism in the air. The brunette announced her name as Kathy, while the blonde revealed her name was Liz. The two frumps boasted about how Syck rescued them from the greasy degenerates. They then described how they left their home in Myrtle Beach because they were sick of the same ole, same ole'.

"That's when we met Ronnie, my asshole ex," said Liz with an overtone of fervor and spite. She then managed a smile as she looked at Syck and said, "Oh, well, I guess we wouldn't be here if it wasn't for them."

Ora and Nina made the girls feel comfortable, and as the night progressed, they opened more and more upon every passing line and drink. Syck then turned to Liz as he stroked her hair from her ear then tantalized her with his tongue. She closed her eyes as she tilted her head back and swirled her tongue into his.

He then turned to Kathy, and he put his hand around her waist before he pushed his tongue into her lips. She quickly submitted, loosening to every touch. Over at the table, Ora became aroused and started pawing at herself while watching the show. Nina then turned to Ora and shoved her tongue into her mouth.

Hector then jumped up, dropped his pants, and yelled, "sex party." Everyone stops and looks at Hector; Syck begins to laugh at him as they all join in laughing and mocking Hector's short endowment. Hector looks at the room, laughing at him, and he quickly pulls up his pants and sits back down.

Dusk was now approaching as Devin walked into the room. He gazed upon his subjects and smiled. Nina jumped to her feet and sprinted to Devin's side, kissing him on his cheek. He whispered in her ear, and a sadistic grin came over her. Nina then suggested that they check out the old ruins behind the mansion, just for kicks. They all become elated and follow Devin down the back trail, giggling in a frolic flight of rapture. They then came upon a clearing, the site of the decomposed ruins. A twenty-foot Pentagram lay on the ground, presenting itself in its venomous, malformed manner.

Liz and Kathy were humored by the painted star, dancing around it in entertainment. They laughed and sneered while making spooky jokes and poking at each other like schoolgirls on happy gas. The sun began to rise over the eastern horizon while Devin softly whispered a prayer in Hebrew. Ora joined in on Liz and Kathy's laughter, asking them how they felt about human sacrifice. They both began to laugh hysterically.

Devin and his disciples just stared at them, the sacrificial lambs who found themselves encircled by a Witch Cult. Kathy suddenly stopped laughing. Liz aimlessly continued, until she realized the seriousness of their situation. Fear struck them like lightning, and both started to squirm and squawk within their circled confines.

Ora then spoke, *"Wary, oh worry your pretty, little hair. Now you need not worry 'cause your head is bare."*

Liz and Kathy's hair instantly fell to their feet, and they cried out woefully. Their bodies shook in convulsions from the horror that presented them. They begged and pleaded while the circle of Witches walked around them in a constant flow of malice.

Syck then rhymed, *"Life is full of little surprises as you fear from what's behind you. So now your face no longer smiles as tooth and tongue they rot in bile."*

The sacrificial lambs felt their mouths. They spit out their teeth and blackened tongues, howling in pain-riddled cries.

Nina then retorted, *"What you do from when you're new, you love the world around you. But when you fall, you aren't so tall,' your bones shrink up inside you."*

The crushing sound of breaking bones filled the air, and their skin wrinkled from the cavities of their crunching bones. Their broken skeletons that filled their once beautiful bodies now stick out from the sacks of skin. Yet, at that point, they were still alive, their muscles and cartilage holding what was left in a hammock of human harrow as their vocals gurgled like dying animals.

Hector then rang out, *"Live and learn is one hard lesson. There are some that never do. You toss and turn, twist and churn, a rotting lot of you."*

What was left of the two women turned inside out, leaving a steaming heap of human hash. The disciples began to circle the painted star as they rejoiced in the ritual of their coven. Afterward, they returned to the mansion while Devin stayed behind. He fused the heaping mound of the carcass into an incinerated pile of ashes from two words of will.

On the way back to his dwelling, Devin noticed a giant buck with great antlers peering at him from afar. Its antlers spread like a royal crown of majesty as the Beast just stood there with adjudicating eyes. For the first time in three hundred years, a slight touch of fear pumped through Devin's heartless frame as he contemplated the antlered creature. He then smiled and turned away as if unconcerned. Two months passed as the group lived each day in a deluge of ungodly Earthly pleasures. Devin and Ora went off to New Zealand for an eclipse sacrifice as the rest of the group continued with their usual amusements.

David Lane was the sheriff of Horry County. Gary Wallace, otherwise known as "Old-Man Joe," retired after thirty years on the force as David quickly got voted in for sheriff. David was mulling over a missing person report on Bud Shaner, who had disappeared almost a week earlier. Bud was the town drunk and had four drunken driving convictions on his record, so his license was revoked, which rendered him to walking and hitchhiking. Buckeye Buck Tavern was his home away from home. The gossip in town was that he may have been hit by a motorist who thought he was a deer, as they theorized his dead body was likely on the side of a road somewhere. A couple of search parties came up empty, and they called off the hunt as the pursuance dramatically reduced the department's limited funds. David Lang was thirty-seven years old and had been a cop for seventeen years, working his first four years at the New York police department.

He met his wife in a penthouse on Park Avenue at a high-class party where he was invited by a politician whom he had saved from a mugging. Sarah was a corporate lawyer who brushed shoulders with some of the most powerful tycoons in the World. She and David connected at the punch bowl, with him cracking a joke about the stuffy stiffs that crowded the party. She immediately took a liking to him for his sense of humor, good looks, and quick wit.

Sarah carried herself with the confidence of a true winner. She could have picked anyone from her wit and beauty, but she picked David. Her brunette hair flowing and inviting like her lightly brown eyes and inviting face of beauty. She was two years older and two inches taller than David, with curves that glided ever so smoothly into her long legs. She made more money, but they both had flexible personalities, which forged a healthy relationship. David was amiable, with thick brown hair and strong facial features and body structure. His moral integrity was that of good nature as he contributed to society with tireless devotion. Time after time, he would put his life on the line for the community and just cause. After nine months into their relationship, they decided to tie the knot. But Sarah feared she would be widowed by their first anniversary, so they moved to David's hometown, South Carolina. She liked the idea of running her own office in a small community away from the suit-cloned cutthroats.

She also liked the odds much better for David's survival compared to New York. David simply liked it because it was home. They resumed their residential ownership in a four-bedroom ranch on ten acres, just eight miles west of Lang Township. Sarah often joked about how David was the King of his self-proclaimed town. But she respected the history of his family name.

The next morning, Old-Man Joe had been hunting in the thick forest on government property adjacent to an Indian reservation where hunting was legal for anyone with a hunting license.

With him was his hound, Tag, his loyal companion and work dog trained for hunting by the "hound brothers," named by their profession.

The air was hot and dry that day. Setting his sights on quail and wild turkey, Old-Man Joe could smell the scent of pine from the sun pounding down. Tag stayed forty feet ahead of him, flushing the game out into the open for a clear shot. The pair had already succeeded in ambushing about fourteen quail, which would find themselves on Joe's kitchen table. But what he really wanted was a nice fat turkey.

So Old-Man Joe continued his hunt into the late afternoon until Tag became unhinged in a thicket. His barks echoed through the forest, signaling trouble. It was then that Old-Man Joe saw what all the fuss was about. He had to cover his mouth to keep from gagging. It was the missing and now decomposed Bud Shaner. The only reason Old-Man Joe recognized him was because Bud was wearing the same old army boots he had worn every day for the last five years.

Joe called his dog, and the two high-tailed it back to his truck, where he quickly put his dog away back of his truck and then called Lang police station. Patrica, the dispatcher, answers the Lang Township Police dept, but everyone just calls her Pat. "Hey Pat, this is Joe. Is David around?" "Old-Man Joe, how do you like retirement?" said Pat, happy and oblivious. "Please. I found Bud Shaner deader than a doornail. I need to talk to "David." "Oh, dear," said Pat and quickly said, "patching you to the Sheriff."

Old-Man Joe then told David where he found Bud's body and the condition it was in. David scanned the giant-sized map of Horry County and pointed out the location Joe described. David then told Pat to call Johnny to the location and then to get on the phone with the state police. He drove to the location where Old-Man Joe stood in front of his truck. David Parked then followed his mentor through the woods. A quarter mile in, Old-Man Joe pointed to the bushes where the dead body lay. David walked through the thick brush that concealed it from visibility as he took in the repulsive spectacle.

He put on some white rubber gloves and examined the remains. Animals and insects had destroyed much of the evidence if there had been any. David then noticed that the sternum was cut, and the torso almost lay inside out, as if it were pried open. Since it was quickly getting dark, David decided to return to his car and wait for Johnny and the state police. When they reached the road, Johnny was pulling behind David's squad car and had a curious expression on his face.

"What's going on?" he asked as he approached them. "Pat told me on the radio that Old-Man Joe found Bud's body. Is that true?"

"I'm afraid it is," David said with an appearance of remorse on his face, shaking his head in disgust. David turned to Joe and told him he should go home to Emma, his wife. He added that he'd keep him informed if anything else popped up and thanked him for leading him to Bud Shaner.

An hour later, a convoy of official vehicles littered the side of the road. There were two state troopers, a rolling crime lab unit, and a coroner taking up the rear. They brought two small generators and ten tripod halogens, along with an assortment of high-tech gizmos. David and Johnny led the assemblage of officials through the trail that began to take its ill-gotten form. Upon the recovery of the corpse, David and Johnny answered questions as they watched the crime lab technicians do their job. The landscape was yellow-taped and lit up like a small baseball field. After two hours of investigation, the coroners zipped the cadaver into a body bag and loaded it into their vehicle.

Soon after the state lab boys wrapped up their operation, they trudged back to the road. The coroners were the first to leave the scene while the rolling crime unit and state trooper cars remained parked along the road. David pondered questions of who, what, and why as the vision of poor Bud Shaner persisted in his mind.

"What kind of sick puppy do you think did this?!" Johnny blurted out.

"Let's not jump to conclusions," replied David as he pulled away from his lumbering thoughts. Johnny was full of zest and zeal and the craving to conquer Evil in his boyish fantasies.

Before the crime team took off, one of the state troopers approached, saying they would stay in contact and keep them informed. Johnny felt shortchanged when David told him he was heading home, but he accepted the predicament and followed suit.

When David returned home, he found Sarah waiting in anticipation. After not answering his cell phone, she called the station afterward, and Pat gave her the scoop. David was greeted at the door with hugs and kisses from Sarah and their three-year-old daughter, Lisa. Sarah quickly asked with concern about the young man they found in the woods and what happened to him. David told her how Old-Man Joe found the body of Bud Shaner during his usual hunting spree. Then he said, "Enough about my day. How'd yours go?"

"I've got a mound of paperwork that will keep me busy for the rest of the week."

Sarah's office was in the den. There, she filed taxes, prepared adoptions, and practiced divorce law. All she had to do today was to start filing taxes for Jack Longley's General Store. David liked the fact that Sarah worked at home. He didn't have to pay for daycare for Lisa, and dinner would always be ready. And if he was lucky, he could sneak home, get a little "nooky," and then slip back to the station.

David set Lisa down, rushed towards the oven, and peered inside, "Mm-mmm, really smells good."

"Well, you go wash up, and I'll set the table."

David smiled, "Okay, mom." Sarah snapped a dish towel at his buttocks as he half dashed for the bathroom. They ate dinner in the dining room, with David and Sarah playing footsy under the table while seductively staring at each other and smiling through their meal. David then retired to the living room and grabbed the remote while Lisa still played with her food. He turned on the tube to see a reporter standing in front of the coroner's building in Harrisville, a little over fifty miles away. She gave a vague outline of Bud Shaner--- his name, age, and how long he'd been missing. She also spoke of the decomposed condition in which he was found.

Sarah walked in and caught the last part of the report. "Oh my God. We moved down here to get away from the violence, not to pick up where we left off."

David then told her if ten people were murdered every day, it still wouldn't come close to the numbers in New York City.

She just shook her head as she walked away.

David clicked off the TV and proceeded to chase after Sarah, grabbing her from behind. Then he picked her up, and she let out a short, high-pitched yelp. He kissed her on her cheek, as she quickly gave in to his touch. He sat her down as they savored one wet kiss.

Sarah quickly put Lisa in her room, and she and David rushed into their own bedroom, where they peeled each other's clothes off in a passionate race. David then picked her up again and sat her gently on the bed. He climbed on top of her and stuck his tongue down her throat. Between each kiss, she'd gaze into his eyes, whispering, "I love you."

He then put himself inside her, and she cried out amorously. He peered into the depths of her Soul, ogling down with every erogenous motion. She flung herself on top of him while stroking herself up and down. David howled, "I love you," as they continued in poetic motion.

Sarah wailed out in ecstasy as she went into an orgasmic fulmination of spasms. David erupted into her as they both cried out their love. Sarah laid her head on David's chest while squeezing herself on his side. She ran her fingers through his chest hair, rejoicing in their love. Soon after, David fell asleep. Sarah smiled, shook her head, then went to check in on Lisa and locked up the house. The next day, over a cup of coffee, David viewed the giant-sized map of Horry County in his office with Johnny Morgan. David mentioned how vast Horry County was and that it would take a lifetime to cover it on foot. Johnny suggested that a couple of dirt bikes could cover any terrain. David agreed, continuing to stare at the map, David agreed. Johnny offered his dirt bikes for the job. David nodded, exited the building, and they both climbed into Johnny's truck.

Johnny lived on a two-hundred-acre farm he inherited from his father, who died at the age of fifty-nine from mouth and throat cancer. It used to be a tobacco farm until the farmer's union took over the region. The land had been passed down from father to son for generations. Johnny's father used to say he'd go to the union when pigs fly, and he'd spit a brown wad of tobacco juice from his mouth.

The cops pulled into the long, dirt driveway leading to Johnny's house. His two boys and dog saw his truck coming toward them and ran to meet it. Johnny's wife Amanda was hanging clothing on the clothesline in the fresh country air. She was wearing a sundress that graced her slender, young figure, giving her the wholesome disposition of a true country girl.

She had flowing red hair and fair skin, with a pinch of freckles that spread like a stunning constellation of beauty. Her smile glowed with a gentle luminance. As the two men pulled up to the house, Johnny's dog Bandit reached them first, greeting his Master with hyper excitement and tail wags. Johnny's boys then reached him as they shouted, "Daddy, Daddy!" They both dived into his legs in a relentless attack of love.

Johnny scooped them up in his arms as his wife approached them with a happy, quizzical look of conjecture. "What are you guys doing here?" she said gingerly as she shifted her eyes from Johnny and David with a curious expression.

"We've come to get the dirt bikes so we can pick up some hill girls in the boondocks," announced Johnny. Amanda poked him with her finger as she laughed, "Ha, ha. There isn't a woman in the county that would fall for the same trick I did."

"She's got a point," David stated as they all laughed in unison.

They then went inside as Amanda packed lunches, and David and Johnny had a sip of lemonade. Amanda worried for Johnny and even David as they explained what they were doing and where they were going. Johnny told her not to fret and he patted his nine-millimeter Glock he had holstered to his side. She hated guns and his confidence in them. To her, they just raised the risk of trouble. If she had her way, Johnny would be on a tractor in the field instead of a squad car on the streets. Maybe that was one of the reasons she and Sarah were such good friends---they shared each of the others' views in that manner.

Johnny and David went outside to the barn and opened its massive doors. Inside were two nineteen-fifty-something Buicks that Johnny always said he would restore, covered with bird droppings and many years of debris.

A 1956 John Deer tractor his father had used to farm the land took up the rear corner of the barn, along with other relics he left in his passing. In the middle of the barn was a small trailer with two dirt bikes that stuck out like a sore thumb next to the antiques. Johnny then picked the end of the trailer up with ease and hauled it out of the barn into daylight. He asked David to guide him as he climbed into his truck. Johnny started his four-by-four, and it aroused the attention of Bandit. Bandit made a dash for him as if he were going along for the ride.

"Keep out of the way!" Johnny shouted out the window as he backed up to the trailer. David then signaled to stop the truck as it came within inches of the hitch. They hooked it up as Amanda walked over with a thick, brown paper bag full of goodies to eat on their expedition. She then gave Johnny a brief peck on the lips and warned them that the weatherman said there was a possibility of thunderstorms. Johnny told her not to worry as they started off at the scene of Bud's crime. Bandit chased the truck to the end of the driveway before he stopped to watch his Master disappear down the road.

After twenty minutes of driving and chit-chat, they were back at the ill-fated location of grim reality. Johnny pulled to the side as they unloaded the two bikes. One was a two-fifty Honda, and the other was a one-twenty-five, which was Amanda's. David quickly volunteered to ride the smaller one-twenty-five, commenting that it had been some time since he'd ridden. Johnny jokingly replied, "Of course you are. You'd probably kill yourself on this Beast." He kickstarted the two-fifty with one try. Johnny may have neglected those old Buicks, but he kept his bikes juiced and primed for any such occasion. David then started the smaller bike, revving up the engine to warm the steel. Johnny locked up the truck and grabbed their lunches. He strapped a homemade milk crate attached to his seat with the brown bag inside.

Devin took the lead, and they sped off into the thick forest. They first stopped at the location where Bud's body was found. Turning off their engines as they inspected the grounds for any type of clue that might present itself in the daylight. They searched the immediate area for two hours, where the predisposition of heavy brush and empty fields seemed the only perpetrators, to David's frustration. He then noticed a trail that led off into the dark, dense forest, which raised his inquiring curiosity. He rounded Johnny up as they hopped back on their bikes and rode off down the trail. They drove through heavy terrain, up steep hills, and down deep slopes for an hour until they came to a split in the trail. David signaled to stop. They dismounted their iron horses, had a bite to eat, and conferred about the area.

Johnny and David had grown up in those parts, but because most of the region was restricted Indian reservation land, they could only guess as to which way to go. Johnny advised David that the Waccamaw River ran north, northwest, not too far from here, and that they were on Indian land. David looked up at the sky and saw a veil of murky clouds forming but decided that the rain would probably hold off until late evening. After filling their stomachs with sandwiches, they decided to split off to cover more ground. David didn't know what they were looking for but thought it would be interesting to see where those trails would lead. He told Johnny they should meet back at the main trail after they'd searched and thoroughly scrutinized the area.

They started their bikes and went their separate ways. Johnny took the trail toward the river and David the other. After a half hour of riding, David stopped on the trail. He shuffled around the bike, stretching his legs as he took in the scenery. He then heard thumping steps behind him and whipped his head around.

A giant Buck with a majestic crown of antlers stood fearless on the trail. David couldn't believe his eyes as he wondered what the buck would do. David then slowly approached the majestic animal, praising him, "Good boy. Easy does it. Good boy."

The four-hundred-pound Beast was an awesome spectacle. Something seemed to pull David toward the Buck while their eyes met in mutual respect. David reached out his hand to the magnificent giant and said, "So you're Buckeye Buck." He gave a patch of soft-coarse hair between the buck's antlers about five good strokes. With their eyes locked upon each other, David felt the Beast stare into his Soul and transcend what could only be described as some sort of divine powers. The buck tapped its front hoof upon the Earth as he nodded his giant head three times. Then he dashed off into the dense forest.

David stood in dismay at what he just witnessed, wondering if anyone would believe that he just petted Buckeye Buck. The huge animal gained his name over the years after hunters swore they targeted him dead on in their sights, yet they pulled their triggers in vain. The legend of Buckeye Buck went back over two hundred years, told by Indians and hunters alike, whose bullets and arrows could not render the Beast. Old Man Joe even had him in his sights one time with a thirty-odd-six and, to this day, swears he hit his target. And so, the legend continues.

Bewildered and amazed, David got back on his bike and rode for three miles before it started to rain. He then turned around, deciding to meet up with Johnny and call it a day. But the rain poured harder with every foot he covered, and it began to mix with hail. David slowed to a crawl as the sting of hail on his skin became unbearable.

He parked the bike and set off on foot to try and find some shelter. He was scouting for a house, building, or anything that would save him from the dime-sized ice fragments.

Halfway up a hill, David heard Johnny's bike. As he turned, he saw Johnny's beet-red face being punished by the deluge of shredded ice. Johnny gallantly drives through the storm shrapnel to get to his chieftain and friend to tell him they should turn back. Johnny saw the parked bike off to the side by a tree and followed suit, looking around for David. Shouting through the loud storm, David's voice barely made it to Johnny's ears. Johnny turned and started up the hill toward David as a curtain of clouds black with hatred; God was releasing his mighty wrath in the manifestation of a roaring downpour.

Johnny used elm and oak saplings to pull himself up when his feet tried to slip from under him. Finally, he reached David, and they continued to trudge up muddied inclines and washed-out gullies. They made it to the top only to find another hill at the bottom of the one they were standing. Thick, red mud wore heavily on their feet, and a deep, dark dejection began to deteriorate their spirits. Johnny placed too much faith in a frail sapling, and it sent him sailing down the steep slope. He shrieked out in pain while tumbling in chaotic injury.

David rushed down to his scathed friend, where Johnny lies, holding his left ankle with his forehead gushing blood after encountering a jagged rock during his fall. David quickly tore a piece of cloth from his shirt to bandage Johnny's head. He slung Johnny's arm over his shoulder, and together, they continued through the storm. The torrent seemed relentless, yet they slowly made their way. They both slipped countless times, but their inborn animal instinct to survive kept them pressing onward. As he aided his deputy up another hill, David started to wonder if he made the right decision in leaving the trail. His confidence began to slip along with their feet, and he even began to question whether they would make it out alive.

David could see the color draining from Johnny's face, his pale skin dulled with the appearance of impending death.

His discouragement began to show, along with the feeling of hopelessness, when from the point on which they stood, David could see Buckeye Buck at the bottom. David felt a sudden surge of strength, seeing Buckeye Buck like that. It seemed to give him faith and inspiration to continue. With his newfound strength, he pulled Johnny up the hill and in the direction of the buck. When they reached the apex, the alluring animal faded into the dense surroundings.

David then saw a shimmering light through the torrential hail. He shouted to Johnny that they had made it. Johnny's face lit up as David pointed to the beacon. They hurried down the hill as best they could in a new excitement of hope, and the sight of a large cabin came into view. Closer and closer, they came to what seemed like an oasis of land in the middle of a vast ocean. The pair reached a driveway, and sanctuary seemed only a stone's throw away. Shuffling toward the porch, Johnny started to burst out in joy. The cabin was only eight steps away. Suddenly, a huge German shepherd lunged from the porch.

David didn't have time to reach his gun, so he put himself in front of Johnny, stretching out his arm. The shepherd clamped down with ease, tearing into his skin. David shrieked out in pain, and its death grip seemed impossible to break. Even in agony, David's mind was still coherent as he reached with his other hand to his gun. Instead of shooting the dog, he shot into the air three times and yelled. The shepherd finally let go and ran behind the cabin.

David holstered his gun and picked Johnny up from the ground. By that time, there was a man with a shotgun standing on the porch. David and Johnny started their way until he pointed the gun at them. David reached for his wallet and then raised his badge. "Police!" he shouted, but the man still held his sights on the two maimed men.

Once the man saw their mangled state, he lowered his weapon, and the two officers shuffled the last few feet. As they drew closer to the man, David noticed he was in his seventies and that he was Native American. The man extended his arm, gesturing he'd help get Johnny into the house. He escorted them inside and set Johnny on a sofa by the fireplace. Looking around, David could see trophies of what seemed like a hundred animal heads on the walls. He also noticed no gadgets of any sort, no TV, no radio, no nothing, just the firelit room with all the eyes staring back onto their lookers. The man told them to wait where they were, and he momentarily disappeared.

The aged Indian then returned with a bowl of water, bandages, and a small leather pouch. He asked David to hold out his arm, but David told him to tend to Johnny first. The old Indian turned toward Johnny, taking off David's makeshift bandage. He began to clean his wound with a rag that floated in the bowl.

"What's your name?" David asked as the old man tended

to Johnny.

"Nathan Tuscarora," the Indian replied in a low-key tone.

With a touch of anger in his voice, Nathan told the officers they were on his land, which was part of the Indian-owned reservation. David explained how they had found themselves lost while searching for evidence in the death of Bud Shaner. He then told him how he had come upon Buckeye Buck. Nathan paused as if caught off guard; those words seemed to strike a soft spot. He instantly changed his tone to slightly upbeat as he remarked how lucky David was for such a sight. He said a man could live a lifetime and never catch a glimpse of the great ghost Beast, and David had managed to spy on him twice in one day. Nathan apologized with empathy for his dog's fanged-tooth hospitality as he put the final touches on David's arm as Johnny stood by the window trying to get a signal on his cell.

He then asked if he could use Nathan's wall phone to call his wife. Nathan shook his head, telling him his ancestors didn't have one, and neither did he. Johnny just looked at him like he couldn't believe it, then asked if the phone worked as he pointed to the wall. Nathan just shook his head while Amanda's words echoed through his head: "Thunderstorm, be careful." "You have your phone on your boss?" he asked, already knowing David never kept it on him as it was always lying on his desk or in the console of his car. "No," he confirmed.

Nathan then explained that his nephew would be there in the morning, and that's when he could take the officers to town. David seemed to accept this fate, but Johnny couldn't, as they kept trying to get a signal. He kept staring out the window and his cell phone and the phone on the wall knowing Amanda was probably calling the Air Force, Army, and National Guard, everyone short of NASA. Nathan walked to a cabinet where he grabbed three glasses and a bottle of Backwoods whiskey. David shook his hand, refusing to drink, but Nathan poured anyway. He held out the glass to David until he finally gave in. Johnny gratefully took the glass, hoping the dark liquid would ease his soreness. After two shots, they began to enjoy themselves and forgot about their pain and the rain.

The old Indian laughed hysterically as David told him some of his stories about New York City and how he escaped death on more than one occasion. At first, Johnny looked at him like he was crazy, but the contagiousness began to set in when David chortled in the same manner. They drank for hours by the firelight, as it seemed Nathan never received much company from outside the reservation as he hung on every word in laughter.

Nathan suddenly became silent, his face growing long and serious. "You modern men of the World walk through life with your eyes closed. Apparitions of our forefathers cry out in the winds, saddened by the way you live without nature.

You build your skyscrapers up to the clouds so your sons and daughters never get to see the beauty of the eagle taking its prey. You isolate yourself in your concrete buildings with your central air and never get to smell the southern winds pushing through a field of wildflowers.

You take from our mother Earth and never give back, as she gets sick from the poisons you feed her rivers and the filth you flood into her skies. You rape our women and kill our children, as our buffalo no longer walk the earth in great numbers. You push us to the corners of lands you don't want and call them reservations as you strip our ancestral holy grounds."

The old Indian's eyes watered for a moment while David

and Johnny became speechless at the undeniable truth that was presented to them. Nathan stood up and walked out of the room. David and Johnny looked at each other dumbfounded as if they themselves were responsible for the anarchy of which the old man spoke.

Nathan walked back to the room carrying homemade pillows and handwoven Indian blankets. He reminded the officers that his nephew would be there in the morning. David thanked him as he turned in for the night.

The next day, Johnny and David woke to the sound of a truck speeding up the driveway and their heads pounding from a hangover. David stepped up to the window and saw Nathan on the porch, smoking a tobacco pipe and his nephew slamming his truck door. They stumbled outside with squinting eyes to greet the bright, clear sky as Nathan introduced them to his nephew Lofton. Lofton stood seven feet tall, with proud features and a powerful physique. Lofton reached out his giant hand to David, and they shook in mutual respect.

Johnny then blurted out, "Oh, shit!" as white fang approached them in a predator's slow manner, with a low, rumbling growl. Nathan shouted something in Indian. The German shepherd stopped dead in his tracks and sat still.

The officers thanked Nathan once more and then hurried into the truck that would take them back to Johnny's truck. As they drove through the muddied roads, Lofton asked if his grandfather had bored them with his sanctimonious speeches.

David just grinned and said, "Oh yeah, I guess you can say that and more."

Lofton laughed, "He probably gave you his 'white man killed the land' sermon."

Johnny added, "And the poisoning of the rivers, and the

killings of women and children, and everything else on God's green earth."

Lofton smiled, "The old man is still bitter over the long lawsuit our tribe had against a big corporation. We won, but it was a heartfelt battle. That's why he lives in that cabin, to bless those animals mounted on the walls by the last owner we won the property from."

David and Johnny pondered the perplexity of the story. They then talked of other things and chuckled on and off all the way to Johnny's truck. When they reached the truck, Lofton volunteered to pick up their bikes to save them from the trouble. Johnny quickly took him up on his offer, though the thought of going back into those woods made his stomach turn.

They said their goodbyes, and Lofton was gone. When they reached the station, David ordered Johnny to have his head and ankle looked at and to take the day off.

When David walked through the station door, he was bombarded with questions. "Where were you?" Are you all right? Where's Johnny?"

After David explained, Pat told him how Sarah had been worried sick and that she'd called the station a million times. David thanked her, went into his office, and closed the door. He called Sarah and told her what happened. Then he went to the police computer to review the local happenings in Horry County and the ticket distribution. In the last month, there were two drunken drivers, one domestic dispute, and a retail fraud, along with fifty-three tickets.

He skipped straight to the citations and analyzed each one. Most of those involved were locals; twenty-two of them were just passing through, and one was a new resident whose name came up with red flags.

David leaned back in his chair while a long list of felonies flashed on the screen. He saw the address of the felon's residence and made note that the property in the valley had been vacant for a very long time. The place was owned by an out-of-towner, or so he thought. "What was it the Indians called it …? Okay, yeah, the Valley of the White Snake."

He then noticed the time correlation between Bud's disappearance and the arrival of Thomas Syck in the area. He also saw that the house was owned by Devin Demas.

David decided to pay Mr. Syck a visit, but first, he would stop at home to reassure Sarah visually that he was okay, get a quick bit to eat, and change his clothes. Afterward, he would pay Mr. Syck a visit to the so-called Valley of the White Snake.

David pulled up to the enormous mansion a number of sophisticated vehicles lined the wide portion of the approach at the top of the driveway. He sat there for a moment, taking in the spectacle of this out-of-place palace, before he walked to the front door and rang the greeting bell. He waited thirty seconds until he rang it again, but still, there was no answer. Peeking inside the window, he saw no one. He decided to walk around to the other side of the house, and as he turned the corner, he could hear a radio blasting heavy metal. He continued walking, and it became louder as he drew nearer to the rear of the mansion. Finally, he came to some hedges, which created a privacy fence. He peered through the branches, taking notice of a twenty-something-year-old female sunbathing in the nude, singing to the weighted metal song.

He didn't want to bother her, but he also didn't want it to be a wasted trip, so he hollered out hello and half-covered his eyes.

"Hello," he shouted once more, finally catching her attention. The woman reached over and turned off the radio nonchalantly, then stood up, standing in her nakedness without a single shred of shame.

David looked to the side. "I'm here to see Thomas Syck."

"Who's asking?" the woman responded in a heavy, European accent.

David pulled out his badge and replied, "Sheriff's department."

She paused for a second and then told him to walk toward the back of the hedges, where there would be an entry to the pool. He followed the hedge line to the entrance, and by the time he saw water, she had robbed her naked body. She stood by the front of the pool, inquiring as to the reason he wanted to see Syck. David disregarded her question while he took notice of her long, wet hair that draped down like a black curtain enshrouding a perfect Masterpiece of beauty.

He then asked her name. "Nina," She responded in a soft voice with a heavy Italian accent.

She studied David's features as if he were a long-lost acquaintance. David moved toward her, as she offered no words, just a bewildered look, until she caught herself staring and then asked why he needed Syck.

"Just a couple of questions," he said, his eyes finding it hard to resist the cleavage that protruded from her robe. "Well, he's not here," she stated sternly. "Has he done something wrong?" "No. I just wanted to ask him if he knew a Bud Shaner." She shook her head, "I doubt it. We just moved to this area." David looked at her sharply, then said, "I didn't say where he was from." She quickly replied, "I assumed you were the local sheriff? "I am." David paused. "Did you know Bud Shaner?" She looked lost at the sound of the name and shook her head.

"How about Mr. Demas?" David inquired. "Could I talk to him?"

Again, she said he wasn't there. "He's out of the country."

He scrutinized her face for lies, which showed a hint of deceit, but thanked her anyway as he walked off. When he reached his car, he looked up at a window and saw a curtain fall back from a curious spectator. Being a cop for almost two decades gave David an aptitude to sniff out a lie, and, to him, this smelled like Bud's rotting carcass.

Two weeks later, Devin returned home from the other side of the globe. Even though he had dwellings all over the World, to him, the valley seemed home. Nina told him about his good twin, the sheriff, and how he was asking questions about the sacrificial pigeon that christened their estate. Devin was slightly moved by the news. He had already seen David in his visions. He informed his clan that True Alliance delegates from all over the World would come to the valley for an eclipse ceremonial celebration.

He then told them that every ten delegates would bring their own unexpected sacrificial lambs and that they would have a smorgasbord sacrifice in just three months. All eyes lit up as they were also promised immortality and provincial authority in Devin's dark World.

That day, David decided to go see that crazy, old Indian, Nathan. He would thank him and his nephew for their hospitality and for retrieving Johnny's dirt bikes. As he drove through the reservation, all eyes were on him, as if he were a deliverance from hell. He drove slowly through the cold stares until he reached Nathan's cabin. When he pulled up, Nathan was sitting on his porch, smoking a pipe, with White Fang by his side.

David shut off the car engine and yelled out the window,

"Is it safe to come out?"

Nathan waved his arm and gave a command to his dog, which then ran off behind the cabin. David waited until the fanged creature disappeared before climbing out of his car.

Nathan noticed that David's puncture wounds had mostly healed, and he cheerfully stated as David approached. "Thanks to whatever you put on it that day," David responded enthusiastically. "My doctor said he could make a million off the remedy."

Nathan half smiled while David sat down on a chair next to him, taking in the serene surroundings of dense timberland. "You sure do have it made out here, old timer." Nathan smiled again as he replied that he was now just a mere living creature on the skin of great mother Earth. David thought how deep this old man could be as he drew silent. The aged Indian then divulged an unexpected stunner as he told David his family name was anecdotal to his tribal ancestry. David's face looked puzzled as he continued, "Haven't your elders ever sat you down and told you about the valley of the White Snake? Have they not told you of your sixth great-grandmother, who bore a child from a Devil man with strange powers?"

David recalled how his mother used to tell stories of a Witch Man-Warlock who owned the valley, but only around Halloween as a joke. Nathan went on to explain how David's sixth great-grandmother bore two boys. One was mutilated during one of their rituals, and the other was freed by his tribal ancestors, who saved him from the malicious Demigod. He also told him stories of the "confessor" and how he lived with his ancestors in his deformed state due to the White Snake's Witchery.

Nathan's exorbitant stories sent chills crawling down David's skin, especially the thought of mutilated babies and

110

hooded-robed men, which repulsed him beyond belief. Even more so, the thought of him being kin to this ghastly, vile man appalled him.

David shook off the horror as he thought of how Indian folklore often proclaimed eccentric fables of horses dancing on clouds and spirits that whispered in the wind. Nathan closed by telling him that a great spirit, in the form of the antlered buck, was somehow connected to the opposite force of the Evil that ran rampant throughout the valley.

After an hour of old teller tales, David decided he could spend his time in better ways than listening to a crazy old coot. He said his goodbyes and headed back toward town, but he couldn't stop thinking about his family tree and how far back his name went. Just to kill the curious cat, he decided to pay his mother a visit since she wasn't far out of the way. She lived in the same house in which he was raised, located in the hundred-year-old district just outside of town. David pulled into the old driveway, which had more cracks in it than a frozen lake in April. He could see his mother in the backyard, pruning her white rose bushes. He walked around back, and she smiled when she caught sight of her son.

"Hi, mom," he said as he pecked her cheek with a kiss. David was an only child, and although he tried to visit as frequently as possible, it was still never enough for her. Ever since his father died from a rare blood infection at the age of fifty, he tried to spend as much time as he could with her.

"To what do I owe this unexpected treat?" she asked with a smile.

David smiled back. He told her that things had been hectic lately, and he just wanted to see her bright face. She turned to the prickly, flowered shrubs with a sentimental sigh. "You know, David, your father planted these roses when you were just seven years old. You remember?" David nodded, and his face grew long, reminiscing about the day oh so many eons ago.

She went on, in a slightly shaken chord, "Every summer when they'd come to full bloom, he'd say those damn shrubs would outlive him."

David smiled and said, "I remember."

Her eyes tinted in modest tears while she straightened her posture, lightened her chords, and quickly changed the subject. "I'm starving. You eat yet?"

David shook his head, no, and they headed inside the old Victorian-style home. They had soup and sandwiches and went on reminiscing about old times and faces.

David loved his mother very much, and it pained him to see her alone. He often offered to have her move into his place, but she always declined. He then dropped the bomb, asking her about their family tree and if she knew anything about those stories, Nathan told him.

"Whatever did you bring that up for?" she queried.

"Just curious. I've been talking to a crazy, old Indian who told me some weird things about our family history."

She paused as she looked at him like she'd been holding onto a secret for years. "Well, David, there has been a story your grandfather used to talk about Devils and Witches out there in the valley."

David just listened with an expressionless face as she told him how his great-grandmother, over three hundred years ago, fell in love with an unsavory fellow. She divulged how he seduced her with trickery and lies while killing her mother and

112

her newborn child. Word for word, her testimony was that which came from Nathan, but she didn't believe any of those stories, dismissing them as fairy tales you'd tell around Halloween.

She then got up from her chair. "I've been meaning to give this to you," she announced as she walked to a glass cabinet in the corner of the room. She opened the antique door and reached in for a five-inch-thick book that had a decorative front cover with a tree made of tin. She labored her way back to David and handed him the family tree album.

She told him she knew she was getting into trouble when she took the Lang name, but she wouldn't have traded one day for a lifetime with anyone else. David smiled as he looked at the cover and opened the book to the first page. There was the Lang name, embellished in red with a picture of a tree.

After a cup of coffee, David told her he had to get back to the station. She told him to give Sarah and Lisa her love as she kissed him on the cheek. She looked out the front door as he pulled out of the driveway. David honked his horn and waved to her then sped off.

The second shift was clocking in as David walked into the station. Johnny was at the front desk talking to night shift deputies Jim and Scott. They were talking about the biker gang Jim and Scott had busted the previous night for drinking in public and disturbing the peace at the Berry Bush Motel just outside of town. They also talked about Liz and Kathy, whom Ron, the biker, told one of the deputies about after the deputy asked him who gave him the black eye.

Johnny took notice of the description of Thomas Syck through the story they conveyed from the biker. When David heard the news, he became frustrated, wondering what the hell Syck was doing in Horry County. Johnny then told David that

Ron and his goons were locked up in the back, waiting for the county wagon to pick them up. They may have just received tickets. However, they would all need to be processed at the county jail since they all had warrants in four different states. But first, David would have a chance to have a talk with them while they were still his prisoners.

David told Johnny to go home and tend to his injured ankle. Though Johnny wanted a piece of the interrogation, he reluctantly walked out the door. Charley, the night deputy dispatcher, pushed the button on the panel to let David into the back of the jail section.

He grabbed a chair and walked down the row of cells, some empty and some occupied. David stopped, then queried aloud, "What cell is our Mr. Ron Wallace in?"

A voice rang out toward the end of the row, and David planted his chair in front of the caged man, surveying Ron's hardcore mannerisms.

"Who dotted your eye?" asked David as if stirring up a bee's hive with a stick. "Go fuck yourself, you are fucking oink-oink bitch! I'm already going to county, and you fucks towed our bikes away, so ahh ..., go fuck yourself!"

David shook his head as the other bikers joined in on the mockery.

David stood, turned, then picked up the chair and smashed it to bits. He then yelled at the top of his lungs, "Now do I have your attention, you fuck!?"

Perplexed by the sudden disruption, Charley popped his head in the Plexiglas window to check on things. David stood in silence as he just stared at Ron, acting like he was about to open the cell and unleash his anger.

"Alright, alright," announced Ron as he signified his compliance. "I don't know who the asshole is, but he sure knows how to swing a pool stick. He threw cash around like it was nothing. He kicked our asses, then took our bitches. There. You fucking happy now?!"

The untamed blockhead humbled in his cell as David nodded and turned to the exit of the confines. Ron pushed his face into the bars, blurting out, "Just to let you know, that boy isn't right."

David turned to Ron's divulgence and froze to the incoming information.

"Something isn't right about that boy. Just trust me on this one. Man, my boys have taken out other gangs, thugs, and even a couple of cops. But this guy, this guy scares the fuck out of me. Man, I mean to tell you that boy ain't right."

An outlandish ghoul began to saturate David's mind with its phantom questions. He then tapped the door as Charley peered through the window and buzzed him back in. He half waved at Charley and said good night, his mind somewhere between heavy contemplation and reality. Charley half waved back, still confused, then turned to stare once more at the broken chair.

Outside the station, David looked about the darkening sky, deciding to have a drink and talk with Rick, the owner of the Buckeye Buck Tavern. David took notice of the regulars before he walked to the bar, where Rick was already pouring his usual draft. He placed a frosty mug of beer in front of David and asked, "What's new?"

David looked first into the frothy foam, then raised his eyes, looked directly at Rick, and questioned him unexpectedly. "Heard you had a little ruckus around here a couple of days ago."

Rick shuffled a bit, caught off guard. He quickly explained that he didn't call the station because the blonde-haired man paid for the damages.

Once David was satisfied with Rick's recollection, he gulped his beer, said his goodbyes, and stepped out into the night air. He stared up at the full moon. Witches and goblins, he thought to himself as he shook his head. A black Mercedes-Benz, with black tinted windows and the True Alliance logo on the license plate, was stopped at the corner light. David thought to himself that he'd seen that logo somewhere but couldn't remember where. He watched the car turn the corner, heading toward the old church and cemetery before it disappeared from his sight. David drives home pondering where in the hell he had seen that logo. It started to eat at him the more he thought about it.

When he arrived home, his riddle was forgotten once he saw Sarah and Lisa's faces. This was his favorite time of the day, coming home to his excited daughter shouting out, "Daddy, daddy, daddy!" along with his beautiful wife's smile. He walked in and set the family tree album on the table as his daughter rushed him like a miniature linebacker. Sarah had spaghetti cooking on the stove. It just couldn't get much better for a man in this World. He truly felt blessed every time he walked through that door.

While it was another late family dinner, Sarah was used to it after ten years of marriage. She became proficient at keeping dinners warm and her spirits up, though she worried every time David came home late.

After their usual footsie play under the table and another delicious meal, David grabbed his family album and went into Sarah's study to deliberate its contents. David ran through the names of the noble stock of his progenitor lineage. He saw his name at the top of the tree, along with his cousins. He saw his grandfather and his great-grandfather, then his great, great-grandfather, who was a sheriff just like him. All the way down to the bottom of the tree, he read about his heritage, which took him to where his name derived: England. He looked on the mother's side of the tree and saw he had taken the Lang name from Dianna's side, along with her son James. He went to the father's side and found an empty spot where his name should be. David thought that was a bit peculiar since unwed mothers just didn't exist back then unless the father had died, but his name would still be printed on the tree.

David turned to the back of the book where it gave information on each of the names and the history of each family member, no matter how small the detail or how ordinary they might have been.

He saw that Dianna's father was handpicked by the Vatican in Rome and that he died unexpectedly of a heart attack. All night, he studied the book until Sarah nagged him to come to bed. He closed the metal cover and then turned out the light.

That night, Devin was at St. Andrew's Cemetery, which lay at the edge of town. He was searching the necropolis for the Lang burial plots. He ran across a few familiar names from his first stay in the valley. He then came to the Lang ossuaries as he went through the most recent to the colonial era which was barely legible. He found Dianna's epithet on the sepulcher. It read "Devoted Mother & Wife," but he was still left in the dark. He assumed she had been killed, as she was supposed to be sacrificed for dessert in their black worship.

"Enough of this shit," he said. He drew the shape of a large bell into the air. A deformed, hellish blue bell appeared, encompassing Evil itself. He held out his fist and swung it, clanging the giant hellish bell that rang out its destruction upon the cemetery. The ground started to shake while his third orb opened. Upright gravestones fell flat, and tomb sepulchers crumbled. The Earth gave way in the vicinity of each plot, the crust pushing itself outward while violent palpitations echoed throughout the churchyard.

Devin beheld a glorious dishevelment of caskets that unearthed themselves from the soil that enslaved them. He opened Dianna's sarcophagus and seized her skull, raising it to his face. He gaped into the chronicles of her life. Even after all those years, his anger for the confessor impinged upon him for a moment as he walked upon the casket of his son, James Lang. Devin looked down in disillusion as he stared at James's skeletal remains that were muddled and in disarray. Knowing he had a son to whom he passed on his mortality stirred a slight overtone of sentiment into his heartless, soulless frame. He then gathered James's bones into a burlap bag and drove off into the night.

The next morning, reporters filled the town. Everyone from *The Enquirer* to the local channels showed up, and even CNN wanted a piece of the action. David walked into the station and asked what the hell was going on. Pat told him about the coffins that surfaced at St Andrew's cemetery. "Johnny's there now, holding reporters off the scene until you get there."

"I'm there. Take my calls."

Pat nodded as David flew out the door. When he reached the cemetery, a flood of reporters saturated the surrounding grounds with a plethora of company logos. Johnny had the front entrance sealed off and was holding off a tidal wave of reporters. Father Hemmings stood dumbfounded. David saw him moping about the grave plots as if appalled by the confusion. David found a spot to park and then walked toward the scene. "What the hell's bells is going on here?" he promulgated.

Johnny shrugged his shoulders and said, "I'd say grave robbers, but only two caskets were opened." David shook his head. "Anything taken?" he queried with a touch of contrition in his voice. Johnny gave a remorseful look as he told David that one of the caskets was empty. David started to walk toward Father Hemming as Johnny said with reverence, "Uh, just one more thing."

David turned to him with a dreaded apprehension as he thought he could almost finish Johnny's sentence. "The two coffins that were opened were Lang caskets, and one of them is empty." For some reason, David feared it might have been his father's casket as he hastened toward his family plots. He saw that his father's casket did partially surface apparently still closed. He then peered upon the primordial plots with his family name that lay open before him.

Father Hemmings approached David with compassion, expressing his condolences. David looked inside one of the coffins, taking notice of the sixteenth-century decor, while Father Hemmings rambled on about how it must be the Devil's work.

David's face flushed. The words hit him hard as he gazed at a skull that lay between the two open caskets. He knelt down and studied the skull, pondering a logical rationale for this disheartening dilemma, as opposed to Father Hemmings's condemnatory conceptions of the Devil's handiwork.

David stood up as he noticed Dianna's gravestone. He remembered her name from his family album. He then observed the stone next to hers, recalling the fatherless moniker. The name "James" barely presented itself after the erosion of time.

Father Hemmings squabbled away, fretfully sighing as he chased after a fallen sepulcher. David watched him scurry, his

119

mind drifting into dark dimensions until he suddenly remembered the Mercedes was in the proximity of this atrocity.

David thought it seemed strange that Lang Township was a quiet and "unheard of" town until this Mr. Demas arrived. He then walked the perimeter of the grounds, studying the geology of the cemetery. He pointed around like Detective Columbo at a crime scene as he hypothesized about the petulant phenomenon. After he circled the graveyard a couple of times, he walked up to Johnny. A plethora of microphones suddenly pointed his way with a million questions. He told the press he had no comment and pushed back upon being prodded.

David and Johnny locked the gates, waving and shouting at the crowd of reporters to step back. David told Johnny he was going to pay Darren Johnson a visit and asked him to send the crews away. David worried whether encroaching reporters could get injured trying to breach the encompassed area as he studied the closed confines and the mass of journalists outside of it.

On his way back to his car, he continued to get bombarded with a barrage of questions. David spun away as the media turned their attention to Johnny. He could see Johnny shooing the reporters away in his rearview mirror as he headed toward Darren Johnson's.

Darren and David had been friends since childhood and remained so, but they both lived such different lifestyles that they hardly crossed paths. Darren and his father ran their own excavation company, Earth Movers USA, about a mile from David's house. David thought if anybody could help him figure out what pushed the caskets out of the ground, Darren could.

David pulled into the Earth Movers USA yard and asked one of Darren's workers where he could be found. He pointed to a small office building with a sixty-foot antenna perched on the side. David parked his car and walked inside. He was greeted by Darren's sister, Karen, at the front desk. David and Karen were high school sweethearts back in the day, but when they graduated, David dumped her for his first love, law enforcement. He left his small-town blues for big-time blues in New York City, graduating at the top of his class at the police academy in upstate New York. Karen waited for him for almost two years before she married one of the truckers who worked for her father.

Karen lifted her eyes from her work and uttered hello to David in a quivery voice. Part of her still carried a torch for her first love. He half smiled as he returned her hello. David tried his best to keep it impersonal whenever he saw Karen since he still felt a touch of guilt for ditching her.

"Is Darren in?" he asked, as if inquiring about a ninety-year-old nun.

"He's in his office with a client," she responded as if replying to a long-lost love. She then pushed the intercom button, looking into David's eyes while announcing his presence.

Darren acknowledged her and said he would be wrapping up momentarily. David cringed as time began to stretch. He decided to pick a chair in which to sit that might keep him from Karen's direct view.

Karen resumed her work. The phone rang, breaking the tension for a moment. Just as she finished her company spiel to the caller, Darren walked out with his client. He shook his hand and told him they'd break ground next week. Darren spied on David as the client headed for the door. His face lit up. He always thought it a pleasure to see his old friend.

"How yaw doing there, Mr. Sheriff?" he jested as he shook

David's hand.

David asked him if they could talk in private. Darren looked puzzled but held out his arm and motioned toward his office. David walked in, and Darren offered him a cup of coffee. He declined since he thought Karen would have to fetch it. Darren closed the door and then took his seat behind his tidy desk. Darren liked having a friend who was a sheriff, as it gave him a small sense of leniency and the courage to push the envelope for legislation into shaky areas of law. Yet, he knew not to put David on that spot because he would be a cop before a friend if the situation ever arose.

"What brings you here?" asked Darren, sipping his coffee and peering over his cup with curiosity.

"What do you' suppose might push a bunch of coffins out of the ground without being dug up?" divulged David in a hesitant voice.

Darren set his coffee down as he repeated half of the question. "Push a bunch of coffins out the ground?"

David then added, "St. Andrew's Cemetery."

Darren asked if it was a joke. David just stared at him with a serious look on his face that Darren remembered oh so well. Darren paused silently in a brief chain of thoughts before he said, "Well, I personally have never seen that before, but I have heard of floods and underwater streams that uncovered whole cemeteries. I could give you a couple of guesses, but like I said, I have never seen anything remotely like the scenario you just described."

David asked Darren not to take up his time with his theories and gave him a look that said he was all business. Darren shook it off and stated, "Well, you got weather erosion, but that mostly happens in the badlands where there are no roots to hold the ground together. Since we're in the southern states where 70% percent of the Earth is red clay, granite, and that would make all three scenarios obsolete." He hesitated before adding, "Are you sure this isn't some kind of fraternity prank?"

His eyes suddenly widened. "Hey, isn't your father buried there?" said Darren with a tone of sympathy. David shook his head yes, then replied, "It's like a giant hand came out of the sky and pulled them up from the ground."

Darren's curiosity was too much for him. He asked if he could see the damage for himself. David answered yes. He advised him to tell Johnny to let him in the gates and that he'd call him later. Darren wasted no time as he told Karen to cancel his eleven o'clock call and to take his calls. David decided to tell Sarah the news, heading west as Darren went east toward the cemetery.

When David drove up to the house, he saw the same Mercedes Benz sitting in his driveway that he had seen on the street near Buck Eye Buck Tavern. It had black windows and a license plate that read True Alliance. "What the fuck?" he stammered as he sped up the drive.

Upon entering his home, he heard two voices coming from Sarah's office.

He turned toward the sound of his dreaded worriment, stepping silently as if walking on eggshells, and propped himself near the door, trying to catch a hint of their conversation. He positioned his hand on the handle of his holstered gun. He halted near the entrance, hearing a nonthreatening consultation about taxes and land contracts. Lowering his hand from his pistol, he walked into the room with a slight feeling of fear.

When David entered the room, he was somewhat

surprised. The man Sarah was talking to somewhat resembled him, except for Devin's bald head and younger skin. "David," said Sarah with a bright smile. "I'm glad you came home. This is Mr. Demas."

They both stood in awe for a moment until Devin stood and extended his hand.

"Mr. Demas just hired me to do his taxes and close on a foreclosure he's trying to buy in Brunswick County."

David motioned for Sarah to follow him out of the room and said politely, "Sarah, I need to talk to you for a minute."

Devin stared forward, looking at nothing as if he didn't hear anything until Sarah excused herself. "No problem," Devin replied. "Take as long as you need."

Sarah followed David, clueless to his concerns.

When they reached the kitchen, David turned to her, locking his eyes on hers. "Sarah, I don't know about this guy. There have been strange things happening since he moved here."

Sarah stared back quizzically for a moment, then asked, "What kind of things?"

"Well, Bud Shaner, for one. And my family plots were unburied at St. Andrew's for two."

Sarah gazed at David as if he were going mad, and she began to giggle. "Listen, David, Mr. Demas is a very rich man. Why or what would he have to gain by killing a drunk or digging up a couple of coffins?" Just as those words left her lips, she remembered that David's father was buried in that cemetery a couple of years ago. She asked if the plot was disturbed.

David shook his head yes, then asked if he could talk to Devin. "I'm sorry about your father's plot, but you shouldn't bother Mr. Demas about such things, David. For Christ's sake, he's the CEO of True Alliance." David nodded his head, "It's either here or the station; take your pick." Sarah looked at him as if he'd lost his mind and reluctantly agreed. She then followed him back to her office as if ready to defend her new client against her off-the-deep-end husband.

"Mr. Demas, do you mind if I ask you a couple of questions?" Devin was nonchalant as he answered comically, "Do I need my lawyer?" "Na, not at all," David answered back. "just a quick chat, but it does appear that you got the lawyer anyway." He glanced up at Sarah. Then he laid it on, "Do you know, or have you ever heard the name Bud Shaner?" Devin wore a puzzled guise as he answered no.

David studied his unexpressive face as he continued to pour out his questions. "Okay, I take it that's your Mercedes out in my driveway, with the plate True Alliance on it." "One of many, you can say," answered Devin, as if counting cattle.

"Oh, then I wouldn't be off base if I told you that I saw your one of many Mercedes drive off toward St. Andrews's cemetery last night." Sarah piped up, "David, you off base. Mr. Demas is well respected all around the World." "It's okay," Devin replied. "Yeah, that was me. I was driving around trying to get familiar with the area, but I didn't notice any cemetery." David returned sarcastically, "So you're trying to get familiar with our town. You drive past a cemetery with a giant steeple church next to it, but it didn't catch your eye?" Devin just smiled and raised his palm upward as if clueless.

"Come on, David," said Sarah, "Give the guy a chance. Why on God's green Earth would Mr. Demas vandalize a church, for Christ's sake? Are you listening to yourself?" David waved his hand as he smiled affirmatively, "I was just curious about Mr. Demas. After all, a new guy in town here, in my home, with my wife and kid. Need I say more?" David drew silence as Sarah apologized to Devin, her face turning red from embarrassment.

"No, I'm sorry," David interrupted as he began to turn away. "I'll let you get to your work. My apologies." He turned to Sarah while he apologized once more, glanced at Devin taking his seat, and then withdrew from the room. He checked in on Lisa and saw her sleeping peacefully, then stuck around for a bit to procrastinate his stay, heading for the kitchen to take a bite to eat. He retreated to the living room with his Dagwood sandwich and soda. By that time, Lisa had woken from her slumber and climbed onto David's lap, rubbing her eyes from the light. David offered her a bite, but she quickly refused, burying her head in his chest. He then fumbled to set his plate on the table, and he reached for the remote. Sponge Bob Square Pants flashed on the screen and Lisa's eyes became glued instantly upon the multi colors and characters.

Fifteen minutes later, Sarah and Devin emerged from Sarah's office, their conversation continuing to the side door. Lisa heard her mother and sprang from David's lap at the sound of her voice.

Before David could set his sandwich down to keep her in the den, she had already escaped. David then scrambled from his seat and followed her. Lisa had her arms wrapped tightly around her mother's leg.

Sarah smiled with embarrassment as Devin bent down to the toddler's level and announced, "Well, well, and what do we have here?" Lisa smiled as she half hid behind the sanctuary of her mother's limb.

David just froze in horror, his heart sinking into his stomach at the sight. Devin then waved his hands like a cheap circus clown, and a red-swirled peppermint candy appeared. Little Lisa's face brightened, and she felt safe enough to come out of hiding and reach for the shiny, wrapped candy. Devin smiled as he cupped her cheek with the palm of his hand and remarked how she had her mother's eyes before he stood upright.

David gasped as if he just swallowed a jagged glass, while Sarah simply smiled and repeated the acknowledgment of their next meeting. Lisa returned to the comfort of hiding behind her mother's leg as Devin said goodbye. Devin opened the door, turned his head toward David, and nodded with a slit smile of approval. Sarah followed his gaze to David, and her face had that look that said *don't say a word*. She quickly closed the door behind Devin and peered out the window. Then she glared at the source of her anger.

Sarah tapped her fingernails on the counter as she shook her head and sighed with disappointment. She was searching for the words of her anger. She mustered out, "You know ..." as David intervened with offsetting politeness.

"Honey, I got a bad feeling about this guy," he said quickly. "Some crazy shit's been happening since he's been in town, and I just want to check him out before."

"Before what?" Sarah interrupted. "Before I can finally work with the big wigs again and break this fucking boredom?" "Boredom? Boredom? Really? All I'm saying is let me check out his background before you meet with him again."

Sarah shook her head and looked away, convinced about Devin's legitimacy. "You don't have a clue," she yelled. David shrugged off her coldness and spoke in a low voice of persuasion, "Listen, all I'm asking is to give me a little time to figure this guy out before you get chummy with him, huh?"

Silence instilled the air as she stood adamantly high upon

the granite rock of her arrogance. Sarah suddenly snapped. "Ten percent of four hundred thousand dollars. Can your small-town mind register that?!" David felt his stomach knot, along with his mind, his upper hand lowered by her strong will. He then lashed out in anger, "Why the hell are you fucking questioning me? I know what the hell I'm doing."

An awkward silence filled the room but was quickly drowned out by little Lisa crying. Sarah turned, then snatched her up and walked away. David stared in shock at this stranger taking his child from the room. He then turned to the door. He wanted to slam it ever so loudly but decided not to. Instead, he walked to his cruiser, his head to the ground, with a sick feeling as if he had lost something. He drove back toward the cemetery, confused. Devin's untimely visit derailed him momentarily. In a strange sequence of timing, this Devin character pervaded his mind with a quandary of mind-numbing questions.

When he reached the cemetery, he noticed Darren digging around and pointing his finger around like a detective trying to find an answer. Johnny stood next to him with a coffee in his hand as Darren poked away at a mound of dirt around a coffin.

There were only a couple of reporters left sitting in their vehicles parked half a block away. When David walked into the cemetery, he saw a bunch of shovel-sized trenches in various locations on the grounds. "Find anything out?" asked David as he approached the human mole. "As you can see, I've been digging around, checking the texture, color, and composure of the dirt," Darren returned. "I didn't notice any underground pockets of water, and I'll tell you, my dad put a shovel in my hand when I learned to walk. I've excavated from here to the Ozarks to the Florida swamps, but I never seen anything like this. It's like a giant groundhog decided to throw all his old furniture out into the street. I don't get it."

Even though David was still despondent from his argument with Sarah, seeing Darren's face reminded him of the mole to which he spoke, and it made him laugh for a moment. David asked Darren if his company would assist the church's groundskeepers in reburying the caskets. Darren felt a bit creepy by the whole mess and would rather be elsewhere, but since he and David were old friends, he agreed to help him out.

David told Johnny to give Darren the key to the gate and to finish the remainder of the day on his beat. He then was off to Buckeye Buck's for a stiff one. Only two people populated the entire tavern when David walked in. Emma and Old-Man Joe were sitting at the counter drinking Pabst Blue Ribbon. Their shot glasses of tequila had been emptied. "The usual?" announced Rick from behind the counter.

"A round of shots for the bar!" declared David. "What's bugging you," asked Emma like a wise old owl with a keen eye for trouble. "What makes you say that?" David responded like a kid caught with his hand in a cookie jar. "Well, for one, your face is as long as a yardstick, and, for two, you're here drinking-Ta-kill-ya' with us retires. What gives?"

All six eyes were fixed on David, and he saw no escape from her probing. After a moment's pause, he gave in by divulging eight little words: "I got myself in an argument with Sarah." All motion in the place resumed as he continued, "Yeah, well, that big shot that just moved in the valley got things stirred up by throwing his money around. I came home to her making a four hundred-thousand-dollar deal with that asshole. And to top it off, the guy kind of looks like me, except for his bald head and maybe a couple of years younger. Man, I'll tell you, we kind of look like we could pass for brothers or something."

"All this stuff sounds kind of creepy if you ask me," divulged Rick as he topped off David's shot glass. "Tell me about it," said Joe. "Finding poor 'ole Bud like that really threw me for a loop." David then added, "Yeah, and then seeing all those coffins sprung like mushrooms really freaked me out." The whole tavern drew silence as their imagination filled their heads with fear and loathing.

Joe broke the silence. "You say this Mr. Demas guy looks just like you, huh?" "Man, I tell you, he looks just like my twin brother, but younger and bald and … oh, there's one more thing. I not only saw Buckeye Buck, but he let me pet him, too."

"What?!" Joe exclaimed. "Come on, now. Now you have been mixing 'wacky tabacky' with them there 'Ta-kill-ya', or are you just losing your mind?"

"C'mon, Joe. That ain't fair. You even said you saw him before." David stated, trying to get Joe to side with him.

"Wait a minute now. I just said I shot at a buck once within a forty-foot range and missed, but maybe instead of trying to shoot him, I should have petted him. Ha-ha-ha!" Old-Man Joe could barely get the last word out as he and Emma burst out laughing, "Petted Buckeye Buck, ha-ha-ha!"

David threw a ten-dollar bill on the counter and turned to the door as all three were now cackling. Rick then hollered before he reached the door, "Hey, maybe you can start a petting zoo with Buckeye Buck, ha-ha-ha!"

David left the tavern feeling like a fool, echoes of their hysteric laughter ringing in his head. He then remembered where he saw that logo: it was in New York on a high-rise in downtown Manhattan when he was a street cop. That symbol, a silhouette of a man on top of the World, with a flame emitting from his two hands cupped together, stuck in his mind.

"Oh, my God," David said to himself. "This guy may be bigger than I thought." He now understood why Sarah worried so much about losing his business. He walked to his car in heavy contemplation as his mind raced to all those unanswered questions. David drove around aimlessly, somewhat scared to go home, so he decided to return to the station and check on things. He made a U-turn and headed toward the sanctuary, carrying his heavy load of mounting problems.

There was just an hour left on the day shift and David wanted to hear his messages personally from Pat. "Hello, Sheriff," she said with a smile that seemed to give refuge.

"Hello, Pat. Any calls?" "Yeah," Pat loyally returned. "County Jail called and said they couldn't make it until tomorrow to pick up the prisoners." "What?! You got to be kidding!" David replied.

Pat added, "Nope. They said they're short-staffed and that they'll try to be here in the morning." David grew even more frustrated. "Try? Well, if they're not here by lunch and I'm not here, you have my permission to let them go."

"OK," she said as if she were setting locusts free on a ripe green crop. "Have they eaten anything today?" asked David.

"Just a pint-sized carton of milk and a muffin for breakfast," Pat informed him. "County would've taken care of that if they had come."

David reached for his pocket. "Here's twenty bucks. Buy 'them some hamburgers or pizza or something. I don't want Lang Township to be known as torturers." Pat smiled, "Oh, Sheriff Lang. You're all heart underneath that thick alligator skin, aren't yaw?" David smiled back, "Don't give me away, huh."

Pat's smile grew, "No problem, Sheriff. I'll see you

131

tomorrow. Have a safe ride home."

David wondered why she said that. Maybe she could smell liquor on his breath, he thought. He blew it off and started toward home. When David arrived home, all was quiet except for Sarah's voice on the phone in her office. David stuck his head in Sarah's office. Lisa was playing on the floor with her Fischer Price toys. Sarah smiled and waved, holding her conversation. Lisa looked up and yelled, "Daddy!" and made her usual linebacker rush toward him. David picked her up and walked out of the room. He went into the living room, where she could express her excitement without disturbing Sarah. He held her in his arms as he daydreamed out the window.

Sarah walked into the living room with a smile. "Well, just got off the phone with the bank, and the ball's set in motion," David told her how he was happy for her with a crooked smile and a congratulations. Sarah strode up to him and apologized for her earlier antics and inappropriate manner, but she ended with, "You got the wrong guy."

David ignored her comment, smiled, and asked, "What's for dinner?" Sarah stated that she'd been on the phone all day and that they'd been invited to dinner with Devin Demas. David was surprised. He really wasn't up to rubbing elbows with his number one suspect. But it made Sarah happy, and that was good enough.

"I called Amanda," she said, "and she doesn't mind watching Lisa. We could drop her off on the way to Mr. Demas's house."

After an hour and a half, they were dressed and ready for the night out. David wore one of two suits, and Sarah wore an evening dress. They drove to Johnny and Amanda's place. Lisa always loved seeing the boys since she hadn't had anyone to play with in their rural community. Sarah said that she'd run her in, knowing how to keep David and Johnny separated so they couldn't talk about Devin Demas. Sarah returned quickly to the car as if she were Alice in Wonderland late for the queen's ball. They headed toward Devin's house as the sun sank, casting an array of colors across the evening sky.

As they pulled into the long driveway, Sarah's eyes bulged out of her head. David often wondered if she resented leaving the sophisticated social circle of New York City. Her bulging eyes didn't help build his confidence as he thought for a moment about how she might be if they had stayed in New York. They rang the doorbell and waited momentarily until Nina opened the door. She was wearing a low-cut evening dress, which hardly left anything for the imagination. When they walked in the door, Sarah's eyes widened even more as she stated how beautiful the house was.

"Hello," said Devin as he walked into the room in a three-thousand-dollar suit. He flashed a "glad you could make it" smile. He then told his guests that his company helicopter was on the way. Sarah's smile was uncontainable as she repeated the word "helicopter" aloud in a happy I can't believe it tone of voice. David seemed unimpressed and asked where Devin planned to take them.

"C'mon, David," Sarah jumped in. "Where's your sense of adventure?"

David had a tone of scourge as he said he'd had all the adventure he could handle in the last couple of days, and he looked at Devin with innuendo. Sarah put her arm around David and countered, "It takes a couple of minutes for this ole coal engine to warm, but we'll be fine; sounds fun. Right honey?" she said as she turned to David and squeezed his hand.

She felt his gun through his suit jacket and became angry again but decided to keep it to herself. Devin offered them a drink, led them into his lavish living room, and walked behind the bar. Sarah asked for a Bloody Mary. David said that he'd have the same. Devin then joked about how he liked a woman who could drink a glass of blood. David said nothing, keeping his comments to himself with restraint.

Devin announced that his helicopter should be arriving at any moment and handed them their drinks. David asked where he was taking them. Sarah was at the edge of her seat awaiting the answer when Devin told them they would be dining at one of his establishments of French cuisine.

"And where would that be?" David asked again in an almost rude tone. Devin laughed, then stated, "Devil's in the details, huh?" He then added, "Off the Atlantic coast, twenty miles south of Charleston." "That's over a hundred and fifty miles away!" David quickly responded.

Devin smiled and told him the trip was a twenty-minute flight, that his Euro-copter could go three hundred miles per hour, and that they'd be back before midnight. "Could you make it before eleven?" David then retorted. "Some of us have to work for a living."

Devin would normally crush someone into a can for such insolence, but he found it amusing, as it came from his progenitor counterpart. Nina sat silent, sipping her drink in disbelief. She had never heard anyone speak that way to her Master.

A chopper rumbled onto the estate, its blades cutting into the sky. "Ah, sounds like our ride," Devin held out his hand. "Shall we?"

David expected it would land in a clearing outside, but instead, it landed on a chopper pad upon the roof. Devin led his guests through the living room and into the family room, where there was an elevator. "You have an elevator in your

134

house?" Sarah sang out.

Devin then joked, "Second floor, lingerie; bottom floor, hell; top floor, heaven."

David stood with disrespectful eyes as he gazed at Devin and Nina, who were staring at him. The door opened, they walked in, then Devin pushed 'R' for the roof.

Sarah's face had a smile from ear to ear. "You sure don't see something like this every day," she stated.

Devin smiled back as the door closed. There was a moment of silence until Nina asked how long Sarah had been a Lawyer. "Almost fifteen years," she declared with pride.

A soft bell rang as the doors opened on the roof, where there was an eight-man X-3 Euro-copter. It was black and white with Devin's company logo on its side. Devin opened its door and motioned for everyone to pile in. After they were all buckled in, Devin gave the OK for the pilot to take off. Sarah had her nose to the window like a kid on her first plane ride. David sat next to her, seemingly still and unimpressed. They flew over the valley, accelerating to over one hundred and ninety miles per hour. Devin reached into a small refrigerator, "May I offer you a drink? All I have is imported beer and wine coolers." Sarah chose a cooler while the other three had beer.

"Thank you, Mr. Demas," Sarah said as she took her first sip.

"Please, just call me Devin now that we're all friends."

David remained silent but found himself beginning to like this Demas character as time wore on, yet he dared not show it.

They reached the restaurant in an astounding twenty-minute circling until they came to a launching pad with the True Alliance logo on it. They landed perfectly as they descended from the clouds. Devin opened the door and motioned for everyone to climb out. He slammed the door, and they ducked under the blades until they were clear. They followed Devin until they were greeted by a doorman who treated them as if they were sovereignty. When they entered the restaurant, men in red jackets catered to Devin's every whim. He ordered a bottle of wine with a vintage made before David was born, along with Worldly appetizers of a savory delight. Their table overlooked the ocean and had a view the gods of Mt. Olympus could even appreciate. Devin ordered a small portion of almost every dish the house had to offer, and a team of waiters served them like royalty.

Sarah announced that she had to use the ladies' room, and Nina jumped up to join her. This was the opportunity for which David had been waiting. Devin smiled as they walked away. "Your wife is very beautiful, with a brain that goes with it," he said as he turned to David. "You're a lucky man."

"Yeah, she's a New Yorker, and I'm just a small-town sheriff, but we make it work," David replied comically with a quizzical smile. "Why Sarah? I don't understand?" said Devin."

"Oh, I think you do," David returned.

"Again, why, my wife, when I'm sure you have a skyscraper full of cut-throat lawyers to do whatever it is you do?" Devin remained silent for a moment. Then stated, "I need a local lawyer who I can trust, that's all."

"That's all, huh?" David asked rhetorically. "OK, let me ask you another question. What brings you to our little community when you can live anywhere in the World?"

Devin smiled again. "I inherited the valley from a family member who died, so out of respect, I decided to move there."

David decided to play the game. He told Devin he was sorry about his family member, and then he asked when that person died and whom. Devin told him that it happened a long time ago, and he just recently decided to move to the valley. Yet he never divulged who. David wanted to drill him further but decided against it when he saw Sarah and Nina making their way back to the table.

They returned laughing as if they had been friends for years. Devin smiled and asked what was so funny while the ladies slid back into the booth. Sarah pointed at David and Devin. "You two," she quipped, barely able to speak the words in her hysteria.

"I don't get it," said David.

"I told Nina that looking at you guys is like looking at two twins in a parallel universe!" Sarah offered, "You better not touch each other, or you guys will explode." David and Devin looked at each other like they didn't get it. Trays of food started to roll in, and even David anticipated the variety of French cuisine they were about to be served. They sat for two hours, eating the best of the best the World could offer while gazing at the rolling waves down below. They polished off the last of the intoxicating elixir and left the building.

They climbed back into the helicopter and made it back to the valley by eleven-thirty, so Devin apologized to David for the extra half hour. Sarah thanked Devin for the glamorous evening, and she admitted to never having tasted wine so fine nor eaten such delightful foods. Devin promised many more such evenings in the future with even more prospects if she so desired. Sarah's eyes were filled with stars as her imagination of the Worldly delicacies of far-off places riddled her mind.

They said their farewells and drove toward Johnny and Amanda's house. After retrieving Lisa, they returned home.

Sarah was still excited when they walked in their door. She put Lisa to bed and slipped into a slinky night dress. It didn't take much to seduce David. They started making love in the hallway just outside of Lisa's room. He picked her up and took her into their bedroom, laying her ever so gently on the bed. She seemed more kinky than usual, reaching for his package and putting him in her mouth. This was a rare treat for David as he tangled his fingers in her hair. Sarah then came up for air and pushed him back, shoving her muff onto his face. She gyrated herself in a frenzy of excitement as if they were strangers pleasing each other's fantasies.

David pulled away and turned her over, reaching for a pillow to prop up her hips. She screamed out in ecstasy while he deeply drilled his passion. Nearly twenty minutes later, they released their passion together, with Sarah wailing and convulsing. She jerked in spasms, then turned over like an animal who achieved what it wanted and went to sleep. David lay awake as he thought how freakish their sex was that night, with no "I love you-s" nor any eye contact. It was as if Sarah was a possessed sex fiend.

The next day, right at six in the morning, the Horry County paddy wagon showed up at the Lang Township Sheriff's station. David was still asleep, worn out from the previous night's activities. The County deputies loaded up the prisoners as part of their usual routine. Don, the head deputy, had a thing for Pat, and he always found a reason to make small talk in his once-a-month visits to Lang Township. This time, he found the courage to ask her out, and she promptly accepted his invitation.

He left the station in high spirits for the mundane trip back down desolate Highway forty-four. Don was singing that old cowboy song, "Oh Suzanna," but changed the name to Patricia.

On the side of the road up ahead, Don saw a black Viper. A blonde-haired man was leaning against the fender, and a Hispanic man was standing next to him. Syck walked to the road, mumbling words of death while Hector just watched in glee. The county prison wagon held steady as Syck rhymed out louder and louder, the wagon drawing nearer. Syck sang out: *"My ears were a-ringing from your song you were a-singing, a song about my name. Now your heads are a-swelling as your bodies sent a-sailing, your wagon crashed and burns."*

Suddenly, a blood vessel exploded in Don's brain, and the truck flipped in a frenzy of carnage. In the rear confines of the thrashing cabin, Ron and his goons suffered the same ill-gotten fate as Don, grabbing the sides of their heads. The metal then twisted into a rolling mess, and the sound of screams behind the violent crash filled the air. Syck and Hector burst out in laughter, like two kids that just destroyed a toy for kicks. They jumped up and down in the middle of the road while tormented shrieks continued amidst the inferno of the burning wreckage.

After Syck's little celebration, he and Hector climbed into the Viper and drove past the flames, heading out of town toward Atlanta. They wanted to do some gambling and pick up some bimbos for some fun until the solar eclipse was sacrificed. Syck hit speeds of as much as one hundred twenty miles per hour as they blasted a Nocturnal Machine CD and passed a joints and compact mirror full of coke.

Johnny was sitting behind a water tower with his radar gun as the two black magic renegades zoomed past him. He quickly got into his car and sped off in pursuit of the black Viper. But this time, he knew with whom he was dealing.

Hector noticed the flashing lights. He nudged Syck to his side and pointed behind them. Syck inhaled the joint and said, "Oh, this fuck-head again." He then threw the Viper into sixth gear as Hector gave Johnny the finger.

Johnny floored the pedal as he spoke aloud, "You're going to jail this time, Mr. Syck."

They played cat and mouse as Syck taunted him by letting Johnny catch up before he'd lose him again. This went on for umpteen minutes until Johnny suddenly stopped. Syck became pissed as he watched him make a U-turn. Johnny had just received the call about the paddy wagon that lay in ruins. He was perturbed about having to stop his pursuit of Syck, but he was the only cruiser on the road, so he had to turn around.

When Johnny arrived at the wreck, his jaw dropped as he witnessed the mound of charred remains that lay before him. Pat called David in tears, telling him about the wreck after she found out from Johnny that there were no survivors. Within twenty minutes, David was on the scene, followed by the Horry County Fire Department, the Dillon County Fire Department, and ambulances. "What the hell happened?" queried David in confusion.

"I don't know yet. I was chasing that loose cannon, Thomas Syck when I got the call. I called Brian's Towing, and as soon as the coroner pulls out the bodies, they'll tow it to the yard."

David walked away in heavy contemplation as Johnny supervised the cleanup. He backtracked fifty yards while observing the contrast of the road. On the side, David saw wide tire tracks, like that of a high-performance car. As he studied them, he also discovered two sets of footprints that surrounded the entire circumference of the tire tracks. It almost appeared as if two people were square dancing with all the shuffled prints that were present. David walked back to his squad car and backed up to the tracks. He then opened his glove box and grabbed his digital camera.

He took dozens of pictures of the tire tracks and shoe prints until he was satisfied; he had enough. He drove up to Johnny and told him about the tracks as they loaded the last of the charred remains. Johnny told David that Syck was driving a Viper and to compare the pictures to a Viper's tracks on their evidence charts. David agreed and said he was also going to put out an APB for Thomas Syck and see if they could get some answers.

Bri-Guy Towing pulled up as David took off. David thought about how so much had happened since the arrival of Devin Demas, and he couldn't pass it off as a coincidence. When he reached the station, he noticed that Pat's eyes were swollen from crying, and tissues were wadded up on her desk. David offered to call Charlie in for a double shift, but she said she'd be alright.

Pat then told him how Don finally worked up the nerve to ask her out.

David smiled and said, "At least he died a happy man, knowing you said yes."

She nodded with watery eyes.

David told her if she needed anything that, he'd be in his office on the computer and to notify him if anything came up. She nodded again as he walked into his office and closed the door. He grabbed the digital camera from his pocket and loaded the file into the computer. Instantly, images flashed on his screen as the download from his high-tech camera spewed into the Lang Township Police data files. David clicked on the stored info on different makes of cars and trucks, then scrolled down to "tread tracks." He pushed the "find" key after loading the picture, and many treads flashed on the screen until a match was found. They were Firestone treads on the 2017 Dodge Viper, just like Johnny said. David imagined that this process might have taken days, maybe even weeks, years ago. He then went to Pat's radio to call Johnny to tell him he was right. Johnny replied that he smelled a rat and a very rich one.

David sat down in his chair as he remembered how smooth Devin was and how he seemed to have an answer for every question. He decided to call Sarah and tell her what happened, but no one answered the phone. He wondered where she could be. When he had left for work, she was awake and feeding Lisa. Did she go back to sleep? Maybe she was outside playing with their daughter, but she wasn't much of a morning person. So many questions ran through his mind until he thought of the worst scenario: is she with Demas? David had to satisfy his curiosity, so he told Pat he would be on the road and that she should call him if anything came up. He almost dashed out the door.

When he arrived home, Sarah's car was gone. His instincts started to scare him. He thought she may have gone to Amanda's to brag about the frivolity of the previous night, so he went inside to check whether she had left a note. No note was to be found. He decided to call Amanda, who told him Sarah had dropped Lisa off and left. David threw a plate that was within reach, and it shattered on the floor. By this time, he started to feel like a fool who had been betrayed as he slammed the door on his way out.

David was a proud and trusting man, but every fiber in his body told him this Demas dude was dirty and that his wife was being sucked into his manipulation. He didn't know the hows, whats, or whys, but he knew the who, and he intended to find out the rest. David desired to confront Devin, but since Lisa was safe at Amanda's, he held himself back. There was nothing he could do at home, and he still had a day's shift to finish, so David decided to check on Darren's progress at the cemetery.

When David reached the cemetery, everyone was busy as

a dozen men with shovels and two small bobcats working the Earth. Darren was in the middle, pointing his finger and giving directions to one of his men. David walked over to Darren. "What's up there, Davey boy?" said Darren.

David just glared at him. He hated it when anyone called him that, especially today. "Any changes in your evaluation?" replied David.

"No. Same as yesterday. It just doesn't make sense. It's as if someone had a cable hooked to a crane and yanked 'them up. I checked with GES, the Geological Earthquake Survey, and they said there's been no movement in the area for ages."

David began to think more and more about the things that crazy, old Indian Nathan had said. David told Darren to keep him informed if anything changed as he walked away in disgust from the deplorable sight of the caskets.

David sat in his cruiser for a moment, watching the workers set his father's casket back in the plot from which it was disturbed. He then called Johnny, who was at the impound lot where the prisoner van was taken, and asked about its condition. Johnny told him there were no signs of foul play, but they were still looking into it and that the van's drive axle was still in place. He also said that there were no signs of blowouts that they could see. He added that David would have a report in the morning and that the investigators would contact them as soon as they knew anything else. Johnny then joked that he would have to charge time and a half for all the babysitting he'd done lately. David apologized, but Johnny quickly said it wasn't a problem and that he and Amanda loved Lisa like family. On that note, David said, "Over and out," and he drove off towards Dana's Diner for a bite to eat and a slice of her famous lemon meringue pie.

At that very moment, Sarah and Devin were leaving town

143

to survey a building. They drove to the industrial section of Harrisville in Brunswick County in Devin's Mercedes. He used his three hundred-plus years of cajolery to build Sarah's confidence and trust, much 1like the serpent did to Eve. She fell for his every trick as he used her desires to reach his objective of the destruction of her very Soul. They looked at a fifty-thousand-square-foot vacant building that used to be a tool and die shop. She asked how it would be used, and he told her it would become a small warehouse for his collection of artifacts, which he had scattered all over the World. This only impressed her more, and she found herself distracted from her mundane life in Horry County.

Devin took her to the best restaurant in Harrisville, but he told her it still fell far short of his usual cuisine. Sarah was swept away by his knowledge of the arts and his past ten years of Worldly endeavors, of which he often spoke. They drank the best wine the restaurant had to offer, and their conversation kept her on her toes. After they had eaten, Devin left a handsome tip of two one-hundred-dollar bills for the waiter, who thanked Devin several times. On their fifty-mile drive back to Lang Township, he picked her brain for clues of any unhappiness she might be feeling. He coerced her into admitting how much she missed New York and its vibrant pace. He told her of one of the many law firms he owned in his own sky tower in Manhattan. He aimed to throw a monkey wrench in the machine of her marriage as he promised her she would have a position anytime she saw fit to return to New York. He added that there was even a daycare center on the second floor for Lisa, the best money could buy. Sarah's eyes were filled with stars. The conversation left no space for her to object.

After they returned to Devin's estate, he offered her a nightcap of rare Scotch that he told her he was saving for an occasion such as this. Sarah asked where his girlfriend Nina was. He replied that Nina was not his girlfriend and relayed the story of how she had been abused by Monastery monks and how he found her in the headlines of Rome's newspapers. The more Devin's words ran through her ears and heart, the more Sarah found herself under his spell. Hours passed freely as they carried on into the evening. By then, her intoxication deluded her perception of time. She suddenly jumped to her feet as she saw the sun dip down behind the foothills of the valley. "I have to go," she said in an apprehensive manner.

Devin impeded her with blighted rapture, confusing her conceptions with tranquility as he whispered, "Relax." The utterance of his voice hit her like a subversive morphine freight train, as a warm feeling blanketed her. She sank deep into the sofa, and her body went limp. Devin then said, "That a girl," as he submerged his hand between her legs and dipped his tongue into her ear.

She fell hard into a felicitous dreamy state, her consciousness becoming submissive to Devin's will. He then pulled her panties to the side, pushing his finger into her hot crevice as she murmured "no" in a squeamish qualm of mustered will. The cajoling ophidian beguiled her once more as he fingered her faster and faster. Her will diminished to an obsequious sex slave to his salacious appetite. He slipped her panties to the floor and lifted her legs into the air before he rammed himself into her with a violent force of entry. Sarah moaned out David's name as her delusions dealt her a self-protective cover. The erogenous marauder answered, "Yes, yes, here I am," as he slithered his skin into her while shedding his lecherous spores. He continued to hammer himself into her as she yelled out David's name over and over. Devin's ancient skills of sexual endeavors made her cry out for more as she lay like a beggar pleading for scraps.

After Devin was satisfied with the damage, he abruptly ripped himself out of Sarah, and she turned on her side, convulsing in a frenzy of sexual desire. Devin then called Nina and Ora downstairs. Ora slipped to Sarah's side and began to kiss her ever so gently. Sarah lost all control of her body and mind as Devin turned her onto her stomach before sodomizing her while she screamed out. She struggled to no avail as Nina and Ora took pleasure in their Master delivering his torture. Nina taunted Sarah with raunchy porn talk as Devin tore into her with Devilish delight.

Sarah then began to fade from her delight as she began to sober from Devin's spell and his warm elixir of delusion. She squinted her eyes as she gazed in thought about her participation in her worst nightmare that had just come true. She flashed hot with guilt and began crying. Devin leaned back onto the couch, smiling as he watched Sarah scramble for her clothes. He sat between Nina and Ora, basking in the mess he created. He then told Sarah not to feel guilty for expressing herself and that David should thank him for liberating her deepest desires. She ran out of the door as the three of them laughed aloud at her remorse.

Sarah went to Amanda's to pick up Lisa, but David had beaten her there. Her heart pounded as she drove home at high speeds, trying to make up for lost time. She stopped at a gas station to clean up the mascara that ran down her face. After nearly fifteen minutes, she came out of the restroom with a deceivingly fresh appearance. Sarah took her time as she mulled over the lies; she would tell David about how she landed the big deal and that it took her longer than she thought it would. When she reached home, all was dark except for the nightlights throughout the house. Lisa was asleep in her crib while David sat in the dark living room as if he were mourning a lost family member.

"Hi, honey. Why are you sitting in the dark?" she said as she clicked on a lamp.

"Where the fuck were you?" he said in a low tone as he

lifted his eyes onto hers. "I just landed a big deal on that foreclosure. I'm sorry it took so long, but I thought ..."

David interrupted as he mocked her in a loud, tonal voice, "Did you fuck him to close the deal?" "I don't believe this. What are you talking about?!" she shouted in unconvincing conviction. "Come on, Sarah, you've been star-struck ever since he came into our lives with the money he's been throwing around." Sarah walked out of the room as she yelled in a castigated voice, "I don't need to take this!" She then lashed out, "I try to better our living conditions, but you're not mature enough to understand!"

David didn't say a word as he reached over to the lamp and shut it off, then resumed his depression in the dark. Sarah lay in bed curled in a ball, and she silently cried herself to sleep.

David left early the next day before Sarah could wake, for he truly didn't want to see her face of betrayal in the morning light. He stopped at a gas station for coffee. Gina, who was behind the counter, asked if Sarah was feeling better.

David questioned why she asked. She then told him how Sarah had come in a crying wreck and that she cleaned herself up in the bathroom, bought a cup of coffee, and left. David tried not to show any emotion while he paid her and gave no explanation then walked out the door. That only confirmed what he already knew. He thought about how he should put a bullet in Devin's head. He thought about how their lives were picture perfect before this Mr. Devil Demon appeared, and he imagined worst-case scenarios of his and Sarah's breakup. He'd never been in such a situation before, and he didn't know where to turn until he found himself headed in the direction of the reservation in search of his new friend, Nathan.

Once David reached Nathan's house, he knocked on his door, but there was no answer. He saw a young girl staring at him from the middle of the road. David turned to her with a smile, which she promptly returned. He then asked where he could find Nathan. The girl pointed toward a field from which David could hear a faint beating of drums.

David thanked the girl and walked out to the open field. The drumbeats grew louder as he continued. The field had tall grass with small rolling hills. He strolled over to a knoll and heard the drumbeats coming from the other side. He then hiked up to the top, breathing heavily. When he reached the summit, he couldn't believe his eyes: Over three hundred Indian warriors danced to the beat of drums as they sang out in unison. Lofton saw David from afar, and he whispered in Nathan's ear. Nathan pointed at David while telling Lofton to fetch him, so he jogged up the hill and yelled at David to join them. David jogged down the hill and told Lofton he didn't want to interfere.

"Don't worry," Lofton said as he patted him on the back. "We are all brothers of our Great Mother."

David was the only man dressed like a white man who was the only white man in the midst of great tribal numbers. He stuck out like a sore thumb as he made his way to Nathan's circle. He was greeted with a hand command by Nathan to sit by his side. "The spirits guided you to the gathering of our war dance, young David. There are reasons you should be here that you do not yet know." David sat silently as his troubled mind had no place to hide.

Nathan sang out with his tribe as the words almost seemed to make sense to David. Nathan then sang; "*Oh, Mother Earth, you make us strong as we drink from your great rivers. Your clouds bring us rain that greens your great forest with life and gives our children nourishment to grow into great warriors. Oh, Mother Earth, your Mountains reach to the heavens where the great eagle reminds us of your strength as it takes your offered prey. Oh, Mother Earth, you bring us our summers, and you replace them with our falls. The weak and old die from your winters as the new is born by your springs. Your great moon lights the night that reveals our enemies and the Evil Spirits that wish us harm. Oh, Mother Earth, you are the very essence of what we are as we return to the soil from which we came. Oh, Mother Earth, our very Spirits dance in the wind as they sing praising your flesh on which we live. Oh, Mother Earth, oh Mother Earth."*

The great tribe sang in different paraphrases of the same song as Nathan opened his eyes and spoke:

"Young David, *a man may have many tribes and many wives as they may all flourish from one seed, but the one seed may die with the man while another man takes his place, and his tribe flourishes on the flesh of our Great Mother.*

*Your seed may spring the greatness of another, or it may unleash the Evil that's sprouted from the loins of your offspring. But the rhythmical patterns of life are harmonious in continuous circles that cycle themselves in many faces. Our Mother Earth harbors evil as well as good, and variation only has meaning from its opposite. The laws of man are superseded by the laws of our Great Mother, as her law holds true to the beholder of the seed who bears his tribe. There is truth in death, and there is truth in life, but our Great Mother gives strength to those who take it like the mighty eagle in the sky.*

*A proud warrior may stand alone as he stands with many. He can love as he hates and crawl as he walks. He can fly with the eagles or slither with the snakes. And as the eagle may sink its claws into the snake and consume him, the limbless snake may slither into the eagle's nest and sink its fangs into the great eagle and consume its offspring.*

Always remember David; *at the end, there is always a new beginning. For it has no means to end, for everything you love you take with you in Spirit."*

Nathan closed his eyes as he sang a verse, then he opened them and warned that a lunar eclipse would soon be upon them

149

and the World would weigh heavily where the wicked grew strong. He closed his eyes again and rejoined his brothers in song. David thanked him and began to walk away, wondering what it all meant.

Lofton jumped to his feet. "I want you to let us know if there's anything I or my tribe can do for you. Our arrows will fly through the hearts of your enemies." He extended a hand to shake David's as they made respectful eye contact. David then turned and walked away.

Syck and Hector got into town around 3:00 in the morning. They checked into the finest hotel on the Atlantic City strip. After they were rested, they were ready for trouble as they walked down the strip with giant egos, wads of cash, and a hormonal rage that demanded relief. They strolled into the first casino they came across and made their way to the roulette wheel. Syck put a five-hundred-dollar chip on black sixteen as he glanced over to a young blonde who was across the table. He winked at her while the wheel spun around. He whispered words of witchery under his breath as the wheel remained spinning. He kept staring at the blonde until the casino clerk yelled out, "Red sixteen!"

Hector watched his smooth friend pick up the beautiful blonde. He admired Syck for his ruthless attitude and good looks, which he lacked. Hector stood four foot eleven inches, with a weight of about one hundred and eighty pounds. He had unusually dark skin, even for a Mexican, as his oddly shaped skull encased a twisted brain. He watched the blond beauty fall for every syllable Syck spoke, her infatuation growing by the minute. Hector could make a woman fall in love with him through his witchery, but his veneration for Syck came from Syck's natural abilities, which he wished Hector lacked. Syck nodded at Hector as he walked away with the blonde by his side.

Louise was the daughter of a wealthy cattle rancher from north Florida. She sang backup for the headlining act, The High Notes. Her dreams of becoming the next Talor Swift filled her head with stars. Her father wasn't happy about her ambitions to become a singer, so he sent her limited funds of only two hundred dollars a month, hoping she'd return home. But she didn't care if he sent her nothing; it still wouldn't prevent her from pursuing her dreams and ambitions.

Syck enticed her to his room with cocaine, playing the role of a noble gentleman on vacation from Los Angeles. He filled her head with lies as he led her to believe he was a producer for a major record label in Hollywood.

After they filled their noses, they took the elevator down to the lobby, and he made his move. When he first asked if he could kiss her, she promptly said yes, so he slowly pressed his lips against hers. They made out all the way down to the first floor. The doors opened, and an elderly couple smiled at the sight of the seemingly happy couple. He held her like a true gentleman as they walked back toward the casino from which they came.

Hector was at the craps table with an enormous pile of chips in front of him and two suspicious security officers behind him. His gains raised their suspicions, as he won every role he threw and smiled all the while. Syck walked up to Hector with his new friend Louise, who couldn't believe her eyes when she saw Hector's winnings. They joined in the celebration, with Syck ordering drinks for the three of them. One of the security officers asked the dealer for the dice, and he handed Hector a new pair. But it didn't make a difference as Hector continued to win with every roll. After Hector had enough, he collected his winnings and cashed out.

The three decided to celebrate by going to the most expensive restaurant in town. They sat in a secluded booth while Syck poured lines out on the table. They laughed and drank frozen daiquiris into the early evening hours. After two hours of eating crab legs and lobster, the table was full of shells and empty glasses. Louise informed Syck that she had to be on stage in forty minutes, and Syck played his part to the tee. He told her in a joking manner he would evaluate her performance and give her a rating between one and ten.

She led the two men backstage at the concert hall and left them to their own while she went to her dressing room to change. Syck and Hector walked toward the curtains, where they could peep at the performers dancing on stage in parallel columns.

Syck had twisted thoughts of some of the things he would like to do to those young starlets if he could get his claws on them. Hector just wanted sex. He told Syck to watch his handiwork as he whispered words of folly. Just then, a whole row of dancers fell into each other, a trail of fallen dominos in human form. The two malicious marauders burst out laughing when the dancers scrambled to get back into their original positions. The music continued while they were out of sync, and a cloud of humiliation consumed the stage.

Hector then tried to outdo Syck. "Watch this," he grinned. He raised his arms, rolled his eyes to the back of his head, and sang out, *"Ghost of old, ghost of new, ghost of grievance, ghost of you."*

The showgirls didn't stand a chance as the stage buckled underneath them and then collapsed under their feet---all the pretty maids fell in a row. Screams echoed through the air as the beautiful Barbies lay broken in agony, their twisted bodies piled up in a mangled mess. Stagehands rushed past the obtrusive sorcerers as they desperately tried to save the injured starlets. Syck and Hector buckled over as they held their bellies in hysteric hilarity. One of the stagehands watched in horror, unable to believe the glee they exhibited from witnessing his friends fall under what was left of the stage. They turned toward the exit, laughing all the way to the next casino and basking in the glory of their dirty deeds.

That night, David drowned his sorrows with whiskey at Darren's house. They drank down the dark elixir from the bottle like they used to do in the old days. Darren's wife divorced him years ago for the love of God; one day, she woke up and found Jesus. She tried desperately to convert Darren from his ordinary day-to-day existence, which couldn't match the all-righteous carriage of Preacher Dan Wallace. She was also unable to bear children, so Dan provided three of his own, along with a plethora of Sunday school kids.

David and Darren drank into the late hours of the night as they vented their woes and talked of high school follies. They reminisced about their football days, calling out the action play-by-play, what had been their part in their rivalry games with the Apaches and Trojans. They sang in a drunken slur their school song until the bottle got the best of them. David ended up passing out on the couch after losing his battle in the eleventh round. Darren stumbled to his room as he, too, lost his battle with the bottle that still had three inches left on the bottom.

Early morning, Louise caught up to Syck and Hector at the lounge where they had partied earlier. She told them with watery eyes that her show had been canceled, and one of the dancers who got killed was her friend. Hector motioned behind her with a victory fist as she cried on Syck's shoulder, elucidating her sorrows. Syck suggested she take a break and come to one of his many homes in the valley that had a sound studio. Louise was reluctant as she worried about the High Notes and her obligation to them. Syck became more convincing. He asked her if she had plans to be a backup singer all her life or stand out like a star. He told her he had some click tracks and would like to see how she would sound in the studio. Her eyes brightened while her mind raced in a daze.

Could this be her chance to show the World her talent?

Once Louise agreed, they finished their drinks and piled into the sports car. Hector drove as Louise sat on Syck's lap. They drove a little way out of town on the highway, and Syck announced he had to relieve himself. Hector pulled over to a secluded spot. Syck opened the door and dumped Louise off his lap onto the ground. She looked up, startled, and he kicked her in the face. Hector jumped out of the car, screaming like a crazed animal. Syck lifted Louise's flailing body and slammed her down on the hood. Hector grabbed her wrists as Syck ripped her dress to shreds and forced himself into her.

Tears rolled down her cheeks as she cried out her terror into the night sky. Syck then slapped Hector's hand in a tag team manner as they traded positions. Syck tormented Louise as he told her the whore she was while Hector giggled insanely, humping her like a dog with rabies frothing from the mouth.

After they had their fun, Hector picked up Louise, threw her into the trunk, and they continued southward. When they got home the next day, Hector dug a six-foot hole behind the mansion grounds. He then retrieved his beat-up naked prize from the trunk. Louise screamed at the top of her lungs in sheer terror. Her misery began to excite him as he dragged her to the hole. He indulged himself once more at the foot of the aperture until he released sickness into her, then simply tossed her in the hole carrying a wicked grin of accomplishment.

He laid a plywood board on top of the hole and then weighed it down with cylinder blocks. He then grabbed an ax and hacked down into the plywood and chopped ax-shaped holes; all the while, Louise screamed. He then put the ax into a wheelbarrow and whistled off toward the mansion.

That morning, David woke to shards of sunlight that bore into his eyes like nine-inch nails. He held his head in his hands as he groaned out, "Never again!" On the coffee table was a note telling him to help himself to anything in the refrigerator and to lock it up on his way out. David leaned onto the sofa, thinking about Sarah and Lisa and what was to come. Did Sarah really cheat on him, or was he overthinking himself? His heart pounded with downtrodden doubt and betrayal as his only revelation was the memory of his once-perfect life. He suddenly became enraged and cursed his current situation. He washed his face in the kitchen sink and locked up behind him as he left for the station.

On his way, he passed the cemetery and noticed all seemed to be in its rightful place and work men gone along with all the reporters. When he walked into the station, Johnny and Pat were in heavy conversation. Pat looked up at David and abruptly became silent.

"What now?" he queried as if expecting the worst. Johnny turned to David with a look of disbelief. "You're not going to believe this," he said with an overtone of skepticism. "The forensics report just came in ten minutes ago. Every person, including Donny, suffered brain hemorrhages before they died of burns and smoke inhalation. "There's more," Johnny added. "They also said that Bud Shaner's body had its organs surgically removed and that the FBI was keeping a tight lid on this one."

"Well then, why did the pathologist tell you?" asked David, confused.

Johnny then divulged, "Sherry, an intern, told me on hush-hush terms, hoping we'd explain what's going on because the FBI is not saying shit."

The three drew quiet as their imaginations cast tall shadows from the strangeness that pervaded their town.

"Any word on our angel, Mr. Syck?" asked David.

155

Johnny said no, as he told me how Syck's hide would be hung out to dry soon enough. Johnny took that as his cue. He stormed out of the building like a gunslinger that had just been challenged. Even with his troubles, David smiled, admiring Johnny's young gung-ho spirit. He then retreated to his office and sank into his comfortable, worn chair. He thought about how Ronnie and his cronies seemed in good shape before their deaths. He remembered how Ronnie tried to warn him about Syck and his strangeness. He remembered Father Hemmings's presumptions of the Devil's doings, his fictitious imagination forging a Beast in David's mind.

He also thought of Nathan's warning of an upcoming solar eclipse drawing out the wicked, but was it metaphorical or fact? What if the two diviners were right?

Pat tapped on David's door and stuck her head in, letting him know Sarah was on line two. David thanked her as he picked up the phone and said hello in a downbeat tone of voice. In a tenor of concern, Sarah asked why he hadn't come home last night. David told her that he was too drunk to drive, so he stayed at Darren's house.

Sarah said with an affectionate voice that he could have called, and Lisa cried for him last night. Her voice was almost soothing if it weren't for the thought of her with Devin, jarring his nerves. Sarah then told David she had to go to Brunswick County one more time to finalize the deal and that Lisa would be at Amanda's house. She then confessed that this would be the last time she dealt with Demas and that she was going to stick to her small-town clients.

There was a moment of awkward silence until Sarah said, "I love you," with a shaky voice of verity. David returned her, "I love you," then hung up before she could speak another syllable. He wondered about her and her demeanor. He barely smiled and then turned to his work.

David would use the department's cyber tools to find out more about Devin Demas. He booted up his computer and punched in the program. Once it flashed on the screen, he moved his mouse into the encrypted FBI files that listed the names of every U.S. citizen ever born on its soil. He typed in Devin Demas and waited for a response. "– No Access" flashed on the screen. He tried again and again, but it kept flashing the same response. He sat back in his chair and started to wonder what kind of man Devin really was and why his file was closed even to police access. He then remembered True Alliance. Jumping over to the Internet, he typed in www.truealliance.com.

Multiple formats of various programs within its system appeared on the screen, along with the many companies in which it was involved and the World organizations it sponsored. He checked into the CEO attendance roster as the screen spewed out two lists of names and the specific descriptions of duties they performed, along with the location of their administration. It took over an hour to search both programs, but no Devin Demas was found, or anyone close.

Pat popped her head in the door and told David a bus that was filled with teenage Catholic schoolgirls had been found empty, and the driver and teacher shot execution style. They were headed upstate on a field trip, and the bus was found in a rural area on a dirt road just two counties away.

"What the hell's going on?" David asked Pat with confused conviction.

She shook her head and then said, "Welcome to the year Hellennium."

David shut down his computer and advised that if she needed him, he'd be at Dana's Diner, and he walked out the door.

Devin had called Sarah earlier and told her to meet him in downtown Harrisonville at 293 Main Street, the City Administration Building, to finalize the papers. She told herself that this would be the last time she would ever deal with him and that she was going to take the money and run. When Sarah arrived, she saw Devin's Mercedes out front. Parking as far away as she could, she walked inside and was directed by a security officer who told her, "Top floor." She thanked him and took the elevator.

When the elevator doors opened, she was greeted by a receptionist behind a curved desk. The receptionist acknowledged her appointment and then led her to the closing room, where Devin was surrounded by "suits."

He stood up from his chair when she entered the room, and all conversation halted. "Everyone," Devin announced, "this is Sarah Lang. She will be handling the foreclosure proceedings."

All the suits stated their names, and then Sarah took the only seat that was open next to Devin. The paperwork was handed to Sarah, and she intensely scrutinized the smallest detail. She answered that all was in order, and she handed the paperwork back to Devin. He signed the papers and handed them back to Sarah. She quickly scrutinized them once more, signed as a witness, and stamped her authorized stamp of a notary. After other witnesses signed, Devin asked everyone to leave the room except Sarah, who loathed and feared being alone with him.

When the room had been cleared, Devin immediately handed Sarah a check for fifty-thousand dollars.

"I'm afraid you made a mistake. There's an extra ten thousand dollars here," she advised him.

"No, that's an incentive for you to join my team," Devin

explained. "There will be many more transactions like this if you decide to come aboard the True Alliance team."

Sarah handed the check back to Devin. She told him this would be their last transaction and that he should rewrite the check for the amount on which they agreed.

"I'm sorry to hear that," replied Devin. "But I want you to keep it as a reminder of my friendship." She took the check and told him never to call her again and that she liked her life the way it was. She put the check in her purse, turned, and left the room.

Syck and Hector pulled up to the mansion in a Semi truck and honked the loud horn obnoxiously. They drove around back, shut the giant diesel engine down, and jumped out from the cab, hooting and hollering in the glory of another dirty deed.

Ora and Nina ran out of the house and marveled at the giant semi as they, too, began to jump up and down in the joy of their accomplishment. "We got ourselves thirty cattle of the best prime rib this side of the Mississippi!" Syck rang out. They all held hands while they bounced about like kids in celebration. Hector then strolled to where a Dfr-520 pole digger tractor machine had been delivered two days prior. Its full rounded blade ranged 2 ½ feet around, along with razor-sharp teeth and a giant hydraulic pole. Nina and Ora returned to the mansion as Hector fired up the pole-digging tractor while Syck directed him where to dig. They dug thirty holes just beyond the hedges of the backgrounds, then drove off to the lumberyard, where they purchased a truckload of four-by-eight panel boards and cinder blocks.

Afterward, they went back to the mansion and cut the panel boards in two, with two small openings for breathing and provisions. They brought out each of the quarry creatures one by one and threw them into their pitted prison. They marked each board with spray paint, indicating each prisoner's attractiveness: Brown was dog meat, blue was tolerable, and red was "smoking." After all the kidnapped schoolgirls were imprisoned, Syck and Hector retreated to the mansion.

David and Sarah woke the next day in each other's arms, with things almost seeming normal. David still held suspicion in the back of his mind but decided to conceal it, giving her the benefit of the doubt in consideration of the many happy years they had been together. Sarah, guilt-ridden, decided to stay silent for the benefit of their marriage. She was aghast by her performance and questioned how she could have lost control of Devin's advances. She just wanted to forget the whole thing that ever happened and go on with the picture-perfect life they once had.

That same morning, Syck drove down Route 44 in the semi with Hector behind him in his black Suburban. Syck was carrying on a conversation with a dead trucker who sat in the passenger seat, stiff and discolored.

Syck then found himself behind Johnny's cruiser and shouted. *"Hee-Haw! It's Quick Draw McGraw. What a stroke of luck! Now let's have a ball!"* Syck accelerated to a high speed as he rammed the rear of Johnny's squad car. Johnny glared in his rear-view mirror, but all he could see was a grill that read Freightliner, all the while the truck slamming him again. He started to radio in for backup, but the impact of the third hit sent him over an embankment and down a hillside. An airbag deployed as the cruiser hit a tree just yards from a drop-off into a strong, moving river. Johnny's neck reeled in pain from the whiplash. He struggled to reach his mic, but he blacked out instead.

Syck and Hector sounded their horns as they drove past the broken cruiser in a playful sonata. When they reached the freeway, they pulled over to the first rest area and put the stiff in the driver's seat as a sick joke. Hector had a line on a mirror waiting for Syck when he climbed into the Suburban. They headed home after a job well done.

David was soon called to the scene of Johnny's accident after the station was notified by a teenager on his motorcycle who saw the whole thing from the side of the road. The paramedics had Johnny in a neck brace and on a stretcher. It took four men to carry him up the hill. David rushed to Johnny's side when they reached the road, asking about his condition in a tone of concern. The paramedics told David that Johnny was going to be okay and that they had to take him in for X-rays just to make sure. Johnny wanted to get up and walk away, but the medics insisted that he be admitted to the hospital.

After David commanded Johnny to do as they advised, Johnny relaxed and let them take him to the hospital. The ambulance scrambled away, and David walked over to the teenager and asked him what he saw. He told David that his bike had broken down, and he was on the side of the road when he saw a big, green diesel run the officer off the road. He then told him that a black Suburban was following the diesel, honking its horn when it passed by.

He also told him that he saw two men in the semi and that the black Suburban's windows were tinted too dark to see the driver. David thanked the teenager and waved Deputy Scott over. He asked the deputy to take the boy and his bike home. David drove in the direction of the green killing machine until he came to the freeway. He halted momentarily to pick his way. He thought to himself, the highway or the side roads. He decided to turn right on the freeway, which looked like the easiest route for a getaway.

After driving twelve miles, he came to a rest stop where,

low and behold, there it was out in plain sight … a green diesel with a trailer. He stopped near the driver's side and drew his weapon, then approached the door with caution. David saw a man with a cap sitting upright, looking straight ahead, as he yelled, "Put your hands on the steering wheel!"

David saw no response, and he raised his voice in command, barking out once more, "Put your hands on the steering wheel!"

The stiff almost seemed to be mocking David with the cold shoulder. The angered sheriff tapped the window with the barrel of his Glock. David opened the door, grabbed the nonresponding stiff by its shirt, and ripped it out of the cab. To his horror, he discovered the cadaver in its discolored condition.

David turned his attention to the cab, creeping up and into its confines. Afterward, he called the station to explain the situation and told Pat to contact the state troops and FBI. Twenty minutes later, two state troopers arrived on the scene. David told them what he knew, then made a quick exit in the direction of Bi-County Hospital to see how his sidekick was doing.

Upon David's arrival, Johnny was standing on his own at the front desk, talking to a nurse. Johnny smiled when David approached them and said, "Hey there, boss. Well, looks like I got a clean bill of health." He then laughed about how he'd probably glow in the dark from all the X-rays and full body scans.

The head nurse jumped in, "Yeah. It's a good thing for airbags and seat belts, or ER would be removing a steering wheel from your forehead."

David then threw in a punchline, "Well, that might have been an improvement."

Johnny sang out as he retorted, "Ha-ha-ha!" while David and the nurse snicker softly.

Johnny and David thanked the nurse, got into the cruiser, and drove toward Lang Township. David grilled Johnny the whole way, trying to piece together a puzzle that seemed to have no Master link.

Johnny's answers left more questions to the same riddle, as he explained the only thing he saw---the front end of a chrome grill. David changed the subject to Dana's hot apple pie, which would be his treat, as he noticed a slight tone of despondence from Johnny after the day's unwelcome excitement. Johnny thought to himself, surprises like this could leave his wife a widow and his children fatherless.

When they reached town, David treated Johnny to lunch at Dana's, then gave him the rest of the day off. David spent the rest of his shift cruising the backroads and the inner dwellings of the rural parts of Horry County. He returned to the station and briefed Jim and Scott about how Thomas Syck was wanted for questioning and the vehicle he drives. David requested that Charlie call him if any more mishaps occurred.

"You got it," returned Charley in an upbeat tone.

On that note, after a day of stress, David found himself at the foot of his driveway. Suddenly he halted to study a burgundy BMW that was parked in the spot where Sarah's minivan usually was. As he rushed up the driveway, David noticed Sarah's smiling head popping through the window curtains. He scrutinized the vehicle with contempt as he could hear Sarah and Lisa scurrying in a beeline for the door.

"She's a real beauty, wouldn't yaw say?" announced Sarah as she approached David with a kiss. David half kissed her back as he asked where the minivan was. "Junkyard compactor, I hope," Sarah chaffed. When they entered their house, Sarah showed David the toys she bought Lisa and a new HD LED TV for David that he'd been eyeballing whenever they went to Harrisville Mall.

She confessed she would never deal with Devin again, explaining how she couldn't work with his lawyers and that she was better off on her own. The good news calmed David during ill-gotten toys. The statement hit his ears with a welcome delight, which gradually made him slightly upbeat. They ordered Tony's Pizza as David relished the company of his family and they him. After they had eaten, David clicked on the new TV that somehow Sarah put together turning the channel from Nickelodeon to the local channel. A reporter stood by a bus explaining how the driver and a teacher had been shot execution style. She then said that they were on their way to a field trip when it appeared that a semi, later found in Horry County, was used to force the bus off to the side of the road. She added that the driver of the semi was found dead, and he was known to be an honest family man with no criminal record and served as a volunteer for a kid's foundation.

"That's horrible!" Sarah said, standing behind David.

"Tell me about it," admitted David. "I was the guy who found the dead semi-driver."

Sarah nudged David with a love punch, "Why didn't you tell me?"

David hunched his shoulders sympathetically, still rattled from the day's events. He then pulled Sarah onto his lap as he smiled and said, "You know me ... not much of a talker." Sarah froze and tilted her head as she strained to listen to the faint cries that came from Lisa's room. She immediately jumped from David's lap and uttered, "Lisa!" Sarah rushed through the hallway to her crying baby's room with David just two steps behind. Lisa stood in her crib; her knuckles flushed white from gripping the top rail while her face flashed shades of red and purple. Sarah shrieked out, panic-stricken as the mechanism of motherhood took its place, grasping the child in her arms. David leaned into Sarah as he told her to lay Lisa on the floor. He then placed his finger into the toddler's mouth to make sure she wasn't choking on something.

Sarah was on the phone but not with the hospital. She called Devin so he might fly them in his helicopter to Brunswick's Bi-County Hospital. Nina answered and said that Devin wasn't home, but she told her she could call him on his cell phone if it was an emergency. Sarah told her about Lisa and that she needed his helicopter to get her to the hospital. Nina then told her to hold while she called Devin on his cell. Seconds later, she had Devin on the line as he was already in his chopper heading toward his house, just a minute into Horry County. He told Nina to let Sarah know that he'd be there in five minutes and that he was only a couple of miles away. Sarah thanked Nina, hung up the phone, and rushed to her baby. Lisa was crying for her mother as the sight of her only child in her dire condition tore Sarah apart.

Sarah told David that Devin was on his way with the chopper, which took him by surprise. But David didn't dare object. He surrendered Lisa to Sarah and turned every outside light on, looking for the best place for a helicopter to land. There was a clearing in the back, so he waited with his flashlight to guide them down. Two minutes later, Devin circled until the pilot saw David's makeshift landing pad. He landed with ease as Sarah ran out of the house with her limp child. Lisa was now comatose, and Sarah's panic grew with every passing moment.

They climbed into the helicopter, and Devin told the pilot to take off. By that time, Sarah was crying as she took Lisa in her arms. David took her from Sarah, and she continued to breathe in a laborious manner while the pilot scaled the rolling hills with precision. After what seemed an eternity, they reached the big city lights. It took only fifteen minutes. The pilot landed atop the hospital like a hornet in its hive. They were greeted by nurses and doctors at the entrance, and David ran toward them with his little girl in a desperate attack against Lisa's illness and handed her over. They immediately put her on a rolling stretcher and started her on IVs and oxygen. They extracted blood into three vials. And afterward, she was off to a scanner.

Devin, David, and Sarah waited in the lobby for word from the doctor. Devin then offered the grieving parents access to the best doctors in the world. David was now helpless in his servitude to this corporate giant as he was ready to sell his soul for the life of his precious child.

One hour later, the doctor entered the lobby and told the glum, grieving parents that they didn't have any answers yet. He said Lisa was stable but still in critical condition. The CAT scan showed nothing. He asked Sarah and David about their family history and whether there were any medical ailments in their families. David's face flushed, and he looked white as a ghost. All eyes turned toward him as if they caught the culprit with his pants down. The horrific death of David's father flashed in his mind.

David remorsefully explained how his father died from Congenital Hemophilia ten years prior, at the age of fifty. The doctor told them not to worry because medicine had come a long way since then. The doctor waved his arm and motioned for the nurse. She snapped to his command, handing Sarah and David clipboards with a questionnaire sheet regarding their medical history. Sarah looked disgusted as she took the clipboard. Devin could feel the resentment that stirred in her heart as she shook her head while staring down at the questionnaire. David was too distraught to notice, holding back a dam of tears that welled against his fighting eyes. They scribbled the information each question required in silence, all the while Devin hovering like a vulture awaiting death.

After they finished, they handed the clipboards back to the nurse, and with a desperate tone of urgency, Sarah immediately asked if she could see Lisa with a tone of urgency. The nurse gave her a congenial smile and said the hospital regulations were strict but suggested that she could sneak them in for five minutes. David and Sarah followed the nurse to the elevator. They went up three floors, then down a long hallway. As she opened the door, the nurse repeated that they could only stay for five minutes.

Sarah walked in, and tears poured down her face, seeing her little Lisa asleep and hooked up to tubes and wires that monitored her body. David stood next to Sarah as her tears continued to stream. She held Lisa's hand, uttering words of comfort to the unconscious child. David rubbed Lisa's foot as he fought to hold his tears back. "Daddy loves his little girl," he whispered. They administered their love in the hope that their words would heal their daughter. Sarah pleaded to God not to take her little girl.

The nurse popped her head in the door. "I'm sorry, Mr. and Mrs. Lang, but it's time to go." Sarah bent over and kissed her daughter's forehead as she whispered, "I love you" in her ear.

When they reached the lobby, Devin was talking in heavy conversation on his cell phone until Sarah and David approached. He gave a thumbs up to the emotionally drained, grief-stricken parents. "I'll get back to you," he told the receiver of his call. He then announced, "I just talked to my good friend Dr. Joseph Miranda from New York, one of the finest doctors in the world. I told him that money's no object in this matter and to get here right away."

Even thou Devin offered words of salvation, David couldn't shake the feeling that a snake was slithering in his midst. He drifted into a daydream as Devin continued his alluring professions of his connections and access to the greatest doctors in the world. A compiling conceit of malevolent propensity kept casting tenebrous feelings into David's heart as if they were lambs being led to slaughter. Devin rambled on as David's daydream-double-vision brought an obscure sight of Devin's stealth demonic caliber. Devin's voice twisted into a hissing snake of spellbinding promises, and David's intuition screamed, "Beware!" Devin's soulless eyes were without any glint of life as they entranced Sarah like a doe caught in headlights.

David came out of his dismayed, clouded state as Devin was offering to put them up in a hotel nearby. But even in her slight hypnotic condition, Sarah was resolute and adamant in disregarding her own comfort. She said she would stay in the waiting room until they heard word from the doctor. David felt relieved as the pressure was taken off him from accepting a minuscule more of anything from this Charon-bearing gift. Sarah made direct eye contact with Devin as she made it clear she would use his medical associates at any cost the assurance Lisa's recovery. David looked askance at Devin, and Devin took David's sideways glance as his cue for departure.

He gave Sarah the number to his cell phone and told her to call any time, night or day, if she decided to take him up on his offer. Devin gave her a sympathetic hug, nodded to David, then disappeared around the corner back to his helicopter.

Sarah and David crawled back to their corner of sorrow as they sought solace in each other's company in the dismal waiting room. Not only did David worry about his precious little girl, but he also worried for Sarah as she sat silently with her head in her hands, praying for her daughter's healing. Minutes turned into hours, and hours turned into years; it seemed an eternity waiting on word of Lisa's prognosis. Sarah would not be forgotten as she pestered every passing nurse with an array of questions, using her courtroom tactics for an air of urgency. But her method was useless, as the hospital staff was used to inquiries with every conviction imaginable. Whichever staff member happened to cross her path they would give her the same answers in varied reprisals of their own recollection.

Finally, at four in the morning, a different doctor approached them. He opened with "Lisa's fine" but ended with "she has Congenital Hemophilia disease."

Sarah sank deep into a chair as the information took hold.

David had almost foreseen the diagnosis, given his family history.

The bearer of the bad news explained how the disease worked and how they could try to counterattack its effect. He explained that the liver and pancreatic hormones couldn't produce white blood cells, creating a lack of glycogen polysaccharide levels, which caused chronic deficiency. He talked about the procedure of dialysis, along with medical breakthroughs that held promising healing. David was horrified that the disease had reared its ugly head in the form of a family curse.

Sarah asked the doctor when they would start the procedure and if there were any other life-threatening possibilities that might present themselves. The doctor shook his head no and said he would almost guarantee a healthy recovery, though he emphasized, "We must act right away!"

Sarah said she might have a doctor from New York oversee the procedure. The doctor on duty made no qualms of opposition but said it wasn't necessary.

David stepped in and said, "I think we should just go with the staff here because, one, we don't have time; two, I'm sure they are very capable; and three, I really don't want to owe Mr. Demas any more than I have to."

Sarah glared egregiously, but she knew he was right, so they gave the doctor the go-ahead. The doctor made a short, reassuring speech and then disappeared into the fluster of the medical staff. Sarah carried a ton of trouble back to the waiting room. David sat next to Sarah as she gushed a stream of grieving tears. He put his arm around her waist while the stream became a deluge and the deluge a drowning pool of bewailing sorrow. She buried her face in David's shoulders as he embraced her with a warm blanket of sanctuary. Emotionally drained, Sarah fell asleep upon David's shoulder, a shell of her once happy self.

David was careful not to move and wake Sarah as he watched *CNN Headline News* on the TV screen that sat high upon the wall. A reporter was talking about the Smithsonian Institute in downtown Washington, DC. It had been burglarized by a Criminal Master syndicate. The news footage showed an empty glass case, which once enshrouded the *Egyptian Book of the Dead*, also known as *The Necronomicon*. The reporter went on to say that not a single alarm sounded, and two of the guards were found in an odd condition.

He then added that their physical structures collapsed into themselves, leaving two heaping mounds of human hair to be found in the proximity of the stolen book. Two priceless Adolf Hitler paintings were also stolen, baffling FBI and police officials with no apparent clues.

David envisioned the Mastermind capable of such sick deviance and pondered the lengthy measures to design such a scheme. He began to doze off to the tiring humdrum news that was disseminated, his head resting upon Sarah. Two hours later, the attending physician, Dr. Hogart, walked in with an update on Lisa's state. David and Sarah simultaneously woke as the doctor called out, "Mr. and Mrs. Lang?" in a low, polite manner. He smiled with an amicable aura and was about to give his report. A nurse shared his disposition and quietly stood behind him. "Lisa is doing fine currently, but it's still too early to tell if the dialysis is working. More tests will be needed."

Dr. Hogart then told them more papers would need to be signed to continue her treatments and tests. He nodded at the nurse as she handed them papers on a clipboard. After they signed their lives

upon any paper, David excused himself to call the station. Sarah remained, talking to the nurse, asking when they would be permitted to see Lisa. "Soon," the nurse replied.

Charlie answered at the station. David told him of this new, undesired dilemma that had unfolded before him. Charlie expressed his sympathy as he relayed comments about the uneventful evening back in Horry County. David told Charlie that Johnny was in charge and that he didn't know when he'd be back at the station. David hung the phone up, knowing Lang Township would be in good hands under the command of Johnny Morgan and his team, Jim and Scott.

He walked back to the waiting room and found Sarah talking to an older man dressed in a suit. David approached them as Sarah smiled. "This is Dr. Joseph Miranda," she said, turning toward David. "He flew in from New York."

David reached out his hand as the doctor gave a cold, clammy handshake. Sarah gazed upon the doctor admirably as she explained to David that she gave Devin the "go-ahead" to call in Dr. Miranda. She gestured David to the side as she elucidated her opinion on the matter, overruling any objections David might have. He realized she was unmovable on the issue, and since the highly recommended doctor was already here, he gave his consent. And besides, all that mattered was Lisa's recovery.

A nurse popped her head into the waiting room door with a smile as she announced that Lisa was ready for a visit. Dr. Miranda, David, and Sarah followed the petite nurse to the elevator. She took them to the third floor and then led them to Lisa's room. Little Lisa lies awake, sitting up in bed, playing with an array of Barbie dolls. Her face lit up when her mommy and daddy walked in the door. Dr. Miranda stayed behind as he requested to see the medical reports and confer with Dr. Hogart.

Sarah held back a dam of tears that welled up in her eyes as she rushed to her baby girl's side. Lisa hugged her parents before she showed off her new dolls. David noticed the new toy boxes and a United Parcel Service box on the floor. Lisa's elation filled the dismal room with cheer, and it seemed contagious. Sarah hid her grieving emotions as she surveyed the wires and tubes attached to Lisa. David sat on the side of Lisa's bed opposite Sarah as they coddled her with love.

Lisa almost seemed oblivious to her illness as she nonchalantly asked when they would go home.

Sarah then explained why she was there, and she continued to fight a river of tears all the while. David jumped in, telling her that once she was well, they would take her to the zoo to see the zebras and lions and monkeys. Lisa's eyes shimmered as her imagination danced with monkeys and apes on bicycles and tight ropes putting on a show just for her.

Dr. Miranda walked in on the excitement, and Lisa quickly drew silent, his appearance triggering fretful anxiety. Sarah sensed her daughter's uneasiness, and she introduced the doctor to her with assuring approval. Then she told her, "He's here to help you."

"Hello, Lisa," he said with a pleasant smile.

Lisa turned to her mother and asked if the doctor was going to stick her with more needles. Sarah hugged her as she confirmed with a soft overtone, "He's only here to help."

Dr. Miranda read the clipboard that hung at the foot of her bed. He commented on what pretty dolls she had, which diverted her wariness to the plastic figurines whose hair she caressed with affection. Dr. Miranda seemed to have a bedside manner that would charm a cat down from a tree or, in this case, a child into compliance. He asked for Lisa's left hand as he slowly started to win her trust. He simply took her pulse. "Now that didn't hurt at all, did it?" he asked as he released her wrist and smiled.

Lisa agreed as she turned her attention to her dolls. The cordial nurse walked into the room, and she announced that the concierge from The Berkshire Hotel had called and announced that Lang's room was ready.

"I didn't order any room," David responded.

Dr. Miranda intervened by stating, "Mr. Demas and I took the liberties and ordered you two a room." He jokingly added how they got the suite while he got the servant's quarters.

He then told them Lisa would be fine and that they should get some rest. "Doctor's orders," he said with a smile. David nodded at Sarah as they acknowledged their exhaustion through facial expressions and, finally, verbal admittance. Sarah turned to Lisa with a shaky voice as she told her to listen to the good doctor and nurses, and then she hugged and kissed her. David reminded her of their zoo trip as he also hugged and kissed her goodbye. David slipped his arm around Sarah's waist as he gently urged the hesitant mother to leave her child. As they left the room, Sarah glanced once more at her daughter, who was immersed in her toys. The doctor followed behind to offer more words of comfort, with Sarah hanging on his every syllable. He told them he would call them if anything new presented itself.

A short, pudgy man patiently waiting behind them addressed them with a heavy Italian accent. "Mr. and Mrs. Lang, I'm-a-here to take you to D-hotel. Please follow me."

David almost expected this as he speculated that Devin spent considerable thought and money on their situation. But why? They followed the comical punster to the elevator as he chattered with foolish flattery about David's good fortune for having such a beautiful wife and comments about the weather. "Oh, you're a-going to like the Berkshire Hotel. How you say … ah, yes … it's very elegant."

They descended through the floors as the man introduced himself. "My name is Al-Franko, but they call me Big Al. You can call me Big Al if you like."

The small cubicle was filled with endless babble as Al-Franko went on. Finally, to the relief of Sarah and David, the door opened in the main lobby, and they received a brief break from his endless prattle. "Oh, you're a- going to like-a my cab," he then continued. "It's a-nice and clean."

They walked outside to a remake of a model 1957 Chevy cab in mint condition. Al-Franko scurried to the rear door and opened it by the time the couple reached him. Sarah scampered into the vehicle as David paused and asked Al-Franko to hold down the conversation because Mrs. Lang wasn't feeling so well. Quieting Al-Franko seemed impossible as the cabbie apologized a hundred times, even more annoying. They proceeded toward the hotel, and the Italian cabbie glanced in the rearview mirror as if it was painful to hold in his words. David looked at Sarah, who was staring into a dreamy void of despair, and decided it might be helpful to keep Al-Franko talking. "So, how long have you been a cabbie?" he asked.

Al-Franko seemed elated that he now had permission to unload a tonnage of words. "Ever since I arrived in this beautiful country, America, for twenty-two years."

David's face drooped when Al-Franko asked if they had a sick relative back at the hospital. "Yes," David said, and he told him briefly about Lisa.

Al-Franko expressed his sorrow and mentioned that his brother was a Catholic Priest. He said they would pray for the Lang family later that night. David wasn't much on religion, even in the face of these embittered events, but accepted Al-Franko's offer to return; thank you.

Soon after, they arrived at The Berkshire Regal Hotel. Giant porticoes graced the entrance with mid-seventeenth-century carvings on the great pilasters. Sarah gazed in awe. Al-Franko pulled up to the front entrance, quickly threw the cab in the park, and raced to reach the rear passenger door before David and Sarah could exit. David had the door half open when Al-Franko intervened with snap-finger service. Sarah stood with her head tilted toward the giant pillars as David reached into his pocket and asked how much he owed for the ride.

"The first one's on a-me," Al-Franko said as he handed him a card. "You call a-me any time of night or a day." But David tried to pay anyway. The good-natured man waved his hands, gesticulating that David's money was meaningless to him.

Al-Franko scurried to the driver's door as he declared, "We

pray for your daughter tonight. You will see Mother Mary, who will smile and bless your family."

David thought to himself that good people still existed and thought himself how he was wrong about the cabby man being one of Devin's employments. They turned and entered the hotel as a doorman welcomed them and held open the door. Stepping into the long vestibule, they gazed at the mid-seventeenth century décor. Authentic paintings of early-century folklore lavished the surroundings. The place reeked with refined pleasantries. They walked to the front desk, and the concierge bid them welcome. When David announced his name, the concierge snapped to attention with overwhelming courtesy. "Oh, yes, Mr. Lang. You are to have the best suite in the house."

David glanced at Sarah out of the corner of his eye. He noticed those old stars in her eyes coming back to haunt him, but still, she deserved a little pampering at that point. The concierge personally escorted them to the sixth floor, then down the long corridors to suite 66. The hotel manager showed them around the expansive suite as he stated, "Anything and everything is paid for, so don't hesitate to ask for anything."

David attempted to hand him a tip, but again, his money was refused. His money seemed worthless in Harrisville. "Enjoy," the concierge said as he closed the door behind him.

Sarah stared out the huge window and took in the giant spectacle of the surrounding area. But Lisa's illness wouldn't let her enjoy it as she defused into a soft slumber upon the silken sheets. David called the station again and gave Pat the phone number to the hotel as they were talking about the day's events.

After he hung up with Pat, he sunk his fatigued frame next

to Sarah upon the silken sheets. They slept in a heavy slumber until early evening when a knock on the door woke them. Sarah remained in bed as David labored to the door. Dr. Miranda stood at the entrance with an expressionless face.

"Dr. Miranda! Is everything alright?"

"Everything's fine," the doctor calmly replied.

"David, I just wanted to tell you your daughter will go through dialysis early tomorrow morning." Sarah was now standing behind David in a hotel robe. "Hello, Sarah. I was just telling David that Lisa is going for dialysis treatment early tomorrow morning. I don't expect any complications, but there is a stipulation for my services."

David glanced at Sarah, puzzled while expecting something outrageous or strange. "I request your presence for dinner tonight. Let's just say it's a way of getting to know my patients." David sighed in relief and, glancing at Sarah once more, agreed to Dr. Miranda's terms. "Good. Shall we say eightyish?" David nodded and said, "We'll be looking forward to it."

Dr. Miranda nodded his head as well. "Very good. I'll see you then." He then walked off to his room down the hall.

In Demas Valley, Devin was overjoyed as two of his henchmen FBI agents handed him a briefcase. They were also confreres in the profound atrocities inflicted by their black powers at the Smithsonian, the malevolent legionnaire whose members of the True Alliance were a formidable force on the spectrum of Devin's grand design. Devin called them his rooks, as he used them like chess pieces in the procession of the prophetic battle yet to come. Devin praised their handiwork, which was plastered all over the news stations, as he opened the briefcase.

"Oh yes, my lovely, I've been waiting for three hundred

years to possess you. Finally, you are redeemed to your rightful owner." The two henchmen fell to their knees as Devin held up the *Egyptian Book of the Dead*. Devin declared war as his abounding rapture ran rampant, and he revered their Master, Mephistopheles. Ora, Nina, Syck, and Hector then dropped to their knees as they, too, bowed in the presence of the renowned *Necronomicon*. In unison, they began to sing from the bowels of their Evil Soul, singing psalms in the lowest key a human being could sing.

Four light knocks sounded on suite 66's door at The Berkshire Hotel. Sarah opened the door to two bellhops who rolled in two racks of clothing. "Compliments of the house," the senior bellhop stated as he swept his arm in the direction of the garments like a game show with a prize.

Sarah stood in the doorway, momentarily speechless. Finally, she stood aside and let them enter. David was clueless to the proceedings as he was showering in the eloquent bathroom. The head bellhop stated that the hotel had a direct line to some of the biggest names in fashion, and then he walked to the door. The other bellhop advised calling the front desk if Sarah or David required different clothing. Sarah thanked him and ran for her purse to give him a tip, but the bellhop refused it also.

Sarah marveled at the glamorous evening wear as she laid out the garments on the bed and sampled each dress. "What's this?" David asked as he walked into the room.

"Compliments of the house," Sarah stated as she twirled in a three-hundred-sixty-degree rotation in a red dress. David gazed from afar as Sarah told him the apparel was designed by some of the biggest names in fashion. She then reached for a suit on the main rack and announced how good he'd look wearing that garment. The old phrase "beware of strangers bearing gifts" came to mind as David just stood there at a loss for words.

To keep Sarah happy, he went along with her, being careful not to cause any waves. He tried on four of the suits until Sarah was satisfied with the solid aquamarine-colored suit. David shrugged his shoulders and said, "Do you really think a cop would wear an aquamarine suit? I doubt it unless maybe he was in Miami in the eighties."

Dr. Miranda knocked on their door, and Sarah answered, wearing an eloquent red. "That dress really compliments your beauty," he stated in a formal and polite manner.

"Thank you. Dr. Penelope Cruz wore this piece to the Oscar Awards last year," Sarah said with pride. David walked out of the bathroom fully dressed in style, looking like a Miami vice. "Well, I must say there, David, I could almost mistake you two for movie stars," said the doctor as he looked them over.

"It will do, I guess," retorted David without enthusiasm. "Where are you taking us to see the King of England?" he added with a slightly upbeat tone.

"Nowhere quite that elaborate," the doctor smiled, "but I assure you that it's quite cultured. Shall we?"

Dr. Miranda opened the door and stood in the hallway, awaiting their exit. David closed the door behind Sarah, and they proceeded to the elevators. A soft bell rang, and a hotel staff member greeted them in a formal manner, asking, "Which floor would you like?" "Restaurant," Dr. Miranda returned. Sarah's curiosity was more than she could keep to herself as she had to ask if the restaurant had its own floor.

The doctor smiled as he replied, "In a manner of speaking, yes. It's below the lobby, sort of in a basement."

"Sort of?" Sarah repeated, "How is that?"

Dr. Miranda then explained how The Berkshire was built in 1836 by an eccentric man who didn't follow conventional methods. Simultaneously, a soft bell rang, a light flashed, and the doors opened. A dimly lit vestibule led into the dining room, its walls decorated with medieval Gothic paintings. Sarah and David followed the doctor as he was greeted with reverence and snap-finger service. As they were guided to the rear of the lounge, they passed paintings of Witches on fiery stakes and sculptures of grotesque figures. Colors glowed brightly in the luminance of the lounge's purple, fluorescent lights that dangled above various forms of exotic plants.

They were escorted to a horseshoe-shaped booth surrounded by a trellis with English ivy vines that strained to reach the soft, purple fluorescence. In the middle of the table was a small, early seventeenth-century oil lamp, which was virtually the only light the booth had to offer. They lolled in the furtive seclusion of the exclusive surroundings and the twisted Gothic grotesque artistry.

Sarah then spoke idiopathic as she asked what kind of man this eccentric person was and how he came to possess such a collection of creepy art. Dr. Miranda smiled before expounding the story of a man who inherited a large fortune from his father, a major contender in the shipping industry. But when steam-powered ships came in full effect came the death of his sailing vessel company and his father soon after. So, Sir Paul Berkshire used his inheritance to build the hotel, and he dedicated it to his soon-to-be bride, Madame Anabelle Charlevoix. But with Madame Anabelle's arrival in America came her coquettish aspiration in the Black Arts of Witchery.

"Well, to say the least, she was one of the last to be persecuted by being burned at the stake as Sir Paul watched in horror the love of his life consumed in flames. Sir Paul

Berkshire was quite a renowned artist and was about to become World famous for his creations," the doctor continued. "But after the death of his beloved Anabelle, he piled all his works of beautiful meadows and mountains and set them ablaze. The last ten years of his life were a blur of whores, harlots, and hustlers in a drunken delusion of depression. Some called him a madman as he reached his own blood for the dark pigments of his paintings. This was his studio, and, the story has it, he was found dead in that far corner with a brush in his hand at the foot of that large tapestry."

Sarah and David beheld in horror a painting not quite finished---Devils and Demons dancing around a flame-engulfed preacher trying to shield two small children. The giant tapestry repulsed David as he lost himself in the mournful, morbid vision of Sir Paul.

A waiter brought a bottle of a 1938 vintage and asked Dr. Miranda if he'd have his usual. "Yes, and the same for my friends," the doctor replied.

David and Sarah stared confoundedly at the doctor, who smiled with secretive eyes. After a moment of silence, he finally said, "You're probably wondering how a New York doctor knows so much about the history of this southern town hotel."

"I'd say that's a good assumption," David responded.

The doctor smiled once more as he said, "It's simple. I'm a frequent commuter between here and New York City."

The doctor continued, admitting his partnership in owning The Berkshire Regal Hotel. "So, as you see, I really wasn't going out of my way by responding to the call of duty and coming downstate."

David then said, "Well, I can pretty well guess who your

partner is."

Dr. Miranda replied jaunty, "Well, my dear Watson, you can speculate all you want, but I'm really not at liberty to say." The table had an awkward moment of silence until the waiter reappeared with a tray of exotic foods from around the world. They conversed upon many subjects, including the most important one, the wellbeing of their daughter Lisa. The 1938 elixir softened their inhibitions, going down like a smooth ride in a Rolls Royce. Sarah laughed aloud as the doctor made "quack" jokes about his profession. David remained a tough customer, though he did smile.

After the bottle had been emptied and Dr. Miranda ran out of jokes, they went to the elevator and called it a night. Sarah then made her own joke as she retorted, "I hope you're going to be comfortable on your cot in the servant's quarters."

"I'll try," he replied as the doors opened to the sixth floor.

When Sarah and David made it back to their room, the phone had been ringing urgently. Sarah gave David a look of fear, sobering up with each ring in loathing repulse that it was bad news from the hospital. David picked up the receiver as he, too, was panic-stricken from the unknown that was about to relinquish itself into his ear. He said hello, and Charlie, the night dispatcher, revealed himself on the other side of the line with a tone of trouble in his voice.

"Hello, Sheriff, sorry to bother you, but I thought you'd want to know that both squad cars of Jim and Scott, haven't answered my calls in over two hours."

Even though David was relieved it wasn't bad news from the hospital, it was still difficult to hear. Charlie went on to say that the last time he heard from them was when Scott called the station, stating that he had seen a naked woman running across the road into the forest.

"Where did he call from?" David asked.

"Just north of the Redman's farm on Blane Road," Charlie answered. "Jim was a rock's throw away, so I told Scott to hold off until he arrived there, and that was the last time I heard from either of them."

David told Charlie to call Johnny and have him check it out, and to call him back to keep him informed. After he hung up the phone, he sat momentarily in thought and stared into space.

"What's going on?" Sarah asked. "As she broke the silence with her worrisome curiosity."

David explained the current situation, saying he might have to go back to the station in the morning. Sarah seemed almost unconcerned as long as her little Lisa remained unharmed. "They're big boys," she stated while walking to the bathroom. "I'm sure that they're probably just sneaking a nip of whiskey or something."

David didn't reply to her insensitive comment as she entered the bathroom with her night bag. David sat in silence as he contemplated the geological location of Scott's incoming call. His eyes widened as he realized it was on the outskirts of the valley. Sarah walked out of the bathroom in a black negligee that graced her body like a curvaceous catwalk model. "You're still dressed?" she asked as if he wasn't supposed to be.

David remained in heavy thought until he picked up the phone receiver, stating that he had just one more call to make. Sarah pouted like a little girl who didn't get her way, giving a faint sigh before she walked away. David called the hotel desk and inquired about a rental car for the morning. The concierge told him that a rental would be waiting for him in the morning with the proper paperwork. When he hung up the phone, Sarah practically attacked him like a lioness until he submitted to her drunken, sex-crazed will.

David hardly worked at all as she disrobed and devoured him as if he were a calf wildebeest that had wandered from its herd. He lay flat as she pounded up and down upon him, then changed from frontward to back. After the vampire drained him dry, she withdrew her fangs, rolled over, and then lay fast asleep. This was nothing like it used to be, David thought as he lay there, drained in heavy deliberation. *Has the current perilous condition of our daughter somehow awakened the reptilian parts of our brain? Or have we just advanced to this level from over ten years of delusions of love?*

David sank into the depths of his psyche as his body descended into a deep, dark, dormant dimension. He began to dream of a demented figure that saturated blood-splashed paintings and melded into his mind like a parasitic leech. Buckets of blood-drenched a naked canvas, transforming it into a picturesque panorama of butchery. Mademoiselle Anabelle cried out in pernicious pain as her skin melted in a pyre of persecution. A paragon of tortured souls lost in purgatory spiraled over his head like a helix of nauseating hypnosis. An apparition of Sir Paul Berkshire materialized in a swarthy form that stood before him.

His mouth moved in a stammering mutter as his words contorted from a black dimension, struggling to convey an omen of condemnation. He gestured by pointing upward, covering his fist with his other hand while he held them over his head. He continued this process over and over as his twisted discarded words had a sense of significant urgency. Sir Paul looked around as if he'd be in tremendous peril if caught, warning of the mortality of treacherous times to come. He pointed to the sky once more, then dissipated into the spiral of the condemned Soul.

The phone rang abruptly, waking David from a cold sweat

and back into the living world. He reached through the darkness as he fumbled for the phone. "Hello," he answered as he wiped sweat from his forehead.

"Sorry to wake you, boss, but we have big trouble here in Horry County," divulged Johnny.

"What now?" David asked lethargically, with a hint of disgust in his voice.

"I found Scott and Jim's squad cars, each with their driver's side doors open as if they were in pursuit, and David ...," there was a short pause, "I just heard some God-awful screams in the forest."

David sat up as he asked, "Are you sure?"

"Sure, as I am talking to you," Johnny said sharply. "But I ain't crazy enough to hoof it in those woods by myself. State troopers are on the way as we speak."

"Alright, keep me informed," David stated as he glanced at a glowing clock and noticed it was 4:30 am.

"Will do," Johnny said as he pushed "end" on his new cellular phone.

Johnny felt a touch of fear while he stared at the two vacant squad cars then began bellowing out on speaker phone Jim and Scott's name.

David started to fall back asleep until a flash of information flared a spark of awareness that startled him wide awake. The location of those squad cars was on the opposite side of the valley, at the foot of its prominent slope. He called the front desk and asked how soon he could get a rental. The concierge regretfully replied that Harrisville only had two rental car agencies, and neither one would be open until 8:00 am. David thanked him and then hung up the phone.

He lay there feeling helpless and in the lap of luxury as the call of duty beckoned him. He then remembered good ole' Al-Franko handing him a business card and telling him he could call night or day. He turned on the bathroom light, being careful not to wake Sarah, as he dug for Al-Franko's card. He grabbed the cordless phone and walked back into the bathroom.

He dialed the number and waited until an answering machine picked up with Al-Franko's voice on the greeting. David spoke after the beep, stating his name and the reason he was calling. But before he could finish, a woman about Al-Franko's age, around 60, answered in a heavy Italian voice, telling him to wait for a minute. David could hear the fuddy couple bickering about as Al-Franko labored to the phone. He cleared his voice as he said, "Ah-hello," as polite as one can be after being awakened at 4:45 am. David first apologized for the late call and then gave his reason for calling so early. But before he could finish, Al-Franko intervened midstream, saying "No-a-problem."

Twenty minutes later, Al-Franko's taxi pulled up in front of the hotel, where David waited in view. David thanked him as he emphasized his gratitude, stressing how important it was for him to get to Horry County. Al-Franko kept saying, "No problem, Mr. Lang," as his motor mouth started to warm up like a prop engine on a small boat. He grilled him twenty questions for every sentence David divulged in route. David didn't want to waste any time and directed Al-Franko straight to Blaine Road.

When they reached the dirt road, two state trooper cars were on their sides while Johnny's squad car remained upright along with Jim and Scott's squad car. Al-Franko shrieked, "Mamma Mia!" as David recited muffled paraphrases of

American slang. Al-Franko commented how strange this car accident was out in the middle of nowhere while he put the cab in the park.

David agreed as he stepped out of the cabbie and gazed upon the aftermath of a chaotic puzzle that was missing pieces. He walked to Al-Franko's driver's side door and asked if he had a two-way radio. David glanced at his console and saw that he had not, then he authoritatively commanded Al-Franko to stay put.

He then walked cautiously to the closest wreckage, trying to view the scene without committing his body to an onslaught of who knows not. He slowly circled the demolished vehicle and beheld the torso of a state trooper, ripped apart like a rag doll. David announced loudly that Al-Franko should lock his doors as he reached the wreckage for the trooper's twelve-gauge shotgun. He started forward to the next wreck, where he witnessed the gore of body parts strewn about. He thought to himself how odd it appeared and wondered if he was still dreaming.

Before he reached the next squad car, he saw the missing head from the torso that lay behind him. When he came upon the car, inside was the second state trooper, his head in his lap and his hand still gripping the radio' mic. David anticipated the worst as he continued to Johnny's cruiser, approaching it in worrisome fear. He stretched his neck like a goose, peering and straining to see the contents inside. There was no Johnny and no trace of blood, which gave David hope that his friend was still alive.

He then looked up ahead and saw Scott and Jim's squad cars, unscathed as Johnny's. David reached into the squad car and radioed Pat, reporting the present condition. He told her to call more state troopers as gunfire rang out, along with screams of Johnny's voice, from the dense, timbered forest.

When he stood up out of the squad car, Al-Franko was walking toward him and gawking at the forest to his right. "I thought I told you to stay in the car," David barked.

"You need my-a-help. I-a-help," Al-Franko said bravely.

David glanced back toward the headless trooper and gave in to Al-Franko's brave offering. He reached back into the squad car and grabbed the shotgun that was propped against the console. He handed it to the Italian cabbie and asked if he knew how to use it. Much to David's surprise, the Italian slid the chamber open, peered inside, and saw it was loaded.

David looked at him, puzzled, as Al-Franko simply replied, "I used to be Mafioso in Italy in my twenties, here I'm a cabby."

More screams and shots rang out as they proceeded in the deleterious direction of the outcries.

They trudged through the thick woods as the morning sun embarked upon the landscape and shadows twisted from its continuous ascension into the sky. Blood-curdling roars bellowed into their ears as they paused in terror for a moment. Huge branches were broken more than twelve feet above the ground, and unnatural three-footed impressions, each over two feet wide, of deformed cloven hooves prints into the rich red soil. They halted once more as the conjuncture of morbid realities and the obscurity of the unknown petrified them in their tracks.

Then they heard Johnny cry out again as if he were being tortured in absolute horror. They chased the shrieking sounds of his screams, and as they drew near, they could hear leaves and branches violently breaking, mixed with the baritone grunts that might come from a large animal. David held out his arm, signaling to stop. He crouched behind a stump, and Al-Franko followed suit.

188

"What in seven hells is that?" David queried, pointing through the trees.

Al-Franko made a Catholic sign of the cross gesture from his forehead to his chest as he bore witness to an ungodly sight of terror. An elongated creature stood almost fifteen feet high, with three legs and two arms on each side of its immense torso, fused together in a malformed mutation. It had two heads that were combined in a defacement of loathsome horror, and its cankerous skin was of stomach-wrenching sight. The Beast labored in a chaotic frenzy of odious anger as it battered and shook a tree in a fury of frustration while roaring in a venomous tongue.

David suddenly realized the object of the creature's circumvention was Johnny, who hovered high in the branches as he fired the last of his bullets into its leathery skin. The shards of metal only fueled its rabid rage as its hostile hands seemed capable of shaking the stars.

After David regained his senses, he pointed for Al-Franko to advance left while he flanked to the right. The colossal Beast remained consumed in its present task of toil while David and Al-Franko went unnoticed, and they now stood behind it. David's twisted nerves and worst fears of losing a deputy had no means to obligation and duty of freeing his good friend. "Now!" David hollered as both shotguns fired simultaneously, aiming for the small of the Beast's spine and the back of its head. It let out a clamorous cry, lashing its disproportioned body at the twosome firing squad. They each dislodged the empty cartridges and cocked, locked, and then rocked the giant freak off its hooves with another blast from their steel masts.

They fired again and again as the Beast continued to scramble to its three mis cloven hooves. Shrills of agony pervaded the forest as it rose. The Bestial creature had enough. It ran off into the thicket of the timberlands as its horrific howls reverberated throughout the woods. David then yelled to Johnny, "Are you alright?"

Johnny remained silent for a moment, as if in shock, until David repeated the question. He then shook it off as he called out, "I thought I was a goner for sure."

Shaking to his very bone, Johnny proceeded to climb down the tree as David nervously joked that Johnny had used two of his nine lives in less than a week. Johnny's voice trilled tremendously as he responded, "Man, am I glad to see you, whoever you are," as he shook Al-Franko's hand. David smiled and intervened. "Why is that Big Al?"

"What the fuck was that?" David said.

"I was hoping you'd tell me," Returned Johnny as he regained his voice.

David looked around. "I don't know, but let's get the fuck out of here before that thing comes back." They all agreed as they high-tailed it out of Dodge with a quick step. When they reached the road, Johnny had completed his half of the story as he told them how the creature had ambushed him as well as the two dead troopers. He explained how that giant thing tossed the squad cars around like toys and then ripped those poor troopers to shreds.

David expressed his undying gratitude to Al-Franko as he took the shotgun from him and told him to go home. Johnny reached out his hand and thanked Al-Franko for sticking his neck to save him. Al-Franko mumbled phrases from the bible in Italian as he walked to his cab.

"I'll call you later," David shouted. "And, uh, let's keep this to ourselves, okay?"

Al-Franko looked at him dumbfounded and asked, "Who

would believe a-me anyway? Would you?" David smiled as he watched Al-Franko climb into his cab and drive away.

Twenty minutes later, troopers and ambulances filled Blaine Road, but the fun part was trying to explain a tree-high Beast to an unmoving trooper. Instead of a mystical Monster, they wrote the report as a car accident, and until David had more answers that suited them fine. After an army of tow trucks, coroners, squad cars, and medic vans left the scene, Blaine Road was returned to its mundane desolateness. Only David and Johnny remained momentarily as they rehashed the horrific events. "Screw this, let's get out of here," David said as he heard a small animal rummaging about the edge of the woods.

They regrouped at the station where they could surmise the situation in safety. As they walked in the door, they were instantly attacked with a profusion of questions. The pleasantly plump Pat and walking stick and Charlie stared into space as David explained their mind-bending encounter.

Johnny then said something even stranger than the strangeness of the creature itself. "Man, call me crazy, but I almost felt sorry for that damn thing until it got shot and began ripping people apart. Then I was just plain out petrified! The freaking bastard came out of the sticks gripping its head and wailing about like it was just as horrified as we were. Then those gung-ho, gun-slinging troopers opened fire on it as it seemed to plea for help. They were the aggressors; God rest their Souls."

"But here's what's really fucked up: the more time I spent gaping at that Freak thing, the more I saw a resemblance of what looked like a giant conglomeration of Scott and Jim. It was those eyes on each of those skulls of that giant head. It had two eyes on each side; one side looked like Scott, the other looked like Jim as if they were somehow meshed in one fucked

191

up mess."

Charlie and Pat contemplated Johnny's story like he had lost his ever-loving mind. They seemed to be waiting for the punchline of Jim and Scott walking through the door. But no punchline was told, nor was any sign of Jim or Scott established as they tried to depict a gigantic, grotesque gargantuan in their narrow minds. Pat then changed the subject as if it were too appalling to talk about or just too plain silly to be considered. "I heard about little Lisa; she's going to be alright; I hope."

David regrettably told how she had the same disease from which his father died as Pat held back her tears. He then turned to Johnny.

"I got a get back to Bi-County Hospital to see how Lisa's coming along. Just tell Scott and Jim's wives that we don't know where they're at, at this point and time, and that we're doing everything possible to find them."

David left for Harrisville as Charlie relinquished his command, and Johnny went in person to tell Scott and Jim's wives of their disappearance.

During the forty-five-minute ride, David's mind started to verify the correspondence between events, places, and times. He couldn't shake the thought of the monstrous Beast that killed those troopers and chased Johnny up a tree like a squirrel. When he reached the hospital, his mother and Sarah were sitting in the waiting room in dejection of the unknown. "Mom, what are you doing here?"

She looked at him with a half-smile as she declared, "What? A grandmother can't be there for her granddaughter?" He hugged her and glanced over her shoulder at a seething Sarah. He then explained how Scott and Jim went missing and that he tried to find them.

"Again, they're big boys. I'm sure they can handle themselves," Sarah said sarcastically.

David let her verbal arrow fly, knowing she was heavy-hearted in despair.

"What's the latest news on Lisa?" he asked with fretful anticipation. "We don't know, she's going through dialysis as we speak," said David's mother, Carol.

David sat quietly between his mother and Sarah as they waited together in the air of troublesome worry. His mother broke the silence by asking about the two missing deputies. David gave them a candy-coated explanation of varied theories of where they might be. He left out the part of the giant-sized freak and the wake of death it left in its path.

On the midday local news, the same reporter David noticed at the cemetery stood in front of the coroner's office just two doors down from Bi-County Hospital. Porter Lewes stood at average height with light black skin. He carried himself astutely with a bow tie wire brim glasses and the low baritone voice of a reporter. He mentioned the odd supposed car wreck, which happened in the newly popular town of peculiarity, Lang Township. He went on to remind the viewers about the caskets as a quick flash showed the surfaced coffins, which sensationalized his next comment. "Now two state troopers met their deaths in Horry County, just two miles outside of Lang Township." He added that two Horry County deputies were missing and that there was no search party actively looking for the missing men. He closed his vicious defamatory statements by vilifying Lang Township, proclaiming the roads unsafe as the screen flashed the smashed-up state patrol cars. The screen then showed some potholed roads that could have been anywhere.

Sarah now realized what was weighing down David's

shoulders, and she wrapped her arms around him with mindful consideration. David then stood up and started pacing. He kept his World of Trouble to himself as Sarah remarked how much of an asshole the reporter was.

One hour later, Dr. Miranda walked in with a nurse. He had a smile on his face.

"Good news?" Sarah queried with hopeful eyes as she clenched a ball of tissue.

"Good news indeed," the doctor returned with an upbeat tone. He then divulged that it was just the first stage of the process, but things were looking up.

Before Sarah could ask, Dr. Miranda stated that it would be good for Lisa to see her loved ones. The nurse then waved them on to follow her as the trip to Lisa's room started to become a ritual. Carol carried Lisa's favorite candy, gummy worms, with a teddy bear that filled a sizable amount of space in the small elevator. When they reached her room, Lisa was elated. She cried out in joy at the sight of her parents and Grams.

After a couple of minutes into their visit, she finally settled down as she sank her teeth into a gummy worm as Sarah inhaled the scent of her benevolent brown bear. Lisa was then saddened when she asked when she could go home and why the nurses hurt her with needles. Sarah's eyes welled while explaining how she was sick and the shots would make her better so that she could go home.

"And I can still go to the zoo and see the monkeys?" Lisa asked as she sat on the edge of her seat. David added, "And the lions, and the bears, and zebras, but most of all, the monkeys." Little Lisa shook her hands convulsively as she let out a high-pitched yelp of joy. They spent the remainder of the afternoon with their lonely child until a nurse announced that

194

visiting hours were over. Sarah reassured Lisa once more that she would be all better soon and then she could come home. As the three started to leave, Lisa bellowed in a fervent frenzy, bringing a rain of mother's tears and Sarah rushing back into her arms. Sarah conversed in an inspirational speech that moved mountains, lured Angels, and captured stars as her precious jewel wiped her eyes.

David took advantage of the moment and asked his mother if she'd stay the night in Harrisville. He explained that he needed to go back to Horry County. He didn't bother to tell her of the threatening hideous titan that still roamed about, nor could he tell Sarah. But if he could keep them safely in the dark out of Horry County, he'd be one step up in subduing harm's way. His mother reluctantly agreed and said she'd be more than happy to oblige. David could live with a little unsettling disappointment from his mother, but if anything ever happened to her, there would be no place the Beast could hide from his wrath. They then dined at a locale less gloomy than the hotel restaurant, with a big fat man-boy as its logo.

David wanted to talk of the early events on Blain Road, but every time he thought about it, he considered how it would sound. He himself couldn't nor wouldn't believe such a story and would fear that men in white coats might put him in a straitjacket. After they dined, they drove to the hotel, where David set his mother up in her own room. But she and Sarah would converse and keep each other company while David high-tailed it back to Horry County.

When he reached the station, Charlie was back on duty. Johnny had gone home for the night for some much-deserved rest and time with his family. All had been quiet, except for that noisy reporter still lurking about. Charlie told David how the pesky reporter tried to pilfer information from Pat and then him just an hour earlier. Charlie handed David a business card that the reporter gave Pat. It read "Porter Lewis." On the bottom was the slogan "Messenger to the World because the World wants to know." David stuffed it in his pocket as he retreated into his office, where he sank into his consoling chair. Even though there was a rabid Beast rampaging around and a slanderer for a reporter fussing about, David was still comfortable in his present surroundings.

Devin sat in his study with his new armament---*the Egyptian Book of the Dead*--- for the apocalyptical war to come. He scrutinized every page as he soaked its secrets into his sanctimonious mind. He compared the notes of his mentor Barabis' parchment scrolls to the Necronomicon. Each embodied similar attributes in its anatomy, forboding a nefarious omen to come. Even though they came from different origins and times, they carried the same message; only this testimony trumpeted the triumphal slayings of Angels and the unleashing of the Demonic dogs from the gates of Hell. It relinquished ill-natured incantations of fatal abrasions as it seethed with hatred for God.

Its pages sang a victorious song while ringing out a different outcome than the good book proclaimed. It foretold of a Dark Emissary whose Soul waited in hell while he walked among the living. The ancient pages of the Necronomicon disclosed the projection of the constellation on Devin's birth and his death from mortal life. It depicted times and locations from events past, present, and yet to come. Its venomous paraphrases of abomination contrived terms of capitulation for the occupants of Zion.

The pages chanted in rapturous bliss iniquitous scriptures and sacred psalms of Satan. It was an instruction manual of step-by-step tactics and strategies for the Holy War to come. Cryptic poems delineated the crucifixions of countless Christians, condemning their Soul and cultivating their carcasses into the soil of Earth. It described the Dark Eminent upon his throne of human bones and the wretched of tormented misery at his feet, as the words screamed his title---

*Eminence of* Evil - *The Witch Master.*

Devin sat back in his chair as he relished the fact that he proselytized a great army in numbers ready for dispersion at his will. A solar eclipse would soon fall upon the valley, and his chess pieces were in proper order. The world embarked upon a chaotic future of condemnation. An affliction of turmoil has infected the Middle Eastern nations as the virtue vassalage is but a vague memory in the subverted Vatican. Earthquakes are more profound as the petulance of third-world nations perpetuates their unstinting death toll. Children betray, lie, and kill their siblings and parents, as mothers and fathers rape and lewd their children. Idol worshipers fall to their knees in great numbers, conjuring their pagan gods.

Racial tensions clash in contemptuous contusion as skin color becomes more important than the individual. Fallacious symbols of faithless men cast their tall shadows from the tottering pedestals on which they stand.

Wars are waged by malign aristocrats as the protocol is placed wayward in the thirst for power. Legislation suffocates the impoverished with red tape as innocent commoners waste behind bars simply for the lack of funds to properly represent themselves.

Oil spills, abortions, adultery, murder, famine, and forsaken Souls were just a few attributes of atrocities. He peeked into the pits of hell as his soul stood and stared upward in the stillness of wait. Devin basked as he leaned back in his chair. The time drew near to the ancient celestial, feudal war for the soul of man. Devin would scavenge the broken pieces and reassemble them for a theme of his own.

That evening, David fell asleep at the helm of his desk into the early morning hours of the night. Charlie knocked lightly then popped his head in the door as he reluctantly awakened David to inform him of disturbing news from a call that just came in. Charlie cleared his thought as David lifted his head and adjusted his eyes to the stick man in the doorway of his office.

"Sorry to wake you, Sheriff, but Bob Blanchard called the station half scared out of his wits, saying that there's something in his barn eating his horses." David sobered from his sleep while grabbing an arsenal of weapons. He then volunteered the trembling Charlie to join him in his arms. David stocked his cruiser with four loaded shotguns, a forty-four magnum, and twelve smoke bombs. Chills crawled down Charlie's spine like tiny spiders that sought shelter in the moment of his fear, realizing the serious demeanor in which David carried himself. His quaking gullet clogged with fright as he worried about his balding head. He wondered what he was about to face and why he had to go; after all, he was just a sworn-in dispatcher.

They locked the station and then left for Bob Blanchard's farm. David concocted a plan in his head as a long, drawn-out silence fell upon the cruiser. David drove down a dark dirt road in the direction of a pretty good idea of what he was about to encounter. Charlie gripped the shotgun tightly with sweaty hands with trepid anticipation. He looked over at David and took in his stoical exterior. Charlie was hopeful the drive would never end, but they came upon the Blanchard farm to find horses, sheep, and pigs befuddling from the barn in pandemonium.

The Beast had torn the opposite side of the barn a hole in the wall that fit its giant atrocious figure. Half-eaten horses with their gaping spines riddled the interior. Yet the two deputies went unnoticed as the monstrous Beast licked the blood off its fingers as it leaned against a column with its back facing them.

198

Charlie's knees buckled, and he strained to stay afloat while David proceeded haphazardly, not knowing how to approach the quandary at hand. David almost felt pity for the wretched creature. It seemed to be crooning a mournful, twisted tune as it resided, oblivious to the presence of the prowling gunman. David noticed a five-gallon gas can and singled to a halt while he motioned for Charlie to take his rifle and withdraw. Charlie wasn't about to dispute David's decision if it would save the risk of a direct encounter with the hideous Beast, though he hid his relief while rushing towards his exit.

David stealth his way to the gas can, pinched the top lever, and sloshed its contents onto bales of hay in the inner perimeter, leading out the same way he came.

Charlie almost stood out of sight as David closed and locked the door. David continued to splash gasoline on the sides of the barn as he worked his way to the shredded opening the creature had created. David stood to the side of the jagged aperture, sneaking a peek at the now lethargic, pot-bellied Beast.

David noticed that it started to fall asleep as he reveled silently at the fortunate opportunity for a quick, successful kill. He then slipped back into the barn practically under its nose as he dowsed a large bale of hay that consumed the last of the gasoline. He silently lit the haystack with his pocket lighter and quickly exited to the exterior of the kindling flames. David ran to join the trembling, terror-drenched Charlie and rearmed his assault rifle.

Shortly after a wail of shrieking howls bellowed out from the fire inferno as the crashing sounds of turmoil flailed about the barn. The panic-stricken Beast pounded the sides of the barn's walls and punctured holes through the barrier of its entrapment. Like a big, dumb animal, it stuck its head through an open cavity, thinking it might save him, then withdrew in painful peril. Abruptly, it ceased its wailing and thrashing about as David! presumed; he silenced the creature for good.

Charlie prematurely vocalized a victory dance as a thunderous crash sounded off with a ferocious discharge. The Beastly freak ran through the wall and wallowed on the dirt in anguish and agony, attempting to snuff its flaming back. It mourned out a sonorous, ear-piercing cry as it rolled about the ground in a clamorous, discordant despair. It hastily jumped to its trisected feet as it looked around to soothe its blistered skin with some water. Its distressful eyes glazed about the vicinity as they focused on the source of its pain. David aimed his rifle at the tormented creature, and it seemed to understand what David was doing. The Beast then turned and ran off across a tobacco field while it wailed muffled cries before it disappeared into the nearby forest.

David turned to his pale deputy and poked him, "Well, it's a good thing you were here, Charlie. You must have scared that thing off."

Charlie forced a smile while staring in the direction of the departed creature as he silently breathed a breath of relief. Farmer Bob Blanchard stormed out of his house as his portly wife wobbled behind him. "What in Damnations did you do to my barn?!" he barked as if his tongue lashing would bring it back.

David calmly replied, "Well, I'll bet that thing won't come around here anymore. You should be happy."

"Happy? You burn my barn to the ground and say I should be happy? Boy, I'm just tickled pink. Can you see my joy, Sheriff?! "I'm just tickled pink and all fuzzy inside."

"Come on, Bob," David hollered back, "Just think what that thing would have done to your house and your pretty, little wife. Why, I just saved your ass!"

Farmer Bob stammered, lost for words, as his wife stared silently in disbelief at the glowing embers of a once sturdy structure.

David then broke the silence. "You just make sure you call us if that thing comes back, eh." David turned and ambled towards his cruiser as Charlie stood momentarily in shock. David stopped and then turned to Charlie and said, "Unless you're going to chase after that thing, let's go!"

Charlie snapped out of his daze and quickly shuffled to catch up to David. Farmer Bob yelled at David's back, "I'll make sure I call the fire department before I call you!"

"You do that, Bob," replied David, "you do that."

Bob's wife's fatty jowls nagged for her husband to get in the house as David smiled and walked towards the cruiser. They drove back to the station and David dropped off Charlie to finish his shift. He told Charlie to call him if any more problems arose.

That prospect quietly pained the simple dispatcher as he mentally struggled with the thought, but he verbally agreed. David had handled all the problems he could handle for one day, or so he thought. Just fifteen minutes after cozying up to his new high-definition TV, a dainty rap sounded at the door. "Now, who in the hell could that be?" he complained as he regrettably got up from his chair.

When he opened the door, Nina stood there in the scantiest black outfit, like an enchanting temptress that could chew up a man and spit him out. "What are you doing here?" David demanded in an unwelcoming manner.

"Well, hello to you, too," lashed Nina in a peppery tone, as if her feelings were hurt.

David hesitated as he caught himself slipping from his typical humane demeanor. "I'm sorry, it's been a rough day. How can I help you?" he asked, hoping she'd go away soon after.

Nina seemed to know Sarah wasn't home, yet she asked casually, peering behind him and acting clueless.

"No, she's in Harrisville due to our daughter being in the hospital there," he said, still hoping she'd go away.

"Well then," she started as she nudged her way past him, "you could use a warm meal." She walked toward the kitchen and David couldn't help his eyes drifting to her curvaceous body.

"That isn't necessary," he expressed as he held the front door open, hoping she'd get a hint.

David could hear the kitchen cabinets opening and closing, and he finally shut the door. When he turned to the kitchen, Nina was bent over, gaping into the refrigerator, and his eyes fought to stay off her ravishing, round rump. "You don't have to do this," he insisted as she unwrapped two T-bone steaks.

"Oh," she declared, "I couldn't sleep with myself if I didn't."

David thought I'll bet you don't ever have to worry about that. Her obstinacy was obvious as David turned from the toiling chef and resumed his place at the foot of his TV. Thirty minutes later, she called him into the dining room, where a candle was lit, and the lights dimmed. David took his place in his usual chair and Nina in Sarah's. He felt odd about the present predicament, but after seeing and smelling the feast laid out before him, his hunger suddenly assaulted him. Nina wouldn't allow any awkwardness in the room as she continued her flirtation. But David took notice that she never once asked

202

how his daughter was doing, and he wondered all the while about her true motives. Still, her cajoling lips seemed to absorb his contention as her bewitchery began to enchant.

Just as they finished eating, the phone rang. Due to the events of the day and the present distraction, the furthest thing from David's mind was that it could be Sarah. As he picked up the phone, he expected to hear Charlie's disconcerting words, but instead, it was Sarah's comforting voice. A smile came to David's face as she said hello, but at the same time, a load of problems weighed upon his mind as she looked over at Nina and considered the chance of bad news from the hospital. He took the cordless phone into the living room, turning his back to Nina as Sarah asked about his day. "Just another ordinary day here," he replied.

"Everything okay there in the big city?" he asked, hinting at the news on Lisa.

"So far, so good," she replied, hoping words rang true. "Dr Miranda said more tests will have to be done in the morning. Other than that, Lisa's taking it well."

"She has her mother's will," David honored in praise.

Sarah giggled. "What's so funny about that?" David inquired.

"Oh, nothing," Sarah answered. "I was just thinking that Dr. Miranda fancies your mother."

"What? How did that come about?" David inquired, almost too afraid to ask.

"Well, after you left, Dr. Miranda said there is nothing to be done at the hospital until tomorrow, so he asked us out to dinner again. I told him that I didn't have an appetite and would turn in for the night to get an early start at the hospital.

So, he then turned his attention to your mother and asked her out as if that was his motive in the first place. Carol was just as surprised as I was and was going to turn him down, but I insisted that she should get out and paint the town."

"Why'd you do that?" David expounded as if the thought was too cumbersome to conceive. "Well, your mother may be in her fifties, but she isn't dead. She deserves to have a little fun." There was a suspension of silence as David envisioned his mother and Dr. Miranda doing the tango across the dance floor. "I guess you're right," David admitted. "It's just that he's a New Yorker and all."

"New Yorker? What's that got to do with anything? I'm from New York, and you married me."

David backpedaled. "I didn't mean anything by it. It's just that ..."

Sarah cut him off. "What? Your mother deserves a little break from her lonely life, I'd say."

David could tell by Sarah's voice that she was getting annoyed, as she was now in the defensive mode. He quickly changed his tune and told her he hoped they'd have a good time. But just as Sarah was about to shift back to her normal tone, Nina blurted out, as if on purpose, "Where's the dish soap?" David cringed at the sound of her voice, wondering what Sarah's next words would be.

"Who the hell was that?" she asked as David pondered an incalculable return while considering misleading conceptions she might have. He finally summed up the truth as he told her that Nina wouldn't take no for an answer and that she cooked dinner for him.

Sarah became enraged. "What the fuck does that little tramp thinks she's pulling? Put her on the phone! I'll tell her where she can put the dish soap!"

"No, no, that's not necessary. I'll get rid of her as soon as …" Just then, the doorbell rang.

"Now, who the hell could that be? Her sidekick, that another whore?" Sarah said profoundly.

David couldn't comprehend Sarah's profanity as the bafflement of the day started to short-circuit his brain. When he opened the door, Scott's pregnant wife stood there with a two-year-old boy in her arms and anxiety showing on her face. "Oh, it's Scott's wife," David promulgated aloud with the phone still to his ear.

"Sorry to bother you, Sheriff, but I'm really worried about Scott. He wouldn't just leave without telling me where he was going."

"Come on inside," David said as he held the door open. He then instructed her to have a seat as he retreated to Sarah's office. It seemed he was running out of rooms in which to escape.

Sarah continued to harp on David to get rid of the tramp/trollop/whore/harlot. Almost every word was pronounced, enunciated, and practically spelled out---"Make her leave now." A deluge of confusion came to David's mind, and he remembered that old commercial about some product that said something, something, "Take me away." He told the nipping wife that he'd get back to her. He promised he would work on getting rid of the proclaimed ogress as soon as he was off the phone. Sarah managed to belt out trollop /tramp /whore, one more time. David told her not to worry and then hung up.

When he walked to the living room, Renea's two-year-old was sitting on Nina's lap. Renea stood, and David told her to sit back down because of concern about her pregnancy. Tears welled up in her eyes as she told him she talked to Jim's wife, and she was also worried about her husband during the strange happenings.

"I wish I could tell you something at this point, but I really don't know. I thought the state troopers would help us, but it's as if Horry County has the plague. I had Pat leave a message with the FBI, but they act as if we don't exist."

David studied her face. A moment of silence came over the room, which forced David into a lame, last-minute protocol. "I don't know, Renea, but I give you my word I'll do everything in my power to bring Scott home to you."

Renea looked at David intensely, and the room became quiet again. "You're not telling me something!" barked Renea. "Now, what the hell is going on? I know you know something!"

"What? What are you talking about?" retorted David. "I'm just as confused as you are."

"Really, Sheriff. Then tell me why is Scott's squad car parked in your driveway? Where is he?"

Tears welled up in Renea's eyes as embarrassment flushed David's face. He had completely forgotten she had seen the same cruiser for the last two years, and he couldn't dispute all her incessant inquiries. David knew he couldn't dilly-dally with her intelligence or her growing tolerance anymore, so he decided to try the truth. David glanced over at Nina while she sat with a smug smirk and continued to gently bounce the two-year-old on her knees.

"Come into the office, and I'll tell you everything I know," insisted David as he put his arm on Renea's shoulder in a consoling manner. They began walking down the hall until

David stopped. "Why don't you grab the little one," suggested David as he stared into Nina's untrusting eyes.

Renea wiped a tear from her eyes, turned to her baby, and smiled at Nina as she retrieved the infant from the dominatrix.

They then proceeded to Sarah's office as David began to explain. He gazed into her swollen eyes as she held her baby on her hip.

"I hope you don't think I'm crazy, but you can ask Johnny and Charlie to verify what I'm about to tell you. Charlie called me while I was in Harrisville and told me that Jim and Scott were not answering his calls on the radio. So, I told him to keep trying and to keep me informed. After a while he called back and told me that they still were not answering the dispatch. So, I took a cab to check it out myself. When I reached the scene where they called in from, their squad cars were sitting untouched, but Johnny's and two state trooper cars were demolished."

David went on and recanted everything that had happened, except the raging, giant Freak Thing and the mangled mess of the state troopers. Renea hit him at every angle with questions of inquisition and studied David's face upon with syllable he spoke. David then told her that he and Johnny would comb the area first thing the next morning and that she'd be the first to know what he turned up. That seemed to pacify the pining possible widow.

"I know you're a good man, Sheriff. Scott really looks up to you. Please, please find my husband and bring him home to me!"

David cupped her child's face with his palm as he promised his commitment once more. He then walked Renea to the door, and they said their goodbyes. When David returned to the living room, Nina was sprawled out on the sofa like a satanic seductress. "What do you think you're doing," asked David with disgust and displeasure.

Nina laughed. "I just want to give you something, and that something is me."

"Sorry, Nina, but you're mistaken. I'm a happily married man and a faithful one at that. Now, if you would please leave."

David stood halfway to the front door as he motioned his arm towards the exit. Nina stood, and she shook her shapely hips in a slow, provocative saunter encroaching upon David's comfort zone.

"Awe, come on," said Nina, "I saw the way you were looking at me that day at the pool. Come, let's play. I won't tell."

She wrapped her arms around the back of his neck, and she lingered near his lips. David gently unclasped her fingers, then repeated himself with an alternate phrase: "Get the fuck out of here so I can get some rest, or you could eat your next meal in jail! Got it?"

Nina stood in a sexual stance of defiance, then divulged, "There's no rest for the wicked, and my good sheriff, you are wicked. You just don't know it yet." She slipped her dress off her shoulders, and it gently fell to her feet. She approached him with even more vigor.

Again, David threatened her. "I will have you arrested for lewd behavior. Now put your dress back on and make like a tree and leave."

This only seemed to arouse her as she asked if he was going to use his handcuffs. Then she said, "You can't arrest the willing."

David began to lose all patience as he raised his voice to a roar. "I'm not playing with you. You better put your clothes on and move the fuck on!"

Nina ignited into fiery hysterics as she stood grabbing and taunting. She suddenly ceased her mirth and raised her arms. She bespoke a slow, bestowing spell that seemed to swallow him whole with every syllable. *"Oceans of lust that trounce upon your righteous wretched Soul, tides befall a singing song of me you are enthralled.*

David fell to his knees as he began to weigh heavy with her tempestuous flesh. The entrancing turns of her curves could create torturous enticement and lure a man to his death. Her breasts were like great mountainous peaks of insurmountable latitudes that provoked a climber to scale its razor-edged ranges.

Nina clenched his light head by his thick brown hair and pulled his face to her crotch. The scent of her bewitching womanhood drove him to become a man he knew not, his probing predator tongue piercing into her pique pool of fire. She lifted her leg upon his shoulder as she tugged his head into her, bracing her balance on the physique of his frame, all the while saying, "Good boy, lap it up, good boy."

The phone rang David's deaf ears, with Nina sensing Sarah's rage from afar, relishing her distress while her husband was a slave to her seduction. After the phone ceased ringing, Nina grew tired of her position, and she lured the stumbling, light-headed lapdog to the bedroom, where she fueled David's sexual fire. David's wistful will was at the command of her governess guile, spreading her legs and making her demands. He had a vague reckoning of his activities while he felt the course of his actions, but it was as if someone else was participating in the act.

Nina lay in amusement as David tossed upon her fiery flesh, his hunger pained in an endless pit, which drew a sadistic smile across her smug face. She turned to her side as he pushed himself into her forbidden zone, ramming her rump in a rampant frenzy. Over and over, he immersed himself in the submergence of her desires, performing a puppet dance from her strings. He liberated his poisons into her inferno damnation, yet no relief was offered from his empty, endless need to drink from her fountain well.

Finally, she departed, leaving him in a discorded state of deranged madness, her spell still potent with nymphomaniac passion. David stayed in bed cursing the emptiness it contained, pleasuring himself repeatedly in catatonic strife to find resolution from her soulless scent on the sheets. Eventually, exhaustion claimed his cursed frame as her enchantment enervated him into a deep sleep.

Back at the mansion, Syck and Hector were under stringent restraint of Devin's strict orders not to taunt the Catholic virgins with their vile loins, which meant the repeated raping of Louise. Syck lifted her out of her Earthly prison by the locks of her long blonde hair as screams from the trepid schoolgirls, who thought they'd be next. Theresa was the eldest of them at seventeen years of age. She rang out her moral support to her schoolmates through the wooden boards of her captivation. She strained to prop herself at the top of the dugout, her efforts falling and landing her at the bottom, where her feces lay along with her dejection. She lies there crying as she thinks of home and her parents. She wondered why she was being punished by these twisted torturers. Was this karma for teasing Suzy just because she was overweight? Or maybe trading notes in class with Veronica, her best friend forever.

Or was it because she had impure thoughts of Steven DeCarlo, the quarterback for St. Peter's Lutheran High, after she let him kiss her behind the stands? Or maybe God was mad at her for skipping her prayers and not performing penance for her sins. She began to cry and pray for forgiveness. Her spirits were dropping into despair as she began to prepare for death. She shed her tears upon the cold, damp dirt, and she envisioned the woman's pain through the screams she heard. Louise bellowed out, wailing as her skin was penetrated in pleasure by the warped, perverted lecher.

Theresa could hear Veronica's weeping murmurs two pits down from her and in the background of Louise's haunting cries. She pressed her back into one side of the pit, and she pressed her legs to the other, making a slow crawl to the top. Earth gave way under her feet as she scrambled for footing, suspending her in the air while she dug her fingernails in the dirt. Clods of clay fell beneath her.

She fell to the bottom more than once until her persistence prevailed as she clutched at the six-inch breathing hole. She cried out Veronica's name into the vastness, worried her woeful hails would fall on impertinent ears. "Veronica, can you hear me? Answer me if you can."

Veronica whimpered through her tears, "I can hear you." Suddenly, her forsaken, forlorn spirit brightened with survival optimism as the familiar voice rang out. She strained her composure, awaiting the next syllable, which sounded like almighty Angels singing her name.

"Listen to me, Veronica, I'm going to get us out of here," Theresa commanded, her life-giving words reverberating through her Soul and strengthening her with hope. Louise's screams continued for hours, blending with the pounding, pulsating base from cabinet speakers. Theresa took notice of the soft Earth that was giving way near one side of the board while kicking its vulnerable section. She was elated! Despite her hands being splintered and cut from the pressure of her supporting weight at the breathing hole, she kicked repeatedly in a nervous, frenzied manner as her vision for freedom widened upon every strike.

Finally, a cluster of clay clumps collapsed to the bottom of the pit, creating a cleft large enough for her young, slender body she thought to crawl. She swung her right then left leg through the clearing of the small aperture as she hung suspended virtually by her small hands through the breathing hole. She braced herself, shifted, and squirmed herself into freedom.

Floodlights located high up in the mansion hit her eyes like spikes of twinging pain that made her head throb momentarily. Theresa wiped the dirt from the corners of her eyes while looking around in horror at the thirty prison pits that entrapped her friends and classmates. She called out as she stumbled and staggered about the piles of dirt that girdled the perimeter of the sorrow-stricken pits. She stuck her face into the breathing holes, gaping at the contents they contained, until she came upon Veronica's entrapment. Theresa lifted the cinder blocks with her weakened arms as Veronica's face came to life at the sight of her best friend. Theresa swiveled the wood board to the side, then reached with her magnanimous hand and pulled her to the surface, leaving her mole existence behind.

Peering into a nearby pit, Theresa told Suzy that she'd be back with help and for her to hold tight with faith. Veronica followed Theresa on the path leading to the old mansion as they fled in a panic of serious anxiousness from their fears of recapture. No roads were offered, and no structures were seen, but the vast black forest, which was almost as frightful as the pits they left behind.

Theresa conjectured a contemplative thought as she held out her arm, calling for Veronica to halt, listening to the pulse of the planet for any sign of humanity. To the left, she heard a low, whining tenor of tread tires wailing their glorious call of freedom. They trudged through the dense, wooded timberlands, stopping periodically with straining necks, awaiting and praying for the solace of society. Brush and limbs clipped, bruised, and scraped their skin as they skirmished through the merciless terrain. Closer and closer, they came as their young, tired bones emerged in the direction of their forthcoming liberty. They stood at the top of a hill, from which they could see the asphalt of heaven at the bottom: a highway.

Theresa cried out in a burst of joy. "We made it! We made it! Look, Veronica, we made it!" They scampered down the hill in a gallop of gracious gratification, thanking God the whole way down. Their encouraged mental state brightened in outlook with the perceptions of safety as they encountered the road. They stood to the side, waiting impatiently for a chariot of chivalrous salvation, ready to flag it down.

Finally, a car pulled up, and the woman driving rolled down the window with a gentle smile. "What are you girls doing out here in the middle of nowhere?"

Veronica streamed tears of joy as Theresa explained their situation and from where they came. The pretty woman popped the locks on her Lexus and told them to get in and that they could use the phone at her house. Theresa inquired whether she had a cell phone so they might call their parents right away. The pretty lady told her that she didn't, which Theresa thought odd. Veronica thanked her over and over and practically jumped in the car while Theresa stood momentarily and asked where she lived.

"My house is just down the road," she said with a soft, pleasant voice, pointing forward. Theresa studied the direction in which she pointed as an awkward moment filled the air. "I don't bite," said the pretty lady, using humor to lighten the situation.

"Come on, Theresa," chortled Veronica, "We're finally going home!"

Theresa smiled, then climbed into the back seat as the two held hands in their newfound freedom. The helpful woman hung on every word as Theresa explained the torture from which they just escaped. Just as Theresa finished the story of their capture, they pulled up to the front door of the helpful lady's house. When inside, she led them to the kitchen, where she told them to eat what they wanted while she went upstairs to grab the phone.

The two hungry girls attacked the refrigerator like barbarians, relishing an assortment of edibles. Left to fill their bellies, they smiled at each other in between each bite.

Veronica hummed a little ditty as she chewed her food. She walked over to the kitchen window at the back of the house, knowing she would soon talk to her mom and dad, which made her elated.

She peered through the blinds and then dropped her sandwich. She began to wail out, crying at the nauseating sight that presented its ghastly gloom. "No, no, no!" Veronica shouted as Theresa rushed to her side and gazed at the object of her abhorrent living nightmare.

Outside, past the pool, there were the pitted prisoners they labored so heroically to escape. Nina, Hector, and Syck stood behind them, smitten with smiles. Veronica screamed at the top of her lungs and dropped to her knees. Theresa stood by her side, brave and defiant.

Syck spoke sardonically.

"Well, I guess it's really true what they say, you guys." he smiled at his fellow artisans, "You can take a hen out of a hen house, but you can't get the chicken from the coup." Theresa

214

bent down and placed her arm around Veronica's shaking frame as she looked Nina in the eyes. "You fucking bitch! I had a bad feeling about you!"

Nina laughed and strolled over to the kneeling girls. Then she slapped Theresa with the back of her hand.

The next morning, David woke up feeling drained, dismayed, disheartened, and disgusted as his stomach wanted to vomit at his reflection. He stared at himself in the mirror and wondered, *how did I lose control, and what were those mind-warping words she said before I lost my ever-loving mind? Was that crazy, old coot not so kooky after all? Or do that crazy, old Indian and the ancient Father Hemmings have some validation for their warnings?*

David tried to wash the shame from his body as he stood in the shower under the pounding water. He scrubbed his soiled skin to erase the sin of his adulterated act. He then sat on the bed of his defeat as he wracked his brain, trying to figure out how such a formulated fornication came to be. He dragged himself into a deluge of denigration, distraught at the sight of the blinking, red light upon the answering machine. It took a mountain of strength just to push play, as his heart hammered and fluttered, falling to his feet as he awaited the recorded log.

Sarah's voice rang out a distressful plea for David to pick up the phone, warning him about Nina's twisted perversions without giving herself away. She tried to hold on to her own dignity amid the crisis and turmoil; she would take her secrets to her grave. Her unyielding, unrequited soul stirred her to call three more times with three more pleas of love-torn sorrow. Again and again, she rang out a desperate appeal for David to pick up the phone, calling his name into the vacant receiver. David stood staring upon the spot where it all began as he toiled in a remorseful reproach.

His mental conflict of clouded conjecture wove away a

contemptible daydream of confusion. He was hopeful with delusionary optimism that the hallucinogenic nightmare was the product of his unwanted visions.

The doorbell rang halfway through his resentful recollection, dragging him back to reality. When he opened the door, two FBI agents stood in front of him in their three-piece suits and sunglasses, hiding any hints of discernment. Behind them was an army of forensic lab clones dressed in white. In David's perception, they were there to collaborate on a cooperative assessment of the recent episode of his vanished deputies.

The taller one spoke. "Good morning, Sheriff. We have a search warrant to inspect the premises of your home." He then waved his arm to the lab clones as he asked David to step inside and hand him a search warrant.

"What's this all about?" David demanded as he looked over the legal form in stupefaction. The shorter one, Agent Herbert, spoke up. "I'm sure you already know. Now, if you step inside, we'll remind you all about it." David turned back into the living room as ten men followed behind. He turned around and demanded once more to know what the indictment portrayed and for what reason was, he suspected. The taller one told David to sit on the sofa as the clones dispersed into a thorough search of the house.

Agent Herbert spoke with a scratchy, discorded voice. "Looks like we got ourselves a crooked cop who likes corn holes."

David thought to himself that he'd rather face that vile Beast again instead of confronting the allegations he surmised the two suits were insinuating. The two feds played good cop-bad cop as the tall Fed talked in a warm, low-key voice and the short one like fingernails on a chalkboard.

216

A profusion of questions arose that hit David at every angle with explicit inquisition.

"So, Mr. Lang," Agent Herbert lashed out, "So, you like young girls. They turn you on, do they?" "Fuck you," David shouted back and returned to his silent fume of anger.

Agent Herbert then said, "Come on, Sheriff. Oh no, wait a minute, I'm not going to call you Sheriff because it sickens me to think you're one of us."

The taller fed held back, the shorter hothead with his arm but let him continue the interrogation as Agent Herbert ensued. "So, Mr. Lang, why don't you let me explain what happened last night, and you just nod your head yes or no? Mrs. Nina Saputo came to your house heartbroken over your little daughter being sick and all to ask you how she's doing."

David immediately shook his head no as the accusing fed persisted with headhunting tactics. "She feels sorry for your pathetic, pitiful puss and cooks you a warm meal. Then bam! You take the sweet little dame to your room, where you sodomized her repeatedly! You can tell me, we're all guys here."

David sprung to his feet and lunged for the short Fed. He shoved him off his feet flat and on his posterior. Then he yelled for him to get back up so he could plant him back down. The taller fed jumped in the middle of the two and told his counterpart to go have a smoke and that he'd handle it from here. He waited until his partner left the room before he reached into his jacket for a pack of smokes and then shuffled the contents until two tobacco sticks protruded. He offered one to David. David shook his head as the Fed drew away his offer and stuffed the pack back in his pocket.

The fed commended him for pushing his partner on his ass, telling him how he gets on his own nerves occasionally.

217

David stared at the fed with contemptuous eyes. "You know, it's hard for me to have this conversation when I don't even know who I'm talking to," David commented, referring to the fed's dark sunglasses and no name offered.

The fed apologized as he lifted his wire rims from his long, narrow face, then replied, "Agent Mark Dickerson, from DC." David said nothing for a moment, then stated, "Aren't your feds a little far from home?"

Federal Officer Dickerson smiled, then replied, "Let's just say we were in the neighborhood when we got the call."

David scoffed with sarcasm. "Well, it sure seems funny the impeccable timing you have, along with this convenient predicament I'm suddenly in."

"I'm sorry, Mr. Lang, but I'm sure I don't have to tell you about the procedure. We're just following orders. You should understand that after being a cop for seventeen years and all."

David glared at him with brain-ticking eyes as his thoughts engaged in dark corners where villainous characters hid with pernicious intent. "Let me guess," David said, "He wouldn't just happen to live in a valley, drive a black Benz, and own a billion-dollar corporation, now, would he?"

The fed appeared to be caught off-guard by such a question, as any sign of guilt was barely legible on his trained, expressionless face. "I'm sorry, Mr. Lang, but I'm at a loss as with whom you're alleging I'm acquainted. Though I did take notice of the lavish home Mrs. Saputo is living in when we took the report."

"Well, Mr. Dickerson, I never said Nina lived at your higher, oh, I mean Mr. Demas's mansion. Looks to me like your building blocks have a weak link."

The fed's face became ruby red as if David had struck a nerve. He stammered for words, jumping back to the case at hand. "Now tell me, Mr. Lang, did you have sexual intercourse with Mrs. Nina Saputo? As you know, my lab boys will find out anyways, so you might as well come clean."

David sat silent for a moment as the fed stared deeply at him, awaiting an answer. "I'll come clean, Mr. Dickerson. I slightly remember some intercourse. But I also remember my senses in their usual condition until I ate the little concoction she fed me. Shortly after, I felt like a mouse in her cat's paw game, with no control of my own cognition. So, if anyone's the victim in this dilemma, it would be me. Because I never consented to anything with that little Vamp. In fact, since you and your little lab rats are so conveniently here, I want a blood test."

"That's no problem, Mr. Lang. Now, please, from the beginning, what time did Mrs. Saputo get here? What time did the intercourse take place? How long did the intercourse last? What kind of intercourse did you have? And what time did she leave? I want to know everything; you know the routine."

David sat feeling duped, betrayed, and royally fucked. He did indeed know the routine and recognized when a case was being built against him. He launched into a recollection of his humiliation as he humbled himself, giving the fed an honest description of the hellcat's involvement and his own. After twenty minutes of answering the same questions in varied forms, the phone rang.

David excused himself and walked to the end table where the cordless phone sat. Sarah's sweet voice sang into his ear with its promise of love everlasting as she simply said hello. She immediately plunged into her own propositions of queries, pumping him as to why he didn't answer the phone. David hit new heights of stress as he sat stumbling for words in a syllabicated stutter.

David decided not to cause her more pain than she already was going through with Lisa, so he told her that he sent Nina away and then fell asleep. He asked how Lisa was doing after Sarah seemed satisfied with the explanations he unraveled. Sarah explained how Lisa was in the process of her second dialysis, showing promise for recovery. She then told him Dr. Miranda and Carol had had a good time together the previous evening and would be going out again that night. Sarah began to launch into a long conversation, detailing how they'd make a good couple, until David cut her off, telling her he had urgent business at the station.

"Is everything alright?" she asked, as if still apprehensive after her unanswered calls.

He told her that Jim and Scott were still missing and that he loved her. After hanging up the phone, the lab drones packed up their tools and any possible evidence, including the linens and comforter from his bed.

"Is everything alright?" she asked, as if still apprehensive from her unanswered calls.

He told her that Jim and Scott were still missing and that he had to go, told her he loved her, and then quickly hung up the phone; the lab drones packed up their tools, including all the linens and the comforter from his bed.

One of the Lab-Whitecoat who was cut off from the rest of his colleagues, opened a white, metal case with glass tubes and syringes. He told David to roll up his sleeve and to take a seat. The lab monger sterilized his arm and then pricked his skin, filling two vials with the vitality of his life fluid. He safely secured his instruments and gently inserted the vibrant, red tubes of blood into a smaller case before rejoining his forensic faction.

The two feds emerged from the nooks and pigeonholes of the house. The short, scratchy-voiced Agent Herbert said nothing while the other gave David his card.

"You stay away from Mrs. Saputo and her house. You know the routine; call me if there's anything to get off your chest." David glared and studied Dickerson's face in a moment of pause. "You know I'm missing two deps," retorted David, as if he already knew they knew. The two feds smiled at each other, then paused and studied David's face in the same fashion as he did theirs. Agent Herbert broke the silence and replied, "Well, if they're anything like their crooked boss, they'll probably be up to no good."

David restrained his anger, then calmly spoke in a low, subdued tone, "You better get the fuck out now before he has to crawl out."

The short, paunchy agent puffed out his chest and cocked forward as his partner halted him once more. This time, David smirked in glee. Agent Dickerson nodded his head sideways towards the exit as he said to his partner, "Let's go." Agent Herbert promised David that he'd see him again soon, behind bars, as he followed his partner out the door.

They exited the house, and David followed them to slam the door. Then he saw Johnny strolling up the walk, gawking at the feds as they passed by. David held the door open as he watched the feds leave and Johnny approaching.

"You guys here because of that giant Freak Thing," Johnny blurted out like a blubbering high school kid. David squinted his face as he murmured to himself, "Damm it, Johnny."

Both agents burst out laughing as they walked past him and got into their car. The young deputy slowed his pace in bafflement, rubbernecking back and forth between them driving away and David standing at the front door.

"What gives?" asked Johnny as he approached the porch.

David just shook his head and told him to go into the house. Johnny followed him into the living room, where David cursed as he sat down, dismayed and silent. Johnny had never seen his mentor so dismayed before as he stood in the middle of the room without a word while David continued his silence.

"What's wrong, boss?" asked Johnny, breaking the silence.

David said nothing as he looked at the floor. Johnny found the sofa and sat quit waiting for David to speak. David just stares out into space until Johnny breaks the silence. "Why did those feds laugh at me when I asked about that giant freak? Let 'me guess. They didn't believe you."

Constrained in heavy thought, David recalled Nina's bewitching words just before he lost it. "I'm sorry, Johnny, what was it you said?"

"The feds, they must've not believed you; that's why they laughed at me, right? Don't pay them no mind. I guess the bureau lowered their standards' any' Putz with a high school diploma could be a fed nowadays."

"Johnny, as long as you've known me, I've always been a standup guy, huh?" Johnny smiled, "The best, boss, the best. Why, you ask?"

David shook his head. "Those fucks think I raped that tramp who lives at the mansion with our Devin Demas and Thomas Syck. Man, I tell you, just between you and me, somehow that bitch got me in the sack last night, and it really looks bad for me."

Johnny looked confounded. "What are you saying? She slipped you a Mickey."

"She must of," said David as he raised his hands in question. "I'm not going to throw my marriage away for a quick roll in the hay. There's got to be a reason I lost my mind like that; there's got to be! She came over and insisted that she cook me a warm meal and wouldn't take no for an answer. Renae came over looking for Scott, and I told her that we'd search for them in the morning.

After she left, my head went haywire. That bitch, Nina, said some weird stuff, like a verse or poem. And what's really fucked up is that I was more than willing. I felt as if I was insane last night. It was as if she was in my brain, making me do things I would never do on my own. I was more than content with being her toy. It was even more than that; I felt like a hungry Beast that couldn't fill its appetite.

And when she left, it was worse, as if she took my mind and my soul. I felt completely lost without her. Man, I tell you, if she wanted to cut my nuts off, I would've handed her the knife."

Johnny didn't know what to say or think as he looked at his mentor like he was human after all in his present moment of weakness. David raised his head and looked straight at Johnny with a look of grave importance on his face.

"Johnny, you've known me for a long time. I consider myself mentally sound and proficient at what I do, but I think what we have here is some kind of Devil Witch Cult. I'm not talking about something like those old fairy tales of old hags on broomsticks concocting a brew. I'm talking about Worldly, powerful people who could turn a man's brain inside out. Or exhuming a cemetery full of coffins without a trace of them being dug up. And here's one you could relate to---two of our own are missing. Then a giant Freak Thing, as you call it, kills two state troopers and chases you up a tree. And now I have the feds up my ass insinuating I raped that woman last night.

To top it off, there's a reporter running around that would be dancing in his shoes if he caught wind of this bullshit charge. The state cops won't come to our county anymore under the illusion their boys died from a car wreck."

Johnny considered David's accusations and theories of the corresponding contrivance while horror crept back into his brain. They both became quiet for a moment as they thought about the recent recourse of the eerie events of witchery. David wondered if Johnny's brain was ticking to the doubt of his story.

David ended the silence as he popped up from his recliner and told Johnny he'd meet him at the station. Johnny walked through the awkward air to the front door, clearing his voice and gripping his hat firmly with both hands, shell-shocked.

"Hey, ah, Johnny."

"Yeah, boss."

"Don't worry about me. Treat this case like any other. Just be honest, okay, Officer Morgan."

Johnny turned toward David as he stood in the doorway, his respect for his mentor diminishing. "No problem, boss. I'm sure we'll clear your good name," he returned as if trying to reassure his own doubts. Johnny nodded in respect while putting on his hat to its normal slight tilt, then exited in silence.

David smiled at his friend, then turned to find the keys of his other deputy, which were now in his possession. Walking into the bedroom, he gazed upon the striped mattress of his disdain, where he noticed his crumpled pants that were left there from his raging hormones. David shook his head in disgust as he reached for the foul reminder of his actions and dug deep into the pockets until he heard the jingle. He quickly turned and shut the door as a sickly slime coated his stomach

224

and began to stir his sanity. He left the house, got into the cruiser, and peeled off towards the station.

When parking in his regular spot, David noticed a red Ford Focus in the visitor's lot. He walked into the station and found Johnny and Pat at the front desk and a reporter sitting by the coffee machine, waiting to see him. He sat there like a stealthy vulture awaiting a carcass for its consumption. The reporter jumped to his feet and announced his presence as David quickly walked past him to the front desk and asked Pat the status of things and if he had any missed calls.

Pat shook her head and rolled her eyes towards the reporter as he sat back down.

All three law enforcement staff members conversed in low whispers, then broke out in a mockery of laughter as Johnny slipped and accidentally caught the eye of reporter Porter Lewis. David caught sight of Johnny's quick break and asked the young deputy to follow him to his office. Pat headed towards the coffee machine to concoct David's normal French vanilla as Porter blurted out to David, "I'm not here to defame your good town, Sheriff. I'm just curious how there are three dead, and all those coffins pop up like that."

David halted at the entrance to his office and turned to the person he despised and recounted, "Oh, I recall someone announcing to the world just the opposite of your claims. I also recall 'someone' disclaiming our good town as mismanaged and incompetent, so ah, if you'd excuse us, we're going to muster ourselves to get some work done around here."

Porter retracted his practiced social smile, and Johnny regained his while following David and closing the door behind them. Once inside the confines of the office, David and Johnny calculated with purposeful intent the locations of the bizarre action spots with red markers on a giant map of the county. Each mark revealed a date and time and the horror of its circumstance with graphic pictures.

Pat tapped on the door armed with David's coffee. When she opened it, both deputies looked past her at the still persistent Porter Lewis, who was sneaking a peek back at them. "Still here, I see," said David as he retrieved his morning brew from Pat.

"Oh yeah," she replied. "I don't think he's going to go away too easy without someone talking to him."

David smiled at the word "someone," knowing that that someone was him. "Just hold all my calls and try to send him away, huh."

"You got it, Sheriff," announced Pat as she reclosed the door behind her.

The two deputies proceeded to analyze and reanalyze every detail while arranging the sequential combination to coincide with recent events. They also had over twenty names on a white marker board, with red letters describing the category of their status.

After an hour of wracking their brains and trading thoughts, David grabbed his sunglasses and told Johnny, "Let's get a bite to eat. We can continue this conversation over breakfast, look at the clock, or lunch."

"I'm up for that," returned Johnny as he grabbed his hat and followed David into the lobby, where, guess what, he was still waiting.

David and Johnny made a beeline past him to the front door until the reporter blurted out, "Devin Demas," which led David to recoil in surprise and curiosity. He halted and turned in the doorway and then smiled and gestured with his finger

226

for Porter to come forward. "You just said the magic words, Mr. Lewis."

Porter straightened and followed with relief. He finally had David's attention, and his value had been reconsidered. Once outside, it was David who was asking the questions. What did the reporter know, and how did he come to know it? Porter looked side to side, showing his paranoia, and told David he wouldn't talk on the street.

"Very well," David replied. "I guess I owe you breakfast for making you wait. You care to join us for some of Dana's famous green grits?" Porter gave a quizzical grin and returned, "I don't know about the green grits, but I'll sure have some more of that apple pie she has over there."

David grinned back at the little man and then replied, "Been scoping us out, huh?" Porter smiled and remarked, "Perhaps," as they crossed the street to the place he had indeed been hanging out in for hours earlier that morning.

As they entered the diner, all eyes turned to them in small-town fashion while David led the way to the corner booth away from the curious ears of spectators. Soon after, everyone was in place when Dana approached the table. "More pie and coffee, Mr. Lewis?" she snapped, as if not happy about his presence.

David lifted his hand and froze her in place. He asked Porter to give the good lady his order. Porter smiled and said that more pie would be just fine. David and Johnny both ordered Dana's Southern omelet and her one-of-a-kind green grits. She snapped out once more and said snobbishly to Porter, uh-huh.

After she walked away, David wasted no time as he inquired, "So ah, you were saying about our infamous Mr. Demas."

227

Porter reversed the conversation three hundred sixty degree turn as he stated his good wishes for little Lisa with a tone of compassion in his voice. David said nothing but wondered how this man came to know his personal business as he cleared his cracking voice.

"You were saying about our Mr. Demas."

Porter Lewis straightened again and reframed himself, then said, "You know there's a funny thing about our Mr. Demas; he doesn't exist, no prior trace, no papers, no medical or birth records. Nothing but his ownership of half the planet."

Johnny blurted from the edge of his seat. Yea, everyone knows he's stinking rich, but nobody can live on this planet anymore without being recorded unless you are born in New Guinea or something.

David smiled but said nothing. The look on his face suggested Porter continues. "Right, right," returned Porter, as if caught off guard. "Any fool could be rich. You could call it global domination; I would call it global damnation, in the wrong hands, that is." Porter went on.

"Let me ask you guys a question: ever heard of the True Alliance Corporation?"

"What about it?" said David in quick return. "Oh, you have heard of them, I mean him. Him, as in Demas," returned David. "He is more powerful than the President of the United States," proclaimed Porter. "Hell, he probably has a key to the front door of the white house. Come on," protested Johnny, "that's a little extreme, isn't it?"

Dana abruptly intervened with two Southern plates with green grits on the side and apple pie for Porter. David thanked Dana as she topped off everyone's coffee.

Porter continued, "Extreme? I'll give you extreme. How come whenever there is a solar eclipse in different parts of the world, there is a trail of sacrificed corpses, and your Mr. Demas always happens to be in the neighborhood? Or how 'bout this, wherever in the world he has a residence, the same kind of havoc occurs that your good little town has undergone."

David's brain began to swell from the stress of the new information, but at the same time, he was grateful to learn more about his growing nemesis.

Porter continued, "Or how about that maniacal clique that hangs with him? Bats in the belfry, if you get my drift. And what about that charming fellow, Thomas Syck? When he was just nine years old, he killed one of his fellow classmates because the poor lad gave a valentine to a girl he had a crush on." Porter's voice became melancholy. "The other children witnessed him push the little boy in front of a bus. Syck was acquitted of being so young, and he claimed it was an accident and that he himself was tripped and was a victim. And I'm sure I don't even have to tell you about a lifelong record he's accumulated in fifteen states and twelve different countries. Geez, he's had so many other deputies, state troopers, and every other law enforcement agency go mad trying to put him away. But he has those lawyers from New York and LA that get him out of whatever he gets into."

David's ears began to ring. Distant sounds of utensils scraping the bottom of plates and gnashing teeth throughout the room pounded in David's head. He began to descend into his early morning sickly stomach feeling.

Porter dallied over his pie and continued, "Let's not forget about that vixen Nina Saputo, notorious Priest hacker. The headlines read 'Priest Hacker Found Innocent. Self-defense for being raped? They found the Priest in pieces scattered about the monastery! Oh, and I can guess who came out of nowhere to defend her with the same New York Lawyers who defended our mister Syck. From what I heard, they dismantled the prosecutor's case and handed it back to them in the dissembled pieces. They had the jury eating the crumbs from their palms and had some of the jurors crying in empathy for the young Nina at the time, who never even stood witness in court."

Porter sighed as if relieved to tell all that he knew to someone who might not mistake him for being insane. He went on. "My good Sheriff, if you can imagine all the things they had to defend with top lawyers, and still they basically got away with murder. Imagine all the things they get away with and never get caught."

David nodded his head as he stared deep into the green grits on his plate, swirling them about as he had lost his appetite. Dana once again approached the booth and asked Johnny and David if everything was alright. Johnny hurried his last bite and then handed his plate to Dana, proclaiming the food was good as always. Dana smiled and took his plate, then quickly dropped her mirthful grin as she eyed David's hardly touched plate.

"What's the matter, Sheriff? Lost your appetite from the company you're keeping?" she barked as she took Porter's little pie plate.

"Now, now, Dana, you be nice to our new friend here. He's okay, just a little misunderstood right now."

Dana reached with her free hand into her apron pocket, tossed a check on the table, and said, "Whatever you say, Sheriff," before she returned to her other customers.

David turned to Porter, "So, how do you fit into all this mess?"

"My father, my father was also a reporter," Porter replied.

"We've been following the bloody trail of Devin Demas for quite some time," said Porter, pulling out a photo. "Here, here's a famous picture of the Enola Gay aircraft the day before Hiroshima and Nagasaki. See the date on the bottom of the picture."

Both David and Johnny goose-necked to focus on the date.

"Now, here, take a gander at this one. It was taken the same day, just before they dropped those nukes." David stared at the old photograph, aged with time, and saw Devin's unmistakable image in front of the plane that was responsible for taking countless lives. He stood alone under the craft's iconic logo.

Johnny laughed aloud, "You're off your rocker, reporter man."

Porter just shook his head as he retrieved the picture and put it back into his pocket while David studied Porter's demeanor in silence. "Now, let me ask you two a question. You guys of the law are pretty much rational, black-and-white thinkers, only the facts with no in-between, am I right?"

"Well, if your hands are caught in the cookie jar, that pretty much sums it up," Johnny announced as David just listened. "Hmmm," Porter sighed, "I assure you that there are paranormal occultisms of the black arts, and they believe wholeheartedly in their dark messiah and are willing to kill or die for him."

The two deputies became speechless. They looked at each other as if Porter Lewis just confirmed David's earlier assumptions.

"Witches, my good Sheriff, Witches. Have you ever considered their perilous endowments and the downright nasty powers they possess?"

David shook his head, not yet replied, "But I get a feeling that I should start."

"Listen, Sheriff, I'm not a religious man. Hell, I couldn't hold a candle, let alone hold one in church. I'm a man of cold, hard facts, one who deals on the grounds of proof and substantiation, much like yourselves in law enforcement. Affirmative authentication is my bible. As sure as I'm talking to you, it is as positive as I am through a measured calculation that there's a bloody trail leading to Devin's door. And some kind of witchery points out at every angle to be the irrefutable fact. I may not believe in the spiritual world, but they most certainly do, and the morgue's filling up with stiffs to prove it."

"Why, Mr. Lewis, you're not so much the pompous ass half the town thinks you to be and that I myself thought the same just an hour ago."

"I'm sorry, Sheriff, if you're referring to the report of the state troopers' deaths. That was just a shim-sham to keep folks from wandering through your town."

David's eyes lit up with admiration as he commended Porter for his foresight. "Looks like you didn't have much of an appetite, huh Sheriff," Porter commented, looking down upon his omelet still intact.

David shrugged his heavy shoulders. He then went for his wallet until Johnny grabbed the check. "I got this one, boss," he said as he quickly stepped up to the register.

Porter scooted out from the booth as his eyes remained fixed upon Johnny. "Well," said Porter, "At least you have good people on your side; I'd make sure you keep them there if I were you."

David stood as he glanced at the young deputy and agreed that he was lucky to have an honest, good man like Johnny.

After Johnny paid the check, the two deputies walked Porter to his car. The now revered reporter had revealed how Devin most assuredly had something to do with the Smithsonian murder and the thievery of the *Egyptian Book of the Dead*. David recanted the report he had seen at the hospital and the top-of-the-line security and surveillance that had been encroached upon.

Porter climbed into his car and rolled down the window for a last word. "I don't mean to sound so uncanny and blunt, my good Sheriff, but you need to put away all notions of conventional methods and thoughts. These aren't the run-of-the-mill criminals you're dealing with. No, I'm talking about utter immoralities of the most powerful kind. And I'd bet my last dollar our Mr. Demas has the FBI and CIA, along with Congress, stuffed in his shirt pocket."

David's mind drifted to strange Worlds of scandalous espionage as he mumbled out loud, "It all makes sense."

"What's that?" Porter asked as he studied David's face.

David reeled back to Earth and then said, "Oh, nothing, just a hunch on another mishap."

"Very well," announced Porter. "I'll be at the Berry Bush Hotel if you need anything."

"Thank you," David replied. "You've been a big help."

Porter nodded in respect, then drove away. David and Johnny walked back to the station, where they decided to assemble a search team to find their still missing deputies. David called Old-Man Joe and the Willards brothers, who were also known as the Hound brothers, owning a hound kennel just outside of town. An hour later, they were assembled, with a few more gunned stragglers David hadn't accounted for. They crowded in front of the station, where David instructed in the targeted search area.

One of the Willard brothers hollered, "What if that Monster that Bob Blanchard talked about is out there? Hell, it probably ate your deputies."

The small crowd fussed about as the word "Monster" rang out more than once. David shouted above the disturbance, "Hey, hey," hushing the crowd. "Now, I'm not going to lie to you all. There is something out there, something I don't know how to describe. But we have two of our own out there somewhere with their wives and children at home and worried sick, and quite frankly, I'm sick about it too; I mean their family, and right now, they need the best we got to get them home."

The crowd fidgeted and then came to order, drawing courage from David's words. "I can't believe what I'm about to say out loud," David first said to himself. Then, he began to address the group. "I'm not going to candy-coat this situation. There is some kind of Monster thing out there. But that damn thing is more afraid of you than you should be of it. I shot at that thing, and it ran like a rabbit running from a coyote. Now remember, we're looking for my deputies, Jim and Scott. So, if you see that thing, don't, I repeat, don't shoot at it. Just turn the other way and call in on these walkie-talkies we're about to give each of you."

The small crowd gathered in front of Johnny, and he began handing out the handheld radios. The pack of backwoods gunmen scattered to their trucks and headed towards Blain Road, where David would direct the rudderless henchmen. Johnny gave two articles of clothing that bore the scent of Jim and Scott to the Willard brothers. David felt like he was trying to teach adolescent boys with short attention spans how to scout the territory, even though the Willards were equipped with their hounds. Apprehensive with doubt, he let loose the wayward, unorganized stooges into the forest. But at least he had Johnny and Old-Man Joe to somewhat counter the ineptitude of the bunch. He also took the Willard brothers under his wing as they fanned to the left, with Johnny and Old-Man-Joe to the right and the others following from behind.

David gave orders with hand signals as both crews maneuvered a sweeping line of a half-block radius. The hounds began to howl shortly after they caught a scent. They beat past the point where David chased the Beast away from the treed Johnny. Onward, they pushed as the hounds longed to take up their chase while worry for his makeshift enlistees began to weigh on David. They passed old Could Creek and Bob Blanchard's farm, which lay to his left. David began to regret his judgment of involving the locals, but still onward, they marched, and they were now about a mile from where they started. The yelping and yipping of the hounds began to pound in David's head, along with the hunger from skipping the omelet he left on a plate back at Dana's. The late afternoon commenced embarking upon the timbers as David began to lose faith in ever-setting eyes on Jim and Scott again. Still, the hounds howled on, and so must he continue onward.

Suddenly, there it stood, the tri-hooved creature drenched in trepidation and unable to effectively hide behind a tree. The group halted as it squealed out warnings like a cornered animal might react in fear. The Beast cried out as though it knew it was prey to the riffled men. It seemed to be trying to communicate with hand signals and wails of its own. One of Willard's lifted his thirty-odd-six with the creature in its sights. David batted it upward to the sky and commanded, "No!"

The hick cussed at David as if he was short-changed from a kill he had intended from the start. David just stared at the creature, and he began to see the resemblance to Jim and Scott, of which Johnny had spoken. The hounds went nuts in the direction of the giant Beast as David spoke out loudly, "No way, it can't be!"

"What the hell did you do that for?" the younger of the Willard brothers protested.

"I've got my reasons," David barked back. "For one, you're just going to piss that thing off with those mosquito pellets. And for the two, I have a different plan. And as for three, I'm the one wearing the badge."

The two brothers appeared baffled as they protested with disapproving enthusiasm. David remained unyielding as he ordered a strategic withdrawal. The hound boys couldn't nor wouldn't understand David's reasoning as they jaw-jacked about how they could have killed the giant Devil and went on to say that the blood would be on David's hands. David didn't give a rat's ass about their comments and figured they probably just wanted bragging rights at Buckeye Buck's. He then whispered on the radio to Johnny out of earshot of the bickering brothers.

"Let's head back and get rid of these clowns."

"Ten-four on that one, boss."

With displeased huffs and hand signals, David commanded that they turn around as quietly as he could muster himself. The trisected creature continued trembling with its atrocious back to a ravine, trapped and corralled.

David emphatically waved his hand back in the direction from which they came as he stood in between the Beast and the Willard boys and their hounds. The misfits scoffed with displeasure at David's decision. In compliance, they turned, with the cowardly sheriff tight behind them, pushing them back towards the road.

Moments later, David and the Willard brothers emerged

from the trail and were back on the road, where the Willards continued their griping about what would have been a clear shot at the foul Beast. Johnny and Old-Man Joe waited for David by his cruiser as the Willards quickly huddled with the others who were with Johnny. Old-Man Joe, Johnny, and David gathered, with the Willard herd sneering and jeering. They became louder and louder with opinions that deviated from those of the deputies. The elder Willard Ray took the helm of stupidity, shouting out that they were going back out into the forest to kill that thing. At his wit's end, David unholstered his sidearm and shot into the sky three times to get everyone's attention.

"Hear me out. I'm only saying this once. Go home and stay there. If I see you hanging around these sticks, you'll be going to the clinker. Now, I know I brought you all out here, and I assure you I'm very sorry for that decision. But if you stay out here and I see you, you will be prosecuted. Gott me?"

"Yeah, we got you," retorted Ray. "So meanwhile, that thing's camping out in our backyards."

"Well, like I said, you have a choice---a nice, cozy bed at home or a cold, steel tray and a cot at the clinker."

They mumbled among themselves, then got into their trucks and spit gravel from their tires as they drove away toward town. After they disappeared around the bend, Old-Man Joe patted David on the shoulder, bantering about "good intent."

That same evening, Devin hosted a World conference for the United Nations in Geneva and, for the first time, let himself be televised. He somehow had convinced the delegates who represented countries that had been at war with each other for over five hundred years to sit at the same table and talk. Not only did they talk, but they also laid out plans for peace and exchanged public apologies for past conflicts. This unexpected onslaught of goodwill dazed the United Nations Organization, and Devin's name began to appear on the lips of admirers. News agencies from all over the World called him the new political influencer of policy as they praised his name with passion. Cameras panned and focused on Devin as the President from Turkey presented Devin with a blue turban that had a ruby on its front in honor of his illustrious illusion of peace. Even the Secretary of State of the United States presented him with the Nobel Prize for his role in the pacification of raging global hostilities. He stood behind a podium wearing his turban as he raised his award above his head, and a thousand cameras flashed their canonizing lights. Parades were held, and banners were hung honoring the new peacemaker who graced them with his presence.

After Devin departed and applause was given, the ticker tape swept as all that was left was the semblance of a spent-spirited concession. In the prophecy of his scrolls, he was always in precise mathematical conjunction of the constellation and solar eclipse. By following his scrolls, he found himself just a few hundred miles from his birthplace, where he would visit.

Ora accompanied him on his journey as she witnessed the grounds on which he was spawned while being reminded of his first sins. His destiny would rear its ugly head during the ungodly timing of a solar eclipse. Ten of his disciples awaited him in preparation and presented him with two sacrificial lambs.

Two of the disciples offered themselves the promise of immortality as their hearts lay inside a pentagram ripped and deflated upon the soil under the eclipsed sky.

Devin turned his attention to the darkening sky. He called upon the old serpent of deception and cried out for the depravity of mankind and all his works in the World. He shouted words in Latin and Hebrew as the followers chanted foul phrases in the background of Devin's rant. One by one, various corners of the world reigned with chaotic devastations that were indigenous to those areas. Seattle was hit by devastating Earthquakes. Japan suffered a high death toll from the tsunami. Hurricanes ripped through the Bahamian islands, bouncing off the small bodies of land and onto Miami.

Florida was ravaged by an overflow of torrential rainstorms, destroying life and land. Forrest fires and sinkholes consume the planet as if Hell was trying to force its presence into the destruction of those it touched. Many ran to their churches to pray. Others converted in haste to varied denominations across the globe, as others basked in debauchery. After a short time, Devin emerged. He headed up the True Alliance organization, making emergency medical supplies with food drops in the rural areas unattainable by vehicle, his continued illusion of peacemaker.

David sat home as Devin's face was plastered on every channel while the media asked whether he was on the Vatican's list for sainthood. Devin smiled into the camera, almost as if he felt David's eyes on him. "Does a ring and robe come with the title?" Devin joked.

The World news anchor laughed openly as he sucked up every word with great enthusiasm. David almost spewed, becoming sick to his stomach from the Evil before his eyes.

Sarah remained in Harrisonville while David commuted between the hospital, hotel, and home. He was getting worn down from the stress of all the problems that pounded on his shoulders with constant pressure. He had the FBI on his back with false accusations. His daughter remained in peril, her recovery crawling at a snail's rate. His mother was dating Dr. Miranda, who was surely a puppet by Devin's very hand. Sarah was in a shambles and on the verge of a mental breakdown over Lisa's condition. A fifteen-foot Freak thing unsolved murders that no agency wanted any part of, and no correspondence from the coroners. And now, a supposed Devil Cult in his backyard, with a leader dominant in worldly affairs. *How did all this come to be in my town? How did Nina drive me to my knees? What were those words she said? Oceans of lust, something, something, my righteous, wretched Soul?*

David's head swirled with everything going on while he glared at the source of his troubles on the television screen. He was about to turn in for the night when his heart suddenly dropped into his stomach as the doorbell sounded an unwelcome tone.

His mind raced with the thought of unsavory guests. Should I answer? He pondered. Maybe they'll go away. Maybe I'll just go to bed and wake up with little Lisa in between me and Sarah, David thought. But he dutifully dragged himself to the dreaded door.

He opened the door, and the same FBI Agents-- Dickerson and –Herbert stood on the porch, like phantoms in black suits.

"Hello, Mr. Lang. May we come in? I don't think you want any passing motorist to see their sheriff get to read his rights," Agent Herbert advised.

David knew that talking would be useless, so he simply turned and walked back into the living room, where he asked which court he would be bonded to.

Agent Herbert gently seized David by his sleeve and motioned for him to turn around to be cuffed. "We'll know when we get there, now, won't we."

They marched David to a black unmarked Suburban with black-tinted windows. Inside in the back was a custom-captain's chair with its steel frame welded to the floor, chains and shackles for every limb, and a clear face mask on a swivel. "What kind of Hannibal Lecter contraption is this?" said David. "I'm not getting into that thing." Agent Herbert quickly returned, "Well, it can only go two ways, we can put you in that contraption a bloody mess, or you can be a lamb and sit your ass down." David looked to Agent Dickerson as Dickerson nodded his head and softly said, "It's ok, go ahead.

David shook his head and complied as he drew into himself while they secured him into harsh, cold reality. For two grueling hours, they ridiculed and taunted him until they approached downtown Columbus.

They drove to the check-in point of David's new hell---jail, where they handed David to their custody. After he was booked, printed, and deloused, the jail's deputy marched him to his cell. But first, he was allowed to collect calls from a phone on the wall.

David wasted no time and called Johnny to tell him his whereabouts. He asked Johnny to step up and take up as sheriff and not to worry about him. David went on to tell of a twisted game Devin was playing with him and that he had to ride it out to find the reason for it all.

Johnny argued David's point, saying that he was needed on the front lines of Lang Township in its present condition. "You'll be better off outa jail, boss."

Click; David pushed down the lever and then released it. He stood with the receiver in his hand, hearing a hang-up tone. David replaced the receiver on the wall and sat down, just tired and yearning for his family.

Johnny immediately called Charley and told him that Pat was in charge and to call him on his cell phone if needed. He then went home, changed into civilian clothes, kissed Amanda and the boys, and then got into his truck and peeled away. He arrived in Columbia by 3:30 a.m. and was getting the runaround at the front desk about David's situation.

The deputy at the front desk stared into his computer as he told Johnny there would be no visitation until David saw the judge Monday morning, which meant a night behind bars. Johnny told Amanda about the bogus charges they railroaded David with and that he wouldn't be back home till he could help straighten out the mess.

"What could you do?" Amanda asked, concerned about her husband.

"Well," Johnny stammered. "I could ask around the other deputies if they heard anything or know why the FBI is involved. There's lots of things I can poke at."

Amanda paused, then said, "Do what you got to do, champ."

They exchanged I love you-s then Johnny left town. He began to think he made the wrong decision as big city noise and confusion reeled in his head. *How could I leave the station solely in the hands of Charley and Pat? That wasn't fair to them. What the fuck was I thinking?* Johnny regrouped and decided to find a hotel to get a fresh start in the morning.

That same night, Johnny's dog Bandit wandered wayward into the dark, dense forest. This, by no means, was the first time the dog strolled away.

Sometimes, he vanished for days. But this time, he strolled into the path of a strange scent, which pulled his prying nostrils toward its source. The scent lured him past tobacco fields and old cotton plantations and over Could Creek into the basin of the valley. The scent became stronger, its pungent stench of fresh carcass emanating throughout the valley. The malodorous scent drew the enchanted dog to the old mansion where the ancient pentagram spewed black blood from the crevice of its cursed earth.

The blackest of hate bled from the foul mouth of hell with the discharge of volatile deposits. Bandit slowly lingered at the edge of the murky, opaque liquid, where he licked up a bellyful. The dog violently turned from the tarry solution and vomited volatile eruptions. He spewed some of the black, syrupy substance in painful intervals as his stomach palpitated and he gasped for air. Bandit labored to eject the contents, with froth spurting in globules as his ribcage pumped violently. His every fiber struggled to gasp air through the black bubbles from his snout.

After turning away, the dog gagged at every trot, with his head hung to the ground. His ribcage collapsed upon every gasp. By morning, he shivered back home, where he crawled into the barn as if he were hungover from Evil. He dragged his body under the motorcycle trailer in his continuous strain of clog, his coat now drenched with sweat and his frame losing weight. He sprawled in shadows as shards of light shredded through the barn, and his brain screamed in sheer agony.

Teddy, the eldest of the two boys, finished his breakfast and then ran outside to find his faithful, four-legged friend. He called him out into the field in the back of the house, where his voice diffused into the vast emptiness of the enveloping blue sky. Teddy turned toward the barn as he thought he heard a slight movement.

"There you are, hiding in the barn. What-cha doing' in there?" he sang as he skipped towards the whimper. Teddy threw the large door open in a carefree manner while gaping far and wide as his eyes adjusted to the barn's light. The boy's eyes came half focused upon the whimpering dog under the trailer. Teddy wondered if his four-legged friend was alright, and he crawled on the ground to get a closer look.

"What in the World happened to you?" he questioned as he reached out to pet Bandit.

The dog's frame faced forward with his head turned away.

"You're all wet," declared Teddy, pulling out his hand to observe the wetness. He wiped his hand on his pants, then reached his hand under the trailer, this time not looking.

A low, grumbling growl gurgled from the globules on the dog's snout as he sank his teeth into the boy's hand. Teddy shrieked out as he recoiled his hand in shock. He gaped at the puncture wound, jolting in dismay. Teddy jumped to his feet and shuffled towards the door. The Devil dog chased and tripped the boy to the ground by chomping at his ankles. The boy cried out as the demented dog ate into him with piercing bites. Teddy lay balled up until the crazed animal became satisfied and carried his ailing body back under the trailer.

Teddy lay crying and calling out to his mother as black slime frothed upon his wounds. Amanda was preoccupied with her daily chores out of earshot of his pleas. The boy started to stagger to his feet, angering the frothing Beast, who protested his every move, inciting the boy to curl up and cry.

Amanda lifted her head from a load of clothes she was sorting and told little Timmy to find his brother and tell him he had chores around the house. She assumed he was playing somewhere on the farm and forgot his duties of taking out the trash and filling the dog dishes.

Timmy headed outside and called out, "Teddy," as he walked off the porch and heard no answer. So, he stuck out his arms in airplane fashion and roomed towards the barn. Timmy called out again, "Teddy."

Teddy seized his crying into a loathing seethe of hatred. He opened his blackened eyes with a face of detestable, abhorrent anger. He sprung to his feet, then scurried out into the painful light, where he announced his location.

Little Timmy whipped his head around and then ran to the barn. He stood at the entrance and called Teddy's name again before he fortuitously strolled into the barn. "Teddy, where are you?" he called.

He scoped the barn's interior. No answer was heard, and no Teddy was seen as he went further into the bard. He then saw Bandit in his repugnant state and became frightened at the sight of his ill-willed malevolence. Timmy spun around in a fear-stricken state to tell his mother what he had discovered when he turned right into Teddy. "What happened to you?" The vile-induced boy said nothing as Timmy seemed to be staring into a void. "Teddy, you're scaring me. Please talk to me. Why do you and Bandit look so awful?"

Teddy still said nothing as he started to sway to a silent song in his dull, mottled appearance.

"I'm going to tell," said Timmy as he began to walk around the offensive, odorous urchin.

"You're not going anywhere," said Teddy in a deep, distorted voice as he clenched Timmy's arm and hair.

"Teddy, you're hurting me!" Timmy cried while attempting to squirm away.

"You'll feel better in black, my little brother," Teddy ordered.

He then steered little Timmy towards the aversive rabid dog as little Timmy struggled, crying out, "No, Teddy, no!"

His words were unavailing to the bedevil Imp as he continued to push him towards the black-frothed dog. The little goblin laughed insanely as he held out little Timmy's hand to the pernicious Beast. Tears streamed from Timmy's eyes as he envisioned the terror of his torn skin.

The rancid animal roared out from its Devil den and ripped into Timmy's arm, maneuvering his body for a deeper bite. All the while, Teddy was laughing hysterically. Bandit retreated to his den.

"Stop your crying!" Teddy yelled as he twirled Timmy to the ground behind him. Little Timmy lay reeling and crying as he gripped his wound, repeating, "Why, Teddy, why?"

Teddy stood smiling over his brother. He vacillated over the affected boy in a haunting, hovering horror as he rocked left to right, tottering on the edges of his feet. Kneeling on the ground, Timmy's stomach jolted as black globules Frothed and poured out of his mouth, and his eyes went from blue to black. The requisitioned recruit stood with his brother as they stared into space and began to sway to a twisted, silent song that rang in their heads. Together, they turned towards the house in a slow march as Bandit tagged along with malicious intent.

Amanda had just hung up the phone after talking to Johnny and turned around. There they were, standing and staring. "Oh my God! What happened to you?" she stammered as she shuffled backward into the refrigerator.

"Hello, Mommy. We want to play, and the game's called 'Kill Her If- You Catch Her'."

Amanda stood petrified, appalled, and nauseated as she took in the ghastly sight of their soured serpent skin. The taller boy reached atop the counter for the nearest carving knife that came to hand.

"What are you doing? You put that down right now! You hear me, Teddy? I mean it, dammit!" Amanda cried out to reclaim her authority as her eyes welled with tears, and she shuffled in reverse from the room. Her words of love and then warnings of punishment went unheard as the boys quickened their pace with a delirious thirst for slaughter. Finally, she turned and ran towards the stairs, the twisted Imps chasing after her with visions of making her a human pincushion filled with knives.

Amanda fled to the second floor with Bandit nipping at her feet. She managed to make it to the sewing room and locked the hook latch on the door. She could hear pitter patters up the stairs as her confounded thoughts confused her. She sat with her back to the door as all drew silent, and she wondered what mayhem could be brewing. Twisted snickers were heard in the otherwise menacing silence, which shocked Amanda to her core with a fear she had never known. She turned around on all fours to glimpse under the crack of the door. Teddy's black eyes stared back as raw terror seared through her Soul. Teddy half sang, "I can see London, I can see France, I could see my mother, the fucking, little bitch."

Amanda shrieked as they pounded the door while turning the handle left to right over and over. She leaned her back against the door, pitching against it with all her might.

Teddy peeped through the bottom crack and saw the white flesh of Amanda's ankle and slashed her with a long kitchen knife. The implied urchins giggled at her pain as she howled in piercing distress, and her blood spilled rapidly in gruesome gore. She clenched her gushing gash in a fret as her fuddled faculties flirted with a mental breakdown. She hopped and hobbled to the sewing table, where she grabbed some cloth and wrapped her throbbing foot. Amanda bellowed out, bawling as she tied the final knot, all the while being taunted by pounds and scrapes upon the door and bedevil jeers.

"What the hell got into you?!" she screamed hysterically,

banging her palms to the floor.

"Devil's milk, Mommy. Delicious, black, Devil's milk. You want some?"

The vile Imps laughed in a twisted tune of torturous tenor as Amanda cried like she never cried before.

She then heard them skip down the stairs in a demented droll of snickers. Amanda limped to the door, keeping her guard up as she listened, and then turned the handle to catch a glimpse of her escape. All was quiet and empty, so she decided to step out and try for the phone in her bedroom down the hall. Just as she stuck her head out the door, Bandit lunged at her. She screamed and slammed the door on his nose. The crazed dog squealed and squirmed. She relocked the hook latch on the old door, then sat back down and continued her storm of tears.

For a short time, shadowed silence fell upon the house, absent the sound of her boys. Suddenly, the twisted voices returned as they hauled tools up the stairs that they poached from the garage. They brought tools they knew only by memory from their father's use around the house. A drill, a jigsaw, hammers, and electric cords were just a few weapons of encroachment they carried. They made several trips back and forth from the garage to the house until they were satisfied with their bounty. They foiled and fumbled about trying to figure out how to operate the electrical apparatuses. Ultimately, through trial and error, they added a final working drill to the sum.

Teddy took the drill and commenced to punch the first hole in the door. Amanda stood staring and waiting for a miracle, feeling like a trapped animal soon to be gored. The drill tapped its mark as it poked through.

Teddy put his eye up to the hole and then rang out, "Peek-a-boo, I see you!" He then said, "Don't cry, Mother, I just want to stop your living heart because the pounding hurts my head."

Amanda screamed at the top of her lungs, shell-shocked in fear as the Imps feverishly worked on the door, all the while snickering like hyenas on the hunt.

Amanda began to prepare to climb out the window for her escape as she scooped out her options. She guessed her best route was out to the overhang of the front porch, where there was a six-foot drop. She'd then have to sneak back into the house and the kitchen for her purse and the keys to her minivan. When she turned around, the door was drilled in the shape of a devil's head. She was wearing a crooked smile, and Teddy was looking through. She screamed at the sight of its ghastly image as the little Demons used all four hands together to work the jigsaw. She knew any minute now, they would break through, forcing her to make the decision to climb out the window to escape.

Amanda scrambled to evade their slashes, desperately straining to untangle herself from the rubbery limbs and move out of the reach of the jumping, killer Imps. She ripped her dress from the limb that was binding on her. Teddy began to study the shrub and walked to the other side, opposite Timmy, as Amanda plunged into the Earth. They now stood on both sides of her, Teddy to the left and Timmy to the right, with Amanda's back against the house. The demented dwarves laughed in a crazed frenzy of amusement as they poked their blades at their fear-riddled mother.

She turned to Timmy just as he thrust his blade into her thigh. Amanda let out a high-pitched yelp, then seized him by the locks of his hair and tossed him into the assailing Teddy, where they tumbled and fell.

She yowled in horrendous pain as she hobbled with the

knife deeply embedded in her thigh, laboring towards the side door. Streamed tears; she held the blade between her fingers and was in extreme pain with every step towards the door. The Imps took cruel pleasure in their pursuit as they persisted in their perverse predatory preoccupation with her death. Amanda ultimately made it to the door, then locked it behind her as the crazed, diminutive gnomes pounded and smashed the French door windows with their knives.

Amanda turned to see Bandit standing at the entrance of the kitchen and the hallway, which led to her escape route through the living room and out the front door. He slowly edged towards her with a grumbling growl, his shoulders hunched as he bared his canines. Teddy had managed to open the door as he retrieved his arm from the broken window. Amanda gazed down at the foam-frothed Beast and then over at the oncoming dwarves. She reached deep for her bravery and gripped the handle of the knife.

By this time, her fear had become rage as she gritted her teeth and said, "You hungry, boy, huh? Well, eat this."

Amanda plucked the blade from her thigh while letting out a blood-curdling scream. She then stabbed through the skull of the rabid Beast, and his legs collapsed under him.

"You fucking bitch, you killed Bandit!" Teddy yelled as he stormed at her with a long-blade knife.

Amanda stepped over the dead dog and grabbed her keys on the counter, then quickly dragged herself down the hall, her eyes now dry with determination.

"You fucking whore!" screamed Teddy as they chased on with warped faces plotting methods of slaughter.

Amanda threw furniture in their path to enable her to get to the front door. She reached and fumbled with the locks in a frenzy of desperation as the Imps closed in behind her. Amanda cried out in joy as the door opened and allowed her to escape.

She dashed with her two gaping wounds that pained her upon every step. Teddy jumped from the porch with Timmy closely behind as they closed in on the maimed fish-like sharks following the scent of blood. Amanda toiled with the keys, fumbling with yet another lock as she cursed and cried out in a cold sweat of fright. Finally, success and she climbed into the safe sanctuary that separated her from the serpents.

She started the van as they pressed their morbid, little faces against the window, and Teddy yelled, "You're not going anywhere, fucking-little-bitch, you hear me?!"

He then turned for the tires to slash them like he would her skin. Aware of his attempt, Amanda threw the vehicle into reverse and bolted backward, slamming the pedal to the floor. The Imps jumped up and down in delirium with rage upon the driveway as she pulled onto the road. Teddy flipped his middle finger while his brother continued to jump up and down in a reckless fit of delirium. Amanda began to bawl in a blaze of tears as she drove towards the sheriff's station.

After four miles of tears, Amanda limped into the station as Pat was blabbering on the phone in a prattle of small talk and gossip.

"Oh, my God! What in heaven to Betsy happened to you? "Pat announced as she hurriedly said goodbye to her caller.

"My sons," she cried as she slumped in a chair.

"Teddy and Timmy? What, are they okay?" demanded Pat in a soft, empathetic tone.

Amanda could barely get out the words through her tears

and disarray. "No, you don't understand. Teddy and Timmy did this to me," she finally choked out.

Pat's jaw dropped. "I'm sorry, but it sounded like you said that Teddy and Timmy did this to you." Amanda struggled for air, then grabbed Pat by the sleeve and strengthened her voice. "I'm telling you, my two boys did this to me. They were like possessed little Demons running around with knives." Amanda pointed to her wounds. "Need I say more?"

Pat was skeptical but acted sympathetic as she told her not to move while she went to retrieve the first aid kit. When Pat returned, Amanda had her head in her hands, whimpering and wailing in a fervid fuss. Empathy instantly filled Pat's soft side. She rushed to tend to Amanda's wounds and tried to lift her spirits. Amanda stared into space with an expressionless face, then said, "I could hardly recognize them. Their skin was God-awful green with black blotches, and in their eyes were black as Devil's sin."

Amanda could hardly finish her sentence as Pat put her hand on Amanda's shoulder, not really knowing what to say to someone with such a story. She just gave Amanda her ear and tended to her wounds, and all she could muster out was, "It's going to be alright, dear." After patching up Amanda, Pat called Charley. Pat mumbled to herself as she fuddled about looking for the keys to the weaponry deposit. When Pat found the keys and opened the giant gun deposit, Amanda's eyes widened as she uttered, "No, they're still my babies!"

Pat froze as she was reminded, "Oh, right, little ones," she replied as she closed the giant steel door.

She then turned to a smaller cabinet on the wall, with stun guns, mace, and other sorts of gadgets. Pat then told Amanda to stay at the station and asked if she could take any incoming calls.

"I'll do no such thing," returned Amanda. "I'm coming with you."

Pat was amazed Amanda would want to go back to the house and reluctantly caved in, but only if Amanda would stay in the cruiser.

After Amanda said she would comply, they left for the old Morgan farmhouse, where the supposed Demon children resided. When they approached the driveway, the Imps were dancing around ten-foot flames from a bale of hay they burned Bandit in. Pat wasted no time. She sped up the long driveway while the little Demons scurried into the barn. She slammed the shifter into the park, then commanded Amanda to stay put in the car as she tested the stun gun before entering the twilight zone. Amanda yelled out the window, "Don't hurt my babies!" Pat signaled for quiet and then disappeared into the barn.

Pat stood just inside the door and surveyed the interior of the barn, calling their names. She held the zapper in her hand as she hollered, "Timmy, Teddy, come out. That wasn't very nice what you did to your mother."

A shout rang out from the darkness, "That bitch got what she deserved, ha, ha, ha."

Pat was astounded by the remark. "Now, that doesn't sound like the Teddy and Timmy I know. Are you guys sick or something?"

"Yeah, sick of you rat face. Eat my poop."

Snickers rang out in the shadows as Pat switched left to right in a mode of search and seizure.

"Come on now, is that any way for a six- and four-year-old to talk?"

"Poo breath, poo breath, Patty's got poo, poo! Breath."

Pat continued walking while announcing, "It's nice that you guys broadened your English vocabulary, but I really think you should learn words from a dictionary instead of the gutter."

Teddy yelled, "Get naked and show us your boobies." Timmy echoed, "Yeah, get naked! Show us your boobies!"

Pat stretched her neck to catch the direction the foul speech was coming, then said, "Now, that isn't a nice way to ask a girl out."

"Maybe this is!" yelled Teddy as he lunged at her from behind the trailer and stabbed her high in the thigh with a pitchfork. He quickly disappeared into the shadows, leaving Pat in agony as he guffawed. Pat shouted as she yanked out the prongs in one desperate pull. "AAUGH! OOOH, you little bastard."

The wound wasn't that deep, but deep enough for the Devil children to smell her fear. Now wounded and angered, Pat's senses came alive. She slowly followed the trail of the little brats as she yelled, "Teddy, Timmy! You come out right now, you hear me. You're in big trouble."

"Yeah, big trouble," a voice repeated.

Pat whipped her head in the direction of the voice in the dark, confusing layout of the barn. Another voice rang out opposite of the last while she proceeded in a resolute, death-defying March. She heard what sounded like a footstep, then limped to its path. Again, another footstep adjacent to the last. She halted once more and realized she had fallen for an old-school kid's trick when she saw a stone being lobbed from the darkness. She pointed her flashlight at it as a two-by-four swung low from the loft and struck her down. The two Imps cheered out in victory and climbed down the ladder to the nearly unconscious Pat.

Teddy ripped her shirt open and began to fondle her as Timmy stood laughing insanely in a warped cackle. She lay dazed, spinning between black and light. Snickers rang out as her pain and disgust elated the hysterical little Monsters. The twisted Imps worked together as they toiled to take her pants off until Amanda's voice rang out.

"Get away from her!"

Teddy shouted back, "Fuck you, bitch. I'm going to stick my pee-pee in your pie hole." He then told Timmy, "Watch that bitch," as he proceeded in the pillaging of Pat while laughing perversely.

Amanda limped closer. "God damn it! I said stop it right now!"

Teddy jumped up as if offended. "No, not God damn it. GOD damn GOD! You hear me? GOD dam GOD! AND GOD DAMM YOU!"

He then suddenly shrilled out in pain as he became filled with amps from Pat's stun gun.

Timmy turned to his floored accomplice and then attempted to run until Pat zapped him with her stinger. She scrambled to her feet, pulling her clothes back together as she commanded Amanda to grab Timmy while she grabbed Teddy. They carried them past the dwindling fire, with Amanda noticing Bandit's charred carcass in the ashes. They hurried to the back of the squad car, where they quickly placed the unconscious Devil boys. Pat and Amanda climbed into the front of the cruiser exhausted and drained, looking at each other in disbelief until a glance in the back was a quick reminder of the hellish reality. The women calmed their terror and raced off to the station.

As they approached the station, Teddy woke up from his shock-afflicted sleep, kicking and screaming as Pat said, "Well, kid, this is going hurt you more than me." She then zapped him once more, sending him render-less and out once more.

Amanda followed Pat, each carrying an Imp, as they hurried to get them into separate cells before they awoke.

"That should hold the little Taz-devils until we figure out this mess," said Pat.

Amanda stood staring at her once-innocent children as Pat told her to come up to the front and let them sleep it off.

Almost two hundred miles away, David paced back and forth in his cell, wondering what he would say to Sarah. How *could I begin to explain what happened without sounding guilty?* He wracked his brain with his pernicious predicament in disdain of self-loathing grief as he sank into his small, steel-framed bed. He then wondered how high the judge would set his bail the next day. Would he or she allow a personal bond or go extreme and hang him high with an outrageous cash surety bond?

Would he lose the only job he'd ever known, or would it all blow over like a bad dream? And what of Nina? Could she become contrite and ready to tell the truth to the courts? Or was she basking in her glory for flouncing this flim-flam in his lap? Somehow, he thought the latter.

"Gotta face the music sooner or later," he said aloud as he dragged himself to the phone. He then punched in the numbers to the hotel, which he had memorized during his daughter's misfortunate situation. The operator dispatched his call to the front desk, where the concierge answered with formal politeness.

His call was directed to Sarah's room, and she answered in oblivious ignorance of his circumstances.

"Hello Sarah," he said sullenly as if walking to a guillotine at the break of day.

"What's the matter?" she answered, as if expecting a load of gravel to be dumped on her head.

"I'm in jail."

There was a long pause. "You mean you're at a jail," she said with hopeful merit and forced mirth.

"NO, I'm in a federal jail in downtown Columbia. It's serious. Nina is accusing me of rape."

"That fucking trollop! I told you to get rid of her. I told you she was up to no good! I told you; I told you!"

Sarah teared up as David clamored, "Listen, please, Sarah, it wasn't me. I mean, she must've drugged me or something. I just don't know."

Sarah straightened, then interrupted, "I don't want to hear any more about that fucking whore right now. What time is your arraignment in the morning?"

"Yeah, nine o'clock," David returned softly.

"Just hang tight. I'm there for you, honey. We can't get it dismissed until the preliminary. It all boils down to the substantiation of evidence they present and the testimony of the little trollop. Listen, David, don't worry. I don't blame you. We'll get through this. So just try to relax, and I'll see you in court tomorrow, if not sooner. Oh, and David, I love you very much, and I'm not going to let anybody or anything ruin what we have, okay?"

David's eyes welled as he said, "I love you, and thank you for believing me."

"Not only do I believe you, but I also believe in you, and always have and always will. I know you too well, David Daniel Lang. It's not in your nature to do something like that." Sarah's voice began to shake once more until the lawyer in her said, "I'll see you in court, chin up."

David hung up the phone feeling uplifted and a little more relaxed, as his heaviest worry of hurting Sarah with his conundrum almost shut down her understanding voice. He then laid upon the metal mattress bed, with his fingers clasped behind his head, as he contemplated how lucky he was to have Sarah for a wife.

Pat called for an ambulance, given that Amanda's bleeding had not stopped. Amanda was becoming delirious from the loss of blood, yet she protested leaving her sons behind.

"I doubt they'll have an ambulance suited for them, rascals."

"No, you go get taken care of, and I promise I'll watch over the little ones," answered Pat with an 'I won't take no for an answer' type look.

Amanda was too weak to argue at this point as she drifted in and out of conversation. Pat began to panic as she tried so hard to stop the bleeding, all the while checking the clock to see how much time had passed since she had called for the ambulance. Moments later, a Harrison Bi-County ambulance made its way to the station, and Pat stepped out of the way and let the paramedics take over. They gave Amanda a sedative and started an IV. Pat bent over her just before she drifted off.

"Be well, good friend," Pat said.

As they were loading Amanda into the ambulance, one of the paramedics asked Pat how Mrs. Morgan got her laceration.

"Fishing accident," announced Pat, as if she were there herself when it happened.

The two paramedics silently gave each other a weird look until one of them commented, "Sure been a lot of fishing accidents lately around these parts."

The driver then asked Pat if he could look at her "fishing accident," and she returned, "Yeah, the big one got away. I'll be alright. You go take care of that little gal you have there."

The driver looked at her as if she were two marbles short of a set and just shook his head then before pulling away in the direction of the hospital.

Pat figured the little Devils would be awake soon, so she called for pizza and cola, hoping it might help entice them back to good manners. She then turned towards the back to look in on them. She buzzed herself in, propping the door behind her, then walked down the narrow aisle to the incarcerated Imps. Timmy was sitting just staring into space. Teddy was still drowsy and lethargic.

Pat was startled at first sight of Timmy's eyes since she hadn't had the chance to get a good look at them, other than Teddy kicking at her or attacking her in the barn. As she gazed at their green, mottled skin in the light, Pat began to doubt her judgment when Amanda inquired whether they should go with her to the hospital. She shook it off, then said, "Well, I hope you're hungry because I just ordered a large pizza from the Pizza Palace. What you say to that?"

Teddy slowly turned his head, then said, "Oh boy, Molly, can I eat your hairy pie for dessert?"

Pat just shook her head. "Mm, mm, mm, with a mouth like that, who needs extra spices."

Teddy lashed back, "Oh yeah? With a face like yours, who needs an enema?"

The two tempestuous twerps guffaw like sick little gremlins on happy gas.

"Well, it's good to know you still have some humor," returned Pat with a grin. "Tell me, how did two good-looking boys turn into green little Monsters like yourself?"

The laughing ceased with foul oddness in the air until Teddy sang out, "I'll tell you if you let me pet your hairy pussy."

They broke out in laughter once more as Pat put her hands on her holstered hips and then shook her head once more. "Well, if you boys won't talk sensible, I'll have to take my pizza somewhere else where people are more polite."

Teddy yelled as she walked away, "Aw, come on, Molly, we just want a piece of your eye in my pie, eye in my pie, eye-pie." Timmy exploded into laughter, sending Teddy discharged from his wit into eruption as the two crazed lunatics became lost in a twisted land of their own.

Pat thought it was a doctor or a Priest---poisoned or possessed, maybe both. By now, it was only an hour until shift change, yet Pat had no intention of leaving so soon. She slid a tray of pizza into each cell, but they just threw it back through the bars with the chortled exultation of psychopathic theatrics.

Lang Township had no doctors with its meager population. As inconceivable as it sounded, Pat decided to call Vivian Fay, her good friend and veterinarian who had a small practice on the border of Horry and Brunswick County. She might be able to determine the origin of the boys' green skin and bite marks. They also warranted some holy attention from Father Hemmings and his small staff of clergy. Either way, they would be examined and or exorcised.

Vivian Fay was the first to arrive, and her eyes rounded with astonishment at the sight of their big, black orbs and pale green skin. "Oh my, I do declare. What in hell's creation are these little boys… What happened to them?"

"I was hoping you could enlighten me on that little tidbit," said Pat as she gazed upon the Imps Monsters in a cage.

"Well, as you know, I'm not a doctor, but I'll bet you a tuna sandwich; those are bite marks from a small dog on each of those, ah, kids."

Timmy then said in a soft, childlike tone, "Are you the plumber?" Teddy then added, "Yeah, I got a stopped-up pipe I need unclogging."

Father Hemmings showed up soon after Vivian got schooled in obtuse and impish vulgarism. A young Priest in his mid-twenties accompanied him. Pat and Vivian Fay cursed themselves for him being so good-looking behind that clerical collar.

"Goodness gracious, what happened to the Morgan boys?" Father Hemmings uttered with profound loathing as the young priest stood silent in his shadow.

"I think they may have caught the bug from the Devil himself," Pat proclaimed.

Father Hemmings stood appalled, then uttered, "Oh, Lord."

Teddy shot a verbal arrow of malicious fabrication, "Your God doesn't live here, fuck face."

Father Hemmings was jolted by the bolt of brash, brazen words as he stepped back in horror.

"Don't hang on to their words too much, Father. They have been talking that way all day."

"Yeah, Father, don't hang on my words too much, just hang on Dez nuts."

The little Imps went into hysterical fits in a raving workup of self-amusing droll. Pat finally lost her temper as she banged the bars in belated anger while she hollered for them to behave. Vivian announced that she'd never seen anything like it before, and all concurred except the young priest.

"This is the craft of the treacherous and cunning who know no end to the dark, descending path they embrace," said the young priest.

Vivian stepped forward toward the young priest. "I'm sorry, I didn't catch your name."

"Michael," he returned, as if trumpeted by a symphony of harmonic, heavenly song.

The two women were overcome in breathless contentment to be next to this man who spoke ever so softly yet booming, thunderous rapture.

"We know who you are!" shouted Teddy, "And besides, you're too late for these poor Souls. They're tainted beyond recognition."

All eyes froze upon the young priest ---shocked and stumped by the woeful words. The Imp lashed out, "It's too late for these souls to just go."

The priest lashed back, "It's not too late, you infectious

262

troughs and I will not leave."

Father Hemmings then clapped his hands. "Come, come, these boys need a doctor and a child therapist. We can pray for them at church."

"Why, where is your faith, Father?" queried the young princely priest.

"I beg your pardon, young man. How dare you speak to me in such a tone! I was bearing this cross long before you were a twinkle in your father's eye."

A brief silence fell upon the room as the young priest's piercing eyes penetrated Father Hemmings.

Michael broke the silence. "Is not our burden to bear the cross we carry, my good father? Was it you at the cemetery who said that the Devil's work is at hand?"

"Yes, yes, young man, but that was more or less a matter of speech, and how do you know that you weren't there."

Silence dominated the room once more as Father Hemmings turned toward the front of the station while Michael stayed behind.

Taking advantage of the separation, Pat followed and asked Father Hemmings when the young priest arrived at St. Andrews's church. He turned to her bedazzled, "I don't understand it myself. I never sent for anyone of the sort. He just showed up at the church the day after the cemetery incident with the proper papers. To be honest, I didn't know the Vatican knew we even existed, but the proper papers were in order."

They looked back at the young priest as his hands waved gracefully from left to right, speaking Godly words. Father

Hemmings shouted, "Brother Michael! Brother Michael! Let's go!" The young priest lowered his hand and muddled a few more words, then joined the others at the front of the station.

Charley entered the station and gazed at the strange group of people, smelling trouble on the horizon as he fought his feet from taking flight in the opposite direction. The group paid Charley no mind except the young priest, who gently smiled upon the distressing little balding man. The whole ordeal forced Father Hemmings to think more about his role and the reality of the Spirit World. Through time, he had become smug and complacent in his daily rituals of taking confessions and giving exhortations of prayer.

Michael then revealed aloud, "Father Hemmings, you probably realize by now my being here is no mistake."

The elderly priest became red-faced from fearing words that might foil the complacent world he'd maintained.

"We received reports from a source, who I'm not at liberty to divulge, of the supernatural circumstances which I was sent to investigate."

Charley fussed about with his ears wide open as he prepared for the night shift.

Michael went on, "Father Hemmings, I hate to go over your head, but we have an exorcism to perform."

"Exorcism?" shouted Charley. Everyone turned toward him, watching him spill coffee on himself. He repeated himself and wiped the mess from his pants. "Exorcism! What in the world are you all talking about?"

Pat gave the come here gesture with her index finger as she buzzed open the rear door. "Why do I get the feeling' I walked into hell's door," said Charley as he wished he had called in sick.

"No, just the front porch," stated Pat, almost feeling empowered by the man's fear.

When Charley saw those hell boys, he nearly flipped as Teddy announced, "Well, look here. It's rectum, Butt-Hole Man."

The two Imps could have been four inches or twenty feet tall; it wouldn't have made any difference, as Charley feared them the same. "Are those Johnny's boys?" he stammered.

"Yeah, what's left of them," returned Pat. "That little Devil stabbed me with a pitchfork," she stated as she pointed to Teddy, "And the other one there did his mother for a doozy on foot with a carving knife."

Teddy added, "Yeah, why don't you come in here, Molly, so I could put my pee-pee in your pie hole." Pat shook her head. "I don't know why, but he's been calling me Molly all day with his little nasty mouth."

Charley felt as if he were stuck on rewind and playing over and over a haunting nightmare as he gaped into the eyes of hell and they back at him. "You mean to say I got to babysit these Devil Monsters all night by myself?"

"Aw, come on, rectum man, we ain't so bad once you get to know us," said Teddy with a jeer. Timmy climbed high on the bars in a snickering cackle as he repeated, "Yeah, we ain't so bad."

Pat shoved the rest of the pizza under the bars and then told Charley to come back up front. Charley followed the limping Pat as he glanced at the gorging goblins, his back getting goosebumps and chills.

When they returned to the front, both priests were gone, leaving instructions with Vivian that they'd be back in an hour. Pat yawned as she announced how it had been a long, crazy day and that she'd had enough for one shift. Vivian followed suit, leaving Charley alone with the hellions.

He checked the rear entry door lock that led to the cells more than once and sat at the dispatch desk, all the while waiting and wondering when the priests would return.

It was as if the hellions could sense his fear through the walls, heckling him with horrid hoots and howls, all the while hollering out, "butt-hole man, butt-hole man." Charley was getting sick to his stomach from the continuing nightmare as their badgering taunts filled his brain with distress.

Finally, the priests arrived, yet a mountain of stress remained. He buzzed them through the back door as a wave of hellish heat poured into the lobby, and the smell of rotting flesh imbued the air.

Father Hemmings and Charley turned to the front door, clenching their stomachs from the foul odor. Michael simply marched in, appearing unaffected by the horrid smell. All but two light bulbs had burned out and flickered low. The paint on the walls and bars began to bubble and peel slowly. Any normal man wouldn't nor couldn't walk alone down the dark, dismal inferno as Michael disappeared into its obscurity. The Imps became distressed at his presence, bellowing out unwelcome hostility at his encroachment. When he came to their cells, he beheld their blistered, withering skin and shriveled, frayed hair. "We don't want you here! Go away! Go away!"

"No I shall not go away, ever, you Demoness thieves, never shall I shun from the glory of the ever-living light that shines from the truth of God. Nor shall I become crestfallen from my faith, nay old heathen's, I shall not go until I've reclaimed Teddy and Timothy to the lighted luminance of their individual Soul's. It is you who shall go in the name of our heavenly Father who art in heaven."

"Fuck you, Michael," shouted the Ted Imp. "We already claimed these Souls; their flesh is spoiled with the joy of hatred forever!" Father Hemmings stood in the doorway with a handkerchief over his mouth, hacking the phlegm. "Come in, Father Hemmings, behold the Satanic Solders in their malignant form. Behold the troths who disavow the holy of holies."

The old Priest shook his head in trepidation and aghast fear at the sight of the kind of true spiritual contact that he never accepted wholeheartedly. Michael marched toward him as he shouted serpent-stomping scriptures in ancient tongues. He grabbed Father Hemmings by his sleeve and pulled him into the sweltering darkness as he continued barking out parables of rebuking slang. Father Hemmings felt the Earth move as the young Priest persisted, fearless in his attack, his tongue spilling forth the heavens as the imprisoned children screamed forth in their dread. Michael held the old Priest in front of the Demonized Imps, then shouted, "This is our purpose, the battle against its ungodly gantry. We are the weapons against this abomination of God! Behold the slithering snakes as they crawl away from the righteous and hide in the shadows of Satan."

The old Priest cried out, "No!" as the world spun around him and hurled him into the foul plume of the underworld. Michael commanded, "Take up your cross, bear your spiritual brawn to the serpent, and crush him under thine foot."

Father Hemmings reached into his shirt and took out a tiny, golden cross given to him by his grandfather after the war in Europe. It was the last time he had seen him after Germany suffocated in the decimation of Hitler's dream. Father

Hemmings held out his cross with his shaking hand as tears streamed down his face. Michael took vials of holy water and splashed them about as Charley's terror-riddled hand slammed the entrance door shut.

Father Hemmings felt trapped in the jaws of hell but, at the same time, found new faith from the unshakable rock of a princely Priest. Michael appeared to lighten the dismal corridor as Father Hemmings loomed in his wake. The Satanic Imps screamed out shrieking as Michael prayed over them again and again while the old Priest joined in with an "amen" at the end of his every sentence.

Timmy jaunted in a small circle as Teddy paced left to right, cursing aloud, crazed in his confines and being force-fed shards of God-stained glass.

The battle for the two siblings' souls carried on and on as the old Priest's knees buckled from the long hours of standing in ritual. Michael's restless, relentless march raged on as the trapped Demons yelled back at every praise and prayer to his heavenly king. Father Hemmings set down his bible and then turned towards the door in a sick, weakened state. The young Priest ignored his departure as his immersion in the exorcising rites against the resisting fiends proved more than an ordinary challenge. Father Hemmings knocked upon the door with anxious, rapid taps as Charley took no chances, harking to hear a reply as to who was knocking.

After hearing it was Father Hemmings, Charley opened the large steel door, and the feeble Priest rushed out, wheezing and hacking in a continuous haste to get outside into the open air. Charley gaped into the gloom and saw the young Priest standing without stretched hands, ranting in religious rhyme. He hurried and slammed the door, checking it twice for secureness, then fast stepped out to the exterior of the building, flapping a million questions to the gasping Priest. The old Priest said nothing as he straightened from his hunched, heaving haunt, then pushed Charley out of his way, rushed for his Cadillac, and spun away into the darkness. It felt as if it were the longest night in Charley's life. He spent his night shift in sheer terror while screams howled out into the early morning hours.

A world away, Sarah was in deliberation with the prosecuting attorney in downtown Columbia at the federal court building. The prosecutor remained silent as Sarah went into a three-song speech about her demands for personal bond while he concerned himself with other matters. It was as if Sarah's bar registration meant nothing to the magistrate, or she was a ghost trying to communicate with the living. Finally, the rear door opened, and her shackled husband walked through the door with an escort of two officers directing him to his chair.

Sarah approached him seriously, strong and sturdy. She knelt beside him with a sense of battle readiness.

"Hang in there, Hoss," she declared, trying to lighten the dilemma and his dismal, despaired demeanor.

She then looked toward the prosecuting attorney, and he looked at them with unfriendly eyes as she stated what a jerk he seemed to be. "They won't give me any indication of their plans. I don't like the feeling I'm getting about this whole mess," stated Sarah with uncertainty.

"Tell me about it. I feel like a cow in a slaughterhouse, already stamped for approval," stated the starless sheriff.

In the lobby was a slew of reporters being held out of the courtroom, trying so desperately for the inside scoop they scribbled upon their notepads. Just a few hand-picked columnists were allowed into the courtroom without their recorders and cameras.

Agent Dickerson and his short partner Herbert made their presence known, grouping with the prosecutor as if huddling for the Super Bowl Championship ring. Agent Herbert gawked at Sarah from head to toe. David laughed to himself, thinking how that ass wipe wished he could get a woman so fine and smart.

A court officer then shouted for all to rise before the honorable Judge Stranton. The incumbents of the courtroom instantly complied. Surprisingly, a dark-skinned Spanish-type woman in her mid-thirties of pulchritudinous semblance sat at the bench. The courtroom officer then asked for all to be seated, and the two agents sat at the prosecutors' table, whispering injurious plans for David's destruction. The stern-spoken judge told the prosecutor to proceed in presenting his opening statement. The prosecutor walked from his table like a piranha as he passed by the defense until he reached the middle of the floor.

"Your honor, I'm requesting a million-dollar bond, cash surety, and that Mr. Lang be stripped from his duties as sheriff until this case is resolved."

"I object, your honor," announced Sarah in an angry voice."

"Objection overruled!" barked back the judge.

The prosecutor smiled with piranha pearl teeth as Sarah slunk back to her chair.

The prosecutor continued, "Your honor, there is just too much evidence against Mr. Lang to allow him a low or personal bond, which would give him the opportunity to flee the country.

Sarah jumped to her feet. "Your honor, I object. Mr. Lang has been an outstanding officer of the law and has been serving the community for almost 15 years."

"Sit down, Mrs. Lang. Objection denied," lashed the judge with a piercing glare of fire.

The prosecutor continued, "Your honor, a woman has been raped, with Mr. Lang's very own DNA as the evidence. Again, I ask the courts for a million-dollar cash surety. Nothing less will do, your honor. Thank you."

He smiled upon Sarah with his pearl-white grin, strolled to his chair, and took his seat. The radiant judge then questioned, "Has the prosecution anymore to add?"

"No, your honor," said the flesh-eating fish.

"Very well, the Defense may speak."

Sarah stood, "Your honor, as I was saying, Mr. Lang has served the community for almost twenty years and deserves a low personal bond." She glanced at her nemesis as she continued, "The prosecutor's vicious, unsubstantiated remark about my client fleeing the country is a joke and is making my client, my husband, out to look like a vicious criminal. And furthermore ..."

"I think I've heard enough, Mrs. Lang," said Judge Stranton. "Please take your seat."

Sarah knew well by her almost sixth sense what the judge might say next if she continued. She was deflated once more.

The courtroom drew quiet while the judge looked at some paperwork that was laid before her. She then picked up her gavel and announced, "I'm going to take the prosecutor's advice and set Mr. Lang's bond at one million dollars cash surety, and Mr. Lang will temporarily surrender all his duties as sheriff. The court is adjourned!"

The judge crashed down her mighty gavel and then walked away as an officer commanded the half-slaughtered steer back to his pen. Sarah told David she would see him soon and get him out as she gently cupped her hand upon one cheek and kissed the other. David nodded at her as he noticed Johnny at the entrance, fighting his way past the exiting court crowd. A court cop belched out again for David to stand and follow the yellow line on the floor. Sarah managed to tell him not to worry once more, and Johnny managed to wave at David before he was taken from the room.

Johnny approached Sarah as she turned from her ever-loving heart that was taken away by a courtroom badge. "Sorry I'm late, Sarah, but I just got a call from Amanda at Harrison Bi-County Hospital. Apparently, my two sons attacked her with kitchen knives and went on a rampage, lighting a bale of hay near the barn. Dam, they could've set the whole place ablaze! They also got Pat with a pitchfork. I'm sorry, Sarah, but I got to get back there pronto. David told me not to come; I should have listened."

"That's okay," returned Sarah. "What in hell's bells is going on? Is this hell on Earth or what?"

"I don't know," answered Johnny, "But I got to go. I must see Amanda, then check in at the station."

He wished her good luck with David's case, then rushed away, leaving her alone, scared, and unsure of the future.

A court officer tapped her shoulder, breaking her heavy train of thought. "Mrs. Lang, the judge would like to see you in her chambers."

She followed him past the bench to the door, which was adjacent to the one David had gone through. He led her down the hallway and into a large room, where a magistrate stood next to the judge, awaiting her as she signed some papers.

"Mrs. Lang, have a seat," said the judge as she scribbled on the final document and nodded the magistrate away.

The judge leaned back in her chair as she removed the wire-rimmed glasses from her face and peered at Sarah. "Mrs. Lang, I sympathize with your situation, but don't you think you should let someone else handle this case due to the emotional stress involved?"

"I most certainly do not, your honor," said Sarah with a shade of irritation.

"I see," said the stern-faced judge. "Well, it appears you're not even accustomed to practicing criminal law."

She placed a file on her desk and leaned back in her chair. Her poker face implicated the five little words Sarah didn't want to hear: you don't stand a chance.

"Since you've gone through the trouble of checking into my career history, you must have also noticed I graduated at the top of my Class at Harvard University."

"Yes. Mrs. Lang, I also noticed that the FBI has a strong case against your husband, and the rape victim is ready and willing to give testimony. To be frank, Mrs. Lang, I don't think your husband has a chance in hell to beat this case, and your inexperience is going to drown him even deeper."

With restrained politeness, Sarah lashed back, "Well, with all due respect, your honor, why should he have any representation at all? We might as well feed him to the wolves and give his bones to the vultures of time. I mean, the whole situation stinks like a setup. My husband did not rape that tramp. If anything, she probably raped him."

Judge Stranton tilted her head down and rolled her eyes above the rim of her glasses, shaking her head. "Mrs. Lang, I didn't ask you back here to argue your husband's case. I'm merely advising you to let someone else handle it for his own good."

"No, I'm sorry, your honor, but I can't put my husband's freedom on the line with people I don't know."

"Okay, well, just make a mental note that you were advised by someone who has prosecuted, defended, and judged many cases like this. Rarely does the defense ever win, and if they do win, it's usually in the form of accepting a plea or bargaining for probation."

"Well, with wins like that, who needs a guillotine?" added Sarah ironhandedly.

"Tell me, Mrs. Lang, what makes you think you can do more than an accomplished criminal trial lawyer could? What makes you think you can get up from a pile of paper in your quaint little house and jump into a high-profile case like this one? Tell me, Mrs. Lang, what, what?"

Sarah stood, "I'll tell you, your honor --- love. Now, if you'd excuse me, I have a case to prepare."

Sarah turned and started for the door as Judge Stranton shouted out, "If you really love your husband, you won't take this case!" Sarah paused and then proceeded out the door and straight for the detention compound where David was being detained. Since she was his lawyer, visiting hours didn't apply, and he was allowed two visits per day at any time.

A stocky elderly guard buzzed her through the gate, staring at her curves as she walked past. She was directed to a room where David was already waiting. A standing guard opened a plexiglass door and stated, "No physical contact, ma'am." She nodded and entered the room, where her eyes welled up at the sight of her accused husband.

"You are holding up there, big guy?" she inquired with a shaky voice.

He silently nodded, then asked how Lisa was doing, as if unconcerned for himself.

Sarah sighed, "She seems to be getting better but still has a long way to go. Your mother and Dr. Miranda have been going somewhere every day and seem to have become an item."

David slammed his hand on the table, blurting out, "If he's a friend of that asshole Demas, I don't trust him."

The guard standing nearby stuck his head in the door. "You alright, ma'am?"

David stood up. "What the fuck? You think I would hurt my wife?"

The guard ignored David's outburst as he repeated himself. "Everything okay in here."

"It's alright, everything fine. Just a little emotional stress," stated Sarah as she cracked a slight smile at David.

David still stood glaring at the guard as Sarah tapped him on his arm, bidding him to sit before he faced further charges.

"Please, no contact, ma'am," said the correctional officer as he closed the plexiglass door.

David slowly sat back down as Sarah stated, "Don't worry about his ass right now; we have yours to worry about."

David put his hand on her hand, and the guard once more popped his head in the door, repeating himself. "No contact, please."

David was at his wit's end at this point but kept his composure as he held Sarah's hand and blew out the match while his eyes remained fixed upon the rule squawker.

The guard gulped his thoughts, saying nothing, as he felt the fear that was pumped into him from David, the cornered Beast.

The squawker quieted, then looked away as he retreated and shut the door.

David sat back in his chair, gazing at Sarah, then asked, "Why?" as she shuffled the police report about.

"Why what?" she asked, half attentively.

"Why aren't you mad at me? Most wives would let them throw the book at him if they cheated and went to trial."

Even though David somewhat confessed his sin, Sarah still refused to divulge her little sexcapade at the mansion. She used her legal tactics mixed with her female evasiveness and simply replied, "I believe you couldn't nor wouldn't just take someone's virtue like that. And besides, I wouldn't let the father of my daughter fry like that. She needs her father."

David never questioned her again as they redirected their concentration to the case at hand. Sarah went over every detail and never even so much as raised an eyebrow as David told her the particulars of his spellbinding adulterous act. After almost two hours, the guard announced time was up. Sarah once more told David to hang in there as she gave him the number to the hotel on the main strip of the quaint city of Charlotte. She said, "I love you," and assured him she would win the case as he disappeared into the shadows of his confinement.

At the Berkshire Hotel, Carol and Dr. Joseph Miranda

were in each other's arms, as they were now more than just dance partners. Joseph got up and put on a robe over his naked, old body before he walked to the giant glass window and stretched his bones in the early morning light. Carol stretched her arms as well as she said good morning to her only admirer since the death of her husband. She lay there wondering if she should have given in to her outdated body's desires, particularly to this worldly doctor who could probably get women half his age.

"A penny for your thoughts," she said to Joseph as he stared out the window.

"Did you ever consider the end times to come and the battles yet to be fought," he announced, still turned away.

"Well, that's a strange question to ask. What brings that to mind?" she responded as she propped herself against the headboard of the bed.

"As strange as it might seem for me to ask, it's even stranger that you never question such truths."

"My, my, aren't we the deep-sodded soul today? What gives?" She questioned in amusement. He turned but remained where he stood. "What gives is being a doctor for almost thirty-five years, and before that, almost twelve years of college. I've seen death in every manner and form. I've seen the old that seem to cling to life forever while young children like your little Lisa die at a moment's notice. I've seen the diseases lose all their organs one by one, as machines keep them alive due to their wealth. And I've seen those not so merited with assets to get them through a simple operation wither and die as their wealthy relatives turn their heads away."

"Joseph, you're scaring me. What brings this on?"

"What brings this on is the end times to come. Which side

will you be on, and how long do you expect to endure? What if I told you how to immortalize your body as it is? Not a day older will you ever age until the end of the world?"

"I don't think I would want to live to the end of the world," she said with a newfound fear of the eccentric, outlandish man.

Joseph smirked at her, then rushed to the bed and pulled her to her feet with her hair. She let out a yelp and cried, "You're hurting me!"

"Am I? He steered her to the mirror. Look at yourself. You're decaying as we speak. Your bones are shrinking, your hair's falling out, and your organs will be virtually diminished in twenty more years."

"That's a part of getting old!" Carol cried out. "It's what normal people do."

"Yeah, that's what they do, alright. Come here," he redirected her to the window, gritting his teeth in a fit of rage.

"Look out! There, what do you see? I'll tell you what I see. I see dead, walking stiffs. Just as you spend your whole youth learning your craft, you spend your entire adult life learning how to Master it until you're too fucking old to enjoy it. Now, you call that justified. I call it a teasing joke God cursed us with. He sits high upon his throne as we amuse him with our very existence from life until death. And what of us? What is our reward? To reside at his feet for eternity and to have no identity of our own?"

Carol hollered, "You're hurting me!" as she reached for the hand holding her hair.

"I'll show you true pain," he hissed as he threw her on the bed.

She tried to get away as he grabbed her legs and ripped her nightgown. He then turned her over and said loudly, "This is what your God would do to you." He disrobed and pierced her with a penetrating pain she had never known.

Carol cried out, "Why?" As he shamed her in an act, she never in her worst nightmares thought something like this would happen to her. The demented doctor huffed out, "Because pain is the only thing people truly perceive in their pathetic little pea brains."

She lay crying while he shredded her solemnity, serving himself a portion of her inner self. He said aloud, "I want to taste your soul," then stuck his tongue deep into her throbbing hole. Horror had a new face to Carol as the raptorial rapist rendered his reign of terror. Over and over, he flipped her as every Orphus turned inside out. Once he fulfilled his warped desires, Carol ran to the bathroom, a shambled, sick-hearted mess. She cried tainted tears of terror brought on by the twisted tyrant who manifested his true colors of this Devil-Monster. He then dressed as if late for a casual Sunday golf outing. Fully clothed, he put his ear to the door where he could hear Carol crying, and it seemed to bring him pleasure.

He then spoke through the door, "I suggest if you want what's best for your little Lisa, you keep your trap shut." He then pounded on the door, "You got it?"

She broke from a sob and then screamed, "Fuck you, you fucking bastard!

He laughed his way out of the room and down the hall with a swagger of arrogance. He then switched up to a carefree song. "Zippeite doo dah, zippeite aye. My oh my, what a wonderful day ..." as he waited in the elevator. Wallowing in the warm water, Carol tried to wash away her wretched shame and repossess her dignity.

David stood in a line waiting his turn to receive the dung they called food as two muscle-bulging brutes approached him with ill intent. The larger thug bent his head in David's direction and yelled, "Sewee, Sewee, I smell pork."

David turned and glared at him with a 'don't fuck with me' look, and it seemed to incite glee. David glanced around as all eyes fell upon him. Even the guard turned away, smirking. David knew the moment would be a pivotal point in how he'd be treated in the future. He turned with his empty tray and smashed the closest inmate in his face as one more came at him. David belted him in his ribcage and then his head.

Both inmates lay at his feet as he held the bent tray. Then someone shouted out, "You let a pig beat your ass? Fucking fags."

David simply lifted his knee, bent his tray back, and resumed his place in line. After he received his portions, he sat at a table where more of the bastards gave him dirty looks of disdain. The other after the other left the table. David was just about to take his first bite when a guard behind him told him to leave his tray and come with him. He got up and was escorted from the cafeteria with the guard following.

David was directed to the same room where he had his meeting with Sarah. When he walked in, a stunted, greasy, aged man, about thirty pounds overweight, awaited him with papers on the table and pen in hand. He looked up and smiled.

"Ah, Mr. Lang, I take it," he said gaily.

"And who might you be?" Inquired David with a slight snarl.

"My, my," Most people are elated when they see me. I think you're the first in my thirty years as a bondsman who's given me such a poor welcome."

"Bondsman!" retorted David. "Who the hell would put up a million dollars for my ass?"

"I'm sorry, Mr. Lang, but I'm not at liberty to say, but I do have the proper papers right here to have you out in twenty minutes."

David gazed at the documents from where he stood. "Tell your puppeteer to go fuck himself." Then he turned towards the door.

The bondsman momentarily was speechless and then said, "Are you insane? How else are you going to get out if you don't take this bailout?" David paused at the door, then turned around and said, "Auh, fuck it, this is the worst mistake your puppeteer ever made, letting me out."

The bondsman just smiled and handed David the pen. David signed the papers and made sarcastic remarks about how the bondsman's strings were showing. The bondsman told David to enjoy his freedom, and David threw the pen on the table. "Screw you, puppet man."

The guard then took David to where he was first processed, handed him new clothes, and pointed to the changing room.

"Where is my uniform and gun?" he barked.

The guard told him they were taken by his higher-ups, and he was given new clothes in their place. David just shook his head and walked into the room to change.

As he was changing, he thought of the ways he would get to Devin Demas and all his little puppets. He'd have them where he was now or dead. It didn't much matter to him. He then walked out of the dim confines of the jail and into the grayness of soft, pouring rain.

The soothing, warm sprinkles upon his skin began to stem his stress. He commenced to power up his cell phone when Humpy and Dumpty, the two FBI Agents, surrounded him on the left and right.

"I see they just let anyone out these days," said Agent Herbert, grinning with his tobacco and coffee-stained teeth.

"Oh, look who it is, Laurel and Hardy's idiot twins," replied David, praying they would lift a finger so he could bust them up. They flashed their guns under their jackets and then commanded him to walk towards the black Lincoln limo.

"I wonder if you guys know how to roll over and play dead," remarked David.

"No, but you'll be dead if you don't shut the fuck up and get in the limo."

David quickly lashed back. "Oh, look here, he was trained to speak too."

The door was opened by a tall, Ugandan-type driver with coal-black skin, who smiled with a set of teeth that had braces made of platinum. David was pushed from behind by the two agents, and he flopped into the backseat next to Devin. The agents filed in across from them.

"Well, if it isn't the puppeteer himself. To what do I owe the presence of your great Pharaohness!"

Agent Dickerson reached over and slapped David's face. David simply turned back, chuckling, then said, "Auh, looks like scruffy got mad."

The agent reached out to slap him again until Devin raised his arm. The agent pulled back his hand and knocked on the window for the driver to take off.

Devin then spoke in a low voice that commanded attention. "David, I don't think you have any idea as to who I am, do you?" Devin said as he gazed out his window.

"Oh, I know exactly who you are or what you are. I believe the Indians called you 'white snake of the valley,' but I believe the correct term is Devil's right-hand man."

"Very good, David, but do you know what else I am, aside from the words of slang that come off the top of your head?"

David nodded yes, paused, then said, "Yeah, in some fucked up way we're related. Oh yeah, and you're older than sin."

Devin burst out in laughter. "Oh, David, you have my humor, along with my quick wit."

David cut him off, "I puke at the thought of having any qualities that you have, Demas. In fact."

This time, Devin interrupted. "In fact, what? You want facts? Fact. Your last name should be Demas. Fact. Having the Demas name would make you royalty. Fact. You'd already be dead, along with your whole family, if you weren't of my blood. David, I want you to join the True Alliance organization and sit by my side as I rule."

David interrupted. "You're the oldest idiot ever; if you think I'd have any part of anything you are. My life was picture perfect until you poisoned it with your; I don't know what the fuck to call it. All I know is you're the problem that's destroying my life."

Devin finished his sentence, "Let's just say you can call me the solution to all your problems. If you'd just give up your self-righteous attitude, you'd be rich beyond all your dreams. I already was wealthy beyond your understanding."

David countered, "And where the fuck do you get off sucking the life from the living? Does it turn you on to see parentless children and the lives you've changed with your misery?"

Devin smiled, "Well, boys, I think my grandson deserves a little view into my World. What you say?"

The two sadistic henchmen started giggling as Devin's head and hands contorted with twisted burns and bumps of vermillion shades of Evil itself. He began to laugh with his henchmen as hell revealed its ghastly sights and sounds.

David tried desperately to open his door, but all doors were locked. All he could do was sit through it until the slow-motion sounds of laughter ceased, and Devin unveiled his ungodly vision for his timeless, unworldly course. His heart never pounded so hard, nor had his fears been so heavy as the tonnage of terror that turned his stomach. David's blood surged to his face in repulsive, nauseating repugnance as he bent his head down, cupping his brow with the ridge of his hand and awaiting the harrowing horror to pass. Finally, the driver pulled up to a hotel, as all drew silent in the sweltering state of David's angst.

"Ah, look, my son, we are here at the hotel where your wife is currently residing."

David lifted his head from his hand as he looked out the window and then at Devin's returned to form.

"Now, my son, you have a choice. You could step out with the sheep, or you could remain by my side with the wolf. What's that old saying? Oh yeah, free will. The world is no longer the same as you once knew it. It's doomed for big changes, and I will reign superior to all Kings until my and your Master take his place."

There was a quiet interlude until David spoke, "What are the chances of getting my deputies back?"

"Why, David, I believe the courts took your silver star, which means you no longer have any deputies."

It took the sum of David's strength as he repeated, "Please, I'm asking you. Please return Jim and Scott to their original selves."

"David, David, David. Begging doesn't become you at all, and as you say, I'm older than sin. I'm not here to bring joy and comfort to this world. I'm here to bring pain and war, and if you're not on my side, you and your family will be eradicated with the others."

The door unlocked, and David wasted no time getting out. He stood, turned, and said, "You know, I'm not a real churchgoer, but isn't the other side supposed to win?"

Devin became slightly angered, then replied, "So say the writers of the Pious black book, but don't believe everything you read; it just might steer you from your true desires."

Devin smiled as David closed the door and then turned towards the hotel, and the limo drove away. David then rushed through the doors of the hotel and took the elevator to the second floor and into Sarah's room. When she opened the door, she attacked him with kisses, hugs, and tears, along with a million questions as to how he got out.

David came clean with everything he knew up until then, from the giant Freak Thing to his Most recent Monday afternoon drive with the Devil Demas himself. They began to plan how they would rid themselves of the black magic tyrant who was haunting them with doom. They formulated many ideas, from fleeing the country to going to the media or maybe even a deft, swift sniper shot to the head. David relished the thought of pressing the trigger from afar, perhaps from the top of the hills surrounding Devin's Devil castle.

They then temporarily put their troubles aside and exploded upon each other's flesh in a primal expression of making love.

Over and over, they exchanged "I love you-s" in a deep devotion of passion, drowning in each other's souls. Sarah never loved nor held someone so dearly as David. No man nor Devil could trespass upon their indomitable adoration.

They spent the rest of the day and night in each other's arms as they lingered in their love without distraction.

That same evening, Johnny was in the hospital by Amanda's side as she explained in detail Teddy and Timmy and their attempt to end her life. *How could this be? How could two loving boys just turn? How did they metamorphose from innocents to vicious, vile vermin?* Johnny's brain battled with the parallel parodies of the other incidents that had transpired, and he speculated as to how they all fit together.

Amanda had been pleading with the staff to let her see Lisa just two floors down, and they finally gave in and brought a wheelchair. Johnny wheeled her to the elevator and then to Lisa's room. He forced himself to spend fifteen minutes with the two girls, anxious to get to the station and see what was going on for himself. Finally, he found a convenient exit when Amanda began reading Lisa Dr. Sues *Green Eggs and Ham*. He departed with a quick kiss on top of Amanda's head and said, "I'll be back tomorrow."

Nearly one hour later, he parked next to Pat's pickup truck on the side of the station, where he soon ran into a howling scream. Johnny rushed in to find Pat talking on the phone and sitting at the front desk with her bandaged leg up on another chair. She quickly said goodbye and hung up to tell Johnny all the neat stuff he had missed since he was away.

She told him it was Old-Man Joe on the phone and that he told her the hound brothers were up to no good, going against David's orders not to meddle with the not-so-jolly giant.

Johnny quickly disregarded her comments and then asked about his boys. Pat's face became sullen.

"They're in the back with a new Priest, Michael. He hasn't even come up for air since yesterday. I don't know, but there's something strange about him too."

Johnny walked to the door dumbfounded and pained but angered at the same time about Amanda's suffering. Pat buzzed him through, and the foul stench of hell mixed with hideous heat that pervaded and hit him in the face. The paint on the door had softened and peeled in the boiling, darkened confines, and he felt the black hate upon his skin. Down the aisle, he saw a fatigued silhouette in an unsteady stance, tottering and chanting Godly words onto the cells.

Johnny called out into the gloom as he walked towards the mumbling Priest. Pat limped behind, warning him to stay clear of the bars. When they approached, Johnny asked the Priest how he could stand the heat as he noticed his blistering, red skin. He investigated the first cell, where his oldest tossed and turned in an uneasy sleep as holy words spilled from the mouth of the Priest.

"Hello," Johnny said sarcastically. No answer was returned; only the mumbling holy words from the entranced man were heard. Michael's eyes were open, gazing into emptiness.

Johnny tried again, waving his hand in the face of the unrelenting exorcist. "Man, I don't know how to deal with this," stated Johnny in befuddlement.

A voice then hailed out from the secure door entrance. "Hello. Anybody here? Ahh, there you are."

Porter Lewis approached in the dismal heated room. He put his handkerchief over his mouth and nose while commencing upon the foul-smelling stench and furnace. Porter saw the abscessed skin of Michael and the degenerative, blistered boys in their disembodied state.

He repeated Johnny's efforts to awaken the transfixed Priest by waving his hand in front of his face. The result was the same voidness.

"Is this what I think it is---a modern-day exorcism?" he questioned, staring into the cells.

"Do me a favor, Sherlock, and grab his legs and help me get him to the lobby," said Johnny as he wrapped his arms around the Priest's torso.

Porter consented, grabbing hold of Michael's legs as they carried the flaccid Priest to the lobby and set him on a black leather sofa. Johnny told Pat to get some water for the weary Priest. She nodded and rushed to the breakroom. Pat hurried back to the lobby with a tall glass of water. She propped up Michael's head and trickled the life-giving liquid into his parched lips. Streams of water spilled down his cheeks as the Priest struggled to drink, all the while Pat telling him to sip slowly. Porter took up a chair and asked, "What was it you were doing in there?" as all ears awaited his reply.

The young Priest squinted about the eyes gaping back at him, with dead silence filling the room. "You wouldn't understand," he said, looking away and sipping more of the life fluid into his neglected body. Porter continued with his questions. "No, it wasn't the Latin of ancient Rome, but it was a dialect not used anymore. Am I correct?"

The Priest said nothing as Porter went on, "It sounded somewhat Semitic, but still, I've never heard it spoken so fluently."

Michael spoke slowly, "It's the rite of ancient Hebrew to cast out the Demons of those who are possessed unwillingly."

Porter became puzzled but persisted, "I didn't know that the language you spoke still existed. Did they teach you that in the seminary?"

Michael stood, "I'm not here to talk about myself. I'm here to save the lives and Souls of those two boys," he said as he began to stagger back toward them.

"Whoa, you better sit back down, their father," Pat said, clenching his arm. He collapsed back onto the sofa as Pat commented how weird it was to call the almost teen-looking Priest "Father." The Priest forced a smile and said, "I'm older than you might think."

Pat studied his facial features, then asked with a look of disgust, "Why is it so stinking hot in there?" Michael's voice grew stronger, "Because Satan's fire wields close to the hearts of the lost Souls who have been taken. Foul Demons fuel their hatred from the flames of the forsaken pit of lost Souls. They breathe the Beast's curse upon the innocent as they summon hell's fire upon the surface and into the fidelity of their consciousness. The only way to combat the vile spirits is by solemn command of prayer petitions to God."

"So why not in English?" Porter asked as if taking notes.

The Priest answered, "God knows all, and all is God's to know. The ancient tongue is spoken because it so agitates the Demons to hear it."

"A month ago, I would've told you you're off your rocker,

but it's been pretty weird around here lately," Johnny commented. "Listen, I don't care if you have to stand on your head singing nursery rhymes. I want my boy's back, and I will fight or die to make sure that happens."

"Fight we shall," said Michael, "but not a battle with guns nor fists. This is a clash of two Worlds which both contend for the souls of mankind."

"A human tug rope sounds to me," stated Johnny, feeling like a scapegoat for the holy war. Johnny then recanted himself, "I'm sorry, Father, I'm just frustrated over my boys."

Johnny sat down, defeated, and the Priest smiled upon the good-hearted, soured Soul.

"It's okay," said Michael, as if he'd known him his whole life.

"We should put a giant ice cube back there with some air fresheners," remarked Pat, trying to lighten up the mood.

The Priest sprung to his feet as if renewed with energy. "That's it!" he announced.

"What, air fresheners?" Pat counter.

"No, holy blessed ice. That might help thwart Evil from the boys, along with petitions unto our heavenly Father. But we would need large slabs of it. Is there such a place we can attain such quantity of ice?"

Pat's and Johnny's eyes widened as she divulged, "Ole Hanson's Icehouse is just a couple of miles away."

"Can you please take me there?" asked Michael with utter urgency.

"Of course," said Pat. "We can use my pickup truck if it's okay with Johnny."

"Go ahead," returned Johnny. "I'm going to stay here and keep an eye on things."

"May I come?" queried Porter. "I wouldn't want to miss seeing the good Priest in action."

"Sure, come on. There's plenty of room, and we'll be able to use your help if it's alright with Johnny."

Porter's eyes turned to the deputy in charge, and he nodded his head okay. Johnny waits for them to leave before he returns to his inmates. He made his way to the rear metal door and walked down the hall. Raising his two sons gave him little comfort. He was nervous as he shuffled through the darkness. He came upon the first cell and saw Teddy sleeping---a dreadful, eerie sight of welted, parched skin and heavy, hammering breath. As he approached the second cell, Timmy had his back towards him and was lying in the middle of the floor. "Daddy, is that you?" he said in a child's voice.

"Yes, Timmy, it's me. Are you alright?"

"I'm cold and hungry. Please get me out of here. I want to go home."

"Turn around, son, so I can see you."

The boy started crying with his back still turned to Johnny. Johnny's eyes welled up as he asked Timmy to turn around again.

"Please, Daddy, I want to go home. Please get me out of here! I want to go home. I want to go home."

"As soon as Pat gets here, I'll go to Dana's Diner and get

some burgers. What Cha you say to that, huh?"

"Fuck the burgers. I want to eat your soul, Daddy, ha ha." Timmy then turned and rushed to the bars, where he reached out, trying to seize Johnny with his little Devil hands. Johnny stepped back as Teddy was now awake, climbing the bars in crazed laughter, naked from head to foot.

"Yeah, Daddy, why don't you let us eat your soul? I promise it won't hurt," he said as he urinated through the bars, trying to spray him.

Johnny scuffled back out of reach and yelled at him in anger.

Timmy also took his clothes off and cupped his hand under his rump in a straining squat, pushing out feces into his hand. Johnny caught a glimpse of the turd-filled hand and ran for the exit while their cackling snickers added to the stench-filled air.

Johnny slammed the door behind him as he cursed and exploded in a temper, wondering how and why this happened. He sat on the sofa while the Imps giggled and shouted, "Daddy, I have a present for you. It's hot and brown and awful smelly."

Johnny just sat there as he rubbed his closed eyes with the palms of his hands in a depression of lost hope. He then buried his head in his hands in total exhaustion from the emotional drain and long drive from Columbus and Harrisville.

Johnny quickly drew into a deep sleep as dark, demented dreams dominated his discernment with dreadful Devils and Demons. His own sons hacked at his limbs, while hideous troll carrion eaters feasted on his flesh and while the Devil awaited his Soul.

One dream to another, each worse than the last, he tossed and turned for two hours until Pat and the others returned. He woke to the resonant, resolute sound of Michael's voice, which seemed to have the authority to raise the dead and awaken the mind.

Johnny stood on his feet and stretched his cricked neck from the awkward position in which he slept as Pat walked into the station and propped open the door. Porter had his sleeves rolled up as Michael slid a three-foot slab of ice to the tail of the truck. Johnny walked out to help. Together, they bolstered the slab on a dolly, then coasted it into the station, where they all worked to transport the slab to the cells.

Pat buzzed open the door. The Demonized boys started screaming as if they were lit on fire from the holy, blessed slabs that encroached upon them. Johnny opened Teddy's cell while the Imp fussed in a raging fit, jumping up and down on his bed. The Priest slid the slab into the cell as Johnny quickly slammed the door. The process was repeated at the second cell as Timmy also threw a fit.

Charley unwantedly returned to his shift touchy in temper, shaky in hands, and a grumbling, grunting mess behind his desk. Michael remained praying over the fit-frenzy fiends as Pat and Porter stayed for the spectacle that Charley wanted no part of. As disheartening as it was to see his boys in their Devil-infected state, Johnny had to stay.

Michael yelled at the Imps, who were screaming in discomfort at the prayer and chanting psalms. Teddy turned his mattress and used it as a shield as if trying to protect himself from a nuclear blast.

Timmy just cried in a flood of tears, staring at the slab and Priest as if he were in a Chinese torture chamber being ripped apart. Johnny thought that it was a good thing Amanda wasn't there, or she'd surely be in a shambled mess, making the whole thing even more difficult.

After ten minutes of high-pitched screams, Pat grew tired and departed for the solace of her home. Porter was intrigued beyond words at the unworldly show before him. Johnny and Porter stood by while Michael continued his relentless pursuit of weakening Evil's grip. Over and over, the Priest shouted words of Semitic, sacred divinity in ancient tongues of God as the Imps squirmed about insanely.

The heat and ice combined to give an unnerving, menacing effect as steam filled the rear of the jail in a sweltering vivacity. Porter took up a chair only feet from the rite of the holy word. Michael expressed his anger and seemed to have a personal vendetta against the Evil apparitions who had apprehended the souls of the innocent. He waved and flailed his arms about infelicitously commanding sanctification. Johnny retained his position upon the black leather sofa as Charley spoke not a word, nervously reading the *Harrisville Herald* Newspaper.

In the woods, the Willard brothers were treading on the heels of the giant ogre freak with their own personal posse of soused followers. With flashlights, leashes, and guns, they embarked through the forest, hooting and hollering in their drunken stupor, firing their weapons into the night sky. The Beast they were hunting was surviving off the land, staying clear of humans, as it fed on an occasional deer or moose that would cross its path. But the hound brothers, full of zest and rye and dead, set on killing the Beast.

Their courage ran stronger in numbers from their gutless, gunned rendition of search, seek, and destroy. Onward, they marched through marsh and meshed vines, making the pursuit perplexing and difficult. Even though they knew they were close to their kill, they began to tire from their drinking and smoking out-of-shape physiques. They dredged and labored behind their hounds up and downhill until the oldest Willard huffed out "halt." They built a campfire and tied the hounds to the trees, and they resumed saucing their bottle pacifiers of rye whiskey. They mirthfully frolicked, taking turns roaring the flames, spitting whiskey into the fire. They began to exchange stories about the rumored gossip of Johnny's boys, compliments of Charley's loose lips. Their eyes widened with terror as they hypothesized many theories in their hayseed's brains.

"It's the end of the world as we know it," shouted one of the drunken rednecks.

"Oh, sit down, Earl. It's not the end of the world," announced Ray Willard.

A rubicund of embarrassment flushed upon Earl's chubby cheeks as he submitted in humble compliance, taking his stump by the fire.

Ray took command of the conversation as he walked among the encampments. "Now, we all know that ever since them fancy folk moved into the valley and that gigantic mansion of theirs, we have been having some strange things happening. From them damn coffins popping up to the death of our dear, departed friend Bud Shaner and that God-damn Monster running around. I tell you all there's something strange a-going on in that their valley and I can guarantee that old story about Devil worshipers down there has something to do with it."

"Charley told me that the owner's name of their mansion is Demas. Now, if you ask me, that sounds too much like Demon, which means he must be the cause of all this Witchery that's been a-transpiring. Charley also told me ..."

A loud roar sounded fifty yards ahead, and the drunken jackals scrambled for their guns.

"What in hell's bells was that?" stammered Earl, fumbling for his rifle.

The hounds howled out in a crazed frenzy as Ray and his brother, Josh, grabbed their leashes and trekked in the direction of the vociferated roar. The others followed not so eagerly as the stories from the Devil worshipers and the realization of their present situation reverberated in their pumping hearts.

"Maybe we should come back in the morning," said Earl as he shined a flashlight into the darkness. Ray ignored the chicken's request as he and his brother continued to lead the way in a rambunctious, haphazard charge.

They found themselves at the bottom of a gulch, where the hounds were even more furious from a scent that was closer than some cared for. The hounds bellowed in all directions at the Beast, who had urinated all around the perimeter.

"Where in Sam's hell is this thing?" hollered Ray as he rubbernecked the directions; the hounds were howling.

"I don't know," Josh hollered back, "but there must be a dozen of them cause the hounds are yammering' every which way."

"I don't like it," Earl yelled. "Let's come back when there's light!"

The others quickly agreed and sided with Earl as their bickering began to wear on Ray. He finally gave in to their begging as he began to feel the fear in his pounding chest from their poor tactical position. Just as he motioned for them to turn around, the two-ton Beast suddenly pounced on Earl and crushed him with one stomp.

The others all turned and fired, only enraging it with more

fury from its own fear of being stalked. Josh's set of hounds rushed towards the Beast as he held the web of leashes, trying to keep his pack back. The creature charged his hounds, swinging his arm at the tethered dogs and Josh. It swung them over and back upon the ground, ripping off the arm of the dog handler and pummeling the hounds.

Ray momentarily froze in fear at the sight of his fallen, armless brother. He then let his pack of hounds loose, taking aim with his rifle and firing in an erratic, drunken adrenalin rush. The enraged Beast swung the crushed, dead dogs into the live ones, breaking their backs and skulls, and lodged the dead dogs into the hillside. Then it reached out and clenched one of the drunken gunmen with its giant hand and flicked his head off with its thumb as if it were a dandelion on a stem.

Ray lifted his brother, Josh, grabbed Josh's remaining arm and turned back the way they came. The last gunman tried to run up the hill in search of an escape route, only to be snatched up and have his head flicked off like a bottle cap.

The vile creature squeezed the headless body, drinking the blood with its malformed mouth as the corpse concaved itself from being drained. The Beast then scavenged the scattered dead drunks and drained them dry of their life liquid. After all was drunk, the Beast became drunk itself; it was now an intoxicated, angry creature ready for another drink.

Josh was losing consciousness upon every step they took from the loss of blood. And the craving Beast was closing in on them. The sound of breaking branches and the pounding of its trisected feet could be heard as Josh stumbled and dragged. Ray began to exhaust quickly from his own fatigue and the extra weight of his brother and riffle as he dropped Josh's arm. Yet now he faced the haunting horror of the hunter becoming the hunted.

The creature cried out its abhorrent shrills, terrorizing Ray to the bone with its gaining vicinity. Ray looked behind as if it was now in vision. In a moment, it would be on their heels.

He then caught a glimpse of the road up ahead and huffed out in joy to his brother. But Josh soon collapsed to the ground. Ray looked down upon his brother and then up at the approaching horror just thirty paces away. Raising his rifle, he took two shots at the raging, relentless creature as Josh begged his brother to help him back up.

"I'm sorry," Ray cried out and turned for his truck as the Beast halted at the crawling refreshment. The Beast slowed to a hunching halt, hovering over its prey with delight. Josh screamed out in cries of horror. The ghastly Beast then swooped up its prize and sucked on Josh's stubbed shoulder until his eyes were pulled into their sockets. Ray stammered out in tears as he could hear his brother's last cries as he reached the road to his truck. Dissatisfied with the inadequate amount of elixir, the Monster threw the dried limp carcass to the ground and looked to Ray as it hurried to its drink but tripped in a drunken stupor.

The Beast quickly rebounded as Ray fumbled for his keys with his terror-filled shaking hands. In its frustration, it continued to cry out, then trounced upon the pavement just as Ray somehow managed to start his truck. The Beast could already taste the sweet elixir of its impending prey. Ray yelled in rage as he slammed the shifter and gas pedal while the Beast reached out to the end of the tailgate with its giant, meshed hand.

"Fuck you, Devil fuck!" Bill yelled out as he floored it and broke away.

The tailgate swung open, causing the creature to lose its grip. Ray laughed insanely as he looked back in his rearview mirror and saw the Beast jump up and down in a drunken fury. It then battered the remaining vehicles in its rage at the one that got away.

Ray cried all the way to the station, beating himself up for leading his friends and brother to their deaths. It was then that David's words hit him hard: "Leave that thing well alone."

Johnny woke from a deep sleep on the sofa and quickly reached for his holster when the blubbering Ray bolted through the front door.

"That giant Devil killed everyone!" He stammered as he dropped to his knees and bawled.

"Who's everyone?" asked Johnny.

"Earl, Wally, Jed, and my ..." He could barely finish his sentence, then belched out "My, my brother."

"Where at?" commanded Johnny as Charley handed the crying fool a cup of coffee.

"Over off Blaine Road," he cried.

"Now, see what you did after the sheriff specifically told you not to chase after that damn freak."

"I'm sorry, I'm sorry!" shouted the blubbering fool. "I didn't think." Ray's words became inaudible as he slipped from the ledge of sanity. Johnny wanted to really lie to him but figured the loss of his brother was more than he could ever add. Porter walked in from the sweltering stench of the back section of the jail as Ray broke from his tears in anger and shouted, "There's more bedevilment a-going' on back there. I heard all about your two boys being possessed and all."

Johnny glared at Charley in anger, knowing he was the

leaking mouth of the station as he yelled at Ray to go home. Ray stared at Porter for a moment, then blurted, "You're that reporter from Channel 5."

Johnny raised his voice once more, "Go home!" He then grabbed Ray by his shoulders and turned him towards the door with a slight push. Ray halted at the door, turned, gazed at the incumbents of the room, and stumbled out in a mumbling moan. Johnny glared at the bean spiller once more. Charley ignored the calculating stares and pretended to be oblivious. Although Johnny was usually blunt and forward with his opinion, often speaking his mind upon the very moment of thought, the oddness of the times and the repulsion of being in the same vicinity as the spineless mouth man unraveled his mind and he thought about taking him to the murder site. Charley was relieved when Johnny turned to Porter and instead asked him if he'd go with him to check it out. Porter quickly jumped at the opportunity. He was even more elated when Johnny told him to bring his camera. He then told Charley to call the state boys and corners as he and Porter exited the station and climbed into a cruiser. Johnny turned to Porter as he shifted into drive. "How's the Priest holding up?"

Porter shook his head, "I've been mopping the water runoff from those slabs of ice. I hate to say it, but your boys seem to be in the same condition as yesterday. And that Priest," Porter shook his head once more. "I don't know where he gets his energy, but it's unearthly."

Less than fifteen minutes later, they arrived at the scene of two smashed-up trucks and a station wagon. Porter wasted no time as he squeezed off snapshots of the wreckage that lay scattered about the road.

"This thing must be a pretty sizable creature that would be capable of such a mess."

300

Johnny slammed the cruiser into the park, surveyed the premises, and then said, "You don't know the half of it," as he shook his head in disgust.

"No, but I get an uncanny feeling I'm about to," Porter returned as he rubbernecked about. The two men exited the vehicle, with Porter following Johnny past a small patch of field leading off into the timberlands, snapping photos at every angle. They soon came upon Josh's stiff, dried corpse as the dust began to fill the sky. They turned up the trail, and Johnny commenced describing the Beast for Porter, who was amazed at what his eyes beheld and his ears were hearing. But the carnage the creature left in its wake was more than enough evidence for him to believe Johnny's testament of horror.

Johnny followed the trisected footprints surrounding the encampment. They continued their tracking on a fresh trail of broken tree limbs of giant old oaks and maples.

"My God, it looks like a cyclone ripped through here!" Porters exclaimed as his lens eye took pictures of every print in the rich, red soil.

After a quarter mile or so, they came upon the cold coals of a once vibrant campfire. Johnny studied the area as Porter continued to snap his camera like a skilled machine gunman tagging his mark.

"Nothing revealed here," retorted Porter as he intermittently stared and snapped the destruction of broken limbs that reached almost twenty feet in the air.

They continued along the trail as it began to descend from the top of the foothill on which they stood. The path down was deep sand that ran all the way down the hill for a quarter mile. They started down the hill and soon came upon a human leg sticking out of the middle of a gulch. Giant meshed handprints scraped the hillside haphazardly the thick sand, burying the carcasses of its kill, and tiny, three-inch puddles spewed about the ghastly scene.

Haunting echoes filled the hillside as Porter's camera snapped upon each corpse that Johnny dug up with his bare hands. Johnny stepped back and studied the gulch grave and trail of trisected feet that went down the hill.

He then bent over a small puddle and tasted the liquid it contained with his finger, and his face scowled from the salty bitterness. After Porter shot every angle of the scene, they hightailed it back uphill, opposite the direction of the Beast's tracks.

When they reached the cruiser, Johnny cussed as he raised his hands. "Where the hell is everyone?"

He then called the station, and Pat answered. "Where's the coroner and state police?"

He barked, "We got four dead bodies up here."

Silence filled the airwaves until Pat cleared her voice. "They told Charley that we're on our own and that David is no longer sheriff. I tried calling back, but our calls won't go through."

"What the hell's going on?" returned Johnny, feeling lost and abandoned. "What about the FBI?" Johnny queried as if reaching.

"I'm one step ahead of you, boss. Done did that, and they pretty much said the same thing."

Johnny burst out in anger. "What the fuck are we supposed to do with all these dead bodies?"

An awkward silence came over the radio until Pat replied, "I don't know, bury them?"

"I suppose," Johnny answered. "What's up with my boys?"

"I hate to say it, but they're pretty much the same as yesterday," Pat offered. "After the Priest fell over a couple of times, I was finally able to talk him into laying down for a while."

Johnny sighed, "Alright then, I guess I'll drop Porter off at the hotel, then go get a shovel at the hardware store, and listen, Pat?"

"Yeah, Johnny."

"Don't tell that chicken shit Charley anything. I want this under a tight wrap."

"You got it, boss," she replied. "Oh, and your boys are on another rant right now."

Johnny huffed. "I got to go."

Pat echoed, "You be careful out there, you hear."

"Ten-four, over and out," returned Johnny.

"You've got to be kidding," said Porter. "I'm not going to let you bury those poor souls by yourself."

Johnny wasn't going to argue the point as he simply said, "You're a good man, Mr. Lewis," and then drove off toward town. When they pulled up to the hardware store, Jack Longley was sitting out in front without a care in the world.

"What you say there, Johnny?" the old man said with an upbeat tone.

"Not much, Mr. Longley. Just stopped over to pick up a couple of shovels."

"Well, I'm sorry, you came for nothing. I just sold my last two to a couple of young chaps. Ordered more, but they don't come in till next Thursday." Johnny looked at Porter oddly as if another monkey wrench had been thrown into his plan by the monkey itself. Johnny got quiet in momentary thought as he wondered who could have bought the last shovels. He then thought quickly as he told Jack that Porter accidentally hit a stray dog on his way into town and that they needed a shovel to bury it.

"Say no more," Jack offered. "I have an old one out back. You can have it."

The old man sluggishly turned as Johnny thanked him. He then apologized to Porter for using him in his fib. "You don't have to explain to me," said Porter. "Your actions are very understandable due to these circumstances."

Johnny nodded as the old man made his way back to the front of the shop with an aged, old, sturdy shovel. "This should handle the job," said Jack as he surrendered the shovel to Johnny's hand. "Don't bother returning that old thing," he added as he assumed his chair.

Johnny dug deep into his pockets as he approached the old-timer.

"Don't bother digging for gold there, Johnny," remarked the old man, "That old shovel is only worth its weight in scrap." Johnny smiled, then shook the old man's hand and told him not to hesitate to call the station if he ever needed anything.

"You got it, Johnny," Jack replied as he leaned back in his chair.

Johnny walked to his cruiser, then turned and asked, "Mr. Longley, who was it that bought your last shovels anyway?"

The old man thought for a moment, then said, "Two young chaps around your age. Why do you ask?" Johnny retreated from heavy thought, "Oh, nothing, just being nosey, that's all. I'll see you later, Mr. Longley."

The old man waved as Johnny and Porter piled into the cruiser and drove off towards the scene of their disgust. Johnny described his last encounter with his good friend, Thomas Syck, as they speculated as to why the hellions needed shovels. Porter also contemplated his own theories in his mind as he listened to Johnny's testimony and the recollection of David's troubles.

"Take it from a second-generation reporter," Porter commented, "Until I came to Horry County, I thought I had seen it all." Johnny pulled to the side of the road where the empty vehicles were, "Oh, I get the feeling we're just warming up."

Their minds raced as they looked each other in the eye, took a deep breath, and sighed.

"Well, you sure picked the wrong town to report on," said Johnny as he opened his door.

"No, my good man," returned Porter, "I'm right where I should be," as he exited the vehicle. They loathed in their minds their duty as they labored on the trail to the scene of Josh's death. Upon their approach, Johnny blurted out, "I'll be damned. I must be going crazy or what?" he said as he scooped the area near and far.

Porter followed up on Johnny's bafflement as he did the same, searching for Josh Willard's body. "No, it's not you," announced Porter. "Take a look at these fresh tracks. They match the others from that Thingamajigger Monster of yours."

"Hey, he ain't my Monster," retorted Johnny in disgust.

305

"My bad," returned Porter.

Johnny shook off the chills that tingled down his spine, then pointed in the direction of fresh tracks that led towards the other carcasses.

They descended the deep gulch that was scarred from deep-rooted tracks of Beast that trapesed down the gulch. Johnny studied its steep slope and the continuing tracks that scraped down its side.

"What a crazy ride this thing's taking us on," Johnny commented.

Porter concurred with Johnny's remarks, then followed all the while, wondering what horrors lay before them.

Halfway down, they came upon a blockade of piled sand that filled a ten-foot span within the gulch. Instantly, they realized the pile was not made by Mother Nature. Two tree limbs in the form of a cross lay, sticking out from the sand. Johnny studied the surroundings in silence.

"Looks like that thing has somewhat of a conscience after all, huh," said Porter as he stared at the lumped-together cross.

Johnny knelt on the ground and again reached out to what looked like a small rain puddle. He tasted a drop from the tip of his finger. "Salt," Johnny blurted as he spit it out. He then stood and gazed upon the trisected tracks that skipped down the rest of the hill.

"Well," said Johnny, pointing, "That thing buried them pretty good and seems to have gone that away. That means we go back the way we came."

"No argument there," returned Porter as they turned back up the hill.

After they had returned to the road, Johnny called Pat and told her to call Brian's towing to get the smashed-up vehicles off the road. She asked what he did with the bodies and if everything went okay.

"I'll be there in a couple minutes to explain everything, over and out."

"Ten-four," Pat answered.

David and Sarah pulled into the parking lot of Brunswick Bi-County Hospital and headed to the third floor. When they reached Lisa's room, she was being entertained by Amanda. Sarah immediately rushed to Amanda's side after first seeing that her daughter appeared to be well.

"Are you all right?" questioned Sarah as she looked down upon Amanda's leg.

Amanda's eyes began to well, and Sarah soon followed suit. They embraced each other and cried while David stood in his own silence.

Amanda then wailed out, "My boys, their eyes were black with hate. They kept saying how they wanted to stop my pounding heart from beating." Seeing the scope of her anguish, Sarah said nothing. She just embraced Amanda as she gazed upon David and her daughter.

Little Lisa ran to her crying mother and hugged Sarah's leg.

Sarah scooped her up and embraced her, then she gently sat her on the bed. Lisa turned to her father and hugged him, and his heart melted in her hands. He then straightened his voice and asked Amanda if she had seen his mother.

Amanda shook her head, "I haven't seen her since yesterday afternoon."

David said nothing as if linking puzzles in his head. Sarah and David then looked at each other in confusion as a nurse entered the room. David quickly asked if Dr. Miranda was around.

"I'm sorry, but Dr. Miranda had to leave for New York last night, leaving your daughter in the capable hands of Dr. Hogart."

"Well, is he coming back or what?" David inquired sternly.

The nurse returned a low blow. "No, Dr. Miranda relinquished his position as your daughter's physician to Dr. Hogart." She then took Lisa's empty tray and disappeared into the hallway with a fake smile. David went to call his mother, as every ringtone haunted his imagination. A voice finally answered hello.

"Hey, mom, I thought you were going to stay in Harrisville a little longer. Are you alright?"

"I'm fine, David. I just figured that Lisa was doing better, so I came home. Besides, that room wasn't cheap, you know."

"I would've paid for your room," David quickly responded.

"No, but thanks anyway. That city's just too busy for me. I'm more comfortable here at home."

David then told her that he'd be back in town in a few hours and that he'd come by to check in on her.

"That's alright, David; I'm just going to tuck in early and call it a day."

David knew something was wrong and wanted to ask her about Dr. Miranda but decided not to press her now. They said their goodbyes, and Carol resumed her steady, silent sulk. David motioned for Amanda to follow him into the hallway. He wasn't about to just roll over and let Devin win. He had a lot of fight left in him and a couple of tricks of his own that he was soon planning to perform.

Amanda told him what she knew as he stood staring, taking in the information as if nothing more could surprise him. They then walked into the room and found Sarah and little Lisa crying as if it were the end of the world. David shouted over their bawling, "Hey, what's all the tears for?"

Sarah straightened her voice. "Lisa began crying when you left the room, which made me start crying."

"Daddy," Lisa stammered.

"It's okay, I'm right here," he said as he went to her side, and Sarah tried to dry her eyes.

All the tears got Amanda going again, and even David's eyes welled. Soon after, tears turned into laughter as David entertained the room with his rendition of Burt and Ernie from Sesame Street.

Dr. Hogart entered the room on that upbeat note. He smiled and stated, "I'm glad to see everyone in high spirits because I have good news. By this time next week, Lisa will be able to go home. She needs one more treatment. The downside is that she will have to be treated for Monoclonal Acrid for the rest of her life in the form of a pill, and it can be quite costly. But other than the cost and the remembering to take her prescription every day, she should be able to live a normal life."

"That's good news, doc, but what happened to Doctor Miranda?"

"Why, I don't really know. He just called and said he was

going back to his practice in New York with no explanation."

"Okay, well, let me ask you another question. What did Doctor Miranda do that you and your staff couldn't do?"

"Mr. Lang, I did try to tell you that we are very capable and prepared to treat your daughter. Now, I don't want to cause any waves, but Dr. Miranda barely lifted a finger. Your daughter's treatment is routine for me and my staff. Miranda or no Miranda, the results would be the same."

Dr. Hogart looked at Lisa's chart at the foot of her bed, cracked a goose and duck joke, and then exited. Sarah invited Amanda to stay with her at the Berkshire since David was going back to Horry County. One hour later, a nurse popped her head on the door and announced that visiting hours were over. Sarah assured little Lisa that she would be there tomorrow as the darling little girl resisted crying to show how big she could be in exchange for her parents' hugs and dolls. David dropped Sarah and Amanda off at the Berkshire Hotel, then took off towards Horry County with a vengeance of retribution.

At the station, Michael was still asleep, as were the bedevil Imps. Father Hemmings arrived in guilt after his previous day's abandonment. He told Pat not to wake the sleeping Priest as he had her buzz him through the door.

He was armed with vestments, holy water, and a bible. He quivered and quaked as he walked through the murky, morbid chanting, "Our Father, who art in heaven …" He then halted between the boys' cells and fumbled through the pages of his bible, reciting passages of holy ritual.

Teddy woke up coughing, then stood holding his stomach. He then shuffled to the bars, continuing to hold his stomach while his hair hung, hiding his face.

"I'm sick, Father," he said in a sweet, boyish voice.

The gullible Priest stepped up close to the bars and stooped down face level with the Imp. "What's wrong?" he asked, concerned, as he tried to catch a glimpse of his face.

"Well, Father," the little Devil said as he reached through the bars and grabbed both ends of the Priest's vestment, yanking his face towards him. The old Priest tried to yell out, but his mouth became flooded by the black fluid that Teddy regurgitated.

Teddy and Timmy both started laughing while the old Priest's stomach palpitated erratically, and he coiled to his knees. A sharp pin punched his paunch, and he puked, pouring black. The urchin Imps jumped up and down in victory like they had just won a game they invented that nobody else could win.

Father Hemmings staggered to an open cell, where he gargled his mouth with water and tried desperately to dislodge the vile substance. The rusted tap water was met with resistance from the black, oily blood that gurgled in his mouth. He felt its Evil slither down his esophagus like a serpent into its nest. He clawed at his stomach in wrenching agony, and he squirmed on the floor like a worm being hooked. He gagged and gargled in a muffled, chaotic frenzy, becoming crazed for a draw of air. His sapped lungs strived to belch out a cry for help as he flailed and flopped upon the floor.

Suddenly, he seized his stirring about as the seething blackness of hate now sustained his once unsullied soul. He lifted his head, his eyes now blackened with a burning hatred for the pure at heart and the pious.

Teddy stood smiling as the soured Priest smiled back upon the twisted Imp. Father Hemmings looked down upon his vestment and ripped it off with utter disgust for its meaning.

He then turned towards the entrance, where a ring of keys hung tempting with the fruit of freedom. He finessed it quietly off its hook and returned to Teddy's cell and then Timmy's, letting loose the hounds of hell. They all held hands in a circle and did a quick Diddy of "Ring Around the Rosy." They then seized their mirth as the Priest put a finger to his lips and whispered instructions into their ears. The Imps snickered quietly behind their new leader as he knocked twice on the door.

Pat buzzed open the door as the Imps ran past the Priest and scurried towards the front door. She momentarily became speechless before stammering out, "What are you doing?"

The now twisted Priest smirked at her shocked frame and shuffled past her to the front door, where the two Devils awaited his presence. He opened the door as they scampered out past him, where they jumped up and down in elation. The old Priest stood in the doorway and hollered, "Goodbye, goodnight, good riddance." He then lifted both his hands as he flipped off the room, then turned away, laughing hysterically.

"Did you get a look at Father Hemming's eyes," queried Pat as she looked past Michael's shoulder.

"Why? Why did you let him in there alone?" clamored the young Priest.

"I don't know. Since you were in there alone and sleeping so well, I thought it would be okay. I'm so sorry. What have I done?"

Michael then turned to her with tenderhearted compassion. "It's alright; you had no way of knowing. I should have warned you. This is my fault, not yours."

"Why do you think Father Hemmings did that? Is he

affected like the Morgan boys?"

"From the description you gave of him and his actions, I believe that to be true.

"Where do you think they're going?" asked Pat, dumbfounded.

Michael replied, "Thanks for everything."

The young Priest turned; Pat followed him out the door and hollered, "You're going hoof it? I could drive if you like."

"No thanks," he hollered back, "I want to stealth my way without being beheld."

"Okay," returned Pat, as if wondering whether the Priest had lost his marbles.

She went back inside the station, somewhat dumbfounded. An hour later, Johnny pulled into his parking spot. Pat saw him pull up, and after he turned off the engine and opened the door, Pat rushed to him.

"I'm so sorry, Johnny. Please don't get mad, but somehow, Father Hemmings became tainted like your boys, and they all tricked me."

Johnny pounded his fist upon the hood of his cruiser and yelled with utter frustration. "Does this shit ever fucking end?!"

Pat's eyes welled with tears as she hysterically expressed her sorrow. Johnny calmed his anger as he hugged her and said, "It's alright, but where's the young Priest?"

Pat turned and pointed in the direction in which Michael had gone.

At that moment, David pulled in Sarah's new BMW. He stepped out, asking what was new. Johnny opened his cruiser door and hollered, "Hop in; we got a Priest to catch!"

David didn't question Johnny's statement or motives as he simply climbed into the vehicle, and Johnny sped away to the church. At the church, the bedevil Priest secured the double doors by chain and lock.

Meanwhile, the urchin Imps went on a rampage, turning the place inside out. After all entrances were secured, the aged building was virtually impenetrable with its stone walls and stained-glass windows that reached high upon the building. Inside were enough provisions to last them a year, if needed, but all they desired was the sinful bliss of destruction and the defamation of God. The possessed, mesmerized neophytes toiled diligently in joy as they toppled the giant crucifix to the floor. The old Priest then helped them turn it upside down. Then the Imps spray painted the face. After every crucifix was turned and painted, they danced in the middle of the floor, where they cleared the pews for the reverie.

In Johnny's frustration, he expressed how and why the church was built to keep an army out. Then, out of nowhere, the two FBI agents appeared and commanded Johnny and David to halt in their tracks.

"What do you think you're doing?!" yelled the short one in a self-righteous tone.

"My two sons are in that church," Johnny barked back.

The short agent flailed his arms. "I don't care if your mammy, your daddy, and your grandpappy are in there. This is private property, and you, Mr. Lang, are no longer a sheriff. You know the drill, deputy, file a missing person's report, or you and Cornholio here can take a trip back to jail. Now move the fuck on."

David called upon all his strength to hold himself back from punching the living daylights out of the agents, and he had to restrain Johnny from doing the same. All the while, the agents laughed at them.

"Let it go for now," announced David as he stared into the shrimpy agent's eyes and held back Johnny's small frame with his arm.

"Yeah, let it go, Johnny," mimicked the short agent as he and his partner guffawed and hoped he'd jump them.

"Come on, Johnny," David commanded once more.

David and Johnny walked back to the cruiser as the dictators followed, eyeballing their every move. Once in the car, Johnny crashed his fists against the steering wheel as David looked away, feeling disgusted and helpless. The two agents laughed hysterically at the young deputy's anger as they stood watching off to the side. Their laughter roused newfound strength in David as he reached over and firmly backhanded Johnny on his arm.

"Come on, I need you to get it together right now, okay."

Johnny turned, surprised, but still slammed into drive, trying to spit gravel at his newfound foes. He cursed all the way to the station, feeling bruised and bullied by a system in which he once placed so much faith.

Once at the station, David called everyone into the briefing---Pat, Johnny, and Porter.

"Pat, Johnny, as you already know, I'm no longer your sheriff."

"Yeah, about that," blurted Pat as Johnny concurred.

315

"No," said David, "Don't consider me your boss. They took my badge in Columbus, but I'm still a legally bound citizen and a pissed-off one at that." Johnny shook his head in agreement as all ears were tuned in to David.

"I am somehow kin to that sick fuck Devin Demas out there in the valley," David revealed. Johnny's face became flustered, and Pat looked confused as they sat silently awaiting his next words. He then explained how their quaint little town was and is the home of the Devil's man. At that point, Johnny was willing to believe anything, but he was still aghast as to the description of the sorcerer he had not yet met.

At the church, the two agents were welcomed and acknowledged as they invited the foul Priest and his two Imps to the mansion. They quickly agreed under the condition that they could bring their giant crucifix. The two agents shrugged their shoulders and said, "Why the hell not?" and then grabbed the long cross and carried it to their suburban, where they secured it on top. The Priest clasped his hands as he marveled at the scene while the Devil Imps skipped and danced around the vehicle.

Agent Dickerson opened the rear door and coaxed the excited, bedeviled boys into the vehicle. The twisted bunch then drove off towards the mansion with the Imps hanging their heads out the window to the sounds of Primus; Jerry was a race car driver.

When they reached the mansion, they were greeted with open arms. To Nina and Ora, the two Imps were warm creatures they found hard to resist. They stood the cross up just beyond the pits with the imprisoned schoolgirls, and all eyes marveled at its defiled appearance. Even Devin himself came out to see the spectacle of marred Evil and then led his flock to the old ruins. The pentagram was now a blackened pool oozing black hate as the sound of its vile rupture seemed to sound like hymns of hellish veneration.

Devin baptized his disciples in the sacrament of initiation as their drenched bodies glistened with their black hatred. In the brush, Buckeye Buck was beholding their sinful bliss as his presence went unnoticed.

At the station, Pat, Porter, Johnny, and David watched an old thirteen-inch TV tuned in to the local news that was broadcasting live from Dillon in Dillon County, northeast of Horry. A reporter yelled over the blades of a helicopter as a camera showed the devastation of a forest that was being devoured by fire. The reporter then quieted as he received information, cupping his hand to his ear. After a moment, he apologized for the pause and then announced that the fire marshal of Brunswick County was requesting that all neighboring counties help extinguish the blaze.

The screen then flashed back to the news desk, where a refined, busty brunette reporter furnished new information on Brunswick, Dillon, Horry, and a few other counties in assisting with the fire. The newscaster turned to the weather forecaster and said, "It's our understanding that strong winds are the reason the fire's out of control."

"That's right," said the weatherman as camera two flashed upon a little man and a satellite news van. The screen flashed a blackened Earth that the fire left in its path. Strong winds fueled its march over hills and majestic, aged forest as the forecaster swung his arm in the direction of the strong winds.

"I don't know about you, but didn't that look like that weatherman was pointing toward Lang Township?" said Pat with newfound fear.

"Well, isn't that another blow below the belt," retorted Johnny as he flicked off the old television. He turned to Pat and David; this Demas character can eat a bullet now that my

317

boys are involved.

"Now, now, hold on there," returned David with woeful fright that Johnny might ignite an unplanned gunfight. "For all we know, we could be the only defense against this plague that's infesting our lives and maybe the world."

David sighed and expounded on the severity of their situation with un-waving authority as he divulged the beginning of a plan. Johnny and David went back to the church and parked in a hidden cove a half block away. They stealth their way to the edge of a forest, where they scoped out the parking lot for the FBI agents' Suburban.

They crouched behind a bush where they could view the confines. They saw its quiet emptiness. David gave the okay to enter the church's double oak doors. He waved his hand as he crept into the dimly lit building. They walked through the vestibule, and the only sound was of their stilted steps of restraint. David pointed out the spray-painted graffiti in a fashion of devilish demeanor.

They came to two more doors that led to the cathedral with guns at the ready and alertness alarmed. When David opened the door, the young Priest Michael was cleaning up the sacrilegious defilement.

"Are you alone?" David yelled.

"I am," returned the young Priest as he continued his fussing about.

David and Johnny holstered their guns as they approached the toiling Priest.

"Who did this?" Porter replied.

"Satin!" bellowed the angered Priest. "He who bears many

318

faces."

"Satan's infected servants, which your sons and Father Hemmings have become. They serve their Master, who bears many names and faces. From Beelzebub to Lucifer, Mephistopheles to Satan, Belial to the old serpent, or just plain Devil. He may bear many names and Evils with only one quest: the complete annihilation and desecration of our creator's creation, along with the commandeering of his holy city."

David sighed with slight despair, then asked, what about Johnny's boys?"

The Priest looked through David's Soul as he replied, "Why David Daniel Lang, you know very well where they are. The snake is out of his skin, warming himself upon the rock."

"Let me guess," David said, "The Demas mansion."

The young Priest with old eyes nodded yes, with a look of respectful approval. The Priest turned away and returned to his work as David, Johnny, and Porter went out into the night.

At Brunswick Bi-County Hospital, Sarah and Amanda waited impatiently, awaiting news from Dr. Hogart. Sarah's face was drenched with hope, and Amanda was by her side. To Dr. Hogart's bafflement, Lisa suffered a relapse of her rare blood disease. He approached Sarah in the waiting room with a sorrowful, sodden face.

"I don't understand," he said, "She was doing well, and all the tests came back fine."

"Well, apparently, you missed something," barked Sarah.

"I assure you, Mrs. Lang ..."

Sarah interrupted and tearfully babbled, "Where's Dr.

Miranda? She was getting better when he was here."

"Again, I'm sorry, Mrs. Lang, but there's nothing he could do that I and my staff couldn't do ourselves. This could have happened on any doctor's watch."

Sarah lifted her head high. "Listen here, doc, you and your staff better make damn sure my baby lives through this. Or I'll have your medical license revoked and sue the hell out of you."

The gentle doctor shrugged off her words as if he had heard it all before but still sympathized. Dr. Hogart expounded once more his dire dedication to Lisa's recovery and said he would bring all his brightest colleagues on board. Sarah gazed at him and nodded her head in agreement, as he was her only hope. Dr. Hogart placed his hand on her shoulder and then excused himself to return to his work.

That night, Devin and his cabal placed James's bones in a leather sack and smashed them with hammers. They did this until the three hundred–year–old bones were crushed into little pieces. Hector then took the leather bag as he and Syck left together for a crematorium in Brunswick County.

When they arrived at the cemetery, Syck disposed of the security guard by slitting his throat. Syck took great pleasure in his murderous endeavor, watching as the security officer's knees folded to the floor. They then proceeded to the furnace and ignited the incinerating flames. Syck set the temperature at fourteen hundred degrees as instructed by Devin, and he poured the sack of broken bones into a metal trough. Blue-tipped flames emitted from the furnace as Syck opened the cast-iron door and slid the trough into the fiery oven. The two maniacs giggled in their task and reminisced about the torture they had committed recently as they awaited the bones in the furnace.

Moments later, a buzzer sounded, and the flames

automatically shut down. Syck opened the door, and Hector grabbed the trough with asbestos gloves. After a cooldown, Hector dumped the chalky powder into the leather sack, threw it over his shoulder, and they headed back to the valley.

On a hillside overlooking the Demas mansion, David, Porter, and Johnny were scoping out the premises. They took notice of the pits where the restrained schoolgirls were being tortured by the two Imps. They would peep inside the prison pits with flashlights and sing twisted nursery rhymes about their demise. Screams echoed throughout the valley, along with harrowing laughter.

Herbert and Dickerson sat laughing by the poolside as they watched the Imps torture the young girls. Johnny couldn't believe his eyes as he beheld true Evil in his boys' forms.

Nina and Ora joined in on the fun, with Johnny's bedevil boys entertaining them. Devin then walked up to the sitting hyenas, and they became instantly silent in his presence. Devin's third orb closed as he announced they were being watched.

The two Agents jumped to their feet, awaiting orders to assail the intruders. Devin then whispered words of Witchery as Ora, Nina, and both agents began to morph. Each turned into Demon form, tailored to their characteristics and structure. Ora changed into a slender sloth-like creature, and Nina mutated into a tall, harrowing hag that heckled. Agent Herbert transmuted into a deranged dwarf with deformed curvature. Agent Dickerson was recasting in a long-legged lizard with talons that could scissor a man in half. They stood in front of their Master with a thirst for blood, ready for command. Devin smiled at their sadistic skin, then pointed to the hillside in the direction of the encroachers.

Each of the Demons moved in a manner peculiar to their

structure, stalking the surrounding hillside. David, Johnny, and Porter witnessed the Demonic transformations into hellish soldiers now in pursuance of them. David gave the command to run in the direction from which they had come.

Then, suddenly, the hillside began to wave like a blanket on a clothesline. David looked back at the pool after falling to the ground and saw Devin waving his arms in a motion that corresponded to the rolling hill. The Demon Devils began to make their way to David and his confidants, and he began to realize the hopelessness of their situation.

David motioned for Johnny and Porter to abscond as he turned and took a position with a high-powered rifle. Johnny told Porter to keep running as he took a position higher upon the rippling hill. David squeezes his trigger at the closest oncoming creature. It fell, letting out a hissing screech of pain.

The lizard-like creature squirmed momentarily, then scrambled back upon its clawed feet. It lunged uphill in a jagged leap, whereupon Johnny's bullet hit its mark on its narrow skull just as it was going for David's throat. The dwarf Demon and the tall, hunched hag crawled carefully in heed of the flying projectiles that sprayed in their direction. The slithering sloth side-winded stealthily David's lower left.

Between the confusion of the wavering hillside and the coursing creatures, David questioned their fate in his mind. He ran out of ammunition, and likewise, Johnny's rifle became empty of shells. They both scrambled for their side arms in a staggering attempt for balance upon their feet. The sloth-like creature slithered slowly upward as the others diverted David and Johnny's attention. The hillside was ruthless in its rocking and reeling, leaving the three men buckled to the ground. The vibration of quaking left a blur in David's eyes while Johnny managed to trip along with Porter at the top of the hill. David caught a glimpse of Johnny and Porter as he yelled and waved his hand, commanding them to escape.

Johnny hesitated with an unwillingness to leave his friend behind, but he saw David was angry, and his facial expression and hand signals indicated he should leave. Johnny reluctantly obeyed as he and Porter stumbled down the other side of the hill.

The hill gradually slowed its rampant rumbles as David found the slithery, slinking sloth hovering over him. Just as he closed his eyes, ready for death, Ora's skin returned to its original form. Nina and Herbert also returned to their human skin as they stood over a dead Agent.

"I think best you should come along quietly, ay," said Ora in a low, calm voice.

David opened his eyes as he beheld Ora's emptiness. He slapped her hand out of his way and then stood on his own. Ora just smiled, then turned and walked back down the hill.

David stood momentarily, then followed her without a fuss as he decided to face the Devil's drum and not try to run. When they reached the basin, Ed glared with seething hatred to his hatred as David said, "That's one lizard that won't fly no more."

Nina put her arm against Herbert's chest as he began to advance toward the object of his hatred, and David just smiled as he walked past. Devin sat poolside, awaiting his catch as Ora and David approached his deranged domain.

"Welcome again to my humble abode," declared Devin with a Devilish grin and glare of discontent. David said nothing, and it seemed to amuse Devin. "I see your friend's gotten away, but that's alright; at least I have you, grandson."

"Don't fucking call me that," barked David, clenching his

fist in gritted teeth anger.

"You can't deny the truth, David. You know what I really detest? That name your parents gave you. I think I'll name you Devlin, yes, Devlin Demas."

"Never," roared David in a torrent of rage.

A moment of silence bestowed the air until the Imps sounded off in their discontent from David disrespecting their Master. Devin raised his hand, and they were silent.

"You know, Devlin, I can make you a willing party to my plans, but I'd much prefer you sober without the black blood of hell coursing through your vanes. This way, you could think with your mind instead of your raging heart of hate. I'll tell you what's going to happen here. But first, I'm going to tell you what's not going to happen. I'm not going to alter your way of thinking because I want your free, willing mind when you join me in my quest. I'm not going to hurt your family any more than I already have or disrupt your quaint little town any more than I must. It all depends upon you."

Chills crept up David's back as he surmised that Devin somehow made his daughter sick.

"But still," said Devin as he gazed into David's aura, "I think best that you should have a little incentive to stick around for a while so you can learn to respect me."

"That will never happen," replied David as he smiled at his captor.

Devin simply smiled and turned to Ora. "Ora, my dear, remember that little ditty I taught you when you were in love with that quarterback from Michigan State."

Ora smiled from ear to ear. "Oh yeah, he was my little lap

dog till I grew tired of him."

Devin smiled in reminiscence as he added, "Yeah, that little act of yours cost that poor kid his career, but C' Est la Vie. Sing it, girl."

Ora smiled as David flashed back to Nina's bewitching words, bracing himself for the worst. Ora retracted her smile as she gazed at David, then began a stemming spell of old.

*"Try, try, you might well try, from feet that tread so slow. But where you stand, this house, this land, is far as you can go."*

David felt no different as he stood stubbornly stern and stout, with a strong intention to kill if he got the chance. Devin walked into the mansion and said, "My home is your home. Feel free to do as you please." Ora smiled as the Imps just stared at David while the old Priest did the same. They conversed and whispered their joy for their newfound toy. They turned toward David and wanted to play with Devlin. They began to circle David in a hellish dance and chant.

David just stood there, silent and unimpressed.

The four gave a look of disappointment as they ceased their mirth and dance and said, "Let's find someone who's more fun." David waited until they disappeared into the mansion before he proceeded to the pits. The closer he came, the more he couldn't believe the vast area of the prisons that emitted whimpers into his ears.

He came upon the first prison pit, dropped to his knees, and called out. A cry of desperation was heard from below in a frantic plea for rescue. David lifted the cinder blocks from the plywood boards, then slid the boards from the Earthly opening. Inside was Louise with no clothing, dressed only in a tortured gloom. David reached out his hand as she coiled into a ball, screaming in wrenched tears as if he were the cause of her harrowing horror. He shouted down his good intent, which quieted her; she gazed up at his hand with squinting eyes. David continued his words of comfort. To cover her naked, shivering, soiled body,

David took off his shirt and wrapped her with it.

Nina shook her head. "Blue, don't become you," she said in satirical levity.

David turned around as Herbert and Nina stood there gawking in amusement.

"You all are some pretty sick fucks, you know that," David lashed out. "Look at her! You get off in making people miserable and sick?"

"Yeah, it really makes me hot in my spot, if you know what I mean," said Nina as she touched herself in a tasteless, ill-mannered gesture. "This woman needs food and clothing," declared David with urgent intent. Nina laughed and said, "Yeah, well, I need some more of that libido of yours, but you don't hear me complaining. Now throw that little whore back in her hole and come to Mama."

"You got to be kidding," scoffed David as he gazed upon her with disgust.

"We'll see," returned Nina as if on a mission to prove him wrong.

David sighed an audible sound of annoyance while slumping Louise's arm over his shoulder and whispering encouraging words into her ear.

"You heard the lady, put the little bitch back in her hole!" shouted Herbert to David.

David ignored the command as he and Louise continued their shuffle towards the mansion. Herbert shouted once more, threatening harm in the form of a broken skull. David simply halted without turning and stuck up his middle finger. That got Herbert puffing up his chest and marching toward David until Nina intervened.

"Leave it," she ordered. Herbert halted instantly upon her command, like a trained canine obeying his Master. "Go ahead, kitchens to the right when you walk in the door."

David turned his head and smirked at the seething agent, then proceeded into the mansion. He tried to keep the woman's mind active as he asked her name and where she was from. The weakened woman whimpered words of unintelligible woe, and David weighed what was left of her wits.

Once inside, he sat her down on a chair by the dining room table. Then he ran to the refrigerator. Upon opening the door, a pig's head on a silver platter stared back at him in a gruesome guise. David caught his breath from the unsettling sight and rummaged past the platter to some lunchmeat.

He quickly slopped together a sandwich with some rye bread he found in a breadbox, then set the concoction in front of the dismayed Louise. He told her that he'd be back in thirty seconds as he held up his palms in a hold-tight gesture.

Rushing to the bathroom, he found a bathrobe. Upon his return to the kitchen, he noticed that she hadn't touched her food. Louise just stared into space, separated from reality. David covered her naked body with the robe, then lifted the sandwich to her discolored lips, trying to persuade her to eat.

"Well, well, I guess you can lead a horse to water, but you can't make 'em drink, huh," said Syck from behind. David turned around to face the blond, blue-eyed creep who took pleasure in others' pain, especially women.

"Oh, I finally get to meet the asshole himself," said David in turn.

Syck shook his head and threatened, "You know, you keep talking out that asshole you call a mouth, and you're gonna find out really quick what I'm about."

David gazed at the shell of Louise, "How the fuck could you do this to a human being? Look at her! She doesn't even know her name."

"That's funny," said Syck, "She sure knew how to scream when I was giving it to her doggy style. Oh yeah, she screams good."

"You're a real fucking pig, you know that. A low-life, scum of the Earth pig."

"I'm a pig? I'm a pig? You're the toting badge bitch. Oh, I forgot, you no longer carry a silver star, do you, swine boy."

David glared in a burning rage, then turned to feed the void, Louise.

Syck continued, "Yeah, no matter how much you wash your skin, you still stink like swine."

Syck went on and on until David lost it.

David turned and charged Syck in a warpath of impetuous hostility, knocking him off his feet. He pounded Syck's face with furious rage as he sat upon his torso, pinning him to the floor. Syck bloodied quickly, laughing insanely at each slug. David became confused by Syck's laughter, and then the humanity in him bent in mercy. He stood and ceased his attack. But Syck continued his psychopathic cackling. David gazed around the room and saw it was now full of spectators.

Syck jumped to his feet and began to curse with mouth witching words until Devin yelled no. Syck gawked about the room, embarrassed as blood dripped from his face. "Fine, I'll kick his ass the old-fashioned way."

Ora, Herbert, Hector, and Nina cleared furniture while Devin sat in amusement, watching the two bucks. They took positions of war, staring at each other with searing storms of scornful hatred for the other.

Nina had a twisted epiphany as she urged them to wait until she could blast the stereo to the death metal of Slayer. She then shouted, "Okay, go!" as a big smile came to her face.

Both Nina and Ora sat at the foot of their Master as David waved his hand to Syck to commence their battle. Syck let out a war cry like a crazed Indian about to scalp his foe. They rushed each other, clashing at the midpoint as they traded punch for punch upon each other's frame. David was slightly ahead but beginning to bruise from the brutality. The metal music pounded on while the entertainment of the altercation garnered smiles from the wicked onlookers. Syck's young body seemed relentless as he came at David from different angles with every underhanded tactic he knew.

David took a left to his ribcage and a right to his gut, which sent him gasping for air. But he continued the brawl in bold-hearted fashion. Syck's face began to look like pummeled meat. Each man had his reasons to remain resolute in their repulsion for the other. Syck's vain glory and embarrassment of failure in front of his friends, along with his hatred for the police, kept his fight alive. David's endurance was the result of all the afflictions that had been cast upon him since Devin's arrival. His fuel also burned for the wretched Soul.

s bound in their Earthen pits. Even though David's battle

wasn't solely for himself, a small part of him took pleasure in beating the malevolent maverick black and blue with his old fighting skills. Slayer's music played to its finish as the dueling duo discarded into the next CD of "Cannibal Corpse" while each wore the blood of the other upon their fists.

Both David and Syck had the advantage at different points in the confrontation until the older lion began to dominate. A song later, Syck lay at David's feet. David looked down at his floored foe and then up at the sitting amused one who applauded his performance.

"You fucking bastard," David huffed out, "You won't even feed those young girls out there. What kind of a Monster are you anyway? What's to become of them?"

Devin smiled at the wobbling, fatigued David, then announced, "Smorgasbord sacrifice, what else."

David wanted so desperately to continue the beating and redirect it upon Devin's face but decided to take a different approach. He appealed to Devin's passion for cruelty as he told him how he could get better juice from a healthy peach than a spoiled one. He then asked if he could take the prisoners out of their pits for food and exercise.

Devin studied David's bloodied face for a moment, then nodded his head. He agreed under the condition that only one girl at a time would be freed and then returned to her Earthly prison. David tried to argue how their health would deteriorate if put back in the cold, damp holes. Syck stood up in protest in a bloodied mess and said, "Let them out. What the fuck are we here for, Birthday cakes and ice cream? I mean, What the fuck."

Devin smiled at Syck, then turned to David, extended his arm, and nodded in the direction of the imprisoned girls. Syck shook his head in defeat as David smirked at him and began to shuffle in the direction Devin gestured.

Nina rushed to David's side and put her hand up to touch a cut above his eye. He quickly turned away, and her hand froze where he stood. He then shuffled to the kitchen, and his eyes beheld a losing sight of a half-naked Herbert pawing at the shell-shocked Louise. David rushed to them and cracked Herbert's left jaw with a hard right. Herbert fell, tumbling to the floor from the fierce blow, tripping over his own pants. Nina, Ora, and Hector entered the room and laughed upon seeing Herbert and his flabby nakedness.

Louise lay paralyzed, staring into space. David re-clothed her, sat down again, then shouted for everyone to leave the room.

Herbert pulled up his trousers and told David to watch his back. David ignored him as he pushed Louise's hair from her face and went to the sink to fetch her some water. Herbert glared with fiery eyes thinking he might return the favor of a sucker punch.

"Come on, Herbert," said Nina, "Leave him be with that skank whore."

Herbert reluctantly followed orders as he and the rest of the group left the room.

David held the glass to Louise's lips. Suddenly, she grabbed his hand and tipped the life fluid into her mouth.

"Easy," said David.

She gulped it down as if she had been lost in the desert for days. After a dehydrated Louise drank the water, she whispered for more with a weakened voice of desperation. David hurried to the sink, where he filled the glass once again and returned. Louise drank the second as fast as the first. She signaled for yet another refill, and David obliged her request. It was then that she came alive and began to eat the sandwich he made her earlier.

David took a seat next to Louise as he watched her eat like a starving bear consuming its first catch of spring. He asked if she'd like another, and she quickly nodded her head yes. After she was nourished, she asked where she was and who this kind man was during her torment. David explained who he was, why he was there, and that they were both in the house of a satanic Cult. He left out the part about sacrificing the young girls imprisoned with her in the neighboring pits. David told her that he would do everything he possibly could to help her escape. He then walked her outside, pumping her with hope, telling her how she must remain strong so the others wouldn't lose faith in their survival.

After about ten laps around the perimeter, Herbert announced time was up. "Put the little piggyback in her pen."

Never in his life had David felt so sick to his stomach. Tears saturated Louise's face, and he continued to speak encouraging words about reclaiming her life in Texas. And never in a million years did he think that he'd ever tell someone to pray. But he did.

He then grabbed her cheeks with both hands and looked into her eyes. He told her to hold on. She shook her head, yes, and David did the same. Hector and Herbert giggled in the background.

David then lowered her into the hole she had been into, his detestable disgust drying her tears with hope and confidence in her newfound salvation. She watched David slide the plywood board back into its wrongful place as she scooted into a corner and squatted in her new robe.

He then placed the cinder blocks on top. David then went

to the next pit, where he removed the cinder blocks and slid the lid to the side. Inside was a pale-white, overweight girl. It was Suey Sue, or so her classmates called her. David gazed at the sleeping girl as she scratched her nose from the dirt that fell on her face.

"Hey, wake up, wake up. I'm here to help you."

Suzanne fluttered her eyes open as she vocalized her pain from the floodlights and moonlit sky. Other than the meager daylight that shone through the air holes, she hadn't seen a spectrum of light since that ill-fated day of her capture.

David explained who he was, then told her to grab his hand so he could pull her up. But she hadn't the strength to stand and began to cry, thinking he might give up on her and reclose the lid. David then asked her name, and she slowly replied, "Suzanne."

"Okay, Suzanne, I'm here for you. We're going to give it another shot. Stay with me, girl."

David pushed his torso over the edge for a better reach. But it half collapsed upon her, making her misery worse. He scooted back upon solid Earth and then hollered, asking if she was alright. She began to fall back again as Hector's voice rang from behind in broken English, "Good luck pulling that fatty out." David turned to the voice to see Herbert and Hector scrutinizing his every move with insulting jeers and squawks. He then looked about the perimeter and saw a small ladder by a shed. David grabbed the ladder, ignoring their insults.

"Hey, you can't do that!" announced Herbert. "That's cheating."

David simply flipped him off and walked back to the pit. There, he slid the ladder into the pit and climbed down. He lifted the distraught girl as he commenced with his coaching instructions to climb the ladder. Step to step, she stumbled as David strained behind her to keep her steady. Suzanne moaned as she struggled to take the final step and then rolled to the ground. David surfaced two steps later as Herbert made yet another vulgar comment. David said nothing as he lifted her to her feet and began to escort her to nourishment. When she lifted her head and caught a glimpse of Hector, panic riddled her face. Suzanne pulled away in a scared refusal to go into the house as she recalled the terror Hector put her through. She straightened slightly after many words of assurance from David that she wouldn't be harmed as they continued to shuffle towards the sliding glass door.

Once inside, David set her at the table where she lay her weakened head. He rummaged through the refrigerator, where he repeated the process of making her a sandwich just as he did for Louise.

"There you go," he said as he set the sandwich before her on the table. Suzanne slowly lifted her head, grabbed the meat and bread, and stuffed them into her mouth. She began to hiccup and gasp for air as David scooted a glass of water in front of her and told her to slow down.

She gulped down the water as half-chewed food slid down her throat, continuing to eat as fast as she could without regard to consequences. David watched her eat, and he wondered how he would explain to her that she would have to return to her prison pit. Twenty minutes and two sandwiches later, David tried convincing her to walk the perimeter with him to get some exercise. But all she wanted was to call her parents, pleading and pouring fervent tears to hear their voices. David cringed as he dug deep in deceit as he told her that she would get to call her parents after a little exercise.

Hector peeped inside the kitchen, unseen to Suzanne but not to David. He wanted to tell him to get lost or find his buddy Syck, but for Suzanne's sake, he just glared. David walked Suzanne around the perimeter while trying to keep her mind distracted from the situation. But the horror of the pits was a fast reminder that filled her with terror, knowing that her classmates were still imprisoned. After seven laps, Suzanne began to question if she would get to call her parents at all and repeatedly asked in different ways. David saw no way to avoid the truth, and he finally confessed that she would have to go back to her prison pit with no call home. Suzanne stumbled at his words and then crumbled to the ground, paralyzed in her wretched woe. David looked up as Herbert shouted, pointing to his watch, while he and Hector sat poolside and took satisfaction in watching Suzanne suffer.

David apologized over and over as he held Suzanne under her arms. "No, no, no," she mumbled as the cold sweat of horror danced upon her skin. David took her hand to comfort her as she tried once more to collapse to the ground. He did all he could to keep her on her feet as she determined to avoid being put back in the cold, dark hole. She pleaded with her unenlightened sentiment, unaware of the sinister circumstances involved.

She only knew that he let her out and was now putting her back in. For all she knew, David could be the culprit behind this nightmare. "I'm sorry," said David, "But I must check on your schoolmates to make sure they're alright too. I promise I'll do what I can to get you home, but right now, you got to trust me, okay."

Words of hope from David's mouth were all she had as she nodded in silence. He then led her back to her hole, where she began to stammer and throw a fit in her grief. David apologized as he grabbed the kicking lamb around her torso, placed her back into the hole, and pulled up the ladder. Suzanne's screams and cries brought laughter from the iniquitous onlookers.

They marveled at David's handy work as he placed the lid atop the distressed, wailing girl. David glared at the gawking goons, guiling his tactics as he pictured them with slit throats.

He then went to the next pit, where Veronica had lost all hope. She sat with her head on her knees. She looked up without a sound, wondering whether to whimper words of joy or wail out to stay alive. Veronica was in slightly better condition than Suzanne due to her brief time in the kitchen several days prior. David slid the ladder into the hole and instructed her to climb up. As she took her final step, David reached out his hand and helped lift her from her dark cavern.

Veronica appeared emotionless, waiting for whatever awaited her. David pointed the way to the mansion and tried to brace her against him, thinking she was too weak to walk. Misguided instincts led her to shun David's assistance. She pulled away from him and halted, unconvinced of his intentions. David slipped up as he told her to come inside where she could eat and take a break from her imprisonment.

"Take a break, huh? Does that mean you're going to put me in that crap hole again?"

David thought to himself how this one seemed mentally stronger than the last one. So, to save him from the embarrassment of avoiding the truth and her from delusions, he gave her a brief version of the situation. She looked into David's eyes, searching for deceit, and decided she had no choice but to live with the hope of his words. He then walked her poolside, Herbert and Hector, who stared at the young doe with predatory eyes, wanting, wishing, and wondering if they could sink their teeth into her.

After they entered the mansion, David explained his helpless position to free her but told her he was plotting to escape and not to lose faith. She ate, walked, and then quietly went back to her pitted prison without a fuss. Pit after pit, David repeated the process, some kicking in fretted anxiety, but most listened, placing their hope and faith in David.

Around 4 a.m., David's fatigue began to show. His heavy eyelids closed while one of the girls ate quietly, glancing at him and her exit. This one did not believe one word David told her. She had plans other than going back into her hole. The young maiden made a mad, muddled dash for the front door, mustering every fiber she could. Her scampering scuttle woke David as he barreled after her around the corner. When he entered the living room, the girl was struggling in Syck's arms as he smiled with blotted lips and blackened eyes.

"You should train your livestock not to wander off like that because you never know when a big, bad wolf is around," said Syck as he tightly held the squirming girl.

He then inhaled at the nape of her neck and licked the side of her cheeks with his tongue. David lunged in the direction of the girl's cringing face. Syck pushed her at David, and he seized her away from the crazed lunatic.

"Oh, we're going to have ourselves a real shindig with those girls," said Syck sadistically and with a psychopathic smile. David said nothing, then turned to the girl and told her to walk back with him to the kitchen and away from the maniac.

"We're not finished, I can assure you that," commented Syck behind David's back.

David turned before they rounded the corner and flipped him off. "Oh yeah, we'll see, you fucking pig, we'll see!" shouted Syck. They sat at the table. "Okay, let's try this again," David stated.

"Who are these people?" She cried. David shook his head

and then warned, "You know, that little stunt of yours could've cost you your life."

The young girl looked down at her lap while David's face flushed red with helplessness. He then straightened up his demeanor for her sake as he found his voice and explained how these weren't "normal people." He then told a little white lie, telling her help was on the way. Her face lit up with hope as David slid her uneaten sandwich before her. Wretched Soul after wretched Soul David salvaged momentarily through dawn, waking the captives from their slumberous state of grief. Devin peeked out a window, admiring David's stamina as he walked each girl around the prison grounds. Finally, by two thirty in the afternoon, all had been exercised, fed, and returned to their Earthly depression.

David's eyes were draped in the afternoon light as he dragged himself to his appointed room and sank into the luxurious silk sheets. At the station, Pat, Johnny, and Porter wracked their brains, trying to figure out how they would retrieve the boys and David from their confines. In between their conversation, they would peer at the TV as the screen flashed screens of unstoppable fire that was indeed coming their way.

"Man, if they don't stop this fire, Lang Township will be toast," declared Johnny disdainfully.

"They'll stop it before that happens," returned Pat with a pinch of faith.

The news then flashed the disaster from the aftermath of Earthquakes in Seattle and told of the estimated thousands that lost their lives. Johnny shook his head and clicked off the TV. "What the fuck, is this World falling apart or what?"

He then asked if anyone had any idea as to how they would handle their problems in the valley.

Nobody seemed to have any answers for hills that seemed to breathe and come alive and the origin of Demons. All those obstacles were no deterrence to Porter from participating in Johnny's schemes and endeavors. He had no family to speak of and had been a devout humanitarian his whole life, taking after his father.

"What we need is one of those armored ramming vehicles that smashes crack houses, like in Detroit and LA," said Pat jokingly. Johnny's face lit with an epiphany. He sprang up, grabbed Pat's head with both hands, kissed her cheek, and proclaimed, "You're a genius!"

"You're just now figuring that out?" she returned with a slight grin.

"So, uh, what would you do with such a monstrosity?" queried Porter.

"Why ram the bejesus out of that place? What else."

"Well, I doubt that there'd be anything like that for eight or more states away," stated Pat.

"I wasn't talking about borrowing one; I'm talking about making one out of that paddy wagon that crashed last month. That frame looks fixable. We have plenty of material to make a ram jammer Monster truck."

"That sounds like a lot of time and work," said Porter doubtfully.

"You got a better idea?" replied Johnny. "You saw what we're dealing with, and as Pat said, no other jurisdiction will give us the time of day. So, I say we go to the tow yard and put this thing together. You with me?"

Everyone looked at each other and then nodded in

compliance with Johnny's plan. Charley walked in soon after. He looked at all three and could smell trouble brewing.

"What's going on?" he asked as he sat down in his lunchbox.

"Johnny's boys were taken by Father Hemmings, and we're just trying to figure out how to get 'them back," explained Pat. Charley seemed relieved by the fact they were leaving as he trembled at the thought of them wanting his help. "Well, if we're going to do this, let's not waste any more time," said Johnny as he sprang to his feet.

"I'll follow you and Porter," announced Pat as she grabbed her keys.

They exited the building, got into their vehicles, and headed for Brian's Towing, leaving Charley to tend to the station. Brian and his son were taking out an engine from an old Ford when Johnny's cruiser and Pat's SUV pulled into the yard. Brian ceased his wrenching and gave Jr. some instructions before grabbing a shop rag and wiping the heavy oil from his hands. He approached the cruiser as Johnny and Porter got out to greet him, as did Pat. Brian was a man in his early forties with graying-brown hair. He and his son both carried Fred Flintstone's body structure.

"What's going on?" Brian questioned cheerfully.

"If you only knew," said Johnny as he shook his hand.

Brian glanced over at Pat and then Porter. "Hey, you're that reporter from Brunswick County," Brian proclaimed. Porter smiled and shook his hand. Brian then nodded at Pat, his old crush back in high school.

"Do you still have that chassis from that paddy wagon that got wrecked last month?" Johnny asked, gawking about the yard.

"Yeah, it's around back. Why, you ask?"

Well, I was wondering if it were possible to rebuild it."

"Rebuild it? Why in the hell would you want to rebuild that hunk of scrap?" declared Brian with his palms to the sky.

Johnny took Brian aside with a simple gesture, and they strolled into the yard of misconstrued metal of various colors, most rotted with rust.

He then offered a somewhat vague outline of the truth as to why he needed his help. Johnny's words bounced off the Neanderthal's head as all he heard was "badge-toting Mafioso tactics being dictated at him in his yard. Brian Jr sensed his father's discontent as he often did, lifting his head at the noise of his father's voice sounding off at Johnny.

"What? You want to what with that hunk of what?"

Johnny's fangs started to show as he himself began to lose his ever-loving mind dealing with this half-witted man who constantly made money off others' misfortunes from his line of work. "Listen here, you fuck," Johnny retorted as he stuck his finger in his chest. "You're the only towing agency for miles. Man, you probably make three times the amount a year as I do, but you still got to be a greedy fuck don't you."

Brian became flustered with confusion and guilt as his belly was a testament to Johnny's words. Johnny paused and thought, *how would David approach this man?* Inspired by logic, he revamped his approach.

"Listen here, Brian, your town needs you right now. And besides, I'm sure Porter there could probably give Brian's towing a review on the six o'clock news. Could be bad, could be good, that would depend upon you."

"Okay, okay, whatever you want, Deputy, but all I ask is that you come clean. Tell me what you really need this monstrosity for anyway."

Johnny looked upon the tune changer and then sang the sad story of his situation as he told him about some bad people that have his boy David and who knows who else.

"Well, why didn't you say that in the first place? I may be a greedy fuck, as you say, but I still have a heart. Man, if someone took my boy, I'd be all over them sonsabitches like flies on shit."

Johnny nodded his head as he shook Brian's hand, then said, "I appreciate that, brother." Brian fast-stepped with a new mission as Johnny gave Pat and Porter a double thumbs up to follow. Brian brought them into the garage and pointed out some parts he suggested they use. He then tossed a box of plastic surgical gloves for anyone who wanted about to dig into his World of grease and gadgets. Brian yelled for Junior to stop what he was doing and move the Buick out of the garage. Perplexed, Junior wondered what the fuss was about but didn't bat eye or even reply as he simply responded to his father's request. Two minutes later, the garage was cleared as Brian told his new crew to follow him out back. He led them through a path of jalopies and twisted, wrecked models of various types, each with its own story. They then came upon the chassis frame that had nothing on it but steel rims coated in melted rubber from its fiery crash.

A beeping sound rang out as Junior backed the tow truck up to its frame. When Porter asked aloud how such a wreck could be salvaged, Brian just smiled and commented that he could fix anything. Junior positioned the hooks, raised the frame, and secured it to the tow truck. He then crept it slowly under the scrutiny of his father.

After three songs and a dance of Brian's directions, the metal frame was finessed into the garage. Brian hooked up chains that hung from the ceiling and lifted the frame from the ground as he and Junior set floor jacks' underneath. Each let down their ends and set it gently in place.

They then began to strip its charred metal rims and other attachments until the frame was bare naked. Brian then handed Pat, Porter, and Johnny paper masks and grinders, and he instructed them to lightly grind the surface so he could see any cracks or whatnot. He then left them in their toils as he and Junior went into the yard to search for parts that would fill the frame.

They drove the lot discussing their options until they halted at a 442 V8 that sat in an old Cutlass. "Man, I was going to get a nice chunk of change for this bad boy. I really hate to do it; oh well, let's do this."

"You sure, pa? We could probably use that straight six from that E-250 Ford that's been sitting for almost a year."

"Yeah, we could, but it wouldn't be as much fun putting it together now, would it."

Junior shared the same passion for mechanics as his father. He smiled and backed up to the old muscle car. Twenty minutes later, Junior was backing the tow truck into the bay of the garage with an engine and transmission hanging from its chain. Brian inspected the chassis, and all appeared well, though he would still reinforce its mainframe with titanium welds.

He instructed Junior to take a break and go get pizza as Pat announced she had to go home and feed her two Labs. She offered to come back afterward, but Johnny told her to stay home and get some rest for the morning shift. She shook her head and peeled off the thin plastic gloves, then said her goodbyes. The remaining three returned to their work as Frankenstein's Monster being born.

After a short pizza break, the four mechanical crusaders slapped front and rear axles together and jerry-rigged motor mounts for the 442 V8. They then laid electrical and brake lines in place and fitted its floor with one-inch plating.

The morning had come as the exhausted crew took turns napping, keeping the production moving slowly forward. Johnny was both surprised and thankful that Brian and Brian, Jr. pressed on along with Porter into the next day. Finally, by noon, Brian announced that he and Junior could handle the rest and that they would just be in his way.

"Come back tomorrow a little after supper, and I promise you that this eating machine will be ready to devour," proclaimed Brian with a tired, lazy smile. Johnny returned his own lazy smile with a firm handshake and appreciation. He then woke Porter and drove off to the station. He dropped Porter off at his car and then drove to where he suddenly realized he hadn't been home for days. Driving down his long driveway, he noticed with tired eyes the front door was open and flapping in the wind. He stood next to his cruiser and took in the ghostly emptiness of his once vibrant home as he himself felt the emptiness it portrayed. He walked through the house and secured its confines, then went into his bedroom, not even seeing the Devil-drilled door. There, he passed out, sailing into dark sleep in the comfort of his own bed.

The next morning, Sarah and Amanda were at the hospital early as Lisa suffered yet another setback in her illness. Dr. Hogart was still baffled about the outcome, as test after test was performed at the expense of Lisa's pain. Lisa lay in a laborious state of breath as her lamenting mother languished by her side. Even with the assistance of oxygen, Lisa labored for air. Amanda consoled her friend, rubbing Sarah's back as she cried over her sleeping daughter.

The phone rang and cut through the thickened air in the room. Amanda walked to the other side of the bed, where she answered with a mundane hello. She held the receiver covered by her hand as she announced the call was for Sarah.

Sarah waved her hand and told Amanda to take a message. Amanda asked the same of the caller. She then became silent, and her face perplexed. "Ah, Sarah? Mr. Demas here says that you should stop your sobbing and come to the phone."

Something said Sarah Lisa's outcome may well depend upon dealing with this Devil dealmaker. Sarah wiped her tears, then forced herself to take the phone from Amanda and face her terror. Sarah paused and straightened her voice, wiping another tear and placing the receiver in her ear. Amanda walked back to Lisa's side and studied Sarah's facial expressions for some indication of information. But all Sarah offered was repeated yeses in robotic composure for ten seconds or so before she hung up the phone. She froze in contemplation, momentarily staring at the receiver until Amanda broke her train of thought with a "What was that all about?"

Sarah jerked up from the receiver and then said, "I'm not sure." She then asked for a moment alone with Lisa.

Amanda nodded her head, stroked the child's cheek, and complied. Sarah turned toward her unconscious daughter and spoke softly. "I hope you can somehow hear me and understand what mommies got to do. I love you more than life itself, and all that's in it. God's will; I wish I could take your place and make you all better."

Sarah angered, gazing on high, then begged God for

345

forgiveness as she collapsed upon her sleeping princess with furtive tears of surrender. She lifted Lisa's head, stroked her baby blonde hair, and kissed her forehead. "You're going to pull through this, you hear me, little girl. So you dream of little clouds and ponies, and when you wake up, we'll go home."

Sarah kissed her forehead once more, then said goodbye and walked out. When she reached the hallway, Amanda was talking to Dr. Hogart. They both looked back at her with concerned features.

Sarah marched up to them as her fiery, fuming fury sent her neurons into an agitated outburst of indignation. Before she could say a word, Dr. Hogart sensed her anger and immediately expressed his regret for Lisa's setback. Sarah shook her head. "You can apologize till you're blue in the face. I don't want your apologies; I want my baby girl to walk out of here healthy. You better hope that happens because if not, the only place you'll be practicing medicine is in some third-world country."

Amanda touched her arm. "I know you're depressed and tired, but don't be so harsh on the good doctor. He's doing everything he can." Sarah jerked away and screamed, "Don't stick up for this quack! My baby was getting better till this sham came back!"

"Sarah, you're making a scene," said Amanda in a low voice, looking about. Sarah ran to the stairwell, disappearing. Amanda chased after her. She rushed down the stairwell like a fox running from a hunt as Amanda called her name from two flights above.

Reaching the first floor, Sarah ran outside to where Al-Franko was sitting in his cab. She leaped to the rear door, jumping in and hunching down low into the seat. Al-Franko looked up from his newspaper into the rearview mirror, where he strained to get a full view of his new customer, who preferred not to be seen. Sarah watched the entrance of the hospital and commanded the cabbie to drive.

"Where-a-to?" he asked as he still strained to get a full glimpse of her in his rearview mirror. "Lang Township," she barked. A sparkle came to Al-Franko's eyes as now remembered her. He bragged about her husband, his new friend, and the Sheriff. "Yeah, yeah. Can we please go now?" she returned harshly.

Al-Franko straightened up and went back to business, confused but still cheerful, even when the displeasure of her desired location was disclosed. "Mam, are you a-sure? I-a-think maybe the roads might of be blocked from da-fire," he said nervously.

Sarah threw a hundred-dollar bill into the front seat and then another and another until Al-Franko caved, not from the money but her resolute in which he thought she had her reasons. "Okay, Mrs. Lang, but I'm a-going to have to take maybe some back roads."

"I don't care, let's go," she repeated as she caught a glimpse of Amanda looking around for her friend, who seemed to have lost her mind. Al-Franko crept ever so slowly into the bustle of emergency vehicles coming in with casualties from the fire.

Sarah straightened up as they distanced themselves from the hospital while Al-Franko chattered on about how he drove the good Sheriff not so long ago to the same town.

Al-Franko ceased in pause as he thought of the giant ogre Beast, then made the sign of the cross on his chest as he mumbled Mother Mary, Mother Mary. Al-Franko tried to make small talk upon ears that paid no mind to his endless babble. In the frustration of his one-way conversation, he mentioned the giant Beast he and her husband encountered

347

and described the deaths of the state police.

He sparked no interest in Sarah's displaced mind as she only heard a noise, nothing more. She sat there like an Inca child being led up a mountain to be sacrificed to a volcano. Her lack of interest and her heavy thoughts gave her away as a woman who was an obvious, weathered wreck of emotions. Finally, Al-Franko stopped talking after countless tries to get the woman to speak. In the distance, they could see the smoke from the forest fire that claimed its possession in the timberlands.

The wooded area was rippled with signs notifying drivers that specific routes were unattainable due to the fire. Al-Franko drove on past the warning signs and into Horry County as he followed Sarah's instructions. Reaching their destination, he pulled into the long driveway that led to Devin's Devil den. She tossed Al-Franko another hundred-dollar bill and walked to the front door while he thanked her several times. Al-Franko drove away as Sarah knocked upon the giant oak double doors. Syck opened one of the doors as a cynical smile came to his beaten face.

"Well, well, look what wandered to our porch," he stated lustfully, gawking her over from head to toe. Sarah pushed her way past him, asking to see Devin, without a single sliver of cognizance that David was under the same roof.

"You must be Sarah. I heard so much about you," he said, still smiling as if he knew something she did not.

"I need to see Devin right away! Stop jerking my chain and bring me to him right now!"

"Alright, no problem. Follow me," he said, his sneer hidden as he led the way.

He led her down the hall, then to a door on the south side

of the mansion. Syck pointed and told her Devin was expecting her and to just go on in. She looked bewildered but went ahead and opened the door. To her appalling, loathsome disgust, David lay naked in a slumberous sleep as Ora and Nina were sprawled on either side of him. Nina smiled at Sarah as she stroked the sleeping, erect David in his unknowing state as Ora cupped his package. Nina then announced that there was room for one more.

Sarah shouted in distress as she raced to the bed, demanding they get her off her husband. David woke in total shock as he looked up at Sarah while she battered Nina with her fist in an irate mode of built-up anger.

Syck began to laugh as David scrambled for his clothes in dismayed confusion. David gave up looking for his pants and jumped to the door, where he threw a left at Syck's jaw. Syck took advantage of David's naked situation, his confidence growing with him throwing his own lefts and rights.

The room quickly became a battle zone. Ora jumped on Sarah and pinned her down as Nina slapped the cheeks of her face. Nina began to lift Sarah's skirt and dipped her hand underneath, going for her panties. David and Syck continued their brawl as Sarah let out a bloodcurdling scream from being groped.

Devin clapped his hands while yelling out, "Cease this ruckus right now!"

Syck, Nina, and Ora instantly complied, but David used Syck's obedience to his advantage by getting one more lick to his head. "Why the hell did you bring my wife into this?" shouted David in a seething cauldron of hate.

"Oh, my misguided, ossified grandson, why don't you get dressed and come with me? I have something to show you."

David glared at Nina. "What the fuck did you do with my clothes? And what the fuck were you doing when I was asleep?"

"Oh, come on, Sheriff. You know I can't resist a good man like yourself; I consider it a joyful challenge." David wanted to slap her, but Sarah beat him to the punch with a punch to Nina's left jaw. Nina caught herself before she hit the floor. She then twisted her head to a contorted ninety-degree angle and said, "You just fucked up, Deary."

Devin reframed Nina once more as she returned to stand in compliance. She then walked to the closet and picked up pants, a shirt, and underwear and handed them to David with a smile as she admired his free-swinging package. Sarah reached over one more time to slap her face until David stopped her. Nina smiled and walked out of the room as Ora and Syck followed. Devin told David to get dressed as he stood without shame in his nakedness.

David threw on his pants and shirt, and then he and Sarah followed Devin to a chamber at the far end of the mansion.

When Sarah and David entered the room, they witnessed a variety of torture contraptions. They dated from the post Roman era to medieval times, with a few modern marvels from the twisted mind of one of Devin's most trusted of disciples --- Heilwig. A stretching human rack lined the south wall while a guillotine sat adjacent. A pendulum lolled, hanging from a structure high up on the cathedral ceiling over a table equipped with four restraining straps. Another table sat by the north wall that had a fifty-pound boulder on a chain suspended from a pulley that was locked in place. There was a cage armed with blades inverted in its center. It slid together from a device joining two parts that interlocked from a metal bar. The table to its left was riddled with smaller devices---from finger pinchers to nail splinters and apparatus from every era of

Devin's fancy. The walls were clad in red with Adolf Hitler, John Wayne Gacy Jr., and Sir Paul Berkshire's paintings pervading the room with added horror.

On the floor was a pentagram painted by Masterful hand, with ancient words that encompassed its circumference. The west wall contained a glass enclosure that held the scroll parchments and the *Egyptian Book of the Dead*. It also held Barabas's mummified arm, along with other appendages that each had their own place in the history of Devin's past.

David looked at the human rack stretcher and then asked, "Is this where you entertain your guests?"

"Oh, I keep them maintained and in use from time to time," Devin said as he caressed a nearby component.

David shook his head in disgust as Sarah wondered about the suspended boulder. "What in hell's playhouse is this one?" she asked.

"You like it? That's from old, northern Europe," Devin responded. "The torturer would strap his victim's head and legs, then give that pipe. As you can see, the chain attached to it keeps the boulder from crashing down on the pipe holder's skull. The open troughs on the ends of the pipe are where the torturer would pour boiling hot oil. You can pretty much guess the rest."

"People could be so cruel," Sarah said as she strode back to David's side.

"Cruelty," repeated Devin, "Cruelty's just the opposite of kindness. How can one be without the other? Every generation mirrors that in which they have no hand, except that they're human and are in a tug of war. There are those who truly walk in the shadow of their assailer and turn the other cheek as they pray in faith with their perpetual piety. But there are those who have left their mark upon this World with their murderous endeavors, with no regard for consequence. Those were the ones who remained in the minds of lost generations they touched, maybe a grandfather or mother who suffered the afflictions of their plans. Vlad the Impaler, Attila the Hun, Napoleon, Stalin, and my personal favorite, Adolf Hitler. People tend to remember the atrocities cast upon them rather than the boring, old good they may have accomplished."

"That's not true," declared Sarah. "What about honest Abe? And that other guy, what was his name, oh yeah, Jesus?"

Devin smiled at the lawyer in her. "Oh, misguided Sarah, I've been to every corner of this World for three hundred years. How many generations can your schooled mind surmise that I have afflicted, influenced, and, at times, erased altogether? All remember me as the source of their misery, some to the point of madness, forgetting all that was good and knowing only their moment of doubt and pain."

"You can't possibly think Hitler's more known than Jesus," Sarah said adamantly.

"Yes, yes I do, and stop saying that word in my house," returned Devin with a tone of disgust.

David and Sarah gazed at each other as if during a madness from which they had no escape. Sarah walked over to the glass encasement and viewed the contorted cover of human skin that overlays the book. She then became momentarily breathless as she gasped at the sight of the mummified arm that lay next to the grotesque book's left as if it were on guard.

"What happened to this poor guy?" she queried as she shimmied back to David's side.

Devin strolled before the encasement and felt endeared as it stirred warm memories in the hollow cavern where his heart

352

once was held. He tapped his fingers upon the glass as the leathery, dried, rotted hand struggled to do the same. Sarah gripped tight to David's side as he to her while Devin turned and smiled and leaned on the encasement.

"This is the very hand that molded me from humanity. This is the very hand that cursed Christ and was humbly laid before me by my predecessor." Sarah seemed puzzled. "So, you're saying someone lopped off their arm for you?" Devin smiled in silence as Sarah's horror-filled heart hit her hard with the reality of true Evil. "Let me guess," said David, "That's the book that was stolen from the Smithsonian."

Sarah's complexion plastered her face as Devin concurred, "Nothing gets by you, Devlin. I guess you can take the badge off the man, but you can't take the badge out of the man."

David, disturbed by his comment, said nothing as anger stirred deep the brewing hate he bore.

Devin smirked, sensing David's ill-fated feelings as the air suddenly drew splenetic.

"I could turn you inside out, leaving you a heap of human hash, if you prefer," boasted Devin calmly, as if peering deep into David's Soul. Sarah clenched David by his side as she said aloud, "Don't argue with him. Please forgive us; we've been under a lot of stress."

David bit his lip as Sarah dug her nails into his side, indicating he should behave for their sake and their daughter's.

Devin smiled, "Sarah, your beauty is matched by your intelligence. The World would stand to be tamed if we only listened to the rational hearts of your gender rather than man's lust for greed and power. Fortunately for my Master and me, man's vanity is part of the resulting equation that keeps us in business." Sarah stepped forward as she asked, "Who exactly is your Master?" David cringed at her words, not wanting to hear the answer, bracing himself as he thought of the limo drive from the federal penitentiary. Devin nodded his head and grinned upon the frail couple, then turned away and spoke in reverence of his God, Mephistopheles, "Satan my King."

Devin turned and stepped forward in front of Sarah as David tightly gripped her side, half-stepping himself forward in protective mode.

"Let me show you," said Devin while he waved his hand over her head like an Evangelist who just dropped his follower to the floor.

Sarah collapsed in David's arms as he gazed down upon her convulsing frame. He then lifted her head as her eyes rolled white while she hiccupped incoherent words that spilled from her mouth. David looked up at Devin as his eyes glazed red and the room lights flickered. In the shadows, David could make out Demonic images that danced in the darkness in delight of Devin's dominion. David wanted so desperately to knock Devin down, but he himself felt entranced by the very effects Sarah suffered, and all he could do was hold tight through this Demonic hurricane acid trip.

Sarah howled as if seeing something appalling and clawed at the air. David called her name in worry. Feeling as if he himself were huffing paint fumes, he looked up at Devin once more, sickened and weary by the pure Evil that effused the room. Sarah continued screaming in a frantic effort to escape from the visions that were haunting her. David let her go, and she tore about in terror as he himself seemed weighted to the floor. He managed to yell against a pounding force that pervaded as if polarities were unnaturally offset. The room grew cold as the lights continued to flicker, and Sarah continued to mumble but now flailed upon the floor. David reached for her side and cried out her name in the dark. Devin saw the scope of David's love for Sarah and became enraged by the emotion.

He moved his hand as if cracking a whip, and David's shirt and skin tore with every thrashing snap. The Witching whip sounded off, along with the laughter of Demons and trolls in the background, as David cried out upon every crack.

Devin yelled out at every lash, *"Oh ye fool* (crack). Thou art misconstrued (crack). *One must learn* (crack) *what one must do* (crack)!"

Devin loathed human love as Jesus loathed merchants and gamblers in his father's church as he thrashed him over and over, smirking at David's squirming frame before he turned and slowly walked toward the screaming Sarah. He looked down upon her as the visions that plagued her came alive by his own delighted Witching hand. She desperately tried to move away from a taunting, twisted troll that prodded her and two twisted fairies that buzzed around her, ripping off her clothes. Devin shooed them away as if they were flies, then reached and grabbed her long locks, twisting her hair into his fist while he recited a slow, slithering speech.

*"Oh, ye foul thy wretched whore, quote the raven nevermore. Self-conceived for what's in store, he doesn't need you anymore."*

He then dragged Sarah's flailing naked body across the floor while the room lights flickered, and the troll followed behind Devin. The demented fairies buzzed around like hovering dragonflies, playing upon Sarah's fear. Devin halted in the middle of the pentagram, leaving her crying and naked upon the sacred star. He gazed down upon her naked shell, then cupped the palm of his hand on her tear-drenched cheek as he slapped her other with his other. She cried out once more, waking David out of his stupor.

Devin then chanted a spell of binding anchorage onto the

pentagram as the troll and fairies turned their attention to David. The ferries snickered as they swarmed and clawed at his skin.

He swatted the air while struggling to his feet, and one of the little Monsters affixed itself to David's back and chomped into his ear. David yelped out as he ripped it off him and flung it to the floor. Devin then looked at David, and the other fairy fluttered into his face, screeching out and clawing his eyes. David reached out with both hands and grabbed it by both of its wings, shredded it into three pieces, and threw it next to the other. As he looked up from his victory, the troll was in a slow march toward him in a twisted, snickering droll.

David eyed an old Nazi flag and ripped it from its podium, then broke it over his knee. He then rushed the troll and pierced the jagged end through its mouth as it lay dead with the flag hanging from its gore. Devin was angered at the sight of his treasured memory besmirched by David's hand of defiance. David roared out as the last string of his self-control snapped, and he moved in a seething, slow shuffle towards Devin.

Devin snarled at David, then slacked out words of a thwarting spell. His force of will froze David as his every fiber fought Devin's command. Devin strolled before him and looked him over as David's fists curled into his wrists and his arms contorted into a pacifistic manner.

"My, my, Devlin. It looks like we're all cramped up. Let's get you on the stretcher and see if we can straighten you right up." Sarah came somewhat back to reality as she tried to move beyond the boundaries of the pentagram, yet became crippled by her efforts. Devin led David to the human rack stretcher, laying him down and strapping him onto a torturous contraption. Devin expounded on how David made it harder on himself as he turned the caster wheel. Ancient mechanisms clanked and shifted while Devin spun the caster wheel until David became uncoiled and straightened.

"That should hold you till you see things my way," said Devin, locking the wheel in place.

David sobered to his situation as Devin walked away from him and turned before Sarah. He yelled with deadly woe at Devin's back, causing Devin to turn his attention back to him.

Devin leaned down as berms on his face boiled. "Your baseless threats humor me, my dear grandson. This is no place for morals, my son; you will be dead or deviant; either way, you will be changed forever." He then turned and walked from the chamber.

David heard the door slam, and the lights ceased flickering and fully lit the room. He gaped about the room to see what scattered horrors Devin left behind. But none was in sight--- no troll, no mutilated fairies, nothing but himself and Sarah slunk to her side in the fetal position, crying in a critical stage of mental breakdown.

"Sarah, Sarah, come back to me, baby. Don't let him win," declared David in dire despair. "Now pick yourself up and get me out of this contraption so we can get the fuck out of here!"

Sarah stood and tried to move her feet as her muscles cramped to a mélange of malaise. "I, I can't! My legs, something's pulling me down!" Sarah became Puddy, weeping and crumbling once again inside the circle.

David hollered out hope once more. "Please baby, come on, baby, come on."

Sarah quivered in a struggling contrivance as she lifted her head in constricting constraint, trying with all her might to cross the pentagram's line. Her legs buckled once more in a weakened, spellbound state as her mind sank to new levels of depression. David sighed in defeat as he scrambled for his next move, gazing about the room. His hopes slipped away in his strapped situation as he yelled once more his encouragement at Sarah.

"Well, what's all the hollering and boo-hoo-ing about?" interrupted a voice from the chamber's entrance.

David snapped his neck at the sound of Syck and Hector, who stood in predatory composure, gawking at his entrapment and the naked plume upon the floor.

"Looks to me we have two partridges in a pear tree ready to be plucked and fried," said Syck sadistically. They began to laugh insanely as they ran about the room like children being released into a McDonald's playhouse.

"Get the fuck out of here," shouted David in a defensive demeanor.

Syck leaned over David, "Oh, we'll get the fuck out as soon as we get our fuck on with your pretty, little wife. What-ya say to those apples, huh?"

David struggled with his constraints as he seared his eyes upon the hovering Syck and yelled, "I'm killing you, I promise, a bullet in your brain if you so much as touch her." Syck smiled at David's restraints while Sarah began to scream in the background, being groped by Hector.

"Well, well, well, little piggy, you're in no position to talk. And after me and my compadre stick it to your old lady, I'm going to fuck you up. Here's a down payment."

Syck cracked David on his jaw and then walloped him on his stomach. After Syck had his fill of flagellating David's fettered frame, he went to join Hector in the venture of ravishing their devilish delights. David cringed in horror as Sarah's screams pervaded his ears, and Syck's perverse laughter fueled his hatred. The torturers encircled Sarah like a twisted game of duck, duck, goose, and she kicked her legs at each of their ill-fated encroachments. Hector then clamped her wrists, and Syck slapped her face as she yelped out in pain. David yelled at Syck, "Oh, I didn't know you swung that way, you two boyfriend and boyfriend and all." Syck slowly took off his belt as he said, "I'm going beat the living shit out you, then we are going to tag team your wife and give you a real show."

He slapped his belt over and over onto David's chest and stomach as Hector laughed hysterically at each smack. Syck bent over David and then said, "I'm going to take real pleasure ravaging Sarah's sweet rump." David spat in the face of the scornful scoffer, who took great satisfaction in his grief.

Syck wiped the spattered saliva from his cheek and then quoted, "You're going to wish for death when we're done here." He then continued to flog David as he moaned out upon every strike.

Sarah screamed out in desperation as she promised the two lunatics anything they wanted if they would only stop beating her beloved.

Syck smirked, "You stupid bitch, what could you possibly give me that I can't take. I'll take that pussy whenever I want, and your hubby here is going to watch me fuck your brains out."

David yelled obscenities and threats of death as Syck interrupted. "What's that you say? You want some more? No (slap) problem (slap)."

Syck beat David's torso and stomach over and over as Hector watched in glee, laughing insanely at Syck's comments and strikes.

After countless more flog, Nina and Ora stepped into the room and demanded Syck stop. Syck halted, then turned to Nina and Ora, and then told them to get lost as the belt hung from his hand. Nina got in his face, her eyes turning shades of rage as she warned him in a bewitching threat in Latin.

Syck shook his belt at her in a fit of fury, shouting, "You fucking bitch, you dare threaten me?"

Nina reached out and snatched the belt from his hand, then slapped his face with it. Hector stepped back, knowing very well her prowess and power, and yelled out for Syck to back off. Syck stared at Nina a moment and yelled, "You fucking cunt. That's cunt with a capital C." Syck raised his hand as Hector yelled out, "Come on, essay, it's not worth it."

Nina smiled and said, "You better listen to your "homeboy" Essay.

Syck and Hector began to exit the room.

"Oh, Syck," said Nina.

Syck turned to the door as Nina threw the belt into his chest. He grabbed it, shook it in the air, and called Nina a Cunt-whore-bitch. She smiled with confidence due to her black art as she turned her back to him as he slammed the door behind him.

Nina waited a moment in silence as they left, then whispered into Ora's ear. Ora left the room. Nina rushed over to David's side and asked if he was alright while fondling the welts upon his skin.

"I'd be a lot better if you'd get me out of this contraption so I can kill that bastard," he muttered. Nina smiled as she ran her fingers through the hair on David's chest.

360

"Come on, you know I can't do that. And besides, you're in no condition to fight right now."

She closed her eyes and sighed deeply, as if pleased by his pain, then sauntered over to Sarah as David continued to urge her to let him go. Nina bent over the distressed, tear-drenched Sarah with a sweet, comforting tone.

"You poor thing. Are you alright, sweetie?"

Sarah lifted her head to the empathetic voice. Nina cleared a strand of hair from Sarah's face and smiled when she saw Sarah's tear-swelled eyes.

"There she is. There's the little whore I've come to know."

Nina then slapped her face as Sarah sprawled back to her side, sobbing in agony.

Ora came back to the room, where she handed Nina something, said, "Don't break him," and then left the room laughing. Nina turned to David, her long dark hair draped downward. Nina gazed upon David with a crazed smile, then lifted a long pair of stainless-steel scissors before his crotch. She then lifted the waistline of his pants as he began to squirm, protesting in fear of her motives. Nina giggled as she cut down from the waistline to the ankles of his pants.

Nina then lifted the waistline of his underwear to get a glimpse, and then she commented, "Very nice."

David turned in shame. Nina turned his head before her as her breast against his lips. She gazed upon Sarah, curling to her side once more. Nina guided herself onto David as she studied his features. Losing himself again in her madness, Nina smiled once more at the raging animal that grunted under her control. She slapped his chest with the flat of her palm, leaving fervent hand marks on his skin.

She pounded herself on him as his strength began to weaken from her trusting hips. Nina sensed his heat as she ceased her motion while David's stirring arousal made him her slave once more.

He lifted his head to suckle her breasts as she arched herself into his mouth. She slammed him on his back, then herself upon him as she dug her nails into his chest as she yelled at Sarah upon the floor, "That's the best pussy your man ever had bitch," you hear me bitch!

Nina then lay atop David in benumbing sexual exhaustion and laborious breath. David lifted his head as Nina felt his sorrowful eyes pierce past her and onto Sarah's curled frame on the floor. She sighed in green-eyed grudger as her resentment gorged on her ego. She could not comprehend why David still cared for the fettered bitch or why he even gave his attention to her. In her mind, David should have forgotten all about his past and lost himself in her tangled web of charm with no looking back.

But the outcome was quite the opposite, and guilt obtruded into his heavy heart considering his helpless situation. David found himself with no choice but to go along with the unbridled course that flooded their lives with heartbreaking woe. He thought about how he would have to use his inept acting skills to trick Devin and his clan if he were to get Sarah safely out of the picture.

Nina climbed off David and clothed her naked body. "Well, tiger, you better conserve your energy. You're going to need it later tonight," she said with a scheming smile.

"Please don't leave," said David in a tone of dire desperation.

"Well, well, looks like you got cat scratch fever," replied Nina with a swollen head of vain glory.

David poured it on. "Hey, beautiful, why don't you let me go? I can't go anywhere anyways due to that spell; what was it, something, something, this house, this land."

Nina stared at him blankly and then said, "Sorry, lover boy. You know I can't do that."

David sighed with disappointment as he turned his head away. Nina went to his side and began to caress his hair. He turned to her, closed his eyes, and kissed her hand as if taken by her.

"I'll see what I can do," she smiled, but in her head, she rather enjoyed his entrapment.

"Well, could you at least give me some slack here? This thing is killing me," he complained with the best puppy dog eyes he could muster.

Nina studied his ensnarement and reluctantly loosened the caster wheel until his arms relaxed with slack. Just as she finished, Ora walked back into the room with a blanket and pillow, which Nina found perplexing. Ora walked over, covered Sarah's shivering shell, and lay down next to her upon the painted star.

"Well, looks like Ora has a new friend," said Nina in a playful tone.

Nina then put her hand on her hips and commanded, "Come on, Ora, we can play later."

Ora gave a slight protest, then lifted Sarah's head and placed it on the pillow. She then obeyed and marched out as Nina gazed at David once more and left the room.

Once the two Witches were gone, David studied his situation, as his chance for escape was now improved. He lifted his head to see if Sarah was alright, and to his relief, she remained in a vegetated slumber. He then analyzed the manacle apparatus that held his wrists as he struggled to liberate them from their clenching punishment. He rattled the wooden clamp fittings that held his hands high above his head, twisting and turning in its confinements. They remained sturdy and strong, and he struggled in vain.

After fifteen minutes of toil, he gave up, frustrated and seething. David's discordant battle with his shackles was lost, so he closed his eyes and fell asleep. A short time passed in his languid lassitude until Teddy, Timmy, and Father Hemmings entered the room in frolic and mirth. Teddy gaily swung a bucket as Timmy smacked the ladle with the palm of his hand in a motion of catch and release.

The Priest took up the rear with blackened eyes of hostile hatred and a fiendish, unfriendly smirk. David woke to their twisted sniggers, lifting his head to the ungodly sight of their sadistic semblance.

Teddy set down his pail and played tug of war for Sarah's blanket. Timmy joined his impish brother in his game until they danced in triumph. Sarah was left to curl up on the floor to cover herself. Sarah screamed out in terror at the two taunting Imps. They danced around her as if she were a trophy while the Priest stood at the base of the star. David yelled commands at the top of his lungs for them all to leave his poor Sarah alone.

Devin then walked into the room cloaked in a cold, calloused composure but slightly amused by the Imps contrived measures of meddlesome manifestations. Sarah squirmed in suffering hysteria as the Imps giggled and ringed around her while the iniquitous, black-hearted Priest shouted the serpent's sermon. David yelled at Devin to leave her be as the Witch Master smirked at him, then turned to the undertaking of the Imps and Priest.

Sarah's shrilling screams tormented David beyond belief while the Imps groped her as they circled the star. She curled into a ball in the center of the pentagram and tucked her head into herself like an ostrich in the sand. After reciting various passages, the malevolent Priest stepped to her side, and he pulled her up to her knees by her hair.

Teddy then sat the bucket before her as Timmy handed him the ladle. With an unpleasant sneering grin, Teddy stirred the black secretions of hell. He then scooped a ladleful of the thick black blood as the Priest pinched Sarah's jaw while she struggled to steer away from the ladle.

The Imp began to get frustrated as he missed his target, having to refill his ladle twice until the Priest dug his nails into her skin. The third time was the charm. Sarah gurgled and gasped in between mournful cries as if dying from her loving life. The black-souled Priest then released her as she nauseated in a heaving, reflexive reaction while laboring to dislodge the foul liquid from her mouth. Upon her hands and knees, she gagged as her stomach fixated into a knot.

David hollered discordant syllables while the urchin Imps resumed their dancing around her, and the Priest ministered sinful sermons of induction. Sarah continued to convulse in a fervent, violent reaction.

She dug her nails into her eyebrows and mourned out in grueling pain, rocking back and forth upon her knees. She began a metamorphosis as she let out one last bewailing cry, then abruptly ceased her agitated actions.

The room fell silent as the wicked foursome stared steadily, like children awaiting Christmas. Sarah then lowered her hands, and she stared past the Imps and Priest and upon the Witch Master.

David caught a glimpse of the blackness of her eyes, which cast new visions of her nefarious will.

"No!" he shouted in a long clamor of objectionable repulsion as he tussled where he lay.

Sarah turned her head and smiled as the Priest covered her in a red hooded robe.

"Come, come hither, my little lamb," said the Witch Master as he motioned her forward.

She walked past her formally encircled prison and genuflected at his feet. Devin bent over and grabbed her by her arms, lifting her and turning her around. He then commanded the Priest to take her and leave the room. The Priest complied, and the Imps jeered, giggled, and paraded behind Sarah as they left the room.

Devin then walked to David's side, peering at him as if he were analyzing a science project. "What the fuck did you do to her?!" yelled David as he strained at the sight of his most hated image. Devin shook his head with an expressionless face. "Sarah is no longer your wife. Her transcendence is to the subservience of my Master and hers."

"What the hell are you talking about?" demanded David in dire distress.

Devin, angered, "Forget about her. She could care less if you live or die. All she knows now is hate, beautiful, pure hate. You must focus your attention on the pressing issue at hand, the matter of you joining True Alliance."

David turned away a moment in heavy thought, then looked at Devin and asked. "Where do I sign up?" Devin smiled.

"Now you're being sensible. But I'm still not fully convinced of your sincerity, so I will momentarily leave you to your thoughts." David said nothing as Devin smiled and left the room. He laid back, hoping he prevailed and he would be welcome in Devin's circle. For now, he would have to remain uncomfortably composed in his worrisome constraint, wondering all the while about Sarah's condition.

Al-Franko pulled up to Brian's Towing from the directions Pat gave him at the station. He parked his taxi next to the side of the entrance, then got out and looked around for a familiar face. But no such person presented themselves, just cars and trucks.

"Hello," he called out, curving his hand over his mouth as he walked aimlessly about the yard. No answer was returned, just bright flashes from inside the garage and the sounds of welding metal.

Al-Franko approached the aged, worn, painted door and opened it as he hollered hello once more. Porter tapped Johnny's shoulder as he turned, surprised when he saw it was the very man who helped save his life.

"Al-Franko!" Johnny bellowed out in a happy tone, rushing to greet him and shake his hand. "I didn't think you'd ever want to come back to this town after our little encounter with that giant Freak Thing running around."

"I a-dropped Mrs. Lang off at a big-a, beautiful house from the Bi-County Hospital."

Johnny's jaw dropped to the ground as he feared the answer to the question he didn't want to ask.

"Please don't tell me it was the mansion in the valley," he said as he studied Al-Franko's face.

Al-Franko, now in sudden worry, said yes, then asked if he shouldn't have and why. Johnny sat him down and began to enlighten him about the fact that he just dropped her off at the doorstep of hell.

He then told him that it wasn't his fault, that he had no way of knowing. Porter walked over as Johnny introduced the two men while Brian continued to shoot bright flames from his welding gun. Johnny then explained to Porter the new problem they had from Al-Franko's misshape of delivering Sarah to that hell hole in the valley. Al-Franko became long-faced, then demanded they allow him to help and refused to take no for an answer. After Johnny saw how adamant he was, he graciously accepted his offer with another handshake.

The armored vehicle began to take on a formidable shape, with metal spiked protrusions and gun apertures. It had the look of a medieval, modern-day war machine hungry to eat any barricade. But still, it took time to build such a Monster from metal and supplies that began to run thin, which made them innovate with what they had. They had gone through twelve four-by-eight, quarter-inch steel panels, three trucks, and a van they stripped for parts.

After a full day of welding, Brian took a break and walked outside with a can of beer and a smoke. Johnny, Porter, and Al-Franko joined him but refrained from drinking alcohol. They stood under the evening sky as Porter pointed out a large cloud of smoke in the northeastern direction. Al-Franko told of his ride through Brunswick and Horry County and all the signs and warnings of restrictions and detours. The four minds converged, conversed, and conjectured as to how long it would take for the fire to reach Lang Township. They then talked about the giant Ogre Beast and the still missing deputies Jim and Scott. Brian had a hard time swallowing such cock and bull but said nothing to oppose it. He just stared at Johnny as he told his stories.

Al-Franko then gave his version of the day, how he and David scared away the giant Devil that chased Johnny up a tree. He continued by saying that David was one of the bravest and most honorable men he had ever met.

He then added that David thought not of his own life but of his friend and deputy, even after witnessing the horror the vile creature left in its path. Tears rushed to Johnny's eyes, and smiled as he stated, "And that's why I'll never give up on him, because he would never give up on us."

Brian told Johnny there wasn't much work left on the project and that they'd only be in the way. Johnny worried but didn't question him. He only asked when his Metal Monster would be ready to eat house.

Brian reminded him once more of the time and money he was losing by putting the thing together. Johnny cringed while Brian's heart fell as he thought of the poor kids at the hell house. He then looked Johnny in the eyes and, with a strong handshake and nod, promised he'd be done by the next evening. He then nodded his head to Porter and Al-Franko and returned to the garage.

Al-Franko then turned to Porter and asked him where he was staying, as they both wondered what they would do with their time until the project was finished. Johnny interrupted, "Well, my wife is at a safe distance from this crazy-ass town. I have an empty house. You guys are more than welcome. And besides, we got a lot of planning to do if we're going get them sonsabitches."

Porter and Al-Franko both agreed that it would be best to stick together to contrive their mission. They then got into their own vehicles and followed Johnny to the farmhouse.

At the mansion, Devin's first guest, Michi Yakahara, arrived from Japan. He came with twelve of his most accomplished disciples and six vessel virgins who knew and accepted their fate of ritual slaughter. The Yakahara family was a feared name even before the feudal wars of old Japan and still carried a formidable presence. His family controls heroin that comes from Thailand into the shipping docks of Tokyo and onto the shores of San Diego.

He also owns a multitude of sweatshops in Taiwan, Borneo, the Philippines, and Okinawa, making products you'd find at the dollar store.

Michi Yakahara possessed a multitude of black art powers taught by his father, the Grand Master, as his father before him, with the earliest recorded family history in 1045 AD. His school of black ninja sorcery was located on a 22,000-acre estate that housed the Evilest of Evils who thirsted for knowledge and power. The Yakahara syndicate seminary was called Stygian Sheath of the Stoic Sword, which was also a subsidiary of the True Alliance organization.

Ora led the Oracle Priests, along with their subjects, into the mansion, and they marveled at its rich elegance.

"Michi Yakahara, it's so good to see you again," announced Devin as he approached him with acceptance and hospitality.

Yakahara and his coterie fell to their knees with their chins to their chest as he claimed, "The honor is mine that you would let us grace your presence, my Master."

The sovereignty that coursed through Devin's soulless-being accepted the respect from his apostles with a simple nod.

"The last twenty years have been kind to you, my friend," declared Devin as he gestured for him to stand.

Michi stood, and his disciples followed suit as he smiled and said, "A good, steady diet of human breast milk with toast in the morn and a nightcap of youthful blood from my virgins here, mixed with sake."

Devin glanced over at his tribe and then told Ora to escort them to their rooms. Michi bowed once more and followed her up the stairs.

Behind the mansion, Sarah danced freely in a frivolous folly of Evil while she held hands with the Imps as they circled the wrong-sided cross in glee. The venal, black-eyed Priest chanted as he swayed in hypnotic veneration of Demonical malevolence. They ringed the crucifix in a tireless skip, shuffle, and shake, befitting Satan as they scorned God in curse and contempt. Nina and Ora strolled up to the twisted crew holding hands, delighting in the sight of Sarah's altered condition. Ora looked to Nina as if asking permission to join the sadistic goblins and the capricious Priest.

Nina gazed into Ora's kitty's eyes and then told her to go ahead and have a ball. Her face lit up like a child who just got permission to play outside after a long, rainy day. Ora rushed to join the circle as they continued dancing in a loathing denouncement of anything sacred.

Nina watched their merry mirth for a moment before returning to the mansion and the chamber where David was still stretched out. He lay in his nakedness, staring up at the ceiling, lost in thought, as Nina walked in with an armful of clothes.

"Well, I see you're still in one piece," she said as she set down the apparel and gazed upon his naked frame.

David badly wanted to ask about Sarah but decided to play the game. Still, Nina could see it in his eyes and told him not to worry, that Sarah was having the time of her life. David just nodded his head as Nina smiled, walked over to the caster wheel and crankshaft, and released the mechanisms to David's relief. He sat upright and massaged his wrists as he asked where he could find Syck and Hector.

"Easy there, killer, they're not here. They went to Harrisville to get some party favors for the big shindig."

Nina took in her infatuation as David clothed himself. He then sat upon the maniacal contraption from which he was freed and motioned to her with his seduction. A smile came to her face as she was magnetized to his side. He then pressed his lips upon hers, and she moaned out her pleasure.

He continued to kiss her slowly as he reached for a torn piece of clothing cut from the scissors while her sex-hungered body set her trap. David abruptly pulled her head back by the locks of her hair and stuffed her mouth with the chunk of clothing. Her eyes widened with surprise, and she could only vocalize discordant muffles as he strong-armed her into the very contraption from which he was just freed.

He never once took his eyes off her as he finished dressing, and she was almost able to dislodge the cloth from her mouth. "Oh no, you don't," he said as he rushed to stuff the sock deeper than it was before. "You're not going to turn me into a horse's ass with those Devil words. No way, bitch."

He then looked over the confines of her secured ensnarement and slipped out of the room. He crept slowly and made his way to the living room, peering around every corner. He then made his way to the sliding glass door in the kitchen, which led to the backyard. He could make out Sarah and her new friends surrounding the crucifix. He was bewildered by her fatigued, weary march and chanting elation as he slid open the door and stepped into another segment of the Twilight Zone.

David walked past the prison pits to the twisted circle. He uttered Sarah's name as she passed him, singing insanely in glee. David stood momentarily confused as they danced, laughed, and sang as if he weren't there. She passed once more as he took in the horror of four human heads sitting upright on the wrong-sided cross.

Sarah laughed aloud as she passed David, as he snapped out of his horror-filled gaze. He waited for Sarah to pass by again and tugged her sleeve.

"Come on, Sarah, let's go. I'm getting you out of here."

But her mindless, tireless shell just continued to circle the wrong-sided cross, blind-eyed to him. David waited for Sarah to circle once, grabbed her by the wrists, and tugged her from her playmates.

Teddy and Timmy ceased their relentless march and then turned towards David with disgust. The hellish Priest lowered his head from the stars and gazed at the steadfast, ethical man who was stealing a participant from their ungodly games.

Teddy stood defiant, yelling as he cocked out his green-mottled elbows and clenched his fists. "Give her back!" David ignored the Imp as he continued to drag Sarah behind him.

"Come on, Sarah, snap out of it!" he cried as she abruptly came to a stop.

Both imps began to attack David, trying to bite and scratch him, and the malevolent Priest began to make his way towards him as well. David lifted Teddy and tossed him aside, then simply pushed Timmy to the ground. Sarah began to flail her arms at him as the Priest drew near. David foresaw no alternative than to take decisive action for the surety of absconding with his wife as he knocked her out with a right hook. He then slumped her over his shoulder and began to lumber away.

The relentless Teddy grabbed his foot as David kicked him off. The feeble, fiend Priest froze in his tracks while his black, fuming eyes watched David getaway. The Imps stood on both sides of the Priest as he placed his arms upon each of their shoulders. David was now almost a hundred yards from the mansion at the foot of the hill, where he made his entrance almost two days prior.

His feet began to stumble and slow as his mind began to sway. He had the desire to run yet found himself confused as to why he wanted to leave in the first place. He sat Sarah down, then looked at the hill before him and the mansion behind.

At the poolside, he could make out Nina standing next to Devin. Sarah began to wake at the foot of the hill as David continued his confounded confusion with hyperventilated panic attacks. Just then, Devin began to whisper a chant: *"Come home, my son, come home. I am the way and the sight in which you will see. Come home, my son, come home."*

Sarah stood and gaped at David's untainted frame, then howled out screams of displeasure. She abruptly ceased her howling and stared blankly at the estate, then announced how she had to go back. She turned and reached her hand out to David while he fell to the Earth, strained in confusion as to why he was running. He labored to grasp his inner self, then demanded his will by his very might. Devin continued to chant from afar, and Sarah turned and skipped away. David struggled upon all fours, mumbling aloud a speech short of sanity.

His hands and knees were gnawed by jagged rocks as he inched about with his bearings withered, along with his determination. It was as if his body was weighted with iron that was being drawn to the Earth by witching magnets. David rubbed his eyes and yelled at the top of his lungs as he struggled to his feet and fell once more to the ground. He then began to cry and laugh at the same time until he felt and heard hooves clod the Earth and snorting snout. He looked up from his despondent position of hopelessness and into the deep, bold eyes of Buckeye Buck. Devin quickly became angered from afar at the sight of the noble creature as he now realized who and what he really was. The cloven Beast sidestepped the ailing David and scooped him up onto his royal crown of antlers.

David was astounded as he now viewed his surroundings from a crown of antlers, with the Beast grunting and laboring up the hill. Devin became infuriated as he watched the giant buck trudge over the hill. Once out of sight, Devin turned to Nina and slapped her face. Nina said nothing, then turned her other cheek as if it so pleased her Master to strike her again. Devin walked away in the direction of the hillside, then halted ten feet from the dutiful slavish Nina as he hollered out, "I keep my promises," ole hooved one, "Oh yes, I keep my promises."

David could feel the aguish agony of his Jackstraw syndrome dissipate from his body the further he was taken from the Devil's den. He momentarily forgot his problems as he became lost in the moment of this freakish, fluke event. The story of Jonah traveling inside a whale's stomach came to mind as the creature clumped through the forest under a half-moon sky. David could not deny the fact that this was divine intervention and wondered if he himself was deserving of the refuge he was receiving.

The giant buck was stealthy and quiet for a weighted Beast carrying a grown man. David did not know where he was taking him but knew he was going where he was meant to be. After nearly an hour of plodding through the night's forest, David finally recognized the area---it was the Indian reservation. David spoke aloud to the deer as the buck took its last steps to the porch of Nathan's cabin.

"Why did you bring me here?" he asked as if the Beast

might answer back.

The buck slowed to a stop and gently set him down while White Fang whimpered on the porch as if rejoicing at the sight of a sacred supernatural Beast.

"Thank you," David said aloud as the buck stared for a moment and then turned and trotted away.

Nathan peered out his window and saw the buck disappear into the woods. White Fang came before David with new admiration. The old Indian rushed outside to scold his dog, but when he opened his door, David was kneeling and petting the dog as it licked his face in return. White Fang had gained new admiration for David.

"I see you're making new friends, young David. Was that Buckeye Buck I saw, or are my old eyes lying to me?"

"No, that was him," David softly replied as he turned in the direction in which the deer disappeared. "A couple of months ago, I thought you were just a crazy, old coot," announced David, still turned away, "But what I've seen lately puts all that to rest."

Nathan walked up to David and put his hand on his shoulder as they both stared into the woods.

"Come inside, my friend. We have much to talk about," said Nathan sympathetically, as if he already knew of David's trials and tribulations.

David turned and followed the old man into the cabin as White Fang resumed his post on the porch. David sank into the sofa by the fireplace and sighed, staring into the flames.

"You look like you could use a drink," announced Nathan as he walked over to the whiskey cabinet.

David didn't say a word as he continued to stare at the flames of the fireplace until Nathan handed him a glass of whiskey. Nathen took in David's downtrodden soul a moment and then said, "A couple of my tribe's men saw a giant miscreation of nature in the thicket of the forest. Does that thing have something to do with your problems and that you are now sulking?"

David gulped half the contents of his glass and then looked into Nathan's eyes through his own eyes, which had aged since his last visit. "You remember that little story you told me about my family and that white snake of the valley, as you called him?"

Nathan nodded his head in silence as he simultaneously blinked his eyes in a slow squint of cognitive concordance.

"Well, that snake is a man named Devin Demas, who probably owns three-quarters of the valley and is probably bidding for the rest. He owns a mansion in the valley that makes the state capital look like a dollhouse. And to top it off, he kidnapped a busload of kids and changed my wife and Johnny's boys into something I don't know how to describe. He's also the father to James Lang, which makes me his grandson. Oh, and one more thing, he's the Devil's right-hand man, and for some reason, he says he wants me to rule by his side."

David took another swig from his glass and looked to Nathan for any changes in facial expression that would indicate some answers. But his face showed no clues, and David awaited a reply.

Nathen then spoke serenely. "If you cut the tail off a snake, it may grow back. But if you chop its head off, it dies and crosses over into the Spirit World. To save your wife, you must cut the snake's head off that filled her with venom and cast it into the fiery pits from which it came."

David listened carefully as his words no longer sounded like old Indian metaphors, though they brought little comfort to his mind.

David then cried out angrily, "How does a mortal man like me fight such a foe of supernatural strength? How could I even conceive to lift a finger against him? I'm nothing, a nobody. I'm just a kid that used to carry a badge."

He dropped his head into his hands. Nathan then told David a story of lineage legend about how a Demon Spirit was making his tribe sick from a bad strain of corn.

*A boy lost his little brother and his grandfather to an Evil Spirit that howled out victorious cries into the night wind from the destruction and death it caused and carried.*

*Then, one night, the boy went to the corn crop where the Wicked Spirit danced through the stalks, singing its profane songs of scathing stain. The boy walked to the middle of the crop and confronted the Evil Spirit, expecting to die from his war of words when they clashed. But the malevolent Spirt was amused by the boy's courage and made a deal with him. He told the boy if he could walk through the crop and pick the stalk that was pure golden and ready for harvest, he would take his curse and leave. But if not, the boy would have to take his own life by cutting his own throat and fertilizing the crop with his life's blood and body.*

*The boy agreed to the terms, then walked through the crop scrutinizing each stalk only by sight, all the while the Evil Spirit taunting him with jeers and misleading suggestions. Soon, daybreak would come, ending the Demon Spirit's game, and if the boy didn't pick the right one by then, he would have to cut his own throat in the early morning light. Finally, after calculating size and proportion, along with the Evil spirit's encouragement and discouragement, the boy picked an ear from the stalk, and the Evil spirit said nothing at all. The Wicked Spirit tried to tell him he picked the wrong one and would give him another chance if he set the ear of corn down without baring its core. But the boy saw his worry and looked into its Evilness as he shucked its outer husk. He then looked down and saw that he had picked a bright, ripe golden ear of corn and raised it to the sky in triumph.*

*Yet the Evil Spirit tried to renege on his agreement by claiming the boy cheated. He then offered another challenge of an impossible task, knowing no man could ever accomplish, let alone a boy. The Wicked Spirit told the boy that if he could eat every ear of corn by evening, the curse would be forever lifted. But the boy was wise beyond his years. He refused and screamed into the night sky in a fearless Demonstration of his defiance.*

*His cry of triumphant virtue summoned the Spirits of his grandfather and brother, who came in the form of a tornado and swept the Evilness away.*

David stared at the old man for a moment, then asked how and what that had to do with his situation. Nathan shook his head and then said, "You rode in on the head of a Great Spirit in the form of a forest creature, and you question me? It is I who should question you. You are the chosen one to sweep Evilness away. The Spirit of our great Mother Earth recognizes you and you alone as the virtuous one to carry out such a task. Just like the boy in the cornfield, you can subdue the Evil spirit and cast him into the pit of hell."

Nathan's words seemed like a far-off dream meant for another man as David speculated about the situation of his cursed stint. Nathan reminded him how all things come in patterns of rhythmic cycles and that the life force of the living can sometimes compel forces of the nonliving if it benefits their realm or Mother Earth.

"The Spirits stand strong behind you, David. Good and Evil both seek to win your heart. They see you as a vital instrument in their plans to conquer the other. You can be powerful in either world but can only stand in one."

The old Indian drew morose in a sullen gloom as he explained to David how his wife may never be the same. The old man gulped down the rest of his drink before retiring to bed, leaving David with a half-empty bottle and a mountain of thoughts. He would have to wait for one of Lofton's usual visits that he made every morning. David lay gazing into the flames, sipping from his glass as he sparingly spilled a slow stream of tears, thinking about Sarah and Lisa.

He hadn't cried since the death of his father and, before that, childhood. But the sorrow he felt was unbearable, and the only outlet that was readily available was his tears, along with the warm whiskey that permeated his pain to a numbing perception.

That same night, more guests from Frankfurt, Germany, arrived at the mansion. Devin had them flown in from the airport in his personal, commercial helicopter via the True Alliance. The leader of the group was Heilwig Van Higgler, who operated as the chairman of that location. He also headed the industrial meccas of Berlin, Hamburg, and Strasburg. This powerful man bowed to only Devin, who molded him thirty years ago into what he is today. A tall man in his late fifties, he had a red, rounded nose and blotchy skin from his excessive habit of drinking hard liquor throughout his life.

His father had been a high-ranking officer in the Third Reich who took pleasure in his job at the concentration camp of Dachau. Heilwig was three years old when his father took his own life to avoid capture by the Allied forces. This left his mother bitter, raising Heilwig to be the same.

She remarried Dietmar Kaufer, who had soldiered on the German U-boats. After the war, he worked in a post-war cleanup crew for a construction company that had a government contract from the U.S. but got paid next to nothing. He would often come home in a drunken stupor and beat Heilwig's mother, then lock her in the pantry room.

He would then molest the young Heilwig, making him perform oral sex as his mother cried in the pantry. Often, Heilwig's young jaw muscles would tire, or he would gag. He would then be punished for giving up, being sodomized until the foul-stench man had his fill of the young boy.

One day, Dietmar had the idea that he could stand to make money from gay men who fancied young boys. Heilwig was prostituted until he was sixteen, when Dietmar met his fate at work---a fiery load of debris fell from a crane and onto his head. Heilwig would be free from the oppression he suffered for over half a decade. But by then, women might as well have been table lamps, for he grew accustomed to having sex with men and sought no further than that. His mother got a sizeable settlement for Dietmar's death, and she and Heilwig were relieved by his quick departure.

A year later, she died from her hard life of war and brutal beatings. Towards her end, she was a shell of a woman, with no spark left, as she willed herself to die. Heilwig took his inheritance and bought himself a small shop that made gear wheels for watches and clocks. By the time he was twenty-one, his business had expanded threefold, which forced him to buy a bigger shop. Devin took notice of this rising star and took him under his wing, making him one of the most powerful men in all of Europe. He taught him the black arts, which he, in turn, used to abuse young boys.

Heilwig brought three of his disciples with him and six Interns who were clueless, promising a wonderful vacation to the States. He had no problem convincing their families with the premise of securing their sons' futures from Van Higgler Industries. Some practically threw their sons to the Soulless man, unaware of his perverted intentions and sacrifice.

The commercial Euro-copter came down gently upon the landing pad of the mansion as Devin stood waiting for his old friend by the rooftop elevator. Heilwig and his crew disembarked from the chopper, and it quickly lifted off in an eastern direction back towards the airport. Heilwig and his three associates fell to their knees and shouted words of praise as the six young teens looked at each other in confusion.

They then rose to their feet as Devin hugged Heilwig and greeted him in German. They then loaded into the elevator as Quinn, one of the interns, feared Devin's presence for reasons he knew not. After they were in the living room, Nina and Ora escorted all but Heilwig to their rooms. Devin and his old student sat and reminisced over a bottle of 1952 Scotch. But more importantly, Devin caught him up on recent events. Devin then told him that he had a living grandson and the conditions upon which he was rejected from David's acceptance of submission. He went on to say that David would be twisted into knots soon enough. Heilwig knew oh-so-well that his Master held true to his word when he claimed death onto someone. He'd enjoyed many sights in which his Master had dealt death.

Heilwig begged Devin to see the Necronomicon, catching Devin off guard at his request. Devin then smiled and led him to the chamber he called his playroom. Once inside, Heilwig marveled at the old torture apparatuses and some of those he had built himself for his Master. He specified how he'd like to get one of his Interns on the rack stretcher as he pressed his crotch lightly against its structure.

Devin didn't mind that Heilwig was an aberrant homosexual. Ignoring his perverted gesture, Devin opened the glass enclosure and grabbed the Necronomicon. Heilwig approached it with reverence as he stated that he'd waited thirty years to run through its pages.

Devin entrusted Heilwig even more than his present apprentices as he set the ancient book down and told him to enjoy it as he walked out of the room.

The perverse man tore through its pages but couldn't understand a page written in ancient Egyptian. Heilwig closed the cover and went to ask one of his interns to help him unpack his luggage. Quinn von Flegenheimer gladly and earnestly honored his request as Heilwig led him down the stairwell and into the playroom.

Quinn looked around, confused, and asked, "Where's your luggage? Where's your bed?"

"This is where I get to fuck your sweet rump," Heilwig replied.

The young man's face flushed pale white, and his heart dropped to his stomach, flinching away in fear. Heilwig demanded Quinn to take off his clothes as he ripped his shirt open with buttons flying in every direction. Quinn was almost to the door when Heilwig clenched him by his blonde hair and dragged him to the rack. Heilwig announced your family will be well compensated if you do what you are told. But Quinn struggled with all that he had to evade the madman whom he once admired. Quinn's struggle was futile to the adamant psychopath who manhandled him to the stretcher.

He laid Quinn on his stomach and locked his wrists and ankles upon the wooden manacle device. Quinn screamed in trepidation while his body shook convulsively in terror. "Don't worry because, by the time I'm done with you, there won't be anything left."

Heilwig then used pretentious psychosexual propaganda to pick Quinn's mental securities apart by telling him, "I will stroke gently and show you that you are gay; you will have a beautiful erection.

"Nein, Nein!" yelled Quinn as he strained to save his manhood by thinking of the beautiful woman he had dreamed about just hours ago.

"You've been a very bad boy," declared Heilwig as he took the belt from his pants and looped it into his hand. "You see, my boy, I (smack) won't put up (smack) with your insolence (smack). You will do as I please (smack).

Quinn's clamored cries for mercy eco threw out the merciless mansion as his misery became Heilwig's arousal. Heilwig smiled from Quinn's pain and basked in the moment as he entered his vile disposition.

The next morning, David woke to an empty glass in his hand as the fireplace bared black coals with shades of gray. Surprisingly, he didn't have a hangover, though the gut-wrenching feeling of emptiness consumed him. He rubbed his eyes with the palms of his hands, then stood and stretched as he gazed in the direction of the front window. He could make out Nathan's black hat with its Indian tribal calligraphy. David thought to himself how this must be the old man's routine every day, to watch Mother Nature in his front yard.

David shuffled outside in a squint-eyed stagger as he greeted the old man good morning. Nathan smiled and nodded as he gestured for him to sit on an old wooden chair next to him. David sat and stared into the forest and asked if all was quiet on the Russian front. Nathan remained silent for a moment, then recollected never having the pleasure to witness the great spirit of Buckeye Buck. He almost had an overtone of envy as he expressed his sentiment of how he had hunted these lands since childhood and never once laid eyes upon the creature, except its tail end last night. He went on to say it was symbolic that an old coot like him would be lucky enough to sit next to a man who was destined for greatness and to also give him advice.

"But the spirit of our Mother Earth works in strange ways, and I'm not worthy to question," he declared in humble compliance. Just then, Lofton pulled up on the dirt driveway, leaving a dust cloud behind him. He studied the porch as he parked, and a smile came to his face. The seven-foot Lofton climbed out of his beat-up truck, and it raised an inch or two in relief of the giant Indian's dismemberment. Lofton shrugged his shoulders and put his hands out as if feeling for rain while he looked to the sky and then around the front of the cabin.

"Well, I'd ask if a storm brought you in again, but it hasn't rained for a month, and I don't see your squad car. So, did you ride in on the shoulders of that giant Monster running around or what?"

David smiled as he attempted to change the subject.

Lofton's lighthearted tone became serious as he informed them that the fire was getting closer. He went on to say that the morning news stated that due to the lack of rain this summer, the fire was running rampant, and all the counties were working around the clock to stop it.

"Our Mother Earth may never be the same, but we still have hope to counter the Evil with many faces," said the old man as he looked at David.

David studied the old sage's placid self-assurance as if a sacred secret soiled his skin. Lofton seemed confused but said nothing as the reality of the strangeness in the air was obvious.

David broke the silence as he turned to Lofton and asked, "Hey, you think I could get a ride to town again?"

"No problem," said Lofton as he stood and asked his grandfather if he needed anything from town. Nathan shook his head and then said, "Be heedful of your surroundings." David put his hand upon the old man's shoulder as if he'd never see him again and thanked him for the stay and his advice. He turned away, and he and Lofton piled into the small truck and drove off. Soon after, the cabin disappeared in the dust that trailed them, and Lofton began to pour out questions. David didn't care how he sounded at this point, and he told Lofton everything that had happened to date in a condensed version on a ten-minute ride. Lofton was shocked at the things he was hearing but couldn't deny the fact from other witnesses who confirmed a few of David's disclosures.

"How are you going combat such madness?" was Lofton's new question. "Sounds to me like you need Angelic help."

Soon after, they pulled up to the station, and all looked normal except for a slight haze from the far-distant fire. David thanked Lofton for the ride, and the giant replied not to think twice if he ever needed anything; all he had to do was ask. Lofton drove away.

David walked into the station, and upon seeing him, Pat fled her morning coffee task and rushed to David with hugs and questions. David avoided her questions, cutting her off and asking if the hospital had called. Her face went from excitement to sorrow.

"I'm sorry, Sheriff. Yeah, they called. They said that her condition hadn't changed. She's still in intensive care right now. They asked if you could get back to them as soon as possible."

Her eyes began to water as she expressed her sympathy for the rotten hand he'd been dealt. David did his crying the previous night but still felt a wince of pain that pricked him hard as he fought to be thick-skinned. He didn't bother telling her Sarah's condition or her whereabouts, figuring she'd only drill him with more questions that he wasn't prepared to answer. He then retreated to the office and took notice that nothing had been disturbed not even the computer mouse. He sank into his old, comfortable chair, clasped his fingers behind his head, then leaned back to take it all in. Shortly after, Johnny was beside himself as he and the crew walked into the delight of seeing David back at his desk.

"Are you okay? What were those things? How did you get away?" Johnny asked with a mile-wide smile.

David sat them down as he unfolded most of what he knew, stressing the seriousness of what they were dealing with. He reluctantly told them Sarah fell under the same illness as Johnny's boys, that she refused to leave, and that they would have to be taken. They spent the day mulling over their plans for a surprise attack that was worthy of a successful mission, given their timing and execution.

Johnny informed David that Brian had just called him before he left the house and said that the transmission they put in the Monster vehicle was inoperative and that he'd have to hunt one down elsewhere. He went on to say that due to the roads being closed off, he'd take back roads to some of his buddies who had small junkyards. Johnny became discouraged, thinking of his boys and the time-lapse, but David quickly told him his boys were fine. He then added how there was just enough time to pull his plans together and take care of a few things before the war would begin. He then requested that the others leave the room so he could have a word alone with Johnny.

Once alone, David asked Johnny if he and Amanda could raise Lisa if he and Sarah didn't survive. He went on to say he thought his mother was too old to take on a three-year-old girl unless she was adamant about keeping her. Yet it would be best if she were raised with a family.

"Come on, boss, you're not going anywhere. We're going

tear that Devil clan a new asshole," Johnny assured David. "They can die. We saw that on the hill when one of them sonsofbitches ate my bullet. You remember that."

David smiled in fear, trying not to deteriorate the confidence of his star sharpshooter as he said, "Just worst-case scenario."

Johnny then told him it was no problem, that little Lisa was already family. David stood and hugged him and told him that he'd been a good friend and that he'd draw up the proper papers for Lisa's custody, along with financial statements.

Johnny nodded but repeated his declaration of victory as he said, "There will be no talk of death unless it's for those in the valley."

But David thought to himself how Johnny didn't see into the true face of Evil as he himself did or witnessed the knee-bending spells as he truly felt the odds were against him in the Evilest way. David then told Johnny he was going to check in on Lisa and his mother and told him to make camp at a directed point, which he showed him on the map. He once again stressed their safety as a priority.

"Under no circumstances are you to go up that hill without me," he said in a stare-down of stern words.

Johnny nodded in compliance, promising he wouldn't as he looked him in the eye to seal the deal. David then asked if he could borrow his truck and eighty bucks. Johnny didn't bat an eye as he handed him his keys and a Benjamin. He told David that Amanda was at the Berkshire Hotel and asked if he could check on her. David told him he would, knowing very well the pain he was feeling in being separated from his boys. Johnny then walked into the station lobby, where he rounded up his posse and gear and drove off toward David's designated point of the encampment. David sat in silence, hoping he wasn't making poor decisions in his first move of war as he worried about his troops.

He tried to think more positively by remembering the faith that crazy, old Indian had in him, and he held sustenance in that thought. He then clicked on his computer, waiting for it to boot up. He was running with a hunch that kept ringing in his head to check out. After the screen flashed, he logged on to the police access program for the travel industry. Information from various segments of air travel agencies popped up as he went on to the most elaborate Worldwide airline site offered. He then investigated billings as a plethora of names began filling the screen from all corners of the world.

Most were already in flight, and some arrived days earlier, probably lounging in hotels or maybe hanging upside down in caves, for all David thought. One thing was for sure: he knew their destination, and now he saw their names and where they were from. But did that help him? Somehow, he doubted it. Yet it did reveal to him the magnitude of the grand picture and a little more insight to go by.

David then switched off his computer and went to the front desk, where he told Pat she'd have to run the show for a while and that he'd be back around this time tomorrow. She expressed her well wishes for Lisa and told him to be careful out there. He smiled and nodded, then exited the building, got into Johnny's truck, and drove off in the direction of his mother's house.

As he passed by well-known places, David gazed at his quaint, little town, feeling it would never be the same. Minutes later, he pulled into Carol's driveway. She peered out of a window in a paranoid fashion, staring at the unfamiliar truck. Recognizing David, she rushed to the door. He walked up to the porch and through the entrance and gave her a peck on her cheek. Afterward, she beelined to lock the door behind him.

David, sensing her fettered composure, asked what was wrong. She tried to cover up her fears with a makeshift smile and acted as if everything was hunky dory. But David gave her a look that said I don't believe you. She collapsed into a chair and began to cry in a contortion of pain. David went to her side and embraced her as she blurted out that she was raped.

"Who? Who did this to you?!" stammered David as he fought to hold back his own tears.

Carol mumbled the words Joseph Miranda, and David seethed at the sound of his name. He then asked when and where it happened as the cop in him made a mental note.

But the son in him contemplated a torturous death for the doctor, wondering if he'd be hiding at the Demas mansion. Carol then explained everything except the details of the sex act itself. Maybe if it was an officer she didn't know, she could confess the particulars. But not her son, not David, not the man she raised with a virtuous, unscathed image. David refrained from prying too deeply as he sensed her embarrassment and her tenuous emotions, which could trigger a nervous breakdown if pushed.

So, he stayed by her side, soothing her sorrow and ministering to her with love. He then convinced her to take a sleeping aid and get some rest. She nodded her troubled head and shuffled to her room. David then fetched a couple of pills and a glass of water from the medicine cabinet. After she took the sleeping agents, David told her that he'd lock the door behind him after she dozed off. He then assured her Miranda was in New York and said she could rest easy. He kissed her forehead, and Carol smiled at her son. She let him know how proud she was of him. David smiled and whispered to her to sleep. She smiled once more, then closed her eyes and drifted into a World that was unsoiled from wickedness.

David counted the ways he would waste Miranda and the True Alliance organization as he watched his mother sleep in peace. Once he was convinced she was fast asleep, he slipped out the door and locked it behind him. His seething hatred for Devin's Devil clan was a quick reminder that kept his blood at a boil. David then drives to Harrison Bi-County Hospital without incident, except for the fire trucks and buses loaded full of foot soldiers ready to combat against the fire. He went to the hospital's front desk and announced his arrival. The two nurses looked at each other with a bewildered gaze of grief. The older nurse told him to have a seat until Dr. Hogart could talk to him.

"What's going on?" demanded David. "Is my daughter all right?"

"Please, Mr. Lang, have a seat, and Dr. Hogart will be with you shortly."

David saw that it was useless talking to her and that they had no intentions of telling him a thing. Stalemated, he sat down sick-hearted in his most hellish nightmare of anticipation. Minutes seemed an eternity while he waited in a depressed state of gut-wrenching worry, wondering what the doctor would say.

Finally, the stubby, rotund doctor found his way to David with two hospital cops behind him. He greeted David with a crooked, sullen smile from his ruddy-red cheeks. David wasted no time asking about little Lisa's condition and asked if he could see her as the cops glared at him as if he were a child molester.

"Your daughter is still in a coma at this point, and we were instructed to turn you away if and when you came."

David appealed to the doctor and asked why he was being treated as if he had done something wrong.

"Please, Mr. Lang, neither I nor any of my staff is accusing you of anything, but the state justice department apparently thinks differently. The magistrate of the state's Childhood affairs sent us a fax just twenty minutes ago stating you have a criminal sexual conduct charge pending and that you are, at this point, not making any contact with your daughter."

"What! But I'm innocent! How can they?!"

"Mr. Lang, I'm not here to judge you. In fact, I find it damaging to the well-being of my patient not to see her loved ones. But my hands are tied in this matter, as you can quite see," said the doctor as he glanced at the officers to his side.

David fell to pieces as he sank into a chair behind him while the doctor expressed his regrets once more and then turned away. David buried his face in his hands for a moment until one of the officers interrupted his sorrow with a tap on his shoulder and gave him a polite gesture to leave. David was too drained to give his attention to the mindless drones that hovered before him. He simply got up and walked away. He could feel the cold glares of contempt upon him, and then death marched to the exit.

On his way out, he ran into Amanda, who was walking in. David waved her back outside. Amanda had a grave look of concern and asked if Sarah was alright. David hid his pain as he lied for her benefit and told her Sarah was okay. Amanda sighed in relief but quickly returned to depression when asking about her boys. David gave her the assurance that she'd have her boys in a few days. He then gave his appreciation for looking in on Lisa and explained how he was falsely accused of rape and was kept from seeing her. He then told her that he'd wait where they stood and asked her to go inside and see his daughter herself.

Amanda was a little shaken by David's desperation and

admissions but still believed him to be an honorable and loving father. She announced that she'd be back in the same spot in about a half hour, and David nodded. She turned away and into the hospital, as David watched her until she was out of sight. He looked around for a place to sit and kill some time until she returned. There was a brick-laid flowerbed off to the side that was twenty feet from the door, where employees would take their smoke breaks. He lit up as he sat there wondering, worrying, and waiting for her return. David inhaled the gloom as he daydreamed of happier times. His rump began to get sore from the brick bench, and he stood and paced about. Finally, he saw Amanda. She walked out of the hospital, cupping her hand upon her brow to shade the afternoon sun as she searched for David.

"There you are," she stated as she walked up to David with a bounce in her step.

"How is she?" he asked with a tone of desperation and hope.

"She's fluttering her eyes like she's trying to come through but just can't seem to lift her little lids yet. Dr. Hogart told me that it's a good sign, which shows she's fighting."

The news eased David's tensions, but in no way was he relieved.

"What else did he say? Did he mention why she relapsed?"

Amanda shook her head. "No, he only told me what I just told you and that he's baffled by her regression. Oh, he said that she was priority one and that he and his staff would tend to her as if she were the daughter of the President himself."

The new information sufficed for the time being. Amanda then told David about Sarah's hasty departure; she had left her car and said she had been driving it back and forth to the hospital. David then suggested they trade vehicles since he had Johnny's truck. She agreed, and David walked her to the truck. They exchanged keys. She then let it be known that she wanted to go back home, and David quickly told her the roads were all closed and that she'd be better off staying for a couple more days. Amanda became long-faced upon that unpleasant note. But after David explained Lisa needed a familiar face and that he'd be forever grateful, she complied. David grabbed her hands with his and shook them with every word he spoke, promising he would get her sons back. They then hugged each other and went their separate ways.

When David sat in the driver's seat of the BMW, he could still smell the lingering scent of Sarah's perfume, Channel No. 5. He turned the key, and the engine started, purring as if it was made for Sarah's good taste and elegance.

David took off, squealing the tires in protest of banishment from his daughter and the hatred he carried for Devin.

He hit the highway back towards Horry County, flirting with speeds of 125 mph at times. The sun sank in front of him as he momentarily forgot his problems, listening to "Saulsbury Hill" by Peter Gabriel. Finally, after seven songs and a bunch of back roads, he pulled onto the Indian reservation.

Bonfires lit up the hillside while a multitude of Indians danced to the hypnotic pulsations of primal beating drums. David got out of the car and walked through the murkiness of smoke and darkening sky toward the ceremonial festivities surrounding the high flames. Old and young alike danced around the fire as they sang songs of ancient ritual, wearing war paint with trimmings of feathers and knee-high moccasins. David felt as if he were meant to be there and that he was part of a cosmic connection that was related to his destiny.

Once he reached the first fire, he looked around for

Nathan and Lofton. War cries defused to the night sky as a three-quarter moon shone down its illuminating light. Smiles upon smiles welcomed David as if the tribe had a pleasant secret they shared among themselves. David asked around as to Nathan's whereabouts, and only smiles and laughter were returned. Finally, David realized why they were laughing. Nathan and Lofton were only a spear's length away, sitting on the outskirts of the dancing dogs of the decree, decorated with war paint.

David walked up to them as a younger tribesman got up so he could have a seat.

"I see that our war cries have drawn you here, my good friend," remarked Nathan. "Our warriors call out into the night for justice, and then you appear."

David said nothing as he sat between Nathan and Lofton while song and dance flowed in unbroken, synchronized harmony.

"What's the celebration for?" asked David with a smile.

Nathan smiled back and said, "You, David. It is you why we celebrate. You are the reason we sing and dance."

David became red-faced. "Me? What do you mean by me? Why would you do that?" he queried as if Nathan was joking.

"We celebrate the boy in the cornfield. You portray that boy as a symbol of what is virtuous and what will sweep the Evil that surrounds us."

David said nothing as he studied the dancing natives and their compelling chants of ancient lyrical cries into the night sky. He became straight-faced as anxiety hammered him with the acknowledgment of his consecrated duty. Tribesmen threw those old stuffed animals from Nathan's cabin into the giant fire as Nathan waved two squaws over to them. They approached him with great reverence, each of them carrying a bowl of paint. One bowl contained black, the other white, and they set them at David's feet. Nathan then spoke to them in tribal tongue, and they instantly snapped to his command. They then began to unbutton David's shirt, and he began to squirm and resist disputes about their actions.

Lofton reached over and gently pinched his shoulder as he told him it was okay and to relax. David ceased his inhibitions as they took off his shirt and began to finger-paint his face and chest with tribal patterns. Nathan and Lofton sang in a dialect of their ancestors, and three verses later to the tireless song, David stood out in the masses in which he was imbued.

David sat in silence among the spirited natives as a two-foot pipe made of deer antler was passed to Nathan. Nathan drew deep into its secrets and inspiring antiquities, then exhaled into the sky as he bewailed a call of the wild. He then handed David the pipe, and he reluctantly received it, noticing its ornaments of dangling feathers and engraved features of Mother Earth's creatures.

He recalled that old saying when in Rome, do as the Romans do, as he pulled the smoke into his lungs. He quickly passed the pipe to Lofton, who exhaled the bellowing vapor as colorful tunes became vivid depictions of his surroundings. The tribes pulsed out the very rhythms of the Earth as his mind gained clarity.

A half-man-half wolf danced intermittently upon its paws and feet around the roaring flames in time with the pounding beats of the drums. A half-man-wild boar clopped behind, then stood with squirming snakes in each of his hands while grunting out to the natural flow of Mother Earth. The primal disposition of spirited vivacity moved David's most inner being, allowing him to forget about the material world and its motives. One by one, creatures of creed danced in the decree as they rounded the pulsating flames.

Nathan guided David through nature's theatrics of song, dance, and ritual as he himself became entranced by the pounding drums. Nathan then told him that the paint he was wearing represented the spirit of man, who was a mirror image of our Mother Earth. He then explained that all creatures conduct themselves uniquely in their paradox, but all dance to the same song our great mother sings. But the snake cannot hear our Mother Earth's divine songs, for it has no ears, and it cannot dance, for it has no legs.

Men and women alike shimmied around the flames in a chaotic, unstructured collusion of synchronized syncopation. Their fluid motions and their squalling songs stirred David's Soul with Earthly flavors of savory serenity. His present experience would forevermore leave its deep mark within the pours of his inner being, harnessing a purpose and a sense of depth other than his personal preoccupation with individual interest. This was something bigger than himself, something of infinitesimal perplexities that even a glimpse into its magnitude would be a transcending achievement.

David was now peering into the secrets of the universe as it revealed its omnipotent face of timeless mysticism in moments of abstract images. The beating of drums moved him, and the chanting of song struck him as the star-filled sky inhaled him.

The two squaws reappeared and grabbed David, pulling him into their dance. David looked at the others and followed their motions as if he were now a part of a moving picture. Shame had no place for occupancy in the circle of proud tribal warriors who called upon their forefathers. David could feel the presence of great properties working as their chanting calls charmed the Spirits, provoking their curiosity and concordance. He stomped and staggered in the same fashion as those around him as the natural and Spirit World coincided in harmonizing veracity. David felt free for the first time since the purity of childhood, his spirit soaring with the stars and his Soul singing with the trees. He pranced proudly like the bear and wolf as if he were a creature of the forest liberated from humanity into the call of the wild. David's tireless body went on and on in the circumference of the fire as his mind transgressed into a twilling tincture of utopia. The fire itself roared to the sky; its breath of flames and its solemn light of sheer bliss sanctified the Soul that surrounded it.

David's body fulfilled the physical phase of the ceremonial rite, and he was now ready for the metaphysical plateauing into the far reaches of his perceptions. He took his seat once more between the old man and Lofton as they grinned at their accomplishment. David found the pipe once more in his hands as he drew deep, sensationalizing his awareness to the pinnacle of illustrious splendor. David now viewed the world through a kaleidoscope of enigmatic shapes and colors that constructed configurations of consoling celestial beings. They caressed his hair and stroked his skin as they whispered words of incomprehensible composition into his ears. Disappearing as fast as they appeared, they left David longing for their return.

Then, a hooved bestial creature with Demonic features stood shouting foul, boisterous syllables. Behind the Beast was a dark veil of death that followed the outline of a man who was walking towards David. The Beast spoke in tongues of ancient languages, the broken words spoiling the harmony and peace. The ranting Beast bent upon its fours as Barabis walked past the ungodly Beast and gazed at David with fiery, judicious eyes. David stared back without fret or fear, fortified in the strength Nathan reinforced into him, embracing the fortuity of the moment. Barabis spoke blasphemous words of hell, blazing blisters upon David's skin, while every vow inflicted pain he'd never known. He stood defiant in the breath of death, armed only with the shield of his self-righteousness and the pain which he already carried. Barabis took notice of David's vigor as he voiced his venomous rage, then vanished into the veil of murk in which he came, taking with him his Beast.

David raised his head into consciousness as the morning sun poured its gentle, majestic light over the canopy of the forest. The mass of humanity had dissipated as the coals from the fires matched the colors of the rising sun. The old man still sat at David's side, like a tour guide who had one last passenger on his bus.

"Where'd everyone go?" asked David, befuddled from his time-lapse.

Nathan smiled and said, "It's not important where they are, but where you are. Did you learn from your journey?"

David began to tell the old man his visions, but Nathan raised his hand and told him they were his own to grow from and that no man should divulge his Soul. David felt lightheaded and unsteady as he hoisted himself to his feet with the aid of Nathan's extended hand.

"What the hell was in that pipe last night? No, hold that thought. I don't even want to know," he said to the smiling sage as he stumbled into the morning light towards the BMW.

Nathan looked on as he spoke aloud, "Look to skies for the black eclipse to come in, from which the wicked will draw strength."

David turned and questioned, "And your arrows will pierce the hearts of my enemies?"

Nathan nodded his head and said, "We are here for you. All you need to do is call out into the wind." David gazed into the old man's eyes, seeing his sincerity, then turned away and climbed into the car. He drove away feeling more complete and sounder than when he arrived, leaving him with renewed strength and greater knowledge.

During the night, Devin's commercial Euro-copter worked overtime as it flew back and forth from Charlotte airport as Demonic Delegates came from all over the globe. Others drove in lavish motorhomes, limos, and common cars furnished with tents and gear. The estate was now a crowded camp, with members and representatives and their personal clique of subordinate subjects.

Syck and Hector fed their prisoners raw meat and rotten apples as they taunted each other equally. Some ate while others were repulsed by the raw meat, and they nibbled around the rotted parts of the apples. The Imps ran about from tent to tent, cheering on those who were proclaimed from the black-blooded pond out back. The venal-induced Priest chanted within the encampment, giving his unholy blessings to anything that moved and everything that breathed. Quinn stayed in his room, physically and psychologically damaged and ashamed as Heilwig schemed about his next prey. Yakahara and his clan diligently prepared for the sect of the black eclipse, kneeling with their backs to the east, chanting unholy sacrilege. Ora and Nina stuck to Devin's side as he entertained his guests, and they, in return, pedestaled his Godless presence in subjective submission.

A catering company from the True Alliance organization supplied an abundance of delicacies from all over the world. Everything was falling into place as Devin awaited the hour of his Master's destiny and his hand to this world.

Alliance members continued to pour in. Ambassadorial disciples stayed in the mansion, some rich and upper-middle class stayed in their motor homes, while apprentices and lower-class members were in tents. Festive games were played in medieval fashion, with torturous consequences to their sacrificial slaves, who were the focal point of their entertainment. Some clueless subservient lambs were fattened and kept in the mansion. Their minds were occupied with drugs, porn, and sex as, one at a time were taken into the confusion of loud music, video games, and whores, while the others unknowingly awaited a warm bubbly bloodbath.

The immense estate began to resemble a twisted carnival of deranged dimensions that embodied demented dignitaries of Demonic woe. A large haystack sat fifty yards away where a seven-foot disk spun upright before it. It was painted in tri-shaded colors in the shape of a human figure, with straps to hold three prey in place. Off to its side was a sign that illustrated bonus points for each part of the figure. Six hatchets were given to each contestant as the disk would be spun with the mirth of a twisted mind.

Quarters were torched to a bright red glow, then lobbed from little metal cups onto the flesh of a naked man tied to a giant oak table, where he screamed under the canopy of a torture tent. Adjacent to the tent was a man who harnessed from a twenty-foot A-frame structure. It swung left to right as competitors stood thirty feet away and tried to hit him with javelin darts. Across the way, a plexiglass cube stood stilted six feet tall, full of sulfuric acid, as a young boy sat above the pernicious liquid with his face sodden in tears. To his left was a greasy, blubbery man who wore a top hat persuading spectators to play a game of disintegrating death.

Three tents down were the orgy tent, where the carpet was laid in its forty-foot circumference with sofas and curtained-off rooms. Two pythons slithered about the dark murkiness upon and over those who indulged in the flesh. To the far side of the tent was a young woman bound and tied while a leather gimp inflicted her with pain. He was ravished in her flesh, smacking her rump with the palm of his leather hand. The woman arched her back as if pleased by her punishment.

Horry County's eastern horizon was now an inferno of unstoppable flames, to the frustrations of the firefighters. Dillon and Brunswick Counties also suffered from the inferno that claimed its toll upon life and home. The two governors petitioned the White House for emergency relief but were turned down due to other national disasters and the economic meltdown in the capital. Seattle was a death hole of earthquakes while the East Coast continued to get bombarded by hurricanes that crashed inland as far as New York and Maine. War was continually on the horizon as Congress was trapped in congestion from the hurricanes and the pressing stress of war that knocked hard upon the nation's door.

All over the world, countries were suffering mayhem and terror as morality began to diminish and the ugly faces of the wicked came out from the shadows in vulgar display. Pestilence and disease ran rampant throughout Third World nations, spreading its deadly touch of eradication. Neighboring countries in the Middle East and Asia warred as they never warred before, using weapons of mass destruction and tactical techniques of terrorism. Stock markets crashed, the big three were now only one, and the entertainment world was virtually eroded, leaving Hollywood studios in ghost towns. Blackouts were common as power companies failed in a continuous course.

Agriculture ceased to a halt, except for a few government and True Alliance farms and plantations. Metropolitan police agencies remained at half manpower as multiple forces of authoritarian government portrayed characteristics of Big Brother.

In Lang Township, the smell of death filled the air from the smoky haze that marched its way. Johnny reported to David about the loudness of an Ozz-fest metal concert and the

402

continuous stream of helicopters. David sat behind his desk, leaning back in his chair, studying the map, Johnny's location, and the layout. Their camp lay opposite from the side in which they tried and failed to encroach. Johnny then admitted he snuck a peek down into the valley and told David it resembled a freaking carnival. David momentarily stood in silence, his heavy thoughts weighing in a soundless room. Johnny then broke the quiet as he stated he had caught a glimpse of his two boys and Sarah in a dejected tone of helplessness.

David looked up as Pat popped her head in the door and announced that Ray Willard was there and demanded to talk to David. David told Johnny he'd get back to him and said there was no need for him to spy into the valley until they were all together.

"Our plans could fail if you get caught or killed," David added. "And besides, seeing our loved ones right now isn't going to help." Johnny apologized and agreed before hanging up. David looked up from his desk and at a mission-loaded redneck with Pat lolling in the doorway. David folded his arms on his chest, still angered by his endeavor and the toll on human life from Ray's drunken leadership.

"What can I do for you, Ray?" asked David dully in a flat tone as the hick rushed front and center to his desk. Pat took a seat against the wall and she sipped her coffee. "I know what's going on in that valley, and I want to help."

David glanced at Pat as she to him, and she shook her head and rolled her eyes.

David turned to Ray. "I hope you haven't been poking your nose around where it doesn't belong because I will put you behind bars just to keep you safe if I have to."

Ray waved his arms, "No need for that good sheriff. As you can see, I'm completely sober, and I really want to help.

That Monster thing killed my brother, Earl, and Jimmy, and I'll walk myself into that cell if you refuse me."

David unfolded his arms and smiled at the redneck's comical, unyielding persistence.

"Okay, okay," interrupted David. "You're in, but the first time you don't listen …"

He pointed at the jail cells as Ray nodded his head and sat down quietly as if sitting signed the deal. The room remained silent for a moment as David studied Ray's character.

"As you know, we're facing some tough odds. You sure about this?"

Ray shook his head yes and took off his hat. "I have nothing left. My pappy died last January, and now my brother and last of kin. Oh, I'm definitely in, good sheriff."

David cracked another smile as he turned to Pat. "Have you heard when that armored vehicle contraption will be finished?"

"Yeah, I understand that Brian had a setback, but he said tomorrow for sure."

David contemplated the timing, then said he needed to check something out and would brief Ray on the latest.

David then told Pat to call him with any news, good or bad, as he scribbled numbers from Sarah's cell phone that she had left in her haste.

"Where are you going now?" asked Pat as he grabbed his keys and walked to the door.

David turned. "I'm going to visit our mysterious Priest at

the church."

Pat straightened as if star-struck. "What or how is he going to help?" she queried, as if afraid he might get sent to the front lines.

David grinned, "Oh, you never know."

He then left the station and got into the BMW. He drove in the direction of the church, still tasting the colors and sounds left over from the previous night. When he pulled up to the church, all was motionless. He cut the engine and took in the church's gothic charm. David opened his door and climbed out, intently scanning the holy confines once more before he began to walk to the arched, oak doorway as he noticed the graffiti was all gone. "Hello David," rang out a voice from behind.

David turned to see the young Priest standing there. He glanced around to see from where he came. Not a tree nor bush stood that allowed rationalization of the abnormal appearing act.

"Where'd you come from?" David asked as he peered over the Priest's shoulder.

"Why, I've been here all the while. And where might you have been, David?"

David paused, then said, "Oh, I guess you could say hell's backyard."

The Priest seemed unsurprised by his statement as he invited David to walk by his side around the yard. They strolled a step or two in silence as David wondered as to the Priest's thoughts. The Priest suddenly halted and stomped his foot on the ground, heightening David's bafflement. "Stomp the serpent," Michael uttered.

David was flabbergasted by his little outbreak, yet their awkward walk continued.

"So, tell me, how does a small-town man like me pull off such a task?"

The Priest ceased his steps as he spoke in an earth-shattering tone. "You must avow your faith immediately."

The Priest then continued in Priestly counsel as David anticipated his next words.

"Okay," he said as if defeated. "Let's say I avow my faith, as you say. What, then, is God going to give me strange powers to fight this thing? Because I got to tell you, Father, I've looked into the face of pure Evil, and it wasn't a pretty thing. Oh, and his words of Witchery, let me just say, this ain't no backyard gramma curse. I felt its inflictions first-hand, and I can tell yaw, it wasn't pleasant."

Their awkward walk continued with a slight pause while the Priest continued his Godly wisdom.

"It's not the serpent's work you should fear, but the depravity of God and your separation from Him. That you should and must fear."

"I get what you're telling me, Father, but you're telling me not to worry about a guy who, with a couple of words, almost made me into a permanent fencepost to his house."

The Priest gazed towards the heavens as if gazing into its majestic light. David looked to the sky as if searching for something in the direction the Priest was gazing.

Michael then looked directly at David. "If your faith was truly blind, you would have been able to walk away on your own."

David became slightly angered. "So, what you're saying is, because I don't go to church and pray every Sunday, I brought this on myself?"

The Priest returned David's anger and shook his head. "It's your faith and trust in God which you lack. You can never question His motives or reasons, for He is all-knowing, all-seeing, and all-loving."

David looked to the ground, lost in his humanity, as he wondered how, in this giant cosmos, he came to be the descendent of Evil and still be accepted by God.

The Priest spoke solemnly and slowly, "David, are you aware of the solar eclipse to come in just forty-seven hours?"

David halted in his tracks as the Priest continued walking, as if aware he was deep in weighty thought. David paused and admitted that he knew.

"That's what Nathan told me, that an eclipse is going to be a way for the wicked to release their Evil into the World."

"Our Lord smiles profusely on the North American tribes," professed the Priest, "for they respect and love His creation."

"How did you know he was Indian? I never mentioned," David inquired, his law enforcement senses.

"Let me ask you a question, David. How or why did you think you could skate through life being unpronounced and secular and still be immersed in God's blessing?"

David became introspective, thinking how true those words rang. He thought of Lisa's condition and Sarah's disposition. He halted as he trembled with words of rueful guilt.

"What do I do to rectify myself?" asked David, with his head along with his morale on the ground once more.

The Priest stopped and smiled as he turned to David and patted him on his shoulder. "You can start by lifting your head and Spirit."

A slight warmth consumed David's inner core as he formed angelic conceptions of the consecrated Priest.

"Come with me, David, into God's temple, where you will be baptized and blessed," said the princely Priest as he walked away.

David watched him fade from where he stood, then followed in a slow, torpid march. He climbed the steps and walked through the double oak doors as he noticed the place had returned to its holy manifestation from its debasement. The Priest walked to the front of the pews, past the altar, and through a rear door where steps lead to a baptizing pool. He wasted no time as he jumped into the holy water and awaited David's presence. David stood atop the steps, gazing down into the water and the outstretched arms of the devoted Priest who patiently awaited his Soul. He stepped into the water, overwhelmed with the same feelings he carried the previous night, the innocence of a child. The Priest stood facing David and placed his hand on top of David's head. He began to speak in strange tongues. David peered into his fiery eyes as ancient language poured out from the Priest like a promulgation of purity.

A gentle warmness of divinity drenched David's skin as he became submerged in the placid pool by an untroubled hand. David looked up through the water, and his eyes viewed an illuminating light that surrounded a haloed, winged creature. It almost seemed as if he could breathe underwater, with his fears and burdens washed away, while the pool colored into a bath of blood as if of Christ.

Hallucination flashback from last night or true reality, David thought to himself. The blooded water enveloped David's vision as he closed his eyes, and it veiled his face. All became bright like an exploding star, and the moment seemed without end while he began to perceive the boundaries of his mortality. He could still hear the bellowing, hallowed tongue that permeated the water with the virtuous truth of unmistakable sacredness.

Abruptly, the gentle hand yanked him up by the nape of his collar as he opened his eyes to the Priest. David felt renewed and unstained, as if his soul had been cleansed from the inside out.

"How do you feel?" inquired the young Priest in a soft, placid voice.

David looked at the Priest, confused, searching for the depiction. He beheld the water, then onto his skin for red blood, as there was none. No halo lolled over a winged creature, nor no blood upon his skin, just his drenched self.

"How do you feel?" queried the Priest once more as he rested his hand upon David's shoulder.

David shook off his shock from the supposed sights. "I feel uplifted, is all," he replied.

The Priest smiled at him as he seemingly understood David not to be the type to yell out hallelujah but still knew that he had become deeply affected by his efforts to win his Soul to God. David now understood how he lived his life in the separation of God, which was now his greatest fear. But deep down in the far reaches of his mind, all the way from the dark reptilian part of his brain was still in doubt. The Priest felt him slip as his eyes peered into David's Soul. I see your heart still weighs heavy. Did you not say to yourself that you saw into the face of Evil and witnessed the grief it caused? And what now, have you not felt the presence of our Lord cleansing your soul?

David became ashamed of his lack of faith in the midst of all that held true. He thought of Lisa, Sarah, and Johnny's boys, along with those poor girls held prisoner who still suffered as he straightened from a slouch and asked what he could do. The saintly Priest gazed upon him, pleased in his righteous, gallant demeanor.

"Come with me, David," he said as he turned away and departed from the pool.

David followed him down the stairs and back into the cathedral. The Priest told him to kneel where he stood. Michael then walked to the altar, where he placed a holy sash around his neck.

He then approached David and told him to open his mouth. David abided by his request, and a tasteless wafer was placed on his tongue. Told to clasp his hands and bow his head again, David complied. But as he bent his neck down, he noticed the Priest was completely dry. The Priest began to speak in the same strange tongue as before, and David squeezed his eyes shut.

The Priest's voice reverberated throughout the church, and the structure seemed to shake at its very foundation with devout, divine decree. The prayer petitioned arch angels to sing harmonizing songs with triumphant trumpets and heavenly concerto. On and on, the vivacious prayer continued as the afternoon light shone through the gothic stained glass high in the cathedral. David felt its warm light on his face as he snuck a peek through his squinted eyes. Prismatic, trisected colors poured from the windows in illuminating beams of light that danced gleefully throughout the church. David became uplifted, as if Angels held him in adoration of meritorious worthiness for the prospect of his good intentions. Time seemed to stop with his hair standing on ends amid this holy dimension. The pious Priest reached down and gently shut David's eyes and continued his petition to God with his head held high. David's knees weighed heavily, but his Spirit was light and free as his courage became undaunted by the mission he now fully accepted.

The silence was abruptly bestowed in the cathedral as David opened his eyes to find an empty church. Its confines were returned to the shade of gothic gloom, and bewilderment began once again to infiltrate his mind. He looked left and right, over and back, but all that remained was himself as the mystery of the enigmatic Priest continued.

David stood and called out; however, the only return was the echo of his hail. He walked behind the altar to the door which led to the baptizing room and called out once more.

But still, there was only silence as he closed the door and wondered if he was in a dream that he'd wake up from at any moment. He proceeded to walk past the pews and into the vestibule, calling out once more for the Priest. He continued through the archway and down the cobble stairs towards the car parked outside.

As he approached the vehicle, his heart dropped to the ground at the sight of a white rose resting upon the hood. David's eyes welled, and his spine tingled with chill, cutting chill. It had been the same type of rose his father planted for his mother in the backyard of his childhood home. David's shaking hand reached out and gently grasped it by the neck of its blossom. He inhaled its sweet scent, and he gazed around the churchyard for the perpetrator of the unimaginable scheme. But no one could possibly know the symbolic significance of something as simple as a white rose and what it meant to him and his mother. It had been a personal acknowledgment that only he, his mother, knew, and his father took to his grave. David inhaled the white rose's scent once more as pleasant memories of his father ran heavily through his mind, and a single tear streamed down his cheek.

He looked to his left as the gate to the graveyard swung in the wind, squeaking from its rusty hinges. David became compelled to visit his father's plot as if he were beckoned to a parallel World where he could intervene freely.

He walked through the gate and past sepulchers and tombs of old and onto his father's plot. As he approached the grave, the freshly turned dirt was a fast reminder of recent trespassing and defacement.

David stood over his father's grave as an obscure fog surrounded him, the clouds thickening with shadowy downcast. A warm, gentle rain began to fall, and David dropped to his knees and slumped over the gravestone after a weekend wrought with grief.

He clenched the stem of the white rose so tightly in his worked-up emotion that a drop of blood trickled from his pricked palm.

"Why? Why did you leave so soon when we still need you? Is God so alone that he demanded my only influence and the love of my mother's life and the reason for the man I've become? Why, Lord, why do you take a morally worthy person such as my father when Evil men walk the Earth? Why, o Lord, why?" David cried in a cascade of heartbreak and tears as he roared to the sky with his babble.

A voice rang out from behind the wrenched man, who was so immersed in emotion that he barely heard his name being called.

"David, David, my son, why are you so distraught in pain?"

David lifted his head and gawked through the hazy rainy fog as he answered back, "Father, is that you?"

David began to turn. "Do not gaze upon me, my son, but yes, it is I who raised you, your father."

"Why? Why can't I see you? Are you truly my father?" he cried as he fought from turning toward the voice.

The soft-spoken voice came through once more. "Do you remember when you were nine years old, and I took you fishing at Little Bear Lake, and you twisted your ankle but refused to go home? That you caught the biggest fish still to this day."

David's face lit up as he proclaimed loudly, "It is you, Father!"

He began to turn around and caught himself in frustration. "Why can't I see you?"

"I'm sorry, David. In the afterlife, there remain mysteries that are never to be questioned. But I can tell you that the joy you and your mother brought me in my life is just a grain of sand compared to the bliss of everlasting love that awaits. David, I just wanted to tell you how proud I am of you and that I love you. But you have a great task ahead of you that you alone can carry. Your mother will soon join me. Don't be discouraged or disheartened, for she will be forever joyous here."

David uttered under his breath the displeasure of his mother's prophesized death.

"Always remember, the heavens smile upon you as for me for as long as you shall live and ever after."

The voice faded as it repeated, "Ever after, ever after."

David ceased his tears, stood, and marched away with newfound strength. He never looked back, turning his head from where he heard the voice in a symbolic gesture of blind faith. When he reached the BMW, he looked to the sky, and the rain stopped its placid fall, replaced with a vibrant rainbow. David once more took in the scent of the white rose, then drove in the direction of his mother's house. He looked at the clock display and realized that time was not his friend, as two hours had elapsed during his church visit. He pushed the horsepower of the vehicle through the straights and curves of the road. When he pulled up in the driveway, all looked to be normal. The windows and curtains were open, and Carol was sitting on the front porch. David cut the engine, grabbed the white rose, got out of the car, and strolled up the cracked driveway. He looked around and saw that it hadn't rained on this side of town. He approached his smiling mother, gave her a peck on her cheek, and asked how she felt.

"I feel fine, David. I woke up this morning and decided that I'm not living my life in fear." David smiled at her and was glad to see she had overcome her anxiety. David took notice that old Patsy Cline music was coming from inside the house.

"Is that Patty Cline?" he asked in an upbeat tone.

"The one and only," she returned in a makeshift air of cool-headed composure.

"Crazy for loving you ..." caressed their ears as David sat at her feet on the porch. He looked up and saw the small patio table by her side holding a glass of red wine.

"Oh, I almost forgot, this is for you," he said as he handed her the white rose.

A crooked smile came to her face. "Where'd you get this?"

She queried as she cleared her throat as if trying to strengthen her voice from easily affected sentiment.

David slapped together a little white lie mixed with fact as he told her he picked it up from the grounds at Saint Andrew's Church.

"I've never seen a white rose bush at Saint Andrew's," she gaily claimed as she happily took in its scent.

"Oh, it's far back," he replied, wanting to change the subject.

Carol's face became perplexed, trying to picture the churchyard in her mind as she sipped her wine.

"I haven't seen you drink in a while. Feeling good yet?" he inquired with a grin.

"Oh, you know me. I'll be lucky if I can get two glasses down. Just a little glow. So, what'd I do, win the lottery or something? Two visits in less than twenty-four hours. What gives?"

"I just wanted to see my mother. No crime in that, huh."

Carol smiled as she gazed at the rose, inhaled its escape scent once more, and squinted her eyes in confusion. "I still can't picture where that rosebush might be," she said once more.

David looked away and smiled at her bafflement, then asked if the album playing was Patsy's Greatest Hits, as "Walking After Midnight" filled the air.

Carol sighed, "Your father and I used to dance to this song while you would totter in your diaper to the music."

"Those are good memories for me, too," said David, looking at the ground in a daydream.

Carol shook her head and then said, "I miss your father so much sometimes; I wish it had been me instead of him who passed. Sometimes, there are days where I just can't stand it."

A creepy silence came over the porch until David spoke. "I don't want to hear that kind of talk out of you. Dad would have handled it much worse than you did."

Carol sighed, "Yeah, I suppose. He never had the stomach for things like that. Remember when you brought home that stray puppy you found on the way home from school, and a month later, it died of parvo? I think your father took it worse than you did, especially when it seemed it was getting better, and then suddenly died. Oh, I know you did your crying, but he became sick to his stomach when he had to bury the poor little thing in the backyard."

Just then, the record skipped as the needle scratched repeatedly at the end of the old disk. Carol sprang up and asked David if he wanted a beer. He looked up at her and paused in thought as his father's words of her departure came to mind.

"Sure," he finally said with a smile.

She smiled back and then ran to turn over the record to her old Emerson.

David stood and walked to the middle of the front yard, where he witnessed the heavy smoke that poured into the sky with its black hatred, just a little over twenty miles away. Carol came out with a beer in her hand as she asked if the fire was going to slow down.

"I don't know," said David as he grabbed the can of beer and popped its tab. "I think that if they can't contain it by

416

tomorrow, you should run for higher ground."

Carol shook her head, "Oh, David, I'm tired. I'm not running anywhere. If it gets me, it gets me."

David imagined his charred mother, her Soul-stirring sorrow soiling his mind.

Carol turned back to the porch, adamant in her thoughts as David followed her, momentarily speechless. He sat back at her feet and stared out into the yard as Carol broke the silence with a shaken voice and asked how Lisa was doing.

David looked up at her, and her words hit him like a freight train. He just shook his head negatively.

"That fucking bastard!" lashed Carol in a fiery fit of anger.

"Do you know something I don't?" barked David, forgetting who he was talking to.

Carol stammered at the thought of the whole, sick mess as she looked down at the porch. "Miranda said, 'If that if I want what's best for little Lisa, that I should keep my mouth shut.'"

David stood and shuffled in thought as Carol continued to hang her head. He saw her sorrow as he grasped her hand and told her that it was alright.

She then cried out, "Do you think he could have …?"

She began to catch her breath as David turned in contemplation as to whether he should divulge what he knew.

He turned to her, "Mom, I don't want you to feel guilty because there are some pretty sick people out here trying to make my life miserable."

Carol straightened. "What do you mean, sick people? There's more than one?"

David looked her in the eyes as if bracing her. "Ma, you remember a month ago when we talked of Devil worshippers in the valley before the Civil War, and you gave me our family album?"

"Yeah, but what's that got to do with Lisa's condition?"

"Mom, I think Miranda's part of some kind of new-age Devil Cult since he's affiliated with Devin Demas. Devin is the CEO of the True Alliance organization, and let me tell you, that isn't no Lions club."

"Well, what's our family album got to do with it?" questioned Carol, unconvinced.

"Mom, this guy Demas is over three hundred years old and is my sixth-generation grandfather."

Carol began to wonder if David was having a breakdown with all the stress he was under and needed help. David then explained all the mysterious events and Devin's role in them. Carol said nothing as she took it all in.

"Believe me, as far as I'm concerned, this Demas guy is the reason for everything that's wrong in this World. Hell, he probably started this damn fire!"

Carol couldn't believe her ears, but their family name and history quickly chilled her to the bone, and she knew David wouldn't lie to her or makeup stories. He always based his theories on factual evidence.

"So, what do you plan to do about it? I hope you have help. You're the sheriff; can't you call the National Guard or something?"

David forced a smile. "Let's not talk about that right now because right now is important to me, our time together."

Carol smiled as a bright idea came to mind. "Dance with me, for old time's sake."

David smiled, "Old time's sake, huh?"

He set down his beer as Carol reached out her hand to him. They then began to sway to a nostalgic song upon the porch, an old waltz. It was as if the clock had turned back, if only for a moment. A single tear streamed down Carol's cheek as she somehow felt closer to Dan, David's father. Soon after the song ended, the needle thumped once more, indicating the end of the record. Carol rushed inside to the Emerson, where she wiped her tears and then put on some happy bluegrass music. She then two-stepped back outside, and David asked her if she was alright. Carol took her seat with a heavy breath and a smile as she claimed she was just a little winded. David half smiled and nodded his head. His heart sank to his stomach as he turned and gazed at the black smoke upon the horizon. He finished his beer and told her he had to go, though she protested his leaving. He made known his love for her, saying so and embracing her as if he would never do so again. He then repeated the urgency of needing to leave.

Another tear streamed down Carol's face, but she smiled with crestfallen goodbyes as David shuffled to the car. She felt a sickly pain of loss and gain for her love, her son, and her life. An intrusive bell from the deepest knell sounded its theme, and a loathing loom of ghastly gloom consumed her. David waved once more to the one of the three he loved beyond his life. She waved back at him, again and again, as if it were the last time she'd set sight on him. David then climbed into the BMW, gave her a last wave, and drove off. Carol retreated to her chair, where she began to surpass her normal capacity for intoxication.

David drove towards the station, observing the time as 1: 41 p.m. He contemplated his recent Native American and Spiritual teachings. His doubts ran deep; his thoughts ran steeply while his heart pounded, pondering the task he must endeavor. *Can I put into action what I must do? Can Lisa and Sarah hold out just a little longer until I can put everything into play?*

David suddenly jolted as the two-way radio sounded off. He reached for its blurting ruckus and answered.

"David here."

"Johnny here. Just wanted to tell you that Ray's here. I guess Pat gave him directions."

"Yeah, I figured we could use the help since he promised to keep off the booze," returned David.

A sight pause voided the airways a moment until Johnny said, "Ten-four on that." He then reported that Devin's tent party over the hill was growing into a crowded valley.

David replied to keep him informed and to make sure they didn't get seen.

David pulled into the station, parked, and then went inside the building as Pat gave him a cheerful greeting.

They talked a moment before David retreated into his office, where he powered up his computer. He searched for astrology on the Internet, and a multitude of websites appeared on the screen. He decided to go to a site called Eclipse Chasers, which had a logo of the moon covering the sun while a "keep trucking" character was chasing the sky.

David began to flip through its pages of information until he found data on all the solar eclipses in the last two years. He made note of the dates, times, and locations. The site also displayed the upcoming eclipses, including the next one, in forty-three hours and nine minutes in the southeastern regions of North America. David calculated the dynamics of the whole scenario in his mind, taking into account everything that was involved, including the people, tools, and time he had to work with. He then pondered the past solar eclipses as he moved from the stars to the World news pages. He correlated the dates of the eclipse from his list of where the eclipses were seen. Immediately, headlines flashed up on the screen with pictures of human sacrifices.

Over and over, each location had the same consistency of murderous mutilation as cadavers filled the pages. After viewing ten pages from ten different regions, with headlines all casting the same grotesque pictures, David had seen enough. He now had a little more insight into the psyche of Devin Demas as he imagined the pursuit of his agenda. He then thought of Sarah's ordeal and how Johnny described the crowded mansion with RVs and limos. He also wondered why Devin wanted him to rule by his side. "What more could this man possibly want? He already runs half the planet," then David thought maybe it's simply hell on Earth he wants.

David realized that man or thing, Devin, was a perverse, sadistic creature in a man's body who purely desired the complete downfall of humanity.

The afternoon turned into evening as David mulled over his war plan on a chalkboard, with pictures drawn of the valley, along with timelines and his paths of encroachment. The evening brought shift change, and Charley sat at his post like an obedient slave to time. David tried to include him in the groundwork, but his disinterest was obvious. Time finally caught up with David, and he decided to lay his head where it hadn't been for a while---home.

When he reached the house, he opened the door, and

smells and memories hit him at once as he walked into the time capsule of yesterday's joy. He closed the door behind him, walked through the kitchen, and set his keys on the counter. He stood at the edge of the living room where he gazed at the high-definition TV Sarah had gotten him as a gift from her Devil dealings with Devin. David became enraged by its sight and gave the screen a violent kick. He yelled as he had never yelled before, ripping it from its stand and almost tripping in his anger. He stepped back to the edge of the living room, where he admired his handiwork and imagined it was Devin instead, lying broken on the floor. He then sat down in the dining room, dismayed, disheartened, and dejected. He put his head in his hands and sighed.

Suddenly, the thought of the young Priest's statement came to mind: "Lift your head and your Spirit." David rubbed his eyes and lifted his head.

He then went to the cabinet against the wall that held their family albums, retrieved them, and sat at the table with them. He reminisced through the pictures and would laugh at every other page. An hour went by as he viewed every picture several times until he was utterly exhausted by emotion. He then closed the cover of the last picture, walked down the hallway, and into his bedroom, where he sank into bed. A faint scent of Sarah still lingered in the room. He longed for her life-confirming love to permeate his soul. Finally, the relentless sirens of sleep claimed his body as melted sorrows became unconscious dreams.

Devin called out to him in his sleep with his Witching faculties, imprinting his version of a vision of David's vice-royalty upon Earth. All was deranged, estranged, and denigrated to the defilement of his nature. He sat upon a divided throne of tortured souls and the soiled bones of those he abolished, a throne he shared with his Evil ancestor. He answered only to one, the one Evil ancestor who commanded his ungodly gloom into David's ear. Grotesque figures of demented Demons drove doom to the Earth as they cackled in scorn. The surface of the Earth was clad in the charred death of infertile soil, and the oceans and seas were lifeless and still. The skies were eternally darkened as the sun forevermore was blotted out by the moon. Behind the Demas throne was Mephistopheles, his Master, commanding his minions of malevolence.

David cried out his repulsion while the dismal disdain of death dissipated into obscurity. Warm, gentle rain then washed down peace and cordiality.

A light shone down with illuminating rays in prismatic form as David surrendered wholeheartedly. Its pristine prominence bespoke prose in the same tongue as the princely Priest, piercing David's spirit with purity. Suddenly, David found himself naked, walking on the hot desert sand towards a synagogue that stood alone. He came to its giant golden doors and entered its hallowed halls of sanctuary. He gazed upon his body as it was clothed in a white robe with silver trim.

A God-fearing voice rang out. *"In my father's house, there are many mansions, and in those mansions are many rooms where I prepare a place for you."*

A maze quandary came into David's sight as levels upon levels, rooms within rooms, and halls upon halls portrayed the very perplexity of God himself. David ultimately found himself in a vast chamber of majestic proportions, with no ceiling structured overhead.

He peered on high to its eternal heights, through layers of clouds and into the celestial city of God, where angles abet acclaim for their King. His eyes witnessed what no living man since Enoch and Elijah had ever seen as his awe-stricken soul became inspired. The voice burst once more from the heavens, like sonic booms of tranquil harmony commanding his decree and rule. Great spheres of flames roared forth from the sky and onto the chamber below, where they imploded into three-dimensional figures. They revealed man's purpose through depictions of his virtues and vitality. He was then shown the begetting multiplication of humanity, with each generation back to the Garden of Eden.

The roaring flames abruptly diminished as the Godly voice rang out once more. "To every man upon the Earth, death comes sooner or later. *But how can man die more purposefully than facing fearful odds from the ashes of his fathers and the soils of the Earth, for I am the way and the light, and all shall pass before me.*"

Another sphere of fire roared forth from the heavens and descended onto David's skin like a burning bush. The light from the flames consumed him as its brightness consoled his soul.

He abruptly woke as the morning sun shined hard upon his face through the curtains. He covered his pain-riddled eyes with his hand, then turned to his side, taking account his dreams. His soul stirred strangely as he lay alone and pondered the questions that confused him profusely. He thought of the parables that were trumpeted into his mind, which he recalled word for word.

He then glanced at the clock on his nightstand; it read 9:15 a.m., and he thought to himself how strange it was that he slept so late. He sprang to his feet from his guilt of obligation and rushed out the door to the station.

He looked upward as the blackness of smoke screened the sky to a dark gloom. David then thought to himself how everything was beginning to resemble his nightmare of a scorched Earth from the previous night. Minutes later, he reached the station, and Johnny called him on his cell phone.

"What's the latest?" Asked David as he stood in front of the station.

"Man, this place never stops. I think they have a stage with rappers and metal bands playing now."

"That doesn't surprise me," replied David in a mild tone of detachment. "Listen, I just pulled up to the station. Let me check up on things, and then I'll come out to your location and meet up with you."

"Sound's good. Hey, bring some food for the troops if you can."

"Ten-four, over and out," returned David.

He entered the station as Pat told him it had been uneventful, except for the fire headed their way and the ongoing World disasters. They watched the thirteen-inch as it showed the World in torture. Los Angeles was still under a state of emergency as blackouts were causing looting, heinous crimes, and panic as gangs ran rampant. Seattle continued to have aftershocks while parts of Asia were still burying masses of casualties from the tsunamis that bombarded their shores without warning. Over and over, the screen flashed various disasters indigenous to the geological locations in the four points of the weeping world.

"All these disasters make our fire look like a girl's scout campfire out of control," said Pat with heartening optimism.

David smiled as he thought *if she had been stretched on a human rack or transfixed by the spell, she might have thought differently*. He then told her to order food for the boys in the field as he went into his office. He once more studied the correlation of time, along with the terrain and occulted army in the valley. He then called Brian's Towing as Bri-guy Jr. answered and promptly handed his father the phone.

"Hey Brian, David Lang. How's my Metal Monster coming?"

"Hey, Sheriff, glad you made it out of there. I was just about to call the station. She's finished. You can come pick her up. She's got a full tank and is primed to eat something."

"Thanks, Brian, you helped more than you know."

"No problem. See you in a bit."

David hung up the phone and walked into the lobby, where three white bags of carry-out food sat on a table by the door. He told Pat to keep him informed of the fire's progress and that he was going to meet up with Johnny.

Shortly after, David pulled up to Brian's Towing, amazed by the giant metal monster that sat waiting in front of the laboratory in which it was made. Brian and his son were mulling over its composure as David stepped out and walked over to them in awe.

"Wow, you guys really did a good job! This thing's scary looking."

Brian half smiled. "Yeah, well, you pretty much got yourself a tank. Just make sure you make it count."

David grinned at the thought of ramming down the mansion and all that it contained as he gawked at its formidable frame. Brian went over its functions and explained the transmission's five-gear pattern.

He then explained how its four-wheel drive could travel on just about any terrain with its Earth-eating tires. David asked Brian Jr. to grab the food in his car as he made his climb to the top of the rig. The boy ran to the BMW as David received his last-minute instructions about the Beast. David fired up the

426

engine and smiled at its roaring power. Bri-guy, Jr. climbed the side of the Metal Beast and handed David the food, then jumped to the ground. David yelled his thanks once more with a thumbs up, then tore out of the yard and towards Johnny's location.

David called Johnny on his cell.

"Hey, boss, good to hear from you. What's up?" returned Johnny.

"I'm about ten minutes from you. You still on point?"

"Yeah," replied Johnny, "But you'll have to hoof it on foot once you get to the road."

"Wanna bet," said David as he held his cell in the air and gunned the V-8 engine. "Can you hear me now?"

"What is that?" returned Johnny in his puzzlement.

David then explained that he had retrieved the armored vehicle and would see him in a few minutes.

He drove to where the state troopers met their deaths, and he barely noticed Johnny's squad car sitting in the brush. He then turned abruptly into the woods and quickly made a path into the forest. He smashed his way through trees, brush, and mud and began to climb up the hill. David drove about a mile until he saw Johnny's figure high up on a ridge, where he waved to indicate his presence. David acknowledged that he had spotted him on his cell, and Johnny had ceased his waving.

"You're better off parking downhill. You won't make the steep terrain," Johnny clamored.

"Don't get your panties in a bunch," David said to himself. "I'll be there in one ... second."

Just as David finished his sentence, he pulled up to Johnny's side and parked on the level clearing.

"What? I knew I could make it," said David as if defending himself.

He then took in the scene as the pounding beat of drums and bass reverberated with rapping vocals that echoed from the top of the hill.

"Man, that sounds like Sleaze Dog Holiday," said David, perplexed.

Johnny smirked like a kid who thought he knew something that he didn't as he traded his binoculars for the bags of food.

"I've never seen anything like it," Johnny remarked. "You're not going to believe it when you see it."

Porter, Al-Franko, Ray, and even Old-Man-Joe approached them as Johnny reached for a burger before he handed the bag to Porter. David nodded to Porter and the rest of the crew, then said, "Joe" where are you from? Joe returned; well, retirement doesn't suit me, and besides, this old cowboy would love to kill off some of them devil-worshiping baby killers. David smiled and patted his back.

He and Johnny then climbed to the top of the hill. They crawled on their bellies as they neared the top of the ridge for a view of the valley.

"Man, it looks like a circus down there," replied David, astounded by the crowded mansion, where yet another Euro-copter dropped off its load of human cargo. He then took the tents and RVs that covered the grounds. The prison pits were sectioned off as a stage was built into the far side of the valley wall. Sleaze Dog Holiday blasted rhyme to the rhythm as he entranced his listeners in song. David shook his head in disgust, amazed by the well-fortified layout.

He strained desperately to catch a glimpse of Sarah, but no such sight presented itself as the sounds of twisted laughter and heavy-beat music bellowed from below. The valley resembled a hellish World, with its smoke-filled gloom and the warped Soul it contained.

Noon shined its bright light above the soot, while below its luminance was a darkened gloom that lingered like smoke in a bottle. David nodded to Johnny as they scooched from their bellies and onto their feet and down the hillside to the level of the clearing. There, he told them of the eclipse and its meaning to Devin and their followers. He drew a depiction of the mansion, valley, and their position on the ground and went into the details of his plan. They ruminated over and over, beginning to end, scrutinizing every possible angle. David then took his post at the top of the hill as the others sat and ate. He wondered how he could prevail as his concerns and skepticism began to eat at him, thinking of the populated valley below. Then, those enlightening words from his dream came to mind: "How can man die better than when facing fearful odds." Those words somehow brought him comfort after peering into the very navel of Evilness.

Afternoon turned into evening and evening into night as bonfires lit the valley. The stage darkened and silenced as hordes of hooded-robed people grouped around a pentagram in front of the old mansion. Some swayed where they stood as others rang the five-pointed star and bellowed from the depths of their being. Torches were lit, and carcasses blistered in the black pond that seemed to bubble with delight from the worshippers who chanted around its circumference. The group then began to organize as a circle within a circle, chanting unholy rhyme.

One of the hooded men veered from the others as he walked into the middle of the pentagram without regard to getting drenched. He lowered his hood as the swarm of chanters halted and hushed, awaiting him to speak.

Devin gazed at his followers as he stood in the blackest of hate, in the middle of all who adored him and worshipped all that he represented. David scooped from his post with infrared binoculars as the other three strained with their eyes to see what was taking place.

Devin began his speech: *"I am very pleased, as is our Master, by your ungodly presence. The shadow of his wing will soon cast its darkness upon the Earth with all his iniquities exhumed. We are the lightning rod through which he passes as the cry of his triumph will tear from our throats. Through us, he will teach our enemies true grief while they plea for blissful death from our searing, red swords."*

The deviant, devoted worshippers discoursed decanted hymns of hellish veneration as Devin continued in tune. *"Oh, my lord, shades below, the laurels of your siege roar forth from the dying sky as your beacon will one day shine down from Zion above. We together will forever close the eyes of the proclaimed one, and his armies as their gutted corpses will lie and rot at our feet. So, listen well, I say my flock. Knit your Soul to battle for our Master, and what's left of the mortal side of Mt Zion will be yours."* The infamous robes men cheered in rapture from the tongue that promised Armageddon and seventy. The Imps splashed about the edges of the pond as the venal-induced Priest raved where he stood.

Devin smiled upon the Imps and said, "Be as children in your joy of hate and be baptized in the blood of our Master."

A woman disrobed where she stood as the welts of her debauched skin held evident her faithful following. She went forth before Devin, naked in her self-surrendered bliss, then knelt in the blackest of hate.

"I bequeath a blessing of fortuitous favor from the black star of impious divinity," she requested.

"You came with the courage to be first, without thought of consequence or shame," proclaimed Devin. "You are the breed of humanity which will dominate the wreckage of the World."

Devin scooped a palm of the black liquid as he bespoke in ancient Hebrew the rite of unholy blasphemy. He poured upon her head the black blood and continued in his tongue of unearthly dialect. The woman closed her eyes as the blackness streamed down her body with its Devilish deluge of Demonic woe. Devin inserted his middle and index fingers into her mouth as he beckoned the others to ensure her fearless following into the black pool. One after another, they disrobed and stepped into the blackness as Devin's face wore a smile with conceptual condemnation. He baptized his followers in a satanic sacrament of initiation as their naked, drenched bodies glistened with deviancy.

Devin's arm deformed to its Ill-natured sword. as he pointed it at the cold stars of the heavens through the murky haze. He then pointed it at the blackened disciples as he shouted for a willing servitor to offer their life. Quick silence bestowed the blackened mass as their zealousness ceased. Devin became angered by the sudden silence and shouted with a searing scoff.

"Who among you will step forward to pass from this realm and into my father's?"

He pointed his sword at a few who dared glance at him before they quickly turned away, hoping his attention would be driven to someone else.

He then reached for his robe, whereupon he bared his torso and exposed his heartless chest as he announced his

431

anger once more. Finally, the woman who was the first to be baptized stepped forward once more and tilted her head to the stars.

Devin was pleased by her submission as he caressed her cheek.

He then twisted her hair into his fist, tilting her head further toward the heavens as she grunted from her neck being stretched. Devin continued to shout his blasphemy to the sky as he pointed his blade high. She swallowed one last time, the saliva that welled in her mouth as Devin sliced it into her throat, and a few spectators were sprayed from her life liquid. He sawed through muscle and cartilage as he bent the back of her torso on his knee for support. He then sliced his knife behind the flap of her skin and cut through the bones of her neck.

He flung the headless carcass to the side, wiped the blade with his robe, and sheathed the horrid weapon. He then stuck his hand through the gore of its gaping aperture. He smashed his hand into the skull until his fingers popped through the sockets for its eyes and mouth, like a Demonic, inverted bowling ball. He held its gore to the sky, its eyes dangling from nerve endings. He then walked away as the naked assemblage ventured into a chaotic frenzy of orgiastic divulgence. He walked past the carnival and stage as roadies were setting the stage for the next band, Nocturnal Machine. He then strolled to the crucifix, where he laid the head on the crossbeam near the armpit of the Christ figure in a display of contempt. He then turned away as if the evening had been uneventful and walked into the mansion as the multitudes continued their miscreant acts of sacrilege.

"Man, did I see what I think I saw?" said Johnny in a repulsed disposition. David told Ray to keep watch as best as he could through the thickening smoke as Johnny, Porter, and

Al-Franko followed him to the clearing.

"Now you have seen firsthand the sick minds we're dealing with," David stammered.

"Man, that crazy lady tilted her head to his blade. That's just plain nuts," returned Johnny sick hearted.

David nodded silently as he thought to himself, *Would Sarah be next?* He pondered the worst as the sky was colored in a hellish blaze. From the fires west, snakes were being driven by the flames and a summoning supernatural strangeness that seemed to unify their consciousness. Serpents of every size and color slithered in a rapid, agitated motion, crawling atop each other as if racing to the edge of the World. Rattlers, corals, sidewinders, and even garden snakes flowed like swells upon the ocean in the riptide of rolling serpents. They poured upon the pavement, proceeding towards the lights of Lang Township like a fanged army of slithering soldiers angered in hate.

On the ridge, David asked Porter the time and heard it was 12:23 a.m. David then called the station, and silence was his only return. He then asked Johnny for his keys to the squad car, telling him Charley didn't answer his call and that he was going to check up on him. Johnny handed David his keys as metal music began to pound over the valley walls. David nodded his head as he tilted to hear it.

"Enjoy the free concert," he said as he retrieved the keys.

"Yeah, right. Just be careful. We need our star general in one piece," replied Johnny.

David smiled at Johnny and then jogged down the hill, following the path the armored vehicle had carved. The bright moon provided meager light through the murky haze of smoke as chills crept up his spine, thinking about how a Devil Cult was pervading just a valley away. By no means was his holstered pistol any comfort as his eyes widened to the dark unknown. The deeper into the forest he went, the quieter it became, both from metal and mirth in the valley.

Great trees stood as individual icons, handcrafted by an incomprehensible deity that declared its truth from its very roots. As David walked through the woods, he heard a loud crash of breaking branches that consumed him with fear. He quickened his pace as grunts and moving Earth vibrated with each step he took while his heart pounded profusely. David turned his head and peered through the dark as a large figure loomed in the shadows, staring back at him.

He thought to himself, *Is this the way it all ends? To come this far only to be devoured and eaten?* He continued at the same pace, as did the trisected creature behind, and David realized he could never outrun the creature. He then turned to confront the Beast as it halted in front of him in its tall gloom of eye-assaulting horror as it gazed at his small frame. Not a word was spoken as each wondered what the other would do until David called out.

"Hey there, big fella," he said with his hands raised to the sky, "you remember me."

The giant freak tilted his head from left to right, trying to understand the vague language and symbolism.

"That's right, big guy, you remember me. We worked together. I am David, and you are Jim and Scott."

The Beast grunted out harsh syllables with hand gestures.

"That's right, big fella, I'm your friend. Your wives, Renea and Barbara, love and miss you a lot."

A tear rolled from the corner of the Beast's malformed

eyes, and it moaned as if deeply pained. It then lashed out in anger at a neighboring tree, ripping a limb from its trunk and smashing it to the Earth. Then, it pointed the tree toward the valley.

David flinched but didn't move as he smiled in its direction. "That's right, Devin Demas did this to you. He is the reason you are the way you are!" David yelled as he also pointed at the valley.

The giant Beast threw the limb to the side, grabbed its head, and moaned out, "Demassssss."

David's paralyzed body began to ease as he felt his words sinking hard into the Beast. The giant creature smashed its fist to the ground and howled out "Demasssss" over and over as it turned and walked away. David watched the Beast disappear into the darkness and smoke, then sighed in relief before he continued towards the road. Twenty minutes later, he found himself covered with brush before the squad car. He cleared away the debris, then climbed in and drove to the station. The smoke was so thick he had to drive as slowly as if he were in a New England fog. Helplessness reared its head once more as he crept ever so slowly. He tried repeatedly to call the station but got no response. His hail was not returned, and he began to wonder if Charley had deserted his post. David banged his fist on the dashboard in his frustration as the dismally slow drive pushed him to mull over possible conclusions about Charley's disappearance. Finally, he came to the lights of Lang Township, and his drive became somewhat easier with the brightness of town.

When he pulled up to the station, his eyes came into focus. Charley was hanging upside down from the old-style streetlamp, a puddle of blood below him on the street. David exited the car and un-holstered his gun as he glanced at the hanging carcass with a note stuck to its chest as he walked towards the station. Opening the front door, he proceeded in caution, taking aim at every angle in the building. David stood in the trashed lobby where Charley must have resisted in a struggle. He then walked outside, where he was sickened by the sight of the swaying carcass.

The corpse was barefoot, with a thin, metal wire threaded through the cartilage of his Achilles heels. Charley's mouth was stuffed with an apple, and half of his nose was sliced off, revealing the insides of his nostrils to make him look like a pig. David was repulsed as he holstered his gun, untied the cable, and lowered the corpse. He then reached for the knife and pulled on the handle; its blade stuck in Charley's sternum. "Sorry," David said to the cadaver as he placed his foot on the chest and yanked out the knife with one pull. David read the heinous words upon the bloodied paper: "This little piggy won't be squealing anymore, compliments of your good friend, Syck." David looked down upon the cadaver's open eyes. That showed the residue of Charley's fear from his torturous death just before he met his demise.

David looked around, and the streets resembled a ghostly desolation of hell. He propped open the front door of the station, grabbed the corpse under its arms, and dragged it inside all the way back into the cells. He then called Johnny on his cell and told him the situation. He said if, somehow, he didn't make it back before their designated time to proceed without him, he'd attack from the other side of the valley at that time. Johnny agreed as he acknowledged his pincer plan. David said then what had never crossed his lips, "God bless and good luck, my brother." Johnny returned, "Same to you, good brother; I'll see you in the valley as they both pushed ends on their phone."

David sat thinking heavily of their impending battle as the phone on the dispatch desk rang, and he pondered what horrors it might relay. He tried to keep up an appearance of a working system as he answered, "Lang Township Police Department."

A frantic, elderly voice yelled, "Snakes!" over the receiver. David repeated the old man's comment in bafflement, but no answer was returned, only the signing of a dying man.

"Hello, are you alright?" stammered David. "Hello, answer if you can hear me. Hello!"

David listened intensely as the light sound of rattlers flustered through the receiver. He slumped into a chair, cupping his hand over the receiver to make sure he wasn't hearing things, and looked at the caller ID. It read Jack Longley. David's eyes widened as he contemplated Jack's house, which neighbored his mother's. He became panic-stricken as he hung up the phone and rushed to the cruiser, headed for Jack Longley's house.

The relentless soot continued to spew into the air, and the road was barely visible. He drove as if the cruiser was a boat directed by buoys of recognized landmarks. He began to feel his tires crashing and thumping and wondered if he had a flat tire. He stopped, clueless and perplexed. He opened the door and began to step outside of the vehicle until he caught a glimpse of the road filled with serpents, and one snapped in the air for his leg. David pulled himself in, then slammed the door and cursed at his wit's end. David screamed at the top of his lungs as if shouting at the Devil, simultaneously smashing his fist on the steering wheel. He then slammed the shifter in the drive. David was in joy from the smashing sound of crushing snakes as their scaly frames were flattened under the wheels. He soon came to Jack's house, but the son in him wanted to first check on his mother. With his obligation-riddled conscience, he answered the call of duty, cussing as he pulled up on Jack's driveway. He shined his spotlight on the path he would have to take to the front porch. David has loathed the sight of snakes ever since he was a young boy. He witnessed a water moccasin bite and killed a classmate in the river in which they swam while playing hooky at school.

David opened the door and flashed his light on the immediate area where he would set foot. No squirming reptiles were seen, only dense smoke, which brought about deeper fears of the unknown.

He grabbed the steering wheel with one hand and bent over to look under the car, as all presented clearly. He then proceeded on foot at a quickened pace to the front door. He knocked loudly, calling out for Mr. Longley while turning the handle of the door. No reply was heard, and the latch clicked open. David opened the door, and he called "hello" once more as he crept slowly through the living room, ready for anything and everything that might contest his presence. He proceeded through the dining room, then into the kitchen, where he saw Jack lying on the floor, white as a ghost, still clenching the phone, with his eyes staring at the ceiling.

Upon closer inspection, David found multiple bite wounds on the corpse, the bloated white frame grotesque with death. He cautiously walked over to investigate and knelt at its side.

"Man, this bullshit never ends," he said aloud as he shook his head in utter disgust.

He then turned the chin of the corpse and saw a snake coiled and resting in the curve of the body's neck and shoulder; its fangs bared before David. David jumped back and drew his gun when it lashed out with a pernicious attempt. It crawled over the corpse and towards him as if it had a personal mind of vendetta. He sidestepped left to right, and it froze, changing directions to his movements. He had had enough of the fanged reptile and shot off its head with one bullet. He looked down upon the squirming, headless creature rattling its last warning.

David flushed red as he thought of his mother. He then turned and ran along the way. He came with a flashlight shining his way.

He barreled out the front door and jumped off the front porch, running frantically through the smoggy haze, over the front lawn, and to the side door of Carol's house. The handle turned slightly in his hand but held tight to a locked door. He stepped back one step, then smashed through the door with a kick. He ran up the landing into the kitchen, calling out in a desperate tone as he reeled from room to room in a reckless rush to find his mother.

Finally, he came to her bed, where she lay in a peaceful bliss of death, surrounded by coiled serpents of various sizes and colors. David became enraged at the sight of his dead mother and the vile snakes that encircled her. He shook in convulsive anger and pointed his gun at the ceiling, firing off five shots as he screamed a scowling howl. The rattlers just stared at him with Soulless gazes and venomous fangs as they hissed and rattled in place.

David burst out of the room and paced in thought about how he would retrieve his mother from the nest of death. He reloaded his gun and went out back to the shed. There, he grabbed a garden hoe and garbage can. He rushed back to Carol's bedside and carefully scooped up the largest snake in the can as it rattled in disgruntled anger. One by one, ever so slowly by the sweat of his brow, his heart sank low, snake by snake, he thrust in his hoe. But when it was safe to approach, she breathed no more. Her skin was blistered from the poison within. She lay there stiff, his mother, his friend. David sat by her side for a moment, knowing his father's words. He then lifted her and carried her to the cruiser. He placed her in the backseat of the car and drove off towards town. He called out on a megaphone for residents to lock their homes tight, describing the deadly snakes.

He then came upon a river of serpents that streamed towards the downtown area, like rushing rapids that flooded banks with pernicious pursuit. David grinned and gritted as he recalled what the young Priest proclaimed: stomp the serpent. He sped his tires upon the snakes, taking delight in the mangled mess he left in his path. The crunching sound of their breaking vertebrae trod under his tires lifted his spirits, and their thrashing frames thudding in the wheel wells brought insane laughter from his slipping faculties.

He looked in his rearview mirror at his stiff, white mother. "At least we took a couple of them with us, huh, Mom," he quipped.

It seemed an eternity as his tires continued to crush the contemptible creatures, their cold blood and smashed scales saturating the road. David finally came to pass beyond the slithering sea of snakes, and he halted fifty feet ahead of them. He studied their path and speed and was horrified at their encroachment into town. He then sped away through the black soot and smoke.

Minutes later, he pulled into the cemetery of Saint Andrew, where he thought it befitting to bury his mother. He walked to a small work shed, hoping to find an empty coffin. Yet no such thing presented itself, and he wondered what else he could do. He then saw an old shovel sitting in the corner, and a romantic idea came to mind. He would place his mother in his father's arms in one casket. He grabbed the shovel and walked to his father's grave, though he could still hear the rattling song of Satan in the far distance. David ignored the echoing Evil, focusing instead on his father's stone, and began digging in the soft soil. Every shovelful of Earth was a symbol of memory and his love. He dug deep into his sorrow. Twenty minutes later, he hit a coffin. He cleared away the dirt and opened its lid. David gazed at his father's bones in a decomposing three-piece suit.

He slid to one side, then pulled himself up and out of the grave. He returned with his mother in his arms and set her on the edge of the hollow grave. He then climbed down, slid her body into the coffin, and turned her to her side with her arm over her true love. He glanced down once more at his parents and noticed his mother's hand clenched tight to the white rose. David smiled, then went into a wrenching divulgence of his proclaimed love he vowed. He closed the casket, lifted himself out of the grave, and covered his loved ones in earth. Sorrowful shadows were buried where darkness would never fall again.

He then headed back to the cruiser, where he lit a smoke and leaned on its hood. There, he beheld another detachment of snakes slithering upon the road. They seemed to be determined not to venture into the confines of the cemetery and church as they slithered in a cascading curse. David thought to himself *how strange it was that they worked as a unit and did not veer upon the church grounds*. He snuffed his smoke as the sun rose in the eastern sky, relieved by the beautiful dusky morning. He spied on the masses of serpents as the morning sun bared their immense legion.

David climbed into the squad car and barreled over the fanged creatures in the rising sun's direction. Moments later, he drove onto the Indian reservation, taking in its ghostly appearance. He looked far and near as he made a slow drive through an area where children used to play as the old would sit and watch on the side.

He pulled up to Nathan's cabin and knocked on the door but was met with silence. He then walked beyond the cabin to the scorched earth where bonfires pervaded just a sunrise. He called in every direction, but his voice became swallowed up by the smoky sky.

Returning to the cruiser, he called Johnny and advised him to watch for snakes. He commanded that no matter what,

Johnny was not to stray from their plan of precise timing. He then told him he was putting the first step of their plan into action. Johnny said to be careful, and they signed off, declaring their friendship and victory.

As David drove downtown, he witnessed two rivers of snakes merging into one, and they slithered toward the valley in a relentless flow. Maybe they'll kill Demas and his clan and make my job easy, he thought. But he remembered the prisoners in their pits and how their confines could never protect them from having the perfect conditions for snake nesting. David smashed as many of the snakes as he could, his tires squealing upon their scales, and he screamed out the window in spirited success.

He then turned onto a road leading to the mansion, where RVs, limos, and even old, beat-up vehicles packed both sides of the road. He drove up the long driveway of the mansion, and two valet attendants laughed at David's arrival. He parked his cruiser, got out, nodded to their bewilderment, and walked past them and into the mansion as if he owned the place.

No familiar face presented itself as he walked through the crowded living room of youngsters who were being deceived with delicacies of flesh and the grandeur of abounding opulence. Yet some were beginning to smarten up, sitting away from the mirthful crowd, wondering what happened to their friends. David wanted desperately to broadcast out to those who blighted blindly and tell them to bolt if it were not for his mission. He shuffled through the crowded rooms and into the dining room, then on through the kitchen, where he headed into the backyard.

David's eyes came upon an unimaginable horror. A human leg protruded from a woodchipper that was pointed over the pool. Skin, blood, and bone floated in the gore-imbued pool as the wicked swam and orgy in the shallow waters. David walked past a towering, deranged man with hideous features who was feeding the chipper from a wheelbarrow of dismembered limbs of assorted size and color. He then came to a tent where a blistered, scorched man cried out from his ongoing agony as he came in and out of consciousness. Most of the coins melted onto his skin as others rolled off, leaving a visible trail. David's stomach turned as he walked away, repulsed by the immoral brutalities of the varied spectacles.

Out front, Syck was coming from an RV where he just had sex with a mother and her daughter. He saw the squad car and became unhinged, rushing to the parking attendants and questioning them about the pig mobile. After the attendant described David, Syck ran into the mansion to find Hector so they could mangle David together.

Ora was standing by a grandfather clock, laughing at a joke a European told when she spied on an agitated Syck. Syck tore in the direction of the bedrooms, shoving a youngster out of his way while the attendants stood at the front door peeking in. Ora excused herself and walked up to the attendant to see what Syck was all worked up about.

The valets told her of Syck's interest in the driver of the police car as they pointed it out parked at the end of the drive. Ora rushed back inside and saw Syck and Hector walk into the kitchen, heading towards the rear door. She followed them from an undetectable distance, taking in the massive crowd and looking for Nina or Devin. She went from tent to tent, peering into the hellish obscurities of the various immoralities each contained.

She then reached a tent where Nina was giving instructions for the formation of a ritual during the final hours. Ora whispered into her ear the matter of Syck and Hector stalking David. Nina handed Ora the pointer and told her to take over where she left off, then quickly left the tent. She worked her way through the crowd, searching for Syck's bright-blonde hair and Hector's swarthy, dark skin as she studied the hordes of people. Finally, she caught a glimpse of David being pummeled by the Warlocks in a blissful glee of delight as she hurried to intervene.

"Thomas Syck, leave him be!" she yelled.

Syck turned to her. "Fuck you, bitch. Why don't you go suck off the Witch Master's cock? That's what you do best. Now get the fuck on, 'cause you ain't stopping this."

Just as the word "this" left his lips, Syck's mouth closed upon itself, and he dropped to his knees, pawing at his face. His mouth squeezed together as if a vice smashed his lips into each other until they turned into one, sealing his mouth. Syck jumped to his feet and tore at his face as he now had fleshy, wrinkled, malformed skin in the place of his mouth.

He then looked around for Devin in a frantic mode of trepidation, wanting to beg his forgiveness for his ill tongue. But Devin was nowhere to be found, and he gazed at Nina with newfound fear.

"Don't look at me; I didn't do that handiwork," she said as she motioned, sucking a cock.

He then looked at Hector and David and ran off. Nina eyed Hector as he put his hands up in surrender mode, then followed Syck. Nina smiled, then went to David's side.

"Are you alright?" she asked, looking him over.

David brushed himself off and thanked her. Nina just smiled and said, "You still don't get it, do you, Huggy Bear? My Master sees all, and all is his to see."

She then smiled once more and said, "Come with me," and

turned as if confident he would follow. David obliged, and his heart pounded. It was time to act on his deception to the Witch Master himself, his grandfather.

They treaded through a colorful maze of people and blaring base and rap from Sleaze Dog Holiday. David looked toward the stage as two bimbos dressed like hookers danced at his side. David then found himself back poolside, where Devin waited by the befouled water.

"Ah, if it isn't my long-lost grandson."

David dropped to his knees as he stated, "You are my Master, whom I will follow."

Devin smiled, "What changed your mind? You left so quickly the last time I saw you. Where's your antlered friend? Never mind him, what of you, Devlin? Should I believe you? Hmm … prove it."

David looked at him, confused, wondering what twisted test could "Possibly pass for such a deviant." Devin studied David's demeanor a moment, then said, "Bathe in the blood of man and receive the sacrament of our denouncement."

David's stomach repulsed, but his appearance presented no such scare as he walked to the edge of the cesspool. He looked over at Devin and Nina, who watched as if unconvinced. He then glanced at the churning, unmanned machine, where a torso spun and flopped in the bucket, chopping slowly. The sight of the gore-filled bucket with the malodorous smell of death palpated his stomach with involuntary regurgitation. Rather than vomit and show weakness, he dove deep and released his vomit. He then swam towards the shallow end of the Soul-rotted pool. Halfway to the other side, he dared open his eyes as a swollen, white head floated in his path.

He swatted it out of his way, and his hatred for Devin empowered him to push through the gore. He then rose from the red water and climbed up the ladder, looking toward Devin for approval. The Devil's confidante clapped his hands in long cracks as if still not captured by his loyalty.

A voice bellowed from his other side. "That was a nice trick, but can he roll over?"

Looking over his shoulder, knowing that voice was the FBI agent who pushed him back into the red cesspool, David swam to the cement steps, climbed once more out from the pool, and approached his assailant with a left hook and a punch to his belly. The agent bent over, gasping for air, as David tossed him into the pool. Devin smiled with approval, then looked down at the crippled duck. The agent splashed his hands on the water as he demanded Devin take revenge on David. Devin smiled at the lame duck and said, "Devlin is of my lineage. Death will surely come from my hand if he's not truly submitted."

He then turned to David and requested his company as he began walking towards the profane carnival. Devin stopped at the "quarter" tent, where a fresh slab of meat was crying from searing pain. A twisted Carney that ran the tent lowered himself in reverence to the Evil Eminence that stood before him.

Devin gestured for him to rise and prepare the game as the carny jumped to his request and fired up the torch. He brightened a quarter to a bright red glow, then placed it into a metal cup and handed it to his Master. Devin, in return, held it out to David, who grasped the cup and eyed the poor Soul, who was in agony.

"You know, this isn't necessary. Didn't I prove myself at the pool?"

Devin nodded his head. "Oh, Devlin, I'm over three

hundred years old. You need more than a casual swim to convince me. Now toss the damn coin and show me the pain of man."

David stared once more at the young man whose eyes were sodden with tears as he begged in a foreign tongue for his release. David considered the sake of many opposed to the sacrifice of the few and braced himself for the displeasure act. But he then got a break as Yakahara and his clique walked past, and they all, in unison, lowered their heads as they passed.

David used the distraction to his advantage as he spit in the cup and gestured for the young man to keep quiet and play along. Devin then turned to him and glared at the cup and then at the prey of his amusement. David quickly tossed the coin onto the man's torso, and the man wiggled in pain as only the edge of the heat was taken from the coin.

Devin laughed as he patted David on the back and said, "Good job."

Nina then approached and gazed at her Master and David as Devin told him to follow once more. David maintained a cool composure, loathing his next task but complying with the Witch Master while Nina took up the rear. David proceeded through the murk and blasting metal music played by Nocturnal Machine as he tailed Devin's shadow to the cubed bath of acid.

A teenage boy scaled in blisters and wrought in agony sat high upon the seat, fearing another dunk. A blubbery man in a top hat handed David three baseballs as Devin and Nina stood silent and watched.

He gazed upon the third-degree burns and sympathized with how the teen wheezed from his acid-filled lungs. The burned-riddled boy looked back at him as if begging to end his misery. David yelled out in rage, then threw the ball. It

447

plastered the target with a crash. The teen squirmed a moment, then suddenly ceased his fuss. Smiles came to the sadistic faces that watched. The blubbery man rushed to David with a stuffed bear and retrieved the remaining balls. Devin grinned once more as he nodded with approval before walking away. Nina pecked David's cheek and said, "Welcome to the club," then turned to follow her Master.

David then looked over as the blubbery man's assistant fish hooked the white, swollen carcass from the cube. The vile blob himself held a boy by his fear-riddled shoulders, whose turn was next. David walked up to the portly man and told him he could not use the boy because they were low on sacrificial lambs. The pig protested as he pushed the boy to the cube with his grotesque girth.

"Listen here, you fat piece of shit," David yelled. "Do you know who I am?"

The greasy man became intimidated since David had been in the company of the Witch Master just moments ago.

"And whom might that be?" he said with mild sarcasm.

David released his anger as he pointed his finger at the fleshy chest of the sick-minded top hatter with every word he stated. "I am 11th generation to Devin Demas, which makes me Devlin Demas. Now, if you don't do as I say, you'll be swimming in acid in a minute."

The obese man dropped to his knees. "Please, Mr. Demas, can you forgive a fat idiot such as myself for my ignorance?"

"And hold off on any more right now, or you'll be a dead little fish, got me?"

"Yes, yes, Mr. Demas, here's your lamb."

He pushed the boy to David, who took the boy by his wrist and turned into the haze.

"What's your name?" asked David with compassion.

The boy uttered back, "Billy," in a disparaging tone of low self-esteem.

David walked him to the side of a trailer and then told him to run up the hill in the direction of Johnny's camp. The boy's eyes followed the direction of David's finger; then he fell to the ground, his face wrenched in tears. David asked why he was crying when he was now free.

The boy looked up with emotion and said, "Because that was my brother back there."

Riddled in guilt, David lifted the youngster by his shoulders. "I'm sorry for your brother, but he was already gone before I got there."

Billy wiped his tears and then looked up, knowing it was true, as he saw his brother fall into the acid four times before David's fatal throw.

"Where are your parents? Were you taken from them?"

Tears rushed once more down the boy's face as he shook his head.

"Well, where are they?" David questioned, searching the boy's face for answers.

Billy could barely talk as he stammered words of fervent sorrow while looking up at David in shame. "They brought us here and gave us to the fat man!" he cried.

David knelt face level and hugged the distraught boy, then

told him that he was a police officer and that he was there undercover. He then instructed Billy in the direction of his deputy camp once more and told him to run as fast as he could and not to look back.

The boy hugged David again, then turned and ran like a refugee who could smell freedom. David watched until he disappeared into the smoky haze, and then he turned back into the twisted wickedness.

Devin conferred with one of his representatives from the Middle East as Syck approached him, humbled in pathetic Rue. Devin turned to him, and Syck's mouthless face brought him amusement.

Syck muffled out apologetic words that vibrated through his skin. Devin nodded as if not wanting to be disturbed by Syck's persistent grovel. Devin turned from his disciple and shouted his displeasure in fervent anger.

"Why in all dimensions would you dagger my back with displaced tongue?"

Syck pleaded in body language about the misunderstanding of his loyalty.

Devin shook his head once more. "My poor, uninformed man. You, of all people, should know that the Devil is never a maker. The less you bestow, you take. I bestow woe onto thee or any of misplaced tongue that scorns my name."

Syck mumbled once more, his peeve, wanting his return to his good looks. Devin smirked, then circled the air with his wrist, and Syck lifted and turned upside down in suspension as he squirmed like a toad.

Devin reached for his knife as Syck's eyes widened. Devin sliced open a flap for Syck's mouth. Syck became loud and clear as he gurgled out his pain in blood. Devin pinched his bloodied cheeks together and told him that all he needed to do was look in the mirror when he was tempted to stray his tongue. Syck shook his head in compliance as Devin turned and slung his wrist to the floor. Syck fell simultaneously. The crowd applauded Devin as if he had pulled a rabbit out of a hat. Devin returned to his guest as Syck looked about the laughing gawkers. He clenched his gaping flaps, then ran from the room. Hector watched from a safe distance and followed him unobtrusively to his room.

Syck held a towel to his face, reeling back and forth in grueling pain as Hector walked in. "Man, he really did a number on you, Ese' you need to get that Sown up."

Syck just rocked in pain and stared into the mirror.

"Hold tight, Ese. I'll be back in a minute," said Hector as he left the room.

Ten minutes later, he returned with cocaine, Vicodin, Jim Beam, and a needle and thread. Syck gurgled out with his distrust as he glared at Hector, threading the needle.

"Don't worry, bro, I know what I'm doing. But first things first."

He poured the liquor to see the path in which he would sow. He then sprinkled the coke onto the gashes. He then told Syck to open wide as he dropped four Vicodins down his throat. Hector tilted the Jim Beam and, with a spout atop the bottle, drank as fast as he could. He then cut some lines on a mirror and held it out to Syck. Syck inhaled the narcotizing powder as Hector waited and watched him numb. He then opened the window to hear Nocturnal Machine playing their number one hit, "I'm Your Suicide."

Hector tilted Syck's head to the ceiling and asked Syck what the fuck he was thinking when he talked down the Witch Master. Syck closed his eyes, wondering the same as his head jerked from each drive of the needle. Stitch after stitch, Hector sewed the gaping flaps until all were sealed, leaving a small slit for a foul mouth.

Syck walked to the mirror, taking in his new, monstrous features as Hector cracked a joke. "Hey there, Ese, you're as ugly as me," he said, rolling in laughter.

"Ha, ha," retorted Syck. "Yeah, we're just two ugly duckies in a muddy pond."

Hector stopped laughing and added, "Yeah, two ugly duckies that will soon be immortal and run this piss-hole planet, that is, if you don't piss off the Witch Master again."

Syck shook his hands in the air and shook his head as he said never again. They then began laughing once more as they stuffed their noses with coke and their bellies with Jim Beam.

On stage, the blubbery top hatter announced, "Three hours until the eclipse ceremony begins" over the loudspeaker. David walked the confines with emptiness consuming him while the commotion of the carnival quieted as most guests retreated to their tents, RVs, and the mansion, leaving only the Carnies closing game tents and groups of robed men toiled in the task. The morbid, robed men carried the dead in wheelbarrows to the black-blooded pentagram through the gloomy haze. David saw the very man he tried to save from pain in the coin toss tent stacked on another being carted towards the black pond. He then wandered as he endeavored to find Sarah. But she was not to be found, only the emptiness of himself and the premise of hell. David went to the pentagram, where he witnessed mounds of human carcasses decomposing in the blackest of hate. Next to the pentagram was a podium and a sacrificial slate designed for death. David walked to the edge of its seething hate and peered at its ungodly damnation, with its stench of death and the sight of blistered and boiled corpses.

He walked away dejected from all the misery and endless devoid of life, and his confidence began to slip once more. But when he glanced to his right, he was suddenly facing the majestic antlered Beast. The deer stared at him, and David froze. The very sight of the Beast brought hope once more into his distant heart.

Men clad in red robes came walking down the pathway as they carried a headless cadaver to the edge of the black pond. David glanced back toward the majestic deer, and only a tree and bush presented themselves. He somehow felt that he wasn't alone in his fight against the colossal machine of Evil.

David watched the robed men giggle as they swung the headless cadaver, singing one, two, and then three as it splashed into the black pond. They then walked past David, laughing in cheerful mirth as if he were a ghost in a Charles Dickens novel.

Time began to feel like a boulder that cursed his shoulders as he labored through the rough final hour. David followed behind the hooded-robed men at a twenty-foot pace back into the dismal emptiness of the unencumbered carnival. The robed men continued until they were out of sight in the murkiness. David still hoped to find Sarah and the boys. He walked around, lost in the haze, until he came to the defiled crucifix, decorated with a row of human heads on each side of its upside-down composure. Sickened at the vile sight of immoral wickedness, David shook the cross until it toppled to the Earth, sending heads rolling. He then turned to the pits, which were guarded by hooded-robed men with assault rifles. Rain began to first sprinkle and then turn into a downpour as he looked around and saw small groups of robed men practicing their march. The rain mixed with smoke and wet Earth set off a musky scent that brought an ambiance of loneliness of nowhere to go.

David sat on a stump in the middle of the grounds, and when he looked up, he saw the robed men had tripled in number. Hooded devotionals hovered in the smoky rain, waiting, wanting, and gathering in their gloom of assemblage. One by one, two by two, and so on, they continued to mass as their numbers held true to their faithfulness and cause. The loudspeakers announced that another hour had passed as the relentless rain and smoke poured into the valley.

A hooded figure walked David's path through the rain and haze in a slow, adamant march. David lifted his head from the puddled earth. As she approached, she bared her head. It was Nina who smiled upon a dejected David. She then reached out her hand, and David surrendered his.

Nina's smile widened as she reached out to David. He took her hand, and they walked to a tent where David had been given a robe. He covered himself and looked to Nina for her approval. She cloaked his head with the garment's hood, and she told him to remain veiled until told differently as long lines were formed and torches were lit. David thought to himself that if he didn't know better, he'd say it was night, as the sky was screened in dark gloom. Crowds upon crowds continued to amass as the only light was coming from the torches held by faith-driven hands. The masses began to chant in low, crooning hymns as they shuffled into organized squadrons.

David shuffled with his group but dared not utter a sound from his lips, fearing his own damnation from doing so. Along the base of the hill, they death marched, the line stretching as far as David could see, circling to the old ruins at the back of the grounds. Snakes began to surge into the valley, pouring into the black pond as if drawn by its hellish heat. They blistered

454

and burned in the blackness of hate, flopping and squirming in agitation. Nearly half drowned in its blissful cauldron, as those remaining swayed at its edges to the vocal vibrations of chant. On and on Satan's soldiers marched in beckoned call, while Evil chant enthralled, and the heavens cried with a black rainfall.

They began to march in a twisted pattern resembling the number six-six-six. Bonfires were then lit at each point of the pentagram, and the flames roared high with an orange-yellow glow. The prisoners in the pits were exhumed from the Earth and chain-linked together; the thirty vessel virgins now stood before the sacrificial slate.

Yakahara's sacrificial lambs waited willingly in their group as Heilwig's boys lay bound and tied upon the Earth. Other groups were also bunched, tethered, and tied, waiting unwillingly for their time upon the slate.

Syck and Hector stood to the side as the sewn-mouth Monster heckled the young girls. Syck placed his thumb between his fingers, like an imaginary nose, as he ranted, "I got your Soul, I got your Soul."

The young girls never beheld such horrors as the sown mouth. Syck laughed at their displeasure, sending some clasping to the ground.

Devin approached the pentagram as Nina and Ora followed behind. Ora carried the *Egyptian Book of the Dead* and an umbrella to protect it. Nina carried a bucket of white, chalky powder, also under an umbrella. Ora and Nina stood to the side while David blended with the crowd. Devin walked to the podium as he gazed at his chanting soldiers, pleased with the sight of their fated will. He raised his hand, and all quieted except for the sounds of rattling serpents in the background. Ora placed the book on the podium, where she stood in the rain as her umbrella covered its pages and her Master. Devin opened the human-skinned cover and began a Satanic Sermon of sacrilege over his flock.

*"Oh, Mephistopheles, thou bear many names and many faces but only one truth, in which I am your humble servant. Through misery and woe, I beseech my vow, which holds evident in the masses we assemble. My vow is endless faith as we follow you in the battle and victory of the Zion heavens. My vow is true in alliance and legion as we await the assault upon the creator's most beloved creation, mankind. This final hour will forever stand as the testament and reign of your dominion. I bestow to you human blood that spills and soils the Earth in the befouled blasphemy before the heavens.*

*My influences run deep within the fiber of mankind's desires as the ripple effects of my power are spearheaded by the casting mold of your right wing. I made humanity dependent upon your purpose from the immediate comfort of their lives with my great industrial strength. Mothers offer me their children in the dedication of your deity.*

*Husbands offer me their wives and siblings. Kings offer me their thrones while I behest all in your glory."*

Devin walked to the slate, where he drew his dagger upon a servitor lamb from the Yakahara clan as she lay naked in accepted gloom. Devin shouted scriptures from the *Book of the Dead* as he glided the dull of his dagger through her breast and into her heart. She closed her eyes as Devin cursed the heavens once more, and in his loathing hatred, he pointed his dagger at the blackened sky. He was silent as he thrust his blade through the cavity of her chest, and she screeched her last breath.

The schoolgirls screamed at the sight of the gore as Devin carved the bone, cartilage, and vessels from the chest of the cadaver. They tussled in agitated motion as Syck held one side of the chains and Hector the other. Devin held high the bloodied heart, and some fainted. Some resisted, kicking and screaming, and the rest cried out to God.

A disciple approached Devin with a large silver bowl and a pedestal at its base with the inscription of the True Alliance symbol, where the Witch Master placed the fervent heart. Two disciples walked to the slate, where they retrieved the sacrificed lamb and threw it into the middle of the pond.

The next lamb was placed, and Devin went into the second orison of his beseech. The second died as obediently as the first, and all the while, the silver bowl awaited another bloody prize.

Cadaver after cadaver was thrown into the black pool as their blood shamed the soil in the stigmatization of sacrilege. Ora bowed her head to Heilwig as robes men took away one of his lambs.

Heilwig waved to his disciples, and they dragged a young man to the slate. The young man squirmed and screamed, naked upon the cold slate of death. Devin looked down upon his uneasy frame. He caressed his hair with his bloodied hand and told him not to fret over his life from this realm.

He then turned away as he spoke aloud while inspecting the schoolgirls' pacing, each flinching at his ungodly presence. *"Death is not a disaster to be feared and the work of the destroyer not cruel or undesirable. Construction from the creator cannot stand forever; therefore, the divine custodian---death---constitutes its will."* He then walked back to the altar as his alluring words transfixed his followers with blissful damnation.

*"We circle in a symbolic gesture, representing the serpent with its tail in its mouth, the return of unity. Therefore, the serpent circle is everlasting, the symbol of our destructive nature. Lucifer regained his star and diadem as his legions assembled for new works of creation. His flame will shine from the heavens while celestial spirits will plunge to the Earth as their decaying eyes will forevermore peer into my father's Kingdom."*

457

Devin looked down upon the fearful man, speaking words in German that tore him in utter terror, sending him screaming. Devin then raised his dagger above his torso while his disciples strained to hold the lamb in place. He thrust his dagger into the young man's chest as a Soul-stinging scream scathed the smoke-screened sky.

David became sickened by the waste of life as he forced himself to be patient, yet another cadaver was thrown into the black pentagram.

The hollowed corpses decayed at a phenomenal rate in the steaming sulfide that blistered the dead hides. The foul stench of death imbued the air, and vomit rose in David's throat once more. The Imps and Priest stood out from the crowd as Devin nodded to Nina to perform her part of the ritual.

She walked to the blackness as she called upon Demonic Spirits. She then dislodged a chalky-white powder, the granulated bones of James, Devin's son, into the caldron brew of hell. The slaughter continued until all were slayed, leaving only the schoolgirl virgins for the eclipse.

Through the murky haze, David could make out the full moon slowly embarking before the sun while chanting began once more. After six verses, Devin read from the Necronomicon while the chanting lowered to a backdrop for his voice.

*"Oh, come to thee upon the surface of Earth, oh Mephistopheles. Oh, come to thee, thy spirit that curses the footsteps of your enemies. Oh, come to thee before your subjects who take up arms for the final bout. Oh, come to thee, your apostle patron to my last breath.*

*Oh Beelzebub, lord of this World, Master of the abode, I call on to thee and your hellions of dark soldiers to bestow your malevolent prevalence. Yet you are my Master, my God, and we are your servants. I am all that is evident as I bare thy shell of thine skin."*

Devin disrobed while Nina unveiled her hood, and others did the same. David's eyes bestirred with astonishment as he gazed at the faces around him. People from the U.S. Senate and House of Representatives stood to David's left. To his right was Anna Statler, the federal judge who set his bond at a million dollars and now glanced at him with a deviant smile.

Actors, musicians, comedians, and entertainers from all over the World and from all walks of life held torches in the gloom. One face did stick out to David's seething anger--- Joseph Miranda.

Devin walked from the podium and then turned to the multitude of snakes. *"I take thy coldblooded creatures into thy self in the union of consummation before thy true King, Mephistopheles."*

He then summoned the scaly serpents, spurting out snakish sounds of slithering tongue as six hundred and sixty designated reptiles came before him.

His own tongue slithered out once more, a satanic command while the vile creatures crammed under his skin in a rapid state of compulsion. All over his body, their shapes squirmed under his skin as the orb upon his forehead opened. Devin fluttered violently from their inflow as they continued to pour into his frame as if going to their nest. The mass of disciples gave unholy accolades to the phenomenon they were witnessing.

The black rain fell harder and harder as the last of the serpents entered Devin's body. All became silent except for the remaining rattlers, roaring bonfires, and the downpour as Devin opened his soulless eyes. His tongue rolled forth from his mouth with an inverted V slit at its end. He then bared his pearly-white fangs at his tribe, and all bowed to his Evil Eminence.

He walked to the edge of the pentagram as Demonic

shapes began to form in the black pond, spawning in frothing infest.

"Yes, yes, come, come unto thee, for I have waited so long for your nefarious presence."

The moon was now upon the outline of the sun's aura as Devin joined in the continual chant for humanity's doom.

The Demons progressed in their incarnation as Devin hovered, chiming words of a spell for their unholy presence. One by one, they appeared until six Demons stood drenched in black. Devin's Soul then appeared in the middle of the Demons as if they were his protection. Devin's Soul awaits his return to its rightful place as a living being of immortal proportion.

The Demons wiped the blackness from their eyes and gazed upon the surface and Witch Master. The Demons and Devin's Soul remained trapped in the pentagram until the eclipse was full in place.

David could hear the ripping roar of a V-8 engine in the distance, but everyone else was too immersed in their endeavors of heavenly damnation to notice. The moon was now halfway across the sun as Kilgore rocketed from the depths of hell and into the sky, shrieking out its Devil cry.

Barabis then rose, his appearance untarnished by the blackness that dwelled around him. He stood in the middle of the fiendish Demons that hissed and clawed to the sky. A loud crash sounded from the sky, and lightning zig-zagged over Barabbas's head, bisecting the palms of his hands. Another crash sounded off from the front of the mansion as Johnny plowed his way through limos, buses, and RVs. No one had yet heard the destruction as Johnny thrashed about, plowing the premises as the ceremony continued. Billy sat with Johnny inside the Metal Monster and took pleasure in the destruction of all in their path. Ray, Porter, Al-Franko, and Old-Man-Joe followed on foot.

Devin suddenly became aware of the intrusion as he pointed to David, "You treasonous little worm, bring him!" Robed men on both sides of David grabbed him as he was now a prisoner to Devin's anger.

They walked him before their Eminence as three disciples stood behind him with three silver bowls filled with human hearts. David was forced on his knees before the Witch Master. Devin told him he should have killed him long ago, and he looked to the sky. David's eyes followed Devin's as the eclipse was now in its place.

The bonfires remained the only light as Devin's face smiled in twisted, snakish features. Syck and Hector led the chained schoolgirls to the blood-soiled altar. Tears flowed in hysteric mania, knowing their deaths would soon come. Syck grabbed Suzy as the first of them. She resisted with all her being as Syck dragged her to the sacrificial altar. She then sees a knife lying on the slate. She quickly takes it and slices Syck's face, splitting his eye. Syck grabs his face and drops to his knees, wincing out in pain. The other schoolgirls saw Suzy's courage and began to kick and punch Hector as he was caught off guard, and they beat him to the ground, then ran and scattered. Porter, Al-Franko, and Ray were now upon the crowd, shooting all who wore hoods.

Johnny bore through the crowd in an uproar of death as the welded teeth on the front of the Metal Monster ate all that resembled Evil. The Witch Master transformed into a sixty-foot serpent and slithered swiftly through his fallen followers and gunfire ruckus. It came upon Ray, where it rose above his head and snatched him whole.

The last of Heilwig's lambs were upon the slate altar as

Barabis and his six Demons walked upon Earth. Johnny saw the horror of Ray's devoured as he chased the giant snake at gaining speed. Barabis took Devin's place at the altar. The Demons were like untethered dogs of war as they slashed anyone in their path, leaving only those who were bedeviled by black blood. David reached for his nine-millimeter and shot the legs of those who held him. The giant snake slithered its way towards Porter, who shot at its head to no avail.

He turned to run, horrified to be eaten in the same manner as Ray. David emptied his gun upon the mass of robed men as they felt quick in numbers, as they did from the Metal Monster.

The Metal Monster then rammed into the snake as it crashed to a halt, giving Porter a window for escape. The giant serpent briefly recoiled from the impact, then coiled around the armored truck and pecked at its top end. The windows exploded upon every strike, sending Billy screaming for his life. Johnny jumped to the rear of the truck, where he kicked out what remained of the window. The metal confines began to resemble a can being crushed as the coiled snake continued to compress and crush its roof. Johnny yelled to Billy as he reached out his hand.

The boy momentarily froze but complied, taking Johnny's hand. Johnny pushed him through the window. Johnny quickly followed suit, jumping out of the mangled mess. Then he grabbed Billy and took cover behind a snack trailer from where Porter signaled to them.

The giant creature slithered away, satisfied with its destruction and unaware that its prey had escaped. Al-Franko ran out of ammo as he regrouped his thoughts behind some bushes and witnessed Devin return to his human form.

Devin then resumed the helm of ritual as he took in his dwindling followers. Through the destruction and haze, he saw

David, who in turn was smiling back at him.

"You!" Devin shouted at his wit's end.

His anger seared his soulless self as he marched before David, then halted and shook his head.

"You could have ruled by my side, but instead, you chose a dead existence at the foot of God. He doesn't love you; he doesn't want you! That's why he gave you to me, so I may devour your Soul."

David simply smiled, "I've already seen my home, which is already prepared for me." He pointed high. Kilgore screeched a warning cry from the sky, and Devin looked up, fearing the ritual might not be complete before the eclipse passed.

"I'll deal with you later," said Devin sternly as he turned back to the slate of slaughter.

David lifted his Glock and took sight of the back of Devin's head and was tackled by a robed man from behind. Devin revealed Barabis as he bespoke words from the Necronomicon. Barabis headed the slaughter upon the slate and continued to rip out the heart of the young with his clawed hand.

Horrific cries bellowed from the bowels of the forsaken abode as the Imps jumped up and down in joy. The black-hearted Priest praised hell's fire as he swaggered in a drunken bliss of rapture. A grotesque head of immense proportions began to rise slowly as if awakened from a millenary dark dimension. The foul stench of hell spewed forth as the thick black liquid bared its loathsome form of all that is ill-natured Satan. Both Devin and his Soul smiled upon his rising Master, rushing in words of ancient rite and rhyme.

The moon began to strengthen its pull from the sun. Devin

gazed at the sky with a frayed perturb as his very essence of purpose was slipping from the time he had lost. The Witch Master continued his words of summoning the ill-natured Beast as the Devil rolled its head back and forth as if awakened by Devin's screaming rants and the blood-drenched Earth. Three hundred years of knowledge culminated in this moment in which Devin commanded all his will to keep the lunar eclipse in place.

The commotion continued all around him as screams from his hooded flock filled the clash-riddled air. One by one, they began to fall as arrows and spears fell from the sky. Devin's voice began to lose effect as he gazed at Indian warriors pouring over the hillside.

Barabis turned from the altar and threw hell's fire from his hands onto the oncoming assailants. The Demons answered Kilgore's call as they rushed before the Indians and sliced, clawed, and gnawed anything within reach. Dead fell upon the dead as waves of warriors wailed their war cries in attack.

Al-Franko and Porter took up a spear and stabbed at every hooded robe in sight. Johnny took the boy aside and told him to stay put. He then turned into confusion and began to shoot from the hip anything that resembled a Witch, Warlock, or Devil worshipper.

Devin began to stutter as he saw his rising Master and standing Soul flinch from the first rays of the sun that worked to escape the blotch of darkness. Devin yelled with all his rage and desperation as he belted out verses before the moving sky.

Syck came upon David's blind side and threw a fist to his right jaw. David pawed the side of his face and bent over in pain. He glanced to the side to see Syck bent over with his abhorrent sewed smile.

"This is even funnier than slamming your wife," said Syck

in amusement.

Syck then clenched David by his hair with his left fist and smashed it with his right. David's eyes began to fill with blood as he stumbled to block the fist that hammered him like a relentless piston. Suddenly, the last belt lost its edge as it glazed off the top of David's head.

Syck grabbed the side of his neck as blood poured forth from an arrow that strayed from its path. He winced and whimpered as he jerked away from David. David beheld the protruding point that was lodged in the side of Syck's neck. Syck stumbled backward as David smiled and straightened and began to advance toward his wounded foe. Syck grabbed an Indian that warred near and threw him into David's path. David reached out to the Indian before he could stumble and fall and steadied him. He then turned and saw Syck scurry off into the crowd.

Pleased with the thought of Syck dying in a corner somewhere from the loss of blood, David returned to the carnage. Barabis roared forth hell's fire as the smell of human flesh lingered in black, oblong clouds that loomed in loathsome sight. The tribal soldiers carried no fear except the devastation of their beloved Mother Earth as they took up their fallen brothers in arms in a ceaseless charge.

The moon broke from the center of the sun, moving along its God-given course. Devin's failure to consummate the last verse became the moment of his shattering destiny as he pleaded before his Master and Soul, who was now receding back to the pits of hell from which he came. Barabbas saw his own body become a transparent vapor, which held no tangibility to Earth's realm. Devin watched Barabbas wither away, then looked at the pentagram pit, where his Master was no longer; Kilgore plunged from the sky in smoldering flames back into the pit that spawned him. The Demons squirmed and dove into the disappearing pit as it began to fall into itself like a sinkhole.

The black blood that filled hell's hole dried into shimmering slabs of solidified petrifaction. Devin continued ancient rants, mumbling from the *Book of the Dead*, hoping for a Demonic miracle as the moon now nearly cleared from the sun.

The battlefield began to waver as the robed men were diminishing from bullets, arrows, and spears. David caught up with Porter Al-Franko, and Billy was relieved they were still alive. Billy then bent down to pull a spear from a corpse as its top hat fell off its head; they then continued their dauntless destruction upon the remaining Devil followers. Devin enraged from his failure, looked up from the Necronomicon to a sun-filled sky, then at David twenty yards away.

Devin tore towards him, wanting to skin him alive. David himself had his hands full as he was being choked by a seven-footed robed man while Al-Franko and Billy were fending off two others with blood-dripping spears as Old-Man-Joe empty's an old 44 magnum at the assailers.

Devin shouted in twisted tongue from warped dimensions, the curses he wanted to fill David. He could almost taste the blood from under his fingernails after they would dig into his skin and rip out his Soul to feast on its essence.

Devin approached the giant-robed man, reached through the side of his torso, and ripped his heart as its last beats pumped in his hand. The giant let go of David's throat and fell to the Earth.

David looked up at Devin from his knees and started laughing aloud as he rubbed the side of his neck. Devin's eyes filled with fire as he gazed down on David with all the seething hatred he had ever known.

"Ha, what you- know, turned out to be a sunny day after all," David mocked in mirth.

"Not for you, it won't be," replied Devin.

David roared forth in laughter, "Don't you see, you sick fuck, I won, even if you kill me. I won!"

Devin then looked up at the heavens and then back down before David.

"What you don't realize is that those cowardly bastards will have to come down and fight sooner or later. All you did is prolong the inevitable."

Devin smiled as the crack of his mouth stretched wide, and his face contorted into snakish features. David flinched backward as its mouth opened, baring pearl-white fangs and hissing at David's face, with the stench of death on its breath.

The serpent seemed to smile as it held out its arms while they swerved and swayed and altered into curving scales. Devin's left fist curled into its wrist, and they twisted into a vile, snapping serpent. Its other arm is a husked, Demonic, Ill-Natured sword. David shuffled backward as the snake snapped at each side of him, and the serpent's face savored a smile. Seeing no escape, David closed his eyes, expecting to die. Then he remembered once more the words of his dream: "I shall prepare a place for you."

Pain ripped into his armpit as the serpent tore into him and held him elevated before the Witch Master. David never experienced such pain and cried out to the heavens in agony.

The Witch Master opened his mouth as another snake protruded and sprayed David while its Ill-Natured sword raised for a final blow. David began laughing, ready to die. At that moment, the Witch Master was suddenly sideswiped by

Buckeye Buck.

The Serpent Demon was taken by surprise and trapped by the Bucks's royal crown of antlers. The Witch Master retracted the serpent in his mouth and shouted obscenities of recognition to the majestic Buck.

His snake fist began to rupture the Bucks's side as the Witch Master was being driven to the flames of a pyre. The Witch Master spit out his serpent spray and then clamped down upon the throat of the Buckeye Buck as his back at the flames.

The Demon's snaked fist bit into the Buck. But the Buck dug in with its mighty hooves, and the serpent Demon became engulfed in flames. The majestic antlered creature tilted his head downward while it held the screaming Warlock in the inferno.

All the serpents fled from the Witch Master's body at once as if they were being smoked out of their nest. The Warlock's skin melted, and his screams turned into screeches from a Beast of vermillion husk and horn.

The Demon beast seized the Buck with its antlers as it pushed its way out of the flames. In great effort, it wedged its Ill-natured sword into the Buck's antlers, pinning the head as it pummeled the deer's back with its snake fist. The Antlered Beast began to buck its hind hooves to shake off the giant Demon, but the Demon lifted the Buck and threw it into the flames.

All seemed still and quiet for a fleeting moment until the flames suddenly danced with every color imaginable. Then, the highest point of the pyre poured out brilliant, pearl-white smoke. The Demonic Beast awaited as he peered into the flames. Out from the top of the flames exploded the fourth Archangel Michael, who hovered high with mighty wings that spread out like a veil of radiance enveloping the sky.

The glowing Archangel gazed down as it shouted Godly words that descended deep into the Demon's Devilish skin with displeasured dissent. The monstrous Beast shouted back foul syllables of hatred while it armed itself with a hellish sword that melded into its arm. The Archangel levitated high and drew his sword as light poured forth from its holy weapon. The Beast cast the snake off his hand to cover its eyes to shun the light that pained it's him. Michael soared downward as he struck the Beast while it, in return, parried a blow.

The two deities clashed in battle as David scurried his mangled body towards the fire in retreat from serpent snakes slithering towards him with deadly intent.

The foul reptiles hissed and half circled him, with his back now hunched against the flames. David grabbed a flaming stick from the fire and held the burning end out to the snakes as they scantily feared the flames.

The serpents became bolder and bolder, inching closer and closer, rattling and hissing their rage. David could feel the intense flames burning at his back as the enclosure of serpents tightened around him.

All hope seemed but gone, and he loathed the thought of dying this way. He gazed upon the encompassing serpents as a long shadow was cast over them. The trisected malformed giant from the forest jumped onto the scaly reptiles and began to stomp them with its wide cloven hooves. David's face turned from terror to titillation as he took pleasure in watching the squirming serpents splatter before his eyes.

The Angel and Demon exchanged many blows in the heat of battle as either had the edge upon the other, and both began to exhaust. Michael zig-zagged as the Demon dissected every direction with death-deranged determination. The Archangel swooped down, passing rapidly, while he sliced deep into the Demon's thick husk.

The Angel's glide began to confuse the hellish creature as it flailed its fiendish sword into the air with erratic anger. It then took another blow to its thick husk as it studied the conjecture of his assailant's tactical path.

The vile Demon Beast then lunged into the air, and the tip of its sword clipped Michael's wing, and he twisted in the air like a maple seed helicopter falling to the Earth. The hellish creature murmured in mirth as it labored in glorious pain before the grounded Angel. Michael turned in a struggle to face his nemesis as the Demon's sword was thrust into the low center of his torso.

The foul breath of hell spewed from the mouth of the Beast while the Angel was lifted face to face with Evil. The Demon Warlock held him high in the air as he shouted curses of Devilish dialect before the heavens. The Archangel clasped upon the Demon's sword as his wings fluttered in upward motion.

Michael cried out in pain as he shouted ancient Zionistic parables at the Beast. The foul Demon was sickened by the words, and he flung the Angel to the ground.

Michael grasped his gaping, gorged torso as it poured forth bright-blue colored blood. The Demon inhaled the scent of the Angelic blood, then licked his crooked, malformed sword in blissful delight. He shouted triumph, hellish syllables of defiance to the sky once more.

A voice then rang out from behind him: "Hey, sick fuck."

The Demon lowered his head from the heavens and turned around to the familiar voice. David stood armed with a six-foot spear in the middle of a formation of Indian archers. He then waved his hand and said, "Sayonara, sick fuck" as the giant Demon became laden with arrows.

David then made a mad dash for the Demon and pierced its abdomen. In return, he was raked by the flat of its sword. David sailed backward through the air until he was caught in the webbed hand of the trisected creature, who gently placed him on the ground.

The massive, trisected creature screeched out, "Demassss," as it lowered into attack mode in a slow, torpid march before the Demon. Once more, it yelled, "Demasssss!" as if the very sound itself seemed to fill it with rage. It quickened each step as it roared the Demonic name from its deformed mouth. The trisected creature then ran full force at the Demon and thrust its giant, meshed fist upon the Demon's head. The vile Demon screeched out as it bridled its head in a fit of tumultuous rage. The trisected creature attacked once more and was gored by the Demon's sword. It winced out in grueling pain as it slowly began to fall to its knees while wrapping its giant arms around the Demon's waist.

The Archangel Flew high to study the grounds of war. He then took sight of the sizeable cross and then the long chain that was used for the schoolgirls' bondage.

He soared down and seized the chain, then ripped through the air onto the cross. Michael wiped the chain, snagged the cross, and then chased before the clashing Titans. The Demon was about to thrust once more onto the trisected creature as he raised his husked, malformed sword.

Michael then slung the chained cross onto the Demon and snagged its malformed sword as the Angle flew counterclockwise behind and around the Demon. Its sword became pinned to its back as the Archangel continued to round the Demon, who became clenched and helpless with each pass.

The trisected creature lowered its grip to the Demon's ankles as the chain and cross consumed the vile Beast. The Demon toppled to the ground as the trisected creature turned toward the approaching Angel. It then hunched in submission as prismatic rays shone from the very being of the Archangel.

Michael then grabbed his sword as the Demon Warlock squirmed and squawked as the Archangel shouted homiletic words upon its Devil skin. Michael then lifted his sword and thrust it down upon the Demon's neck. The Demon Warlock shrieked out as it caught sight of Michael's sword descending upon him. Its head fell to Michael's feet but continued speaking its Ungodly babble. Michael then thrusts his sword through Demon's head and holds it into the roaring flames of the Pyer. Black smoke and screams bellowed from the flames as the Angle held steady his sword. The roaring flames consumed the Demon's head into black charred coal as its speaking ruckus was no more. Michael then slid it off his sword with the heel of his foot and stomped down as he shouted Glory to thy King thy Lord. He then grabbed the decapitated Demon upon the cross and tossed it into the flames.

Exhausted, Michael stumbled away from the flames, dropped his sword, and collapsed to the Earth. Michael shook and convulsed in pain from the loss of the holy blue sanguine that poured from his wounds. Michael staggered before the giant Beast, laid his hand upon it, and commanded release as Jim and Scott stood dumbfounded. Michael then struggled to reach his God-given sword, demanding his will and might as blood filled his eyes. A soft voice rang onto the grounded Angle as Michael squinted through his blood-strained face to see two hands gently holding his sword.

David placed the handle of the Angelic Sword in Michael's outstretched hand. Michael smiled as he tightly gripped his God-given sword. David then looked down upon Michael as the Angle smiled at him as if David was everything his Maker intended man to be.

"Victory is ours, oh righteous one!" proclaimed Michael.

Descending Angels gently drifted to Michael's side as they spoke Angelic tongue. They then lifted Michael gracefully as he shouted, "Never forget what you've born witness, and fret not for your loved ones, for they await you, as does my father."

David watched them blend into the clouds and noticed the smoke was fading. He gazed about the premises and saw that the trisected creature had gone as his eyes focused on Johnny, Al-Franko, Porter, and Billy in the distance. Johnny caught a glimpse of David and frantically waved to get his attention. That gut-wrenching feeling of loss overwhelmed him as he began to run through the corpse-riddled field. Johnny stood with a sodden look of depression as David approached.

David heard his name and looked down. It was Sarah crying out his name.

"David! Is that you?"

David fell to his knees at the soul-stirring tone as tears welled in his eyes. Through his tears, he noticed that her eyes had returned to their normal color, but she was blinded by the poison that coursed through her veins from multiple snake bites all over her body. She reached up to David's tear-drenched face, looking past him in her blackened sight.

"Don't cry, my love. Shh, don't cry," Sarah whispered. "I spent the best years of my life with you and cherish every minute." David continued to stream tears while Sarah's eyes widened in sightless vision.

"Tell little Lisa her mommy will always love her baby." She clamored out a wailing cry as the venomous poison endured to eat into her brain with grueling agony.

"Hold me, David. I'm very cold. Please hold me."

David embraced her as if trying to stem the reaper's bounty, and he breathed deep into her very essence. He looked down as her eyes stared deeply at a deathly loom while her wrist tilted to the sky.

"No, not her! Please take me, take me!" David howled out to the sky with tears of fire as his Soul screamed in grieving pain. Nathan and Loften stood behind him, along with Johnny as Porter, Billy, and Old-Man-Joe standing at his side.

The old man placed his hand on David's shoulder and said, "She's not gone, just transcended."

David nodded his head as he stroked her hair from her face. He then lifted her into his arms and walked away. Johnny proceeded to search for his boys as the field before him was filled with cadaverous composure. The wicked worshipers either lay dead or fled and left the valley. Johnny called out in every direction until he saw his boys holding onto each other, hunched on the ground. Johnny rushed to them as he called out their names. They answered back in desperation for their father. The two boys sprang up into Johnny's arms in their returned normality.

They remembered nothing except their present moment of surrounded death as Johnny quickly took them away. All the schoolgirls had survived as they crammed into an RV with Louise at the wheel. Nina and Ora boarded the Euro-copter and flew away. Syck and Hector drove off in Nina's Lexus with Syck in the back seat, drinking from a bottle of whisky with his open, sliced eye. Hector drove as he looked in the rearview mirror and said, Man ese, you are defiantly uglier than me now. Syck shouted from his own lips, shut up! Shut up!

David gently set Sarah's body in the passenger seat of the cruiser and left the valley. Slow, steady tears flowed down his cheeks as he held her hand. David took his beloved Sarah to the cemetery, where he built a casket for her from the graveyard shed, all the while in flooded tears. He placed the pine box into the Earth after digging a deep pocket into his family plot. He then made a slow, torpid march to the cruiser, where he lifted his beloved into his arms and stared into her face as he walked to his family plot. He kissed her once more, then gently lowered her into her grave. He gazed upon her once more and said I love you, Sarah. He then slid the lid top of the ruff-cut coffin and shoveled the Earth onto its lid. Upon every shovel thrown, David felt the great loss as his Soul stirred the sickness of loss. Afterward, he stared at the mounded Earth and grieved over the grave.

He felt as empty as a dry drum while the sky above him was bright and clear. He announced his love for her once more as a warm, gentle breeze passed through him, emitting the scent of Sarah's essence. He breathed in deeply her loving spirit, and a single tear rolled down his cheek. He began to feel joy as he thought of the day they would merge as one in the Great Divine.

David then ran to the squad car as Pat repeatedly hailed him on the radio. When he answered, she told him that the hospital called ten minutes ago and said Lisa had made a complete recovery. David covered his face with his hands in relief, falling to the Earth on his knees as he broke down tears of joy.

He shook his hands to the sky as if saying thank you to the Great Divinity of God. Silence stilled the airwaves momentarily until Pat stated that the forest fires had been virtually diminished. She then asked if a tornado tore through the station. David didn't have the heart to tell her Charley lay dead in a back cell. He signed out, thanking her for the good news. He then gazed at the graveyard like a wise, aged sage who somehow understood the connection between life and death.

Has the end ended its unstinting end? "Perhaps" Perhaps.

Printed in the United States
by Baker & Taylor Publisher Services